WEATHERING
THE
STORM

KATE FORRESTER

To Jane,
   Many thanks without your help I wouldn't have realised my dream
         Kate
            xxxx
         June 1st 2012

This book is dedicated to Viv Handy, the best dad a girl could have.

Acknowledgements

First and foremost I have to thank my children Ellie and Hattie, without whom my life would be less colourful. I would also like to thank my mum, Annie for her love and support in everything I do.
I would also like to thank my friends and editors Sarah and Jane, without whom my writing would be far poorer.
And finally, I would like to thank the ladies of C19, who have been with me since the beginning. Without their support and encouragement I'd never have realised this dream.

Chapter One

Will drifted awake, as he always did, long before light. For him there was no luxury of pulling the duvet higher and snuggling down until daylight filtered in through the window. Whatever the weather was like, his day always began at four thirty. He needed no alarm clock or cock's crow to wake him.

The house was silent except for the sound of the long case clock whose rhythmic ticking and deep chimes, even though it was downstairs, could be heard all over the house; a familiar sound, one he had known since childhood. A family heirloom. Will found it comforting to listen to it, just as his ancestors must have done.

There might not be the luxury of a lie-in but he did steal a couple of minutes to stretch out in his large, king sized bed. It was new, like the other furniture in this room, and for the first time he had a bed that could accommodate his six foot two inch frame. A twinge of guilt entered his mind, as it always did when he spent money on himself and not the farm. He pushed it aside. He'd not had the room decorated since he was a teenager and what else, he reasoned, did he have to spend his money on?

He slid out of bed, glad of the central heating. November mornings in The Dales were freezing. In the past there had been many a morning when he'd climbed out to find the floor icy cold beneath his feet. Changes, there had been lots of changes. He walked along the corridor, glancing in the empty room next to the bathroom. Here was the biggest change of all. Even now, after three months, it was strange to see it unoccupied. His hand traced the name plaque on the door: 'Sarah's room'. He smiled. She was off on her big adventure as she called it. A gap year before she went to university. He was so proud of her, as proud as he would have been if she'd been his daughter. He smiled ruefully. She was the closest thing he would ever have to a daughter. He'd never been good with women, too shy, and since Moira's death there had been no one. She'd been the only one – ever. He'd tried to make love to her but it had been such a disaster, he doubted he'd ever try again with anybody.

He walked into the bedroom and picked up a framed photograph. It was of the three of them at his and Moira's wedding. He traced his finger over the faces in the photograph; his heart contracted painfully, as it always did when he looked at this photograph. Sarah and he looked so happy, grinning widely, but Moira looked lost and sad.

He'd known Moira forever, but he should never have married her. It had been a fool's errand. Hadn't he known that at the time? She had never loved him. How could she? She had been consumed by her feelings for her childhood sweetheart, Myles Bishop.

He replaced the photograph and turned to head into the bathroom. As he did, he caught a glimpse of himself in the mirror and smiled. Sarah would tell him that he needed a haircut. He could almost hear her words:

"Just because you're a bear of a man doesn't mean you have to look like a bear."

God, Sarah was wonderful and he loved her as if she were his own. But she wasn't. She was Myles' daughter. He sighed. Sometimes he wished Moira had never returned... but then he remembered he wouldn't have had Sarah if she hadn't.

He switched on the shower and stepped beneath the hot spray.

He had tried to make the marriage work not just for Moira but for Sarah as well. The little girl had deserved a secure, loving home. But, from the beginning, Moira was cold and indifferent towards him. She often disappeared for days on end, leaving him to look after Sarah. Rumours began circulating about her and Myles. There was talk of an affair. At first Will had refused to believe it – but then they'd gone off to the cottage on the moors and committed suicide, and he'd had no choice but to believe it. He sighed as he stepped from the shower and started to get dry. She'd been too young to die and yet he acknowledged she had been one of those people destined never to grow old. For a long time his grief and guilt had consumed him; he had been convinced he'd failed her, believing if he'd been a better husband, a better man, she would not have taken her own life.

It had been Sarah who had finally made him see sense; sensible, adorable Sarah. In the two years that he and Moira had been married she had become like a daughter to him; they had drawn closer as Moira had become more and more distant. He'd never be able to explain how overwhelmed he'd been when she had opted to stay with him after Moira's death.

It had been about three months after the suicide that she had told him to buck his ideas up. She had stood with her hands on her hips, glaring up at him, and then she had let him have it.

"It weren't your fault, Will. Moira, she were never happy. She should never have married you. The only time she seemed alive were when she were with that Myles. They were so selfish. I used to believe that made me bad, thinking that, but me counsellor at school, she said it were honest.

"You need to be honest too, Will. In the two years you were married she weren't your wife and you deserved better. You're a lovely bloke, bit old with dead dodgy fashion sense and you need a bloody hair cut again, but you're really good and decent. A girl could do a lot worse than you, but you need to snap out of it. I lost Moira – I don't want to lose you an' all."

Her final words shocked him; he couldn't believe she thought he would commit suicide. That had been the turning point. In the years after Moira's death, he had slowly started to sort the farm out, no rushing, just laying the foundations to turn the farm around; slowly, little steps, as his gran had said. Repairs had been made, stock replenished and new ventures started. During this last year, he had turned his attention to the house, doing it up and modernising it.

Once he was dressed he went downstairs and lit the range in the kitchen. He looked around at it, a kitchen that was now what it should be: the heart of the home. Rustic pine units were fitted to two walls and an antique pine dresser, another family heirloom, was positioned on the other. Its shelves were full of mismatched china that sparkled and gave the place both a loved and lived-in air. He looked around at the changes he had made; gone was the dark old fashioned room and in its place was somewhere warm, inviting.

Will glanced around again. They'd thrown themselves into modernising the place – both him and Sarah - using the physically hard work as a kind of a therapy. It was Sarah who had seen the potential of turning three of the old farm buildings into profitable holiday accommodation. She had done some research and they'd both been amazed at how much people were prepared to pay to stay on a farm. They'd worked so hard to get the cottages habitable, but it had been worth it. They were a good investment and the money they brought in was being ploughed back into the farm. He'd have to employ somebody to clean the cottages next season, now Sarah was away. She had always done that, saving her wages for her big adventure. He missed her, but there was no sense in moping.

He made his breakfast and mentally went over the jobs he had to do later. Bad weather was on the way – the met office had been forecasting it all week. Not that he had needed the warnings; as his gran used to say, there was snow in the clouds and a lot of it. He would have to head up to the top pasture, make sure there was food for the sheep up there. He made some sandwiches and two flasks for his lunch, one of soup and one of coffee, pausing only to leave a list of jobs for the two young lads he employed before he disappeared into the cold dark morning.

He stashed his lunch in the cab of the new tractor he'd bought and hitched a trailer to the back. Once done, he filled it with feed and hay for the sheep. It was hard work but he was glad of it because it was freezing this morning and at least the activity kept him warm. When he finished, he whistled to his dogs and, once they were in the cab, he jumped in himself and turned the key in the ignition, smiling as it caught first time. The tractor had been costly, but if it started every day like this he'd be happy.

The sheep all came running the moment he began unloading the food. He worked steadily, filling the feeding troughs and putting the hay out. Dotted around the field were water troughs and he painstakingly broke through the ice that had formed on the top. By mid-morning he could see the weather closing in. He had never seen the sky so heavy and with the wind gusting wildly he'd realised that the weather people were right. There was a real storm brewing. At first the snowflakes were light, dancing on the wind, but soon they began to get much heavier. Will watched as the sheep stood together eating, not bothered by the inclement weather. They were hardy animals, bred to stand the harsh winters in the Dales. The snow was settling fast and by lunch time it was showing no sign of stopping. He realised that his two farm hands, Mike and Stuart, would get stranded at the farm if things continued, so he rang them and told them to get off home. He ate his lunch quickly, glad of the hot soup, and then headed back down to the farm.

He spent the afternoon making sure the other animals were warm, dry and fed before he chopped a load of fire wood and dragged it into the porch to keep it dry. By four o'clock, visibility was less than thirty yards and, knowing he could do no more, he went inside to wait out the storm.

****

The first thing that registered was shock. In that split second when she opened the door it was as if she had been hit in the solar plexus. She felt herself staggering as the air was forced out of her lungs in a harsh gasp. As her brain assimilated the facts, humiliation took over from shock. She felt hot, sick and dizzy, all at the same time. Her eyes were drawn to the woman who was riding her husband like some bareback bronco rider. Locked as they were in the heat of passion, neither of them noticed she was there. She stood trapped like a fly in a spider's web, paralysed, unable to move, watching like some sick voyeur as they reached completion. As their final cries of ecstasy freed her from the numbing paralysis, a keening cry was torn from her throat and then she turned and ran from the house, her husband's shout of "Alison" ringing in her ears.

She got in the car and drove blindly, without planning where she was going, not noticing the worsening weather conditions. Minutes became hours as she put distance between her and the scene of the ultimate betrayal. Haphazardly turning left and right, she followed no route, not caring where she was going so long as it was away. Three hours passed before she registered that she had driven miles and that the road had become treacherous – if it was indeed a road.

The snow that had begun to fall earlier was now a blizzard; visibility was almost zero. How could she have been so stupid? It had to happen of course; in fact, it was a wonder that an accident didn't happen sooner, given her complete lack of concentration. The tyres seemed to lose all traction as the car slid in the icy conditions, jolting her out of her painful thoughts. She tried in vain to control the vehicle, but she had realised the danger too late and the car continued to slide down the road, only coming to a standstill when it ran into the stone wall with a sickening crunch as the front of her car concertinaed in against it.

Alison's seatbelt bit into her as she was jolted forward with the impact and was then thrown back. She would be black and blue tomorrow, she thought, but at least the seat belt had stopped her from going through the windscreen. She was lucky she was not seriously hurt. Tears trickled silently down her cheeks. What a mess - in an accident, Christ only knows where. Could things get worse? The smell of burning indicated that they could.

She pushed open the door, clutching her coat tightly. Her battered body protested at moving so quickly but she had to put space between herself and the car. The flames were spreading rapidly. Conditions underfoot were treacherous and she was twenty metres away when she slipped and fell into the snow. For the second time in one day, all the air rushed out of her body as she landed and, even though the snow softened the impact slightly, she landed hard on her shoulder. White hot pain sliced through her and stars appeared in front of her eyes.

How long she lay there she could not be sure. It could not have been longer than a few minutes though, before the biting cold and poisonous smoke from the fire forced her to move. She gritted her teeth against the pain in her arm as she struggled shakily to her feet, the only thought in her head to find some shelter before hypothermia kicked in. Having no idea where she was, and with visibility so poor that she could not see, she made her way to the wall she had run into and slowly walked along the side of it, moving downhill. It was impossible to tell where the road was or even if there was a road.

Alison was glad that she had the wall as some point of reference because without it she would not have known which way was forward. The weather was the worst she had ever known. Snow had always been something that she loved, making the country look like some magical, beautiful winter wonderland; but this wasn't magical – it was just simply terrifying. Her progress was slow and she slipped and stumbled several times, each fall causing pain to shoot up her injured arm. The cold had invaded every part of her body right through to the marrow. She had been shivering violently almost from the moment she had started walking. The bitingly cold wind was cutting through her, vicious as the sharpest knife. She tried to hug her coat more tightly around her, but it was a futile gesture, it wasn't designed for these arctic conditions. The leather boots she was wearing offered little or no protection and she had long since lost any feeling in her feet making it ever more difficult to stand up.

Alison had been walking about half an hour when the wall ran out.

Well, it didn't run out – it came to a corner. Panic welled up. Did she carry straight on or turn and continue to follow the wall? Would that mean she was just walking around the edge of a field and getting nowhere nearer help? The cold had penetrated her brain and she really had no idea what to do. Tears of frustration threatened and hopelessness overwhelmed her.

The energy she was burning because of the shivering had exhausted her and she could barely keep her eyes open. Confused and disorientated she staggered forward but only two or three paces before she fell once again. She tried to push up but, with only one arm to take her weight, it proved an impossible task. She collapsed back in the snow and waited for death to come.

Strangely, she now felt calm. It was as if she had stopped fighting the inevitable. It was as if she were falling into a deep and dreamless sleep. If this is death, Alison thought, it's not as bad as I expected it to be. She was about to succumb to the elements when, through the fog of semi consciousness, she heard a dog whine and felt the weight of its heavy body as it lay down on her followed by its frantic barking.

"Thank you," she whispered against the animal's silky fur before the darkness claimed her.

Chapter Two

The power had gone off about an hour after Will had come in from the farmyard. He had just had time to wash and change out of his dirty clothes before the electric went off. He went to check the telephone, experience telling him, if the power was out, it was likely the phone was as well. The line was indeed dead. He sighed and picked up his mobile, but there was no signal available there either. Unperturbed, he went into the kitchen and prepared himself his tea on the solid fuel range. Since Moira's death he'd learned to cook. It had been a necessity. The chip shop and take away were miles away and in any case he had owed it to Sarah to provide her with decent meals. Several cook books now resided on his bookshelves and several sauce pans had finished up in the bin, but he had finally mastered the art of cooking and, much to his surprise, actually enjoyed it. He dished up the simple meal and let the dogs out so he could eat in peace. He didn't mind the solitude; he was used to being alone, especially now Sarah was away.

The small camping lamps he'd scattered around the room cast deep shadows. Living out on the remote farm, power cuts were always a problem in bad weather, so the current storm had not caught him unprepared. He always kept some gas lamps and candles at the house and there was a plentiful supply of logs and coal. Downstairs at least the house was warm, thanks to the range and the log burner in the living room. He would be able to ride out the storm in comfort. Filling the kettle at the sink for water to wash his dinner dishes, Will glanced out of the window to see if he could see Winston. The other dogs, Drake and Bess, were back and lying in front of the range but Winston had yet to return. The snow was so bad that he couldn't see much so he went to the back door, opened it and called for the dog to come in.

Leaving the porch door open he returned to the kitchen and set the kettle on to boil. Glancing at the radio he debated turning it on to see if there was any more news about the weather but decided against it. Better to save the battery; he doubted he would learn anything new tonight. The country was gripped in a dreadful storm; heavy snow fall and high winds were causing havoc. According to the met office the current storm was likely to be very much worse than any in recent memory, including the snows of 1947 and 1963. Before the power had gone off, Will had caught some of the evening news, where they had already been reporting fatalities.

Will was bone tired, which was not surprising; the work today had been hard and thankless. Once he'd washed up, all he'd wanted was to collapse into a chair with a book and a mug of tea. He read most evenings, preferring his books to the majority of programmes on television.

He turned and walked back to the door; the dog had still not come in. It was unusual for Winston not to come at Will's call; he was a working dog and used to following commands. Will stepped out into the snow, puzzled at the dog's behaviour, but could see little as it was dark now and the snow was still falling heavily. He called again and then he heard it above the wind: frantic barking. The dog was obviously in trouble. He turned quickly and stepped back into the porch. Pushing his feet into his boots, he grabbed his coat, hat and torch before he whistled for the other two dogs. He dropped to his haunches and ruffled their fur.

"Find Win," he commanded softly.

The two dogs shot off into the dark evening.

The heavy snow and wind meant that he had to move slowly. It was already up to the top of his Wellington boots. Warning the dogs not to get too far ahead he ploughed on slowly. He could barely see now. It was almost a total white out, and he could only hope that the dogs were leading him in the right direction. Win's barking was louder now and Will sighed in relief as he realised they were getting closer. They were near to what was known as bottom field. It was just outside of the farmyard, but still further away than the dog would normally go on his own. He couldn't think what on earth the dog was doing out here. Puzzled, he moved onwards. Bess and Drake were barking as frantically as Win now and he could finally see why. Win was huddled up against the dry stone wall lying on a mound of snow.

"What is it, lad? Are you hurt?" Will asked, as he knelt down.

The dog whined frantically but didn't appear hurt. And that was when Will realised that it was not just snow the dog was lying on, but a body.

Taking a deep breath to steady his heart rate – which had suddenly accelerated from a steady sixty to a hundred and twenty beats a minute – he patted the dog softly.

"Ok Win, lad, let's just see what we have here."

The dog moved and allowed Will to brush the snow away. It was a young woman. His mind flew to the day he had found Moira. Cold and dead, she had been as still as this young woman was.

Shaking slightly, he placed his work roughened finger tips on the pulse in her neck. Her skin was like ice and at first he thought she must be dead, but then a faint movement beneath his fingers told him she was still alive. Knowing that time was of the essence, he lent down and lifted her arm up. The whimpers now came from the young woman as well as the dog. Her arm seemed to be hanging at a strange angle. He stopped, cursing. Lowering her injured arm back down, Will picked up her other arm and pulled her up and forward. The only way he would be able to carry her would be over his shoulder in a fireman's lift, and to do that he was going to have to hurt her. Steeling himself against her cries of pain, he wrestled her into place over his shoulder and then slowly stood up.

She wasn't a very big women but moving an unconscious person is not the easy task that Hollywood movies show. It is physically hard work and Will could feel himself sweating at the labour. His knees buckled and he had to reposition her before he began walking back to the farmhouse. The task was made harder by the woman's wet clothes and the dangerous snowy conditions. How, he wondered, as he placed one foot slowly in front of another, could her thin, totally inadequate coat weigh so much. He staggered slowly back towards the farmhouse, stumbling several times, but somehow managing to remain upright.

It normally only took five minutes to get back to the farmhouse but tonight it was taking far longer. God, he hoped he could make it. He wasn't unfit, far from it; he regularly lifted weights far heavier than this woman, but the snow and wind and his fear of dropping her were making it almost impossible to reach the house.

"Thank God," he murmured as the muted light in the kitchen came into view. "Almost there now, lass," he whispered.

Supporting her with one hand, he reached down and pushed the door open. Relief swept over him. He'd made it. Pausing only to close the door with his foot once the dogs were inside, he quickly left the porch and entered the warmth of the kitchen. He didn't linger but made his way to the living room where he placed the young woman gently onto the sofa. Leaving her there under the watchful eyes of the dogs was one of the hardest things he'd ever done, but he needed to collect some dry clothing, blankets and towels, all of which were upstairs. Realising that time was of the essence, he ran upstairs and gathered the things he wanted as quickly as he could.

Laden down, he returned to the living room. She hadn't moved but Winston had climbed up on to the sofa and was lying alongside her, as if he knew that he had to keep her warm. Will had to smile – it was a rule that the dogs were not allowed on the sofa.

"It's ok, lad," Will whispered as he stroked the collie's silky fur. "You've done a grand job. Now I have to get her out of those wet things." He dropped to his haunches and gave the dog a gentle prod to move him away from the woman. "The thing is, Win, where do I start? I'm half afraid to touch her."

But start he had to. Very slowly he eased her into a sitting position. She wasn't shivering which he realised was a bad thing. He volunteered with the Calder Valley search and rescue team and his training with them meant he knew that, when the body temperature dropped too low, the shivering reflex stopped. It was a really bad sign. Worried, he felt for her pulse again and was relieved to find it, even though it was weak.

    It hit him then, as he counted her pulse, this young woman's life was in his hands. Even if the phone lines were not down, an ambulance would never make it up to the farm and the poor visibility, because of the snow, would mean the air ambulance had to be grounded. He felt slightly sick. What if he failed? He looked at her pale face, so peaceful she could almost just be asleep. He mentally shook himself. She needed him. There was no time for doubts. He had to act quickly or she would die. Grateful, as he never had been before for his training with the search and rescue team, he pushed aside his doubts and concentrated on what she needed.

    Speaking quietly he leant over her.

"Miss, I'm going to have to take your wet clothes off. If there were a lass here I'd ask her to do it but there's only me." Will didn't know if she could hear him but he felt better for explaining what he was doing.

His hands fumbled with the buttons on her coat. He'd never undressed a woman before, not even Moira, and he couldn't help but feel self-conscious. He remembered from dressing his granddad, after he had suffered his stroke, that when removing clothes the uninjured arm came first. Her whimpers of pain when he moved her injured arm made him swear under his breath. He would have to look at her arm once he had got her warmer. Her jumper was loose fitting and he managed to slide it off with little difficulty. It was impossible not to notice how long and lean she was. His breath caught in his throat at the sight of her icy blue bra; he'd never seen such delicate scraps of lace. Swallowing hard, he felt his face redden with embarrassment. Gritting his teeth, he pushed it aside and concentrated on the job he had to do. He grabbed a towel and patted her ice cold, damp skin dry. He reached for the rugby shirt he had brought down and slid it over her head, pulling it down over her shoulders and covering her breasts, before reaching behind her to remove her bra. His fumbling of her coat was nothing compared to his fumbling now. He'd never undone a woman's bra but eventually he managed to unfasten it. Once he'd removed it, he carefully put her arms into the sleeves of the shirt, injured arm first. Her whimpers of pain as he moved her arm caused him to pause and offer a soft apology for hurting her.

Sighing, he began to remove her boots, jeans and socks. Her legs were long, toned and as cold as the rest of her. Once he had towelled them dry he placed some socks on her feet. Her pants were a scrap of lace that matched her bra. He swallowed hard, knowing they were covering the most intimate part of her body. He debated leaving them on, but they were damp and would make her colder still if they stayed on. So, swallowing hard once again, he reached up and slowly pulled them down. Once he was done, he hastily covered her over with the rugby shirt.

Settling her back on the sofa he wrapped a blanket around her. Her hair was a problem. It was wet and plastered to her head. If the power had been on, he would have used Sarah's hair dryer but, as it was, all he could do was rub it with a towel. Once done, he placed one of Sarah's hats over her head to prevent any more heat loss.

She still hadn't woken and remained cold and motionless. Telling her he would be back in a moment, he went upstairs and dragged the mattress from his bed downstairs. He placed it in front of the wood burner stove. Making a bed up on the floor he then gently laid her on the mattress, covering her with blankets and a duvet.

He watched for a while, prevaricating, knowing what he should do, but reluctant to. The best way to warm her up would be to use his own body heat, and Will knew it. Turning the lamps off to save the gas and telling himself not to be so daft, he stripped off down to his boxers and slid in beside the young woman. He turned her slightly, positioning her so that she lay spooned against him. He pulled the rugby shirt up so her naked back was against his naked chest. Shivering slightly as her frigid body nestled against him, he wrapped his arms and legs around her, telling her she was safe, that he was only trying to warm her up.

He lay in silence, listening to the sound of his grandfather's clock and her breathing, a million questions in his mind about who she was and what she was doing out in the storm. Periodically he checked her pulse, the soft beat reassuring him that her condition was not deteriorating.

By the time the clock struck ten, she seemed slightly warmer, which was a good sign. Will knew from his work with the mountain rescue that it was important that her temperature was brought up to normal slowly; too fast and her condition could be made much worse. Rapidly warming her external temperature would force cold blood back to the major organs causing them to fail. Will had taken her temperature several times, watching as the level had risen slowly over the last three hours.

He sighed. He was almost certain that she had turned the corner. Her silence was a concern. He hoped she was just asleep and not unconscious. The bruises on her chest and shoulders he'd noticed when he'd undressed her looked like a seat belt injury, which meant that she had been in a car accident. Her arm worried him. She had obviously hurt it quite badly but he doubted it would kill her. With the car crash injuries in mind he gently removed the hat he had placed on her head and ran his hands gently over her scalp, feeling for any lumps or bumps that would indicate that she had a head injury. He didn't find any but he did discover that her hair was thick and silky beneath his hands.

He was both amazed and dismayed at his thoughts. He had

never thought of himself as a sexual man. He was a virgin. He'd only tried to have sex three times in his life and they had hardly been earth shattering experiences. Yet, here he was, noticing things about the young woman that he had no business noticing; she was injured, for Christ's sake, and he was thinking of her like a pervert.

He slid from behind her and padded through to the kitchen to make a cup of tea. If he were in the services they'd have put bromide in it, he thought. While he waited for the kettle to boil, he put more fuel on the range and the log burner and let the dogs out.

"No more damsels in distress, Win. I'm not thinking clearly with this one here," he told the collie.

The snow was still falling and drifts were beginning to form. Will sighed. It would be days before the roads were clear, which meant days alone here with the mystery woman. The thought of that filled him with some unknown feeling. A more worldly man would have recognised it as anticipation, but Will decided it was terror.

Calling the dogs, he locked up for the night and made his tea. When he returned to the living room he saw at once that Win again had snuggled down against the woman. He smiled as he sat on the sofa and sipped his tea, while watching his visitor closely. She was less pale now, which was a good sign. She still had purple smudges beneath her eyes and he noticed her lips were cracked from the exposure to the elements. He disappeared up to the bathroom and returned with a small pot of Vaseline that Sarah kept for when she dyed her hair. She'd laughed when he had looked puzzled at her putting it around her hairline.

"It protects me skin from dye," she'd told him.

He knelt at the young woman's side and, using the tip of his little finger, he placed a small amount of the jelly in the centre of her bottom lip and then gently spread it over the sore, cracked surface. When he finished, he checked her pulse again, relieved to find it stronger and steadier.

He finished his tea and moved Win from the woman's side before sliding beneath the covers once more. The dog really did seem to think he was her guardian angel and lay at her side whenever Will moved.

It hadn't been his intention but, between the warmth of the range, the repetitive ticking of the grandfather clock and the comfort of being snuggled close to another person, Will found himself dozing for periods. He was in that hazy semiconscious kind of state you slip into before deep sleep takes hold, when the young woman moved on to her back, her head turned towards him, her face inches from his own. She mumbled something in her sleep, her hand reaching up into his hair, her fingers playing with the soft waves. Will woke fully as her lips brushed his, softly tracing their shape. The Vaseline he had applied earlier meant her lips slid over his effortlessly. He held himself rigid, paralysed with shock, hardly daring to breathe in case she should stop. She mumbled something else, pulling his head towards her and kissing him again. He felt his muscles go lax as he relaxed into the kiss.

Lord knows, he knew he should stop her, but nothing had ever felt so wonderful. Her lips were exploring his more fully, teasing and coaxing them until they parted; he was completely powerless to stop them. This was unlike any of the sloppy fumbles Will had experienced before. Her lips were firm, yet soft, both tentative and confident, leaving him helplessly needing more. Some hitherto unknown instinct made him hesitantly respond, slowly kissing her once, then twice. His heart hammered rapidly in his chest and he felt breathless and more than a little giddy. Tentatively his tongue slid over hers as he shyly responded to her more assured movements. Her soft moan of pleasure made him jolt away, sliding quickly from the bed, conflicting emotions of disgust and desire leaving his mind in turmoil.

    Struggling to get his ragged breathing under control, he looked down at her. How had he allowed that to happen? Not only was she hurt, but she was married. It hadn't registered before that she wore a wedding ring, but now the narrow gold band seemed to catch his eye as if taunting him. Him, a man who knew more than most about the tragic consequences of infidelity. She must have thought that he was her husband. If only he hadn't responded in the way he had. It was as though he had defiled her. He should regret it, but he couldn't. He touched his lips in wonder at the tingling sensation that lingered there even though he was now yards away from her. How could a simple kiss be so powerful? How in thirty-seven years had he not known? How could something so simple cause such a connection? Because that was what he felt, connected to this woman in a way he had never been to anybody before.

His body ached and he sighed, aware that it was not because of the hard work he had done earlier that day, but as a response to her; a response that shocked him to his core. God knows, he'd wanted her. He still did. How wrong was that? She was sick, injured and vulnerable. She'd almost died and he'd prevented it. He had no right having these thoughts. Was that why he felt this connection? Were his feelings all tangled up with rescuing her? He really had no idea. Confused by it all, he took a deep breath to try and get his emotions under control. He glanced at the clock – it was just a quarter past four. Knowing he would get no further sleep he moved once more to the kitchen and made yet another mug of tea. Without any bromide to cool his ardour, he pulled the farm accounts out of the drawer, intending to force himself to work on the figures.

The cry of pain from the living room had him dropping the book before he could even begin.

Chapter Three

It had been such a lovely dream, until she'd moved. She'd been sharing the most beautiful kiss. Soft and tender, not at all like the ones they normally shared. Rob wasn't normally much of a kisser. It had ended too soon and she had moved towards him. That, she realised, had been a big mistake. Pain like she had never known shot down her arm and a cry of agony was torn from her lips. She bit down hard on those lips to try and get the pain under control.

"Miss, is it your arm?"

The voice startled her, but not as much as the man did when she opened her eyes.

He was stood close to where she was lying, like some huge giant. It wasn't often that she felt small but she did now and it terrified her. Who was this man? Where was Rob?

Seeing how frightened she was, Will stepped away a pace so as not to crowd her and dropped to his haunches.

"I'm sorry, lass, I never meant to scare you."

He spoke so quietly she almost couldn't hear him.

"Who are you?" She glanced around her. "Where am I? And what am I doing here?"

"Me name's Will, Will Barnes. You're at Highcroft Farm, my farm. It's near Hebden Bridge."

"What, do you mean in Yorkshire?"

"Yes, me dog found you collapsed in the snow. I reckon you must have had a car accident. Though why you left a car in the storm I don't know."

She'd been in a car accident? She remembered then, she remembered it all – every single thing. How she had caught Rob cheating and how she had run away. She remembered losing control of the car and hitting a wall. It all came flooding back.

"It caught fire," she whispered. "The car, that's why I left it."

Will swore under his breath. She could have been burnt to death.

"How long have I been here, Mr Barnes? Is that what you said your name was?"

"Aye that's right, but call me Will," he told her shyly. "You've been here about seven hours. Winston 'ere found you, he's not hardly left your side since."

She leant forward to scratch the dog's head but the movement caused pain to shoot down her arm.

"Miss, I need to look at your arm. It weren't a priority when I got you here – getting you warm was. But you're in a lot of pain and I reckon I need to find out why. Will you let me look, lass?"

"Alison, my name is Alison. What do you mean by getting me warm?"

"You were wet and cold when Win found you. Doctors would have said you were hypothermic."

She glanced down at her clothes, belatedly becoming aware of what she was wearing.

"Where are my clothes?"

"I've put them to dry by t'range in t'kitchen."

"Did you get me like this, Will?"

She watched as the man blushed to the roots of his hair.

"Aye, I did," he stammered. "No choice, you see. There's only me here. I'm sorry but I had to."

She glanced around. She was alone here with this man, a complete stranger. A stranger who'd undressed her. She trembled slightly, unable to hide her unease.

"I swear I'll not hurt you. As soon as the storm clears I'll take you down to t'village."

"I'm sorry I'm being silly. It sounds like you saved my life..." She paused as a brief memory stirred in her mind.

"Did you lie here with me? I vaguely remember being held."

"I didn't m –m – m – mean anything by it," he stammered. "It were just to warm you up. In severe cases of hypothermia, body contact is the best way to warm a person." Will flushed with embarrassment. Poor woman, probably thought he was a perverted old man. "I... I covered you over so I didn't see owt," he stammered on.

The poor bloke was dying: his embarrassment was intense. If the pain, both physical and emotional, had not been so bad she would have smiled.

"Will, it's ok. From what you said, I'm guessing it was an emergency. It was, wasn't it?" she questioned, remembering she was alone with him.

"Aye, it were," he mumbled.

"Then I'm glad you did."

He blushed again.

"I best look at your arm."

She tensed as he moved towards her, aware that it was going to hurt like hell when he touched her arm.

"If you breathe in before I touch it and then slowly let the breath out it might not be as painful," he told her. "Ready?" he asked.

She took a breath in and let it out as he touched her arm. The pain was still terrible but he had given her something to focus on.

"It's your shoulder, it's dislocated," he told her, after he had examined it.

"No wonder it bloody hurts. A trip to hospital then I guess?"

"We're in the middle of the worst storm on record; the drifts are up to 12 foot in places. I can't get you to the hospital," Will said, looking worried.

"It's ok, I'll just have to be brave."

"No, it has to be put back otherwise the arm could be paralysed."

"Do you have a doctor in the cupboard, then?"

"No. I guess I'll have to do it." His tone was serious.

"Have you had training?" she asked doubtfully.

"Aye, I have, with the search and rescue team."

"Bloody hell, you're a real wonder, aren't you? I think I was found by a real prince," she told him softly. "Ok, get on with it."

He blushed again at her words.

Will gathered some things and helped her slide her arm out of the sleeve, studiously ignoring the soft curve of her breast. He tucked a sheet around her to protect her modesty.

She smiled up at him as trusting as a child.

He handed her a rolled up flannel.

"To bite on. This will hurt – I'm sorry."

That was the understatement of the decade, Alison thought, in the split second that Will moved her arm back in place. She tried hard not to cry, but failed miserably. The gentle giant of a man was wonderful, carefully placing her arm in a sling and then holding her until her tears were spent.

"Did you comfort the last patient whose shoulder you put back in place?" she asked, clearing her throat and taking the tissue he offered to wipe away the tears.

Will smiled slightly and looked bashful.

"What?" she asked puzzled.

"Don't kill me, but to tell the truth, the only dislocation I've dealt with is on Blue the pig out in t'sty." He said with a shy smile.

Alison looked at him incredulously.

"You're joking, right?"

"Er no, I'm not." Seeing the look of horror on her face he went on quickly. "I've seen it done and assisted the medics out on rescues though."

"So I was a guinea pig for you to practise on?"

"Nay, lass, that's not what it was like at all. If I could have got a doctor up here I would have, but the weather is so bad there wasn't a chance of being able to do that. I were worried that your arm could have been permanently damaged. I'm so sorry if you thought I was wrong."

The sincerity in his voice and tension in his body made Alison realise she was being ungrateful; after all, the man had probably saved her life.

"I don't think you were wrong. I'm sorry for sounding cross. Tell me, did you give the pig a flannel to bite on?" she asked with a small smile.

His shoulders relaxed; she wasn't angry.

"No, Stu held her down."

"Stu?"

"He's the young lad who works for us."

"Where is he now?"

"I sent him and Mike home before the weather got too bad."

"It's that bad?"

"Aye, I've not seen worse. Happen I'll have to dig a path away from the house in the morning." He watched as she moved slightly and winced in pain. "I've some pain killers in t'kitchen. I'll get you a couple and then you need to try and go back to sleep."

Alison watched as he walked into the kitchen. He was right, she was exhausted. She wasn't sure she'd sleep though. Being alone with him was still unnerving her.

He returned with the tablets and once she'd taken them he helped her get comfortable in front of the fire on the mattress.

She looked up at him once she was settled.

"What about you? Where are you going to sleep?" she asked warily.

"I'll just be on the couch. I won't hurt you, lass. I need to stay close in case you need help, but you've nowt to be scared of, I promise."

"Sorry, I know you're just helping me."

"It's ok." He stretched out on the sofa, knowing that he was not going to sleep at all.

****

To her surprise, she'd slept for several hours; the trials of yesterday had taken more out of her than she had thought. Her back, ribs and chest hurt like the devil and a glance under the rugby shirt showed the bruising from the seat belt in all its livid glory.

She pushed upright slowly with her uninjured arm. The house was quiet. Will must still be outside. She slowly stood and walked across the room towards the window. She saw him immediately. He was bundled up against the weather with the three dogs at his side.

Alison watched him working through the window. There was an economy about his movements that was in keeping with what she had learned about him. Of course, a few hours were hardly enough time to carry out a full character assessment, but the one thing she had learned was that there was nothing superfluous about him. The times he had spoken after treating her shoulder were brief; his words, laced with a deep Yorkshire accent, were simple and to the point. The word "taciturn" might easily have been written to describe him. After his admission that the only dislocation he had treated had been the pig's, he'd withdrawn into himself, blushing and stammering whenever she spoke.

He'd been up early despite being awake half the night because of her. He'd made her breakfast, just porridge and toast; simple and plain like the man he was. After making sure she was settled and insisting that she took some painkillers, he'd told her he was going out to check on the animals and clear the snow. He'd been unable to open the front door. Snow had drifted against it and so he had to climb out of the window, which had been no mean feat for a man of his size. That was another thing that surprised her. At five foot nine, she couldn't remember feeling small but Will made her feel tiny. It wasn't just his height and build - although he had to be at least six foot two and hard physical labour had made him broad of shoulders and chest. No, it was more how he treated her, as if she were something rare and beautiful, fragile almost. Rob had never made her feel like that. She moved tiredly back to the sofa and sat down.

Alison sighed. A deep heavy weight settled on her chest that had nothing to do with her injuries. Rob, how could he have betrayed her in such a way? With nothing to serve as a distraction, she was helpless to avoid thinking about her marriage and the events of yesterday.

Like millions of victims of infidelity, she honestly thought her marriage had been perfect. They had made a home together and, so Alison had thought, a life. A life in which she believed they had shared dreams and ambitions for the future. They had been building a future the way that thousands of young couples did. Alison had grown to love the easy familiarity, the way they moved around each other, knowing each other inside out. No mysteries, loving the little shared secrets that all couples have. In the blink of an eye, her perception of her whole life had changed. It had become a lie; all that she knew and believed was a falsehood. Even the image of him entwined with that woman, whoever she was, was at odds with how sex had been between them. What she had witnessed seemed wild, untamed, raw and, in her mind, dirty. An impartial observer would, she conceded, have probably said it was exciting. Was that what had been missing for him, Alison wondered? Had the easy familiarity she had loved become boring for him?

She had so many questions. From the obvious one of who was the woman? To the painful ones like did he love her? What hurt the most was that Rob had brought the woman back to the home and the bed he had shared with her. The headboard his hands had gripped and the sheets tangled about them were theirs. It was bad enough that he had humiliated her by cheating on her, but he had also robbed her of the home that she had loved. In that moment, Alison knew that she could never go back there. With the knowledge of what she had lost came overwhelming sadness. The heaviness in her chest opened like a raw, bleeding wound. Powerless to stop them, hot tears spilled on to her cheeks and she lay silently crying and grieving for what she had lost.

****

Will was thankful that he had thought to bring a spade into the house yesterday because snow had drifted against all the farm buildings including where he stored the tools. He glanced around him; he couldn't remember snow like this. His granddad used to tell him stories about the snows of 1947 and 1963 when ponds had frozen solid and the drifts had lasted for weeks. He reckoned that this had to be worse. The sound of sheep bleating focused his mind.

He had to clear the snow from the doorway to the feed store, hen house and piggery, not to mention the stable. Sarah would never forgive him if anything happened to her horses. He looked towards bottom field. The stone wall that surrounded it was completely hidden under the snow. He shivered, not from the cold, but from realising how close Alison had been to dying. This was the wall she'd collapsed against. Another few minutes outside, exposed to the elements, and he would have been too late to save her. But he had saved her and he told himself to stop worrying about what didn't happen. The sheep had gathered in one area of the field, gaining warmth from one another. Will sighed, wondering how many of the animals had not survived the night.

He worked solidly for the next two hours, clearing the snow away until his arms and back screamed in protest. Once clear, he had set about checking and feeding the animals. The hens and pigs were all rare breeds. They were a new venture on the farm, brought in after Moira had died. Will had a healthy respect for the history of farming and this was his own small way of preserving what was his heritage. Too many of the old breeds were dying out as farming became more intensive. Once the hens and pigs had been fed, he moved towards the stables.

The horses were called Aragorn and Arwen, Sarah's choice of name, not his. She had a fondness for Tolkien and loved both the books and films. The horses snorted at his appearance, steam from their nostrils hanging in the air.

"It's no good you snorting and stamping your feet at me. I got here as soon as I could," Will said to the stallion as his head appeared over the stable door.

Here was another part of farming's dying history. Shire horses had long since been made redundant by tractors; the gentle work horses now served little purpose and the two foals were going to be destroyed before Sarah had begged and pleaded with him to give them a home. She'd promised to take care of them and had been true to her word. She'd even showed them at local county shows and the rosettes they had won adorned the stable walls. He gently nudged the horse out of the way and broke the ice on the water trough before putting food and hay down. The horse nudged Will's back.

"Hey, manners. Wait until you're offered a treat, lad," Will said softly, before extending his hand with half an apple balanced on the palm. The horse took the apple gently and condescended to allow Will to pat his neck and stroke his large, broad nose.

The impatient whinnying from the next stall made him smile.

"Ah, lad, your lady is getting impatient. I'd best go and pay my respects to her. I'll be back later to muck your stall out." He closed the door and moved on.

"Now, lass, what's all that fuss for, hmm?" he said as he followed the same routine of breaking the ice and putting down food. The horse stared at him, waiting patiently for the treat that she knew he had in his pocket.

"Here you go, my pretty one. You could teach that man of yours a few things about manners and patience."

He moved off from the stable, a smile on his face; the two horses meant as much to him as they did to Sarah.

Progress to the fields where the sheep were was slow because the snow was deep. He'd put several bales of hay out in the fields that surrounded the farmyard so he wasn't concerned about food: he was more worried that some of the sheep might have become stuck in the snow. It would be impossible today to check all the fields - the weather was too bad - but he could do the three that bordered the farmyard.

It was difficult climbing the gate as it was slippery and Will could not afford to fall and injure himself; the animals relied on him, not to mention the young woman back at the house. Who was she, he wondered? Why had she been out in the snowstorm? Will was certain she wasn't local. He knew everybody in these parts. There was nothing out this way other than his farm and the moors. She'd not mentioned family or asked about contacting anybody. Maybe that was because she'd remembered him saying the phone lines were down or perhaps she had no family. He looked at his watch, a gift from Sarah last Christmas, it was nearing mid-day. He'd check the sheep and then head back to see that she was ok and make some lunch.

    The dogs had scrambled over the snow-covered wall and were waiting for him. Together they moved around, checking the sheep. Will sighed when he found the first casualty of the storm; animal deaths were par for the course on a farm but he never found it easy. He suspected that this would be the first of several sheep that would not have survived the storm. By the time he'd worked his way around the three fields, it had begun to snow again and he had found three dead sheep. He moved them to the sides of the fields; there was nothing else he could do for now. Exhausted from the morning's work, he headed back towards the house.

    It was Win who heard it first. The dog's frantic whining and barking alerting Will that something was wrong. As he pushed open the door he could hear what the dog had heard outside: crying. Fear clutched at him. Had she fallen and hurt herself? Was the pain in her shoulder worse? Cursing himself for not calling back earlier, he moved quickly through to the sitting room, calling her name.

She was curled on her side, crying as if her heart would break, deep gut wrenching sobs that tore at Will's soul. He hated seeing women cry. For a moment Will stood motionless, unsure what to do. In the end he knelt down in front of her and did the only thing he could: he gently moved her upright and pulled her against his chest and held her, just as he had held Sarah the day he told her Moira had died, not saying anything, just stroking her back and waiting for the tears to pass. As her sobs began to subside so words began to tumble out.

"Why did he do it? I wasn't a bad wife. I can't go back there. Don't make me."

"Go back where, Alison?" he asked quietly.

"Back to our house. Why did he have to take her there? They violated my home. If I go back her scent will be there; in my bed and on my sheets. Don't make me go back. I can't go in that room. I'll see them again, rutting like two animals on your farm. Please don't make me go back, Will."

"Are you talking about your husband, lass?" She nodded.

"You caught him cheating on you, is that what happened?"

"Yes."

"Is that why you were driving so far from home?"

"I ran away and now I've nowhere to go." The sobs began again.

"Shush, lass. You can stay as long as you like. Happen you've not much choice at the moment. Roads will be blocked for several days, I'll wager."

"You're a good man, Will Barnes," she whispered, before she laid her head against his chest, feeling safe and secure in his arms, shudders passing through her body as she tried to regain her composure.

Will reached for the glass of water he had left at her side.

"Sip this. Me gran used to say it helped stop the shudders after a bout of crying."

She sipped the water before handing him back the glass and slowly moving away from him, leaning against the cushions.

"I must look a real sight."

The first thought that crossed Will's mind at her words was that she looked a pretty wonderful sight to him; the second was that her husband must have been a fool. Why would anybody cheat on such a lovely woman?

"It's nothing a warm flannel won't fix, lass." A frown creased his brow.

The concern in his face was really very touching. After all, she was a complete stranger to this man. He didn't have to care, but for some reason he did. Smiling tentatively, she studied his face. She wondered if he realised what a good looking man he was. She wanted to soothe the three small crinkles from his brow and remove the worried look in his deep blue eyes. Beautiful eyes, she suddenly realised, like a lake in winter and fringed with long, sooty lashes.

"It's alright. I'm not going to soak your shirt again, I promise," she told him.

Relief swept across his face.

"That's good. I'll grab that flannel, and is there owt else you need before I get us some lunch?"

"I'd love a bath, though I realise I can't have one. A flannel is fine though and ... Will, thank you."

A shy smile appeared on his face.

"You're welcome, lass."

Chapter Four

Will stood watching her sleep, mesmerised by her. He had work to do, but he couldn't seem to leave her. She looked so soft and innocent, curled on her side, her face relaxed in sleep. Will had never been around a woman who was so utterly feminine. She was tall, but on the slender side. Even though she was injured, she seemed to move with a graceful elegance he had never seen before. The women he had been around were plain, down to earth country folk. In comparison, Alison was like some rare butterfly.

It worried him slightly that she had eaten little at lunch time. He'd made soup and sandwiches, but she had managed barely half of the soup before she had become tired. He wished his gran was here, just so he could hear her say something comforting like:

"While she's sleeping she's healing."

She'd been gone a long time, his grandmother, but he still missed her. She'd been wise in country ways, knowing all about the medicinal values of all manner of plants. Whatever the ailment, she knew a cure. People would come from miles to consult her. A homoeopathic practitioner long before they became popular. When he'd been a young lad he'd been convinced she was a witch, a good one, like Gilda the good witch in the Wizard of Oz, kind and caring and able to cure all his pain.

Will glanced down at Alison again. She seemed peaceful, but he'd like to talk to a doctor about her, just for reassurance that he was doing the right thing. He'd tried both the landline and his mobile, with no luck. All he could do was trust his instincts.

She did look less pale. After lunch he had helped her upstairs to the bathroom, his arm hesitantly circling her waist to support her. He wondered if she was aware of how his skin tingled at being close to her, how the soft innocent brush of her thigh against his leg had caused it to burn? It was as if every nerve he had was tuned into her. He'd waited on the landing, using the time to compose himself, before he helped her back downstairs. His breath had caught in his throat when she'd reappeared. She had washed her face and had brushed her hair, tying it back with one of Sarah's hair bands. The look was plain and unadorned and to Will quite beautiful. He wondered if he had gasped out loud. He wasn't sure but, if he had, Alison had not heard him.

"It'd be easier for you if I stayed up here," she'd said tiredly, as they slowly made their way back downstairs.

"Too cold, you need to be in the warm," he'd told her quietly.

She'd fallen asleep almost as soon as he had got her settled on the sofa, before he had even placed the soft throw over her legs, something he had done as much for his sanity as her comfort. Her legs were endless and the rugby shirt did nothing to hide them.

It was a long time since he had noticed a woman. When he had been younger, girls had not been interested in him, cruelly teasing him for having no parents and having to live with old-fashioned grandparents, who had neither the time nor money to be interested in clothes that were stylish. Not that he had been worried because, since Moira had first come to the farm with her father who had started work there, he'd only had eyes for her. He'd been drawn to her like a moth to a flame, and other girls ceased to matter. His granddad had told him that he was a fool. Moira Shelly, he'd said, cared for nobody but Myles Bishop. His grandfather had called them the M&M kids because even as a couple of ten year olds they were never apart. They'd asked him to be their friend not because they really liked him, but because he knew all the best places to play, deserted farm buildings, old trees and brown babbling streams.

Although he had known his granddad had spoken the truth, it hadn't stopped him silently carrying a torch for her for several years or for marrying her when Myles rejected her.

The dogs' whining reminded him he had other things to do, and so he moved reluctantly away. Heading back out to the kitchen, he pulled on his boots once more and headed out into the farmyard.

****

The sound of a door slamming vaguely disturbed Alison; she turned restlessly towards the noise but didn't wake. Instead, she sighed softly and sank back into her dream, back into his warm embrace. Her soft body moulded to his much harder, firmer one. It was strange; it didn't feel like Rob's body. His wasn't like this; he was usually far slighter and softer. Perhaps he'd been working out. Muscles rippled and tensed beneath her touch before her gentle stroking made him lax and supple. She reached up and pulled his head towards her, eager to feel his kiss again. He seemed so shy. Kissing was something that Rob really didn't do, unless as a prelude to sex, and then it was forceful, his tongue mimicking the act of intercourse. This kiss was somehow more intimate. It was as if they had just found each other and were embarking on a sensual exploration, shy and hesitant at first, tracing and playing with each other's lips, before they parted on a sigh as their tongues softly entwined together and the kisses deepened. It was odd, but he seemed content to let her lead. This was something new. Rob didn't normally like her to be the dominant one. It made her feel strangely powerful. Smiling, her hands teased the soft silken strands of his hair as she deepened the kiss further, causing heat to spread over her body and her breath to quicken. She whimpered, begging him to touch her, wanting him to touch her body in the same, soft, tender way he did her lips, but he never did.

  She turned in her sleep, restlessly, as if she were seeking something that was just out of reach. She settled back down again, frustrated that she could not work out what it was she wanted. She was peaceful for a time, having slipped into that deep sleep stage where dreams did not disturb. However, the dull ache in her ribs and shoulders meant her sleep did not remain peaceful for long and, as the pain returned, so did the memory of the cause of her injuries. Suddenly she was back in her bedroom being taunted with images of Rob and his mistress having sex in her bed, their cries of passion causing her to flee and run from her home and her life.

She wanted to wake fully. She began fighting to try and pull herself through the haze of dreams and back to reality. But she was too tired and she sank back against the pillows as dreams claimed her again. This new place was cold and she was alone and scared for a long time. The darkness began to engulf her and the pain intensified until once more she found herself cradled in a solid warm embrace. She felt lulled, the soothing words and touch chased her nightmares away and again she felt herself drawn into a soft, tender kiss.

****

It was a daft notion, Will knew, but he was certain that the horse could understand everything he was saying. Aragorn was watching Will intently as he cleaned out the stall.

"Am I wrong to be pleased that her husband is a bastard? It's not as if she'll care what I think."

The horse tossed his head.

"At least I'll not toss and turn all night thinking about her tonight, lad. With the lack of sleep last night and all the work I've done round here, likely I'll be asleep as soon as my head hits the pillow."

The horse snorted softly.

"You don't believe me then, lad? Why is that? Don't you lie awake thinking of your lady?"

The horse snorted again.

"So now you're laughing at me," Will said amused. "Of course, big handsome lad like you, what troubles would you have with women?"

He patted the stallion's neck and led him back into his stall which now smelt of sweet fresh hay. Holding out his hand he offered a carrot to the horse.

"See, now I'm spoiling you, but remember it's our secret, no telling Sarah when she comes back."

He shut the stable door and moved on to the next stall, leading Arwen out and tying her in the main part of the stable while he cleaned out her stall.

"What would she see in a man like me, Lady Arwen? She's so graceful and refined, while I 'm a great, clumsy, lummox of a man. Not to mention she has just been betrayed by her husband, who seems like a real prince of a man." Will's voice dripped with sarcasm.

The horse neighed softly.

"She needs somebody who'd treasure her. What do I know about being soft or gentle or how to please a woman?"

Will sighed and quickly finished cleaning out her stall.

"You don't mind my rough ways or the fact that at the end of the day I smell of muck and hard graft but I'm sure she would." He led the horse back into the stall and, just as he had with the stallion, he extended his hand to the mare so she could take the carrot from him. She neighed softly.

"Ah, lass, you like your little treats, don't you? I'd like to give Alison a treat; she's had a rough few days. It hurts to see such sadness. It would be great to ease that sadness, even if it were only for a few minutes."

The horse neighed and butted his shoulder gently.

"I know, foolish, like I have anything she'd want."

He turned and headed out of the stall. It was then that he saw them, eight shiny new stainless steel buckets still in their plastic wrapping. An idea formed in his mind and, smiling, he picked the buckets up and returned to the farmhouse. Maybe he did have something she would want.

Alison was still asleep when he came back in and he moved about quietly so as not to wake her before his surprise was ready. He filled the buckets with water and put them on the range to heat up before heading upstairs to raid Sarah's room. He didn't think she'd mind if he 'borrowed' some of her bubble bath.

It took the best part of an hour, but he considered it time well spent when he looked down at the bath filled with warm water and millions of fragrant bubbles. He'd found some scented candles in Sarah's room, when he'd been looking for bubble bath, which he had lit, their soft light and subtle fragrance adding to the relaxing air he was aiming for. Two large fluffy towels hung on the towel rail. He nodded, pleased everything was ready.

Win's bark told him that Alison was stirring so he went back downstairs.

"It seems you were right about Winston, I think he thinks he is my guardian angel," she said as she stroked the dog's soft fur.

"Aye, he's loyal." Will stood, unsure how to tell her of his surprise.

"What is it? You look worried Will."

"Nay, lass, not worried, it's just..."

"It's just what?" she prompted.

"It's nothing, really... It's just...I've run a bath for you, that's all," he said hesitantly.

"You've run me a bath? Is the power back on then?"

"No, I um, I heated the water on t'range."

The smile that lit her face was radiant.

"You carried enough water upstairs for me to take a bath? After all the other work you've done today?"

Will blushed and nodded.

"Will, you didn't have to do that."

"You mentioned a bath. I... I... I... I thought you'd l...l...like it," he stammered.

"I do. It's a beautiful thought and one of the nicest things that anybody has ever done for me. I think I have an angel in you as well as Winston."

He smiled relieved.

"Can you help me up?"

He moved to her side and gently slid his arm round her and helped her to her feet before assisting her back upstairs. He pushed open the bathroom door.

"If you shout for me when you're done I'll help you back downstairs."

She walked in and sighed.

"Oh Will, thank you for this."

"It's nothing," he said embarrassed. "Can you manage?"

"Yes, I'll be fine."

He pulled the door to and waited on the landing until he heard her sigh of pleasure and the sound of lapping water that told him she was in the bath. He smiled slowly and went back downstairs to have a wash in the kitchen.

Alison almost groaned with the pleasure of it. He'd even thought of bubbles, although, the fact that he had something so completely girly in his house puzzled her. Where had they come from, she wondered? She smiled. No matter where they came from, they were perfect. The warm water and scented bubbles were working their magic, easing and relaxing her aching muscles. How many times had he climbed the stairs to fill the bath? Rob had given her gold and jewellery but he'd never done anything as wonderful and thoughtful as this.

She'd washed her hair with difficulty and then she just lay

relaxing. The bath was huge, but then it would have to be for Will Barnes to use comfortably. She could have stayed in it forever but the water was starting to go cool. Reluctantly, she tried to get out of the water but the pain in her back, chest and shoulder meant she couldn't stand up. No matter how she tried she couldn't get up. How embarrassing was this, she thought? She'd have to call Will for help. Swallowing hard she called his name.

He'd finished washing up and had put the evening meal on to cook when he heard her calling.

He was climbing the stairs when she called again.

"Alison, are you ok?" he said through the bathroom door.

"I'm fine but I feel stupid and embarrassed."

"Why?"

"I'm stuck. I can't get out of the bath. I've tried and I need your help, but I've no clothes on." Her voice sounded small and worried.

"It's ok, I'll think of something," he told her.

He went to his room and grabbed a pale blue T-shirt that Lisa had bought him.

"Alison, I'll come in with me eyes closed. I've got a T-shirt. If you put it on while you're in the bath I can then help you up and I won't see anything."

"Ok."

Will opened the door and handed her the shirt. Then he turned away to face the wall while she made herself decent.

"It's on," she told him a few moments later. "One day I'm sure I'll laugh about this," she said as he turned around.

Will wasn't sure he'd laugh; he could scarcely breathe. Alison was flushed, either from embarrassment or the warmth of the bath, and the wet T-shirt was beginning to cling to her, emphasising her long slender figure and soft curves. The bright blue colour was the perfect match to her eyes. She was like a water nymph, and Will had never seen anything more beautiful.

He moved while he could still think rationally, helping her stand and step from the bath. She slipped slightly as she stepped down, her hands reaching out, grabbing his shirt to maintain her balance. Instinctively, his arms flew around her to stop her falling. The sudden feeling of her body held snugly against his caused heat to spread over him. Every nerve ending tingled and he felt an unfamiliar heaviness at the junction of his thighs. For a few moments he was unable to move, his senses totally overwhelmed by her. It was as if the moment was frozen in time and he had no idea what to do.

"Will?" Her voice broke into the silence.

Shocked, he pulled away, not wanting her to be aware of his arousal. He turned away breathing deeply to try and regain his composure, but he wasn't able to. Without turning to face her, he handed her a towel before mumbling that he would wait outside while she got dressed.

Alison watched as the bathroom door closed behind him. Shaking, she sank down to sit on the edge of the bath, trying to understand what had happened. Had Will realised, she wondered? He must have, why else would he have turned away with such haste.

One moment she had burned with embarrassment and the next with desire. She wanted to deny it but couldn't. From the moment he had caught her in his arms when she slipped, she had been acutely aware of him as a man and not as the Good Samaritan who had rescued her. Why was that? He'd held her before and she had felt nothing but gratitude for his kindness. Maybe, she reasoned, it was because of the intimate nature of the surroundings, the warm steamy bathroom and her being practically naked.

Pulling the damp T-shirt over her head she began to dry herself. She had just been so aware of him and still was, even now. He must have washed and cleaned himself up because his hair had been damp and he'd smelt of soap. No fancy fragrance, just something plain and simple, yet so good. Because of her height, her mouth had been mere inches from his face. She'd been able to see the pulse twitching in his neck and had longed to run her lips over the soft fluttering. Up close, his skin was soft and clear; how easy it would have been to brush delicate kisses along his jaw and across to his lips.

He'd reacted quickly to her slipping, his arms enveloping her. She'd reached out moulding her body to his. God, he was so firm and solid. She itched to explore under the soft checked shirt he was wearing, letting her hands wander over the muscles she could feel rippling as she moved in closer. She groaned. What kind of woman was she to be having thoughts like these?

His sharp indrawn breath had made her draw back slightly. His eyes had been widened in shock and his cheeks had flushed pink. He'd turned and mumbled that he would wait outside. She sighed as she reached for the clean clothes he had left, feeling terrible. The poor man was so shy and here she was, acting like she was going to jump his bones. No wonder he'd pushed her away so suddenly and then scarpered quickly.

Alison could not understand what had gotten into her. Was this some kind of reaction to Rob's betrayal? Did she need hot sex without the emotions as a way of getting back at him? Will was hardly the right candidate for that. She doubted he was the kind of man for a no strings attached tumble in the sack. No, he was nowhere near worldly enough for that. He seemed strangely naïve, innocent almost. Not that she had ever really indulged in any no strings sex, and Will deserved better than being the man she hooked up with on the rebound. A small voice niggled in her head. "Is that what he would be?" She sighed, knowing that he wouldn't be. It just wasn't her way either, sex without emotion.

Will had put a pair of jogging bottoms out as well as the shirt and socks so, when she emerged from the bathroom, she was covered from head to foot. He was sat on the top step of the stairs, his eyes closed, his long eye lashes fanning out against his cheek bones. There really should be a law about a man having such wonderful eyelashes.

"Will?" She spoke quietly, wondering if he was asleep.

His eyes flew open. Amend the law, Alison thought; no man should have eyes that beautiful either.

"You shouldn't have waited up here in the cold. I'm sure I could have managed the stairs." His cheeks were still pink and he didn't seem able to look at her.

"I said I'd wait."

Alison watched as he stood up. All long limbed grace, the muscles of his thighs strained against the material of his jeans as he stood.

"Yes, you did," Alison said, quietly aware that things had changed between them.

Stepping back slightly so her face was in the shadows, not wanting him to see her reaction, she continued to watch him. She swallowed slowly, now acutely aware of how tall and broad he was, how his jeans seemed moulded to his thighs, how his chest and shoulder muscles moved beneath the soft shirt.

Will waited for her to move towards him; instead she stepped away. He sighed and a frown creased his brow. Cursing his stupidity in frightening her, he stood still, holding out his hand, and spoke softly.

"Come on, let's get down where it's warm."

Knowing that he would not let her go down unescorted, Alison attempted to compose herself and hoped that Will didn't look her in the eyes for she doubted that she could have hidden the desire that must surely be burning there. She placed her hand in his. It was roughened from hard work and warm to touch; just the slightest pressure against her skin made her tremble in anticipation.

Will felt her hand tremble slightly but she did not pull away. That had to be a good thing, he reasoned, as they walked downstairs.

"I'll see about tea," he said once she was settled in the living room. She just nodded.

Fifteen minutes later, she was still sitting curled on the sofa, gazing into space. Will sighed, watching her from the kitchen. It seemed he'd both scared and embarrassed her, for she had not once looked at him since he had helped her downstairs. He knew a different person would have said something light and witty and then things would return to normal, but he couldn't be a man like that. Brought up by his grandparents, he'd never learned any social skills. The quiet solitary boy had become a quiet solitary man. He knew he had to apologise but wasn't sure how or even where to begin.

He turned towards the range; the food was ready. Was she hungry, he wondered? She'd eaten so little and now he was worried that his behaviour would mean that she would not be hungry.

"Alison, tea's done. Do you think you could eat owt?" When she didn't answer he moved into the lounge.

"Alison?" She was miles away and a single tear glistened on her lashes.

"Oh Jesus, Alison." He crouched down beside her so as not to scare her further. "I'm so sorry, lass. I never meant to scare you up there." He glanced towards the stairs. "Look, I'll sleep in t'barn - you can have the house. I would never hurt you, but I'm a stranger and you only have my word for that."

She looked at him, puzzled. What on earth was he talking about?

"You can trust me. I promise not to touch you again." He stood and went to turn away but Alison grabbed his hand and pulled him back down so his face was level with hers.

"Will, what on earth are you talking about?" she asked.

"Well, about what happened upstairs; me molesting you in the bathroom. It won't happen again, I swear. It's just..."

Alison was shocked; he thought she was angry with him.

"Will, where would you get the idea that I think you molested me?"

"Well, I um ... touched you in the bathroom when you got out of the bath. I'm sorry, it was just that you're so beautiful and..."

Alison placed a fingertip against his lips to stop him talking. When he fell quiet she replaced her finger with her lips, kissing him softly. He didn't move so she pulled away touching his face.

"Up in the bathroom, is that what you wanted to do, kiss me?"

He nodded slowly, not daring to speak.

"I wanted that," she whispered. "I was crying because I was wondering what you must think of me, behaving like a hussy."

"A hussy? You didn't..."

"You know, for two grown-ups, we're both awfully confused. Let's simplify things. Would you like to kiss me?" she asked softly.

Again, afraid to speak, Will nodded.

"Good, because I know I would love to kiss you."

Chapter Five

She waited a moment or two before realising that he was expecting her to kiss him. She slowly brushed her lips against his fuller, lower lip with teasing light touches. His response was shy and hesitant, kissing her softly. No hot demands, just a soft feather-like touch that left her wanting more.

"Will, please don't mess about. Kiss me properly."

He pulled away, mortified, and stumbled from the room, not listening to her call his name.

Will didn't know why he went to Sarah's room, maybe because she had never been disappointed by him. He picked up her old bear, wishing with all his heart that she was here; he'd not be in this position if she were, that was certain. He could have left her to look after Alison. He could have hidden away in the barns finding work to do. He placed the bear back on the bed and walked to the window. When would he learn that when it came to sex and intimacy he would always be a failure? Not one woman had ever wanted to kiss him. Not even Moira. When he'd tried to kiss her she'd just stood still like a cold statue. What did he know about kissing? It was no wonder he was rubbish at it and that Alison had been disappointed. He brushed his hand through his wavy hair. How could he go back downstairs; she must think him an idiot. He stood, with his head resting against the window, looking out at the snow.

Alison stared at the staircase. What in the world had just happened? One minute they'd been sharing a kiss so wonderful that she had virtually begged for more and the next Will had run like a startled rabbit. Had she scared him off? If she had she didn't know why or how. He was painfully shy so maybe she'd rushed him, but the slow tender touches had been driving her mad. Ten minutes had passed and he had still not returned. There was no noise or movement from upstairs. What was he doing up there? It was no good. She had to go and find him, to apologise. Moving slowly she walked to the stairs.

"Will?" she called.

When he didn't answer, she slowly made her way up the stairs, her hand gripping the banister tightly. God, it was hard. Every muscle screamed in protest and a film of perspiration broke out on her skin. She'd never take climbing the stairs for granted again. At the top, she lent gratefully against the wall, resting for a moment, before she walked along the landing, calling his name. The bathroom door stood open so she realised he wasn't in there. As she walked, she peered in the open doors that led from the passageway, finally finding him in a small bedroom staring out of the window.

"Will?"

He didn't move, as if he hadn't heard.

"Will, please tell me what's the matter. Why did you run away?" Alison stood in the doorway.

Without turning to face her he replied.

"I'm sorry, Alison, I'm no good at kissing or sex." He groaned. What was wrong with him, blurting things out like that?

Alison was certain her jaw had hit the floor.

"Sorry, what did you say?" she said incredulously, moving towards his side.

"I'm no good at sex and kissing." His voice was little more than a whisper.

"Says who?"

He shrugged.

"I do... nobody has ever wanted me to kiss them."

"Then they were fools. The kiss downstairs was wonderful. I just wanted more." She smiled as she spoke.

"But you...you told me to do it properly." He shook his head miserably.

Oh God, Alison silently groaned; what had she done?

"No, Will, you've got it wrong. I didn't mean you hadn't done it right. I meant I wanted to kiss you more intimately."

"I..." Will, swallowed hard. "I don't know how." He waited for her to laugh.

"Sure you do, just go with your instincts." She moved towards him.

"Seriously, I don't know how." There was panic in his voice.

"Will, just kiss me." She reached up and touched his cheek with her uninjured hand.

"I..."

"Will, you need to learn when you have lost an argument and you have lost this one, so just kiss me." Alison's tone was soft and firm.

Sighing he lowered his head and tentatively kissed her. Alison waited, losing herself in the soft, shy caresses until the shyness passed and his lips parted, kissing her more deeply. She stood still until his arms encircled her as she knew they would and when they did she sighed with pleasure, moving her hands over his back, pulling him closer. The kisses seemed endless and it was several minutes before they drew apart.

A memory teased in Alison's mind; there was a familiarity about the kiss.

"I don't know who everybody was, but they must have been pretty stupid if they told you that you couldn't kiss, because on a score of one to ten that was an eleven. You really can kiss, Mr Barnes." She smiled as he blushed. "But you need to explain when we have kissed before."

Will looked at her, horrified.

"Oh God. It were after I rescued you. I were lay by your side, keeping you warm. Like I told you I did. I fell asleep. I didn't mean to but I was shattered. You must have been dreaming. I woke up when you started to kiss me. Nothing happened. I swear. I... moved away from you once I realised ... I mean, you obviously had no idea what you were doing. I reckon you must have thought I was your husband."

"Always the gentleman, aren't you, Will? I might have thought you were Rob to start with, but I think I would have realised quickly you weren't my husband. Rob never kissed me like you do."

She kissed him softly and felt him tense.

"It's ok, Will, I know you didn't take advantage of me."

"You believe me?" he said worried.

"Yes." She reached up to kiss him again but he moved away.

"I thought you wanted to kiss me, Will?"

"I did..., I mean, I do. It's... it's just that I think... I think we should slow down."

"You do?"

"Yes... yes, I do. I think we could be confused, like. What with your accident and your husband being a bastard and then being stranded here. It's not a normal situation. I don't want you to do owt you'd regret. "

She smiled, wondering if he always did the right thing.

"You are a wise man, Will. Do you know what I think we should do?"

He shook his head.

"Get to know each other better."

"Get to know each other?"

"Yes, you know, exchange life stories."

"My life is pretty boring."

"I'll be the judge of that. Why don't we start over the tea you've cooked?"

She took his hand and headed downstairs.

****

Alison's eyes moved slowly around the kitchen. A cosier, more inviting place it was hard to imagine. From the solid flagstone floor to the warmth of the range it was perfect. Old, in the form of the beautiful Welsh dresser, mingled in perfect harmony with the new of the kitchen units. Blue gingham curtains, which should have been twee, framed the windows perfectly and pots of herbs stood on the window sills. The centre of the kitchen was dominated by a huge old pine table, which should be the place for a family to gather around; except, Will seemed to have no family. He seemed to live completely alone.

She watched him as he moved around the kitchen with an easy familiarity preparing food. This had been a surprise. She'd not expected him to know a skillet from a toaster, yet here he was working with the practised ease of a chef.

He'd insisted that she rested while he dished up the tea. She'd smiled; this was evidence that she was in the north; down in Bath they'd have pretentiously called this meal supper. She'd agreed to rest, but here at the table, not on the sofa. She'd been alone too much in the last twenty-four hours and it gave her too much time to think.

He turned suddenly and caught her staring at him.

"What?" he asked warily, as he placed cutlery on the table.

"You are a surprising man, Will Barnes. I'd never have guessed you'd know your way around the kitchen."

His eyes slid down to look at the floor. Embarrassed at her words, he turned away. Alison sighed, he certainly wasn't used to compliments and it seemed he had no idea how to deal with them. Alison sensed that few people, if any, gave Will any praise. Had it always been that way, she wondered?

"So, what's for tea then, Jamie, or is it Nigella?" She teased, hoping to lighten the atmosphere.

He turned back to face her and caught her cheeky grin.

"It's a rare Northern delicacy; I thought you might like to try it?" he said, carefully keeping his face neutral.

"Really, a rare delicacy? What is it?" Alison asked intrigued.

"Tripe and onions."

"Tripe? I've heard of that but have no idea what it is." She smiled. "I have to say the name isn't inspiring."

"It's the lining of a cow's stomach."

Alison was horrified.

"You're joking, right?"

Will's face fell; he looked crestfallen.

"No, it's really popular and nourishing."

"Stomach lining!"

"Aye, I poached it in a little milk with some garlic and Wensleydale cheese. I thought we'd have carrots and asparagus and mash potatoes with it."

He looked so hurt, but there was no way she could eat the lining of a cow's stomach.

"Will, I'm sorry, I'm sure you've gone to a lot of trouble, but there is no way I can eat stomach lining. I just can't. I'll just have the vegetables." Alison felt terrible.

Will turned away silently and began to strain the vegetables, placing them on the table. Alison couldn't meet his eyes; he'd gone to so much trouble and here she was refusing to even try it.

He reached into the oven.

"Well, seeing as how you don't fancy tripe, it's a good job I made cottage pie," he said, placing the dish on the table. He sat down grinning like the Cheshire cat.

The next thing he knew a tea towel hit him squarely in the face.

"You sod, I really believed you. Here I was thinking that I'd really offended you."

"You did, by calling me Nigella." He smiled at her. "We should eat while it's still hot."

"Ok, cottage pie I can manage. Do people really eat tripe?"

"Yeah, you can eat it. It's really nutritious and won't kill you or owt, but it tastes disgusting. Now come on, lass, eat up."

Later, sat on the sofa, Alison was trying to work out the man who was busy doing the dishes. She'd wanted to help but he wouldn't hear of it. He was a puzzle, this man Will Barnes, that was certain. Just when she thought she was getting a handle on him, he would do something that threw her completely. Like the joke with the tripe. She hadn't expected the humour. He spoke in short sentences and seemed so uncomplicated and straightforward. It would be easy to call him simple, and she wondered if people did mistake his shyness for being not very bright. If they did, it was a mistake. There was a shrewdness about Will Barnes that led her to think he was quite an intelligent man, a practical man who'd been blessed with a good dose of common sense.

His life, she suspected, had not been easy; there was an air of sadness about him that was often reflected in his eyes. He seemed lonely and she wondered if living by himself at the farm was born of necessity not choice. His dry sense of humour had taken her by surprise, not least because, like a flash of lightning, it had appeared out of nowhere and then quickly disappeared and he had lapsed into silence once more. His solitary life and shyness seemed to have robbed him of any social skills; small talk was apparently beyond him and he had blushed and stammered at her compliments on the food.

Her own emotions were in a turmoil. Two days ago she had been a happily married woman who had never even looked at another man. The intensity of her feelings towards Will staggered her. Her hand touched her lips as she remembered the kiss. Her physical injuries meant that for the time being kisses would be all they shared and the sensible part of her knew that that was no bad thing.

As Will had said, trapped here alone at the farm it would be easy for things to move too fast and she needed to be sure what her feelings really were for Will before moving on – he deserved that.

She wondered what he thought of her. Was he in the kitchen analysing his feelings about her, as she was him? She already knew that he found her attractive; beautiful was the word he used. Had Rob ever called her beautiful? If he had, it had been too long ago to remember. He'd always called her lanky. It was funny, until today she'd thought of it affectionately, now it just irritated her. Will had called her beautiful and it had made her breath catch but, she wondered, was he curious about her beyond her looks? He hadn't seemed to be. He hadn't asked her any questions, but that could just have been his shyness.

She smiled softly as he came into the room carrying two mugs of coffee. He placed them on the table in front of the sofa before going around lighting candles.

"Sit down, Will, you've done enough today," she told him when he had finished.

He glanced about the room nervously.

"Shall I sit with you, on the sofa, like?" he asked quietly.

There it was again, the socially awkward man; did he realise how gorgeous he was, standing there, shuffling about, unsure what to do?

"Yeah, that'd be good," she smiled at him.

He sat down in the corner and, although he leant back and rested his elbow on the arm of the sofa, his tension was obvious. Alison sighed, wondering how to get him to relax.

"Let's play a game, shall we?"

"What kind of game?" he asked cautiously. "I'm not much good at games."

She sighed. There it was again – the self-put-down. Alison was sure she'd never met a less confident man.

"Oh, I don't know: you've been good at everything so far," she said with a flirty smile.

Will looked at her puzzled. He had never been flirted with before and had no idea how to respond.

"Hey, don't look so worried; it's just like the game twenty questions only no yes and no answers. We each have twenty questions and we can ask anything we like, but first: introductions." She held out her hand, "Alison Rose Robinson."

He took it slowly, his long fingers curling around hers.

"Will Barnes."

"No middle name? Is Will short for something?"

Will mumbled something.

"Sorry, I didn't catch that."

"Wilfred, me first name's Wilfred."

Named after a relative no doubt, and you don't like it much, Alison thought.

He waited for her to laugh, everybody else did, but she didn't.

"But you go by Will?"

"Yeah, I do. Wilfred were me granddad's name."

Something in his tone made Alison realise that Will had been close to his namesake.

"Is he still alive?"

"No, lass, he died six years ago – cancer."

"I'm sorry, Will. That must have been hard?"

"Aye, 'twere. He were such a vital man – big and strong. To see him ravaged by the disease was terrible."

"Did you look after him?"

"Aye, by then it were just me and him. He wanted to die here. Nurses came out but they couldn't stay all day. At the end it were just the two of us."

She barely knew this man but she found herself wishing she'd been around to offer support.

"It was peaceful at the end and for that I'm glad."

She nodded.

"I was thinking we should take it in turn asking questions?"

"Ok," Will said quietly.

"Right, ok. Do you want to go first or second?" she asked.

"I'll go first," he told her, not at all sure what he would ask, but wanting to delay having to answer a question about himself.

"Ok, fire away then."

He studied her for a moment, thinking what to ask. In the end he opted for the obvious.

"I'm...I'm going to be right boring. I don't know where to start. I can't think of owt interesting to ask. So, where is home? Not Yorkshire I'll bet?"

"No, you're not being boring. If in doubt start with something simple, that's my motto. The place I live is Bath, but it isn't home. Home, where I grew up, is Stratford upon Avon. My parents still live there..." Alison stopped talking abruptly.

"Alison, are you alright, lass?"

"Sorry, it's my parents. It's occurred to me that they must be worried." She bit her bottom lip.

"I reckon phones must be out all over t'country. Try not to worry, lass. I bet they think you're safe at home. As soon as there's a signal or t'landline is working you can call them and let them know you're safe."

She moved closer to him.

"Thank you."

"I... I...I think you should ask me my first question," Will said, nervous at her closeness.

"Are you an only child?"

He smiled wistfully.

"Yeah, me parents died when I were a bairn."

"I'm so sorry, Will."

"It's ok, I don't really remember them. What about you? Do you have any family?"

"I have a brother and a sister both older than me. Simon lives in Stratford and Jane in Warwick. I was the one who moved away from home."

"Do they have children?"

"Yes, they do, I'm Aunty Alison four times over. While I left home, you didn't. So how long have you had the farm?"

"It's been in my family for years. My grandmother's family have farmed here since King George III's time. The story goes that Joshua Walters, who farmed a small patch of land known locally as Highcroft, saved the life of a child who turned out to be the son of the local lord of Ripley Castle. By way of thanks, he was given 50 acres of farmland surrounding his croft."

"So the land here must really be in your blood. I mean, did you ever want to leave here?"

"No, and if I had wanted to I couldn't have done that. My grandparents brought me up after my folks died. I owe them everything. My gran died when I was twenty and granddad became ill a few years after that. I promised him I'd keep the farm going. What about you? You loved Stratford, why leave?" he asked.

"I left when I went to university. The plan had been to get my teaching degree and return to Stratford."

"You're a teacher?"

"Yes, I teach English at a secondary school in Bath. It's amazing, working with young people, helping them realise their potential." From the expression in her eyes, when she spoke of teaching, Will realised that she loved it.

"How long have you been teaching?" he said, smiling at her.

"You don't fool me, Mr Barnes. I know you're trying to work out how old I am by asking how long I've been working."

"I'm not, honest, but since you raised the subject... how old are you?"

Alison laughed.

"I'm thirty three and have been teaching ten years and I can't imagine doing anything else. Can you imagine doing anything else but farming?"

"No, but I have had to diversify. We were just sheep farming in granddad's days, but now, although mainly sheep, I've introduced mixed livestock. I have a rare breeds programme for cattle, sheep, pigs and chickens. Then there are the holiday cottages: I have three but am thinking of expanding to five."

"The holiday cottages are a surprise," she said.

"Yeah, a recluse like me encouraging visitors. Strange, I know." His tone was weary as if he was tired of his image.

"Well, you've been hospitable towards me so I wouldn't know about the recluse but I just thought you were a farmer."

"I am, really. The cottages help support the farm and allow me to work with the rare breeds. Farming is changing so I have had to adapt. Farm holidays are popular and we're close to towns and coasts."

Alison nodded, pleased he was relaxing and talking more.

"So why did you settle in Bath?" he asked, reaching for his coffee.

"I met Rob while I was at university. He was going to work for an IT company in Bath so I followed him."

"How long have you been married?" he asked.

"Five years – I thought happily but it seems my marriage is not what I thought it was."

Alison reflected later that the quiet words Will spoke in response to her answer pulled the rug from beneath her feet and stunned her as much as the impact of falling in the snow.

"No, my marriage weren't what I expected either."

"You were married?" she asked incredulously. His confession that he had been married astounded her. She realised the moment she spoke how rude she sounded, but she was just so shocked, she was sure her jaw had dropped open at his words.

"Sorry, Will, that was so rude of me," she apologised.

"Oh, don't be. Everybody reacts like that," he said quietly.

She felt terrible.

"I was the local laughing stock for years after my marriage. My neighbours talked of little else for months," he carried on.

His admission that his neighbours had laughed at him broke her heart.

"I wasn't laughing at you. You just seem as if you have always been alone here. Why would anybody be so cruel as to laugh at you?"

"Well, everybody knew she didn't love me. I suppose they thought I were a fool."

"She didn't love you. Did you marry her knowing that?"

"Aye, I did. I'd loved Moira since I were a teenager and when she accepted me proposal, well, it were like me birthday and Christmas all at once."

"Why did you ask her to marry you? I mean if you knew she didn't love you."

"She was all alone and needed my help. Her Dad had worked at Highcroft when we were kids. After he died she went away. When she came back it was obvious she'd been struggling. She needed a friend and some security."

Looking back, the reason for his asking Moira to marry him was compelling: she needed him. Even now he had remembered how his heart had beat a little faster when he'd realised that she needed him. In thirty one years he'd never been needed by anybody. Family didn't count - he acknowledged they needed him, but it wasn't the same. Not that looking after his granddad had been anything but a labour of love. It was just he was family and he had just done what was expected of him. That some other person should need him, Will Barnes, had been amazing. Not wanted but needed. Wanting something implied you could live without it, but needing, well, that meant you couldn't survive without it.

"And you could provide it. You must have loved her a great deal. May I ask why you say she didn't love you?" Alison's voice interrupted his thoughts.

Will sighed and waited for the pain to develop in his chest as it always did when he thought of Moira. Strangely, this time it wasn't as intense as usual.

"She were in love with the neighbour's lad, Myles; had been for years. But when she moved back he were already married to somebody else. I guess she wanted to move on from him and we were friends."

"So, I'm guessing, because of your comment about your marriage not being what you'd expected, that you're not married now?"

"No, I'm not."

"How long were you married before you split up?

"We didn't split up. The reason I'm alone is Moira died."

He stood up and put another log in the wood burner, staring at the flames for a long time before moving to draw the curtains at the window.

Alison crossed the room to stand at his side. His life, as she'd suspected, had indeed been hard.

"I'm sorry. It was never my intention to bring up sad memories."

"No, it's ok. You weren't to know. It happened a long time ago. I've been a widower as long as you've been married."

"Which means, old man, that you are how much older than me?" Alison asked, trying to lighten the mood.

"Oh, I'm a lot older than you. I'm thirty seven, so four years older. This means I need much more rest than you. So, I'll let the dogs out and make a cuppa before we turn in."

****

Alison lay quietly, thinking. She had never known darkness like it. It was so deep and intense that it seemed to swallow the room. Everywhere else she had lived or stayed there had been streetlights that shone through the windows. Here there was nothing. There was a glow from the log burner that cast a small semicircle of light, but, beyond, it was just inky blackness.

Will, she knew, was stretched out on the sofa, which was completely stupid. It could not be comfortable, but he had said he would be fine. He'd told her that she had to sleep down here where it was warm and that he wanted to be on hand should she need him.

Alison sighed; she did need him but not in the way he meant. She needed him to hold her. It was ridiculous to be scared of the dark but it was more than that. She wanted to feel his reassuring solid strength against her. She wanted to be enfolded in the warmth of his embrace.

Lying there, thinking over his words, she realised what an idiot she had been. She shouldn't have assumed he was a bachelor. Hadn't she thought that his life had been tough and that he seemed sad? He'd lapsed into silence after he'd let the dogs out, saying no more, his expressive eyes filled with sadness.

"Alison?" His deep voice startled her, coming unexpectedly out of the shadows. "You ok? You're very restless."

"I can't sleep," she told him.

"I could make some hot chocolate if you like?"

She smiled in the darkness. Lord, he was so sweet.

"No, it's ok. I'm just being silly."

"Silly? How?" Alison heard him move and swing his legs off the sofa.

"Do you promise not to laugh?"

"I'd never laugh at you, lass." His voice was laced with concern.

"I'm scared of the dark. I've never known darkness like this."

"Ah, lass, lots of town folk say that about the country."

"Do they? Well, I have a request. Do you think you could bunk down here with me?"

He was silent for the longest time.

"Will, I'm sorry, that was wrong of me. Forget I asked."

"I don't want to forget and I could bunk with you ..." Will paused embarrassed. "But if I lie close to you I'd struggle to hide my feelings."

"I'm not sure I'm following you, Will."

"I know we've only just met and I said we should slow down a little, but ..." he stopped, glad she couldn't see how red his cheeks were.

"But you're physically attracted to me. Is that what you're trying to say?" Alison asked quietly.

She heard him exhale sharply.

"Yeah, I guess..." he paused again. "I'd not do owt, because you're hurt, but if I lay next to you... well, um, me body... well, it would be obvious, like," he finished on a rush.

She smiled softly and moved the covers aside.

"I'm attracted to you as well, Will. It's nothing to be embarrassed about. We can take this slowly. I just really need you to hold me. So, please, will you come here?"

There was that word again – need – only four letters but so powerful. Helpless to resist he swallowed hard and moved to the mattress. She was lying on her back when he slid in beside her but she turned towards him immediately. Her face was just inches from his own, so close he could feel her breath on his cheek. He slipped his arm gently around her, being careful not to hurt her injured arm.

"Thank you, Will," Alison whispered, before brushing her lips against his. It was supposed to be light and simple, a token of thanks, but the moment she touched him heat spread through her. She needed this, needed him. The kiss seemed to have a life of its own and Alison just gave herself up to it.

He should pull away, he knew that. He was the one who had said they should take this slowly, but the intensity of the kiss overwhelmed him. Heat and need consumed him and he gave himself into the exquisite touch of her lips. Her hand was stroking down his back and he felt his muscles ripple under her touch. Then he felt her mouth at his throat, feathering kisses along it and down to the hollow in his shoulder. Her hand had moved to his buttocks and she pulled him closer. His breath hissed out as he became aroused. Alison had to be aware of what she was doing to him. He tensed and tried to pull away, embarrassed.

"Hey, it's ok. Remember what I said? It's normal, I'm aroused as well." She took his hand and guided it to her breast. "Touch me, Will, then you'll see that I'm just as aroused as you are."

He hesitantly cupped her breast through the softness of the material.

"You can move your hand. I won't break and you won't hurt me."

"Like this?" he asked shyly as his thumb gently stroked her through the material of her shirt.

She moaned softly.

"Yes. See, I told you I was as turned on as you. Please kiss me again while you do that?"

They lay in each other's arms, kissing and caressing, tentatively taking the first steps in their relationship before tiredness claimed them and they fell asleep, wrapped around each other.

Chapter Six

No signal again. He slammed the phone down, cursing in annoyance. Where was she? And, more importantly, what was she planning? He looked through the window at the snow. There had to be ten or twelve inches out there. Fucking freak weather conditions! If it hadn't been for the snow she'd never have found out. It should have been perfect. Ali had been away on a teaching conference so the house had been empty. He'd liked the element of danger in smuggling Claire in unseen by the neighbours, letting her wander around where Ali had been, and use Ali's things, before screwing her in their bed. Then the snow had arrived. He guessed that the conference had finished early because of the severe weather warnings.

Judging by her expression, Ali had been stood in the doorway quite some time, watching them. Claire had handcuffed him to the bed, which was why Ali managed to get away before he could stop her. By the time he was free, all that was left were tyre tracks in the snow. He'd slammed the door and smacked his fist against it, frustration and anger coursing through his veins. When he'd turned,

Claire was stood at the top of the stairs – naked, her stance and gaze victorious like a lioness with a kill. He couldn't be sure how many times they had already fucked when Ali had found them - all he knew was it hadn't been enough.

She'd looked at him and laughed.

"Did you see her face as she watched us fuck?" she'd asked.

He hadn't. But he'd been so excited thinking about it that he'd screwed Claire right there, on the stairs, hoping Ali would return and see them again – but she hadn't.

As a mistress, Claire was perfect: exciting, daring, dangerous, different, in short, everything Ali was not. She'd picked him up at a sales convention. Like the predator she was, she had eyed him up, liked what she saw and moved in like a hunter stalking her prey. Not that he'd been unaware of her; he would have needed to be blind not to have noticed her. She was dressed like a siren, in some figure hugging dress, displaying more curves than were found on a scenic railway, and bristling with attitude and intention that screamed sex. They'd had intercourse within half an hour of meeting and the flaming desire he felt for her showed no signs of abating.

Claire wasn't the first woman he'd had. There had been several. He'd been seeking something that he just didn't have with Ali but, until Claire, he hadn't found it. He'd known immediately that she was different. There was something wild and untamed about her. She forced him to toss away his inhibitions, encouraging him to act rashly and take risks. With her there were no responsibilities, no consequences for his actions; there was just that moment. Until Claire, he thought he had been sexually adventurous but she'd shown him what a novice he was. She was like a professor of debauchery and he was a willing student. She was as addictive as any drug and he could not give her up.

The problem was though, Claire alone wasn't enough. He wanted it all: the danger and excitement with Claire and the perfect marriage and wife. He had that with Ali, everybody told him. He'd lost count of how many people had told him what a lucky sod he was to have found a woman like Ali. He normally smiled and nodded. Ali was the perfect wife. He'd known she would be from the moment he'd met her at university. She was the quintessential English rose – elegant, polite and charming. He'd realised early on what an asset a wife like her would be. He'd pursued her carefully throughout their first year at university, knowing that she was the kind of woman who wanted romance. They were engaged by the end of their second year and married in her local church just after they had graduated.

That was five years ago and he had not been wrong about her. She had created a wonderful home for them. She had found the house in an executive area of Bath, the ideal place for an upwardly mobile couple such as them. He looked around at the furniture and furnishings, all things Ali had selected and lovingly put together. He acknowledged her taste was exquisite.

They entertained friends and business associates frequently; their dinner parties were becoming famous. He teased her gently about being a domestic goddess to rival Nigella Lawson. Nothing threw her. He could turn up with business associates unannounced, which he often did, and she would welcome them in and entertain them as if she had been preparing for their arrival for months.

She currently worked full time as a teacher – a traditionally female job that she would give up when they started a family. They had not discussed it, but that was what would happen, because he was the man and he made the decisions. He wanted Ali to be the mother of his children and no job was going to get in the way. She'd be a perfect mother, just as she was a perfect wife. He always made the important decisions, and Ali, who knew her place, rarely questioned him. He smiled. She was the perfect wife, and he was neither prepared nor ready to give up the life he had with her.

It was the balance between this perfect marriage and his dangerous and daring affair he was scared of losing. He needed both things to keep him satisfied. One would not work without the other. He shivered slightly, terrified that because of the weather he might lose it all.

He glanced out of the window. It had finally stopped snowing. A part of him was glad as it meant that the services would be reconnected. It was odd how much people took gas, electricity and the phone for granted. Of course though, once things were reconnected Ali's parents would be in touch. They were close to their daughter and she would be the first person they would want to talk to. He had to speak to her before they did.

Ali's behaviour was so out of character. Running was an impulsive action and she was a creature of habit. She never did things on the spur of the moment. Christ, her lists and plans were legendary. All of which meant that her impromptu flight gave him no clue where she had gone. It hadn't been to any of their friends though. Before the phone lines went down he'd checked with them. Unless they were lying, Ali wasn't with them and he guessed she must have gone further away.

Would she have gone to her parents? Rob hoped not. He knew that he stood a better chance of smoothing things over if her parents were not involved. There was no way that they would understand about Claire, and they would see through any assurances he gave Ali. Not that he intended to give Claire up; he couldn't, but Ali was prone to be too trusting and gullible and he felt certain if he could get her alone he would be able to sort this out. Maybe he'd tell her he wanted to make a baby. Sex with Ali, although different than with Claire, was still satisfying. He was a good lover and he knew she enjoyed intercourse with him.

One of the things he really loved was screwing her after he had been with Claire. He could still smell and taste his mistress while he fucked his wife. No, he had no intention of giving up his lifestyle.

He sighed. It was the not knowing where she was, combined with the inactivity caused by the storm, that was driving him crazy. He needed to do something constructive.

A sound from the behind him made him turn away from the window. Claire stood framed in the doorway.

"You need to accept that there is nothing you can do at the moment. It is just a waste of energy. Energy that, if I may say, could be put to better use." She pouted prettily.

He moved towards her, his eyes taking in the silky peach robe she wore.

"For God's sake, Claire, the neighbours might see you."

"Yes, they might. Can you imagine them watching us fuck."

His eyes dilated and his breath quickened.

"Is that Ali's?" he asked.

She nodded as he took her in his arms. Her scent mingled with Ali's causing him to groan.

"I can smell her scent on your skin," he murmured.

"Does it turn you on?" she whispered.

"God, yes." He kissed her neck. "It's like tasting her on your skin."

Claire undid the robe revealing glimpses of the peach underwear beneath.

"Do you recognise these?"

"Jesus, you're wearing her underwear." He cupped her breasts. "They're fuller than Ali's. Look at them straining against the lace."

"Have you had sex with her while she was wearing this underwear?"

"No, she removed it first."

"Of course she did – prim madam. Do it to me while I wear her underwear."

Rob felt himself become aroused at her words. He slipped the gown from her shoulder as he pushed her gently back onto the dining room table. How could he give this up? The answer was he couldn't.

Chapter Seven

Alison turned, searching for Will's solid warmth as she slowly came awake. Her eyes flickered open and disappointment washed over her when she realised she was alone. The pillow still bore the imprint of his head and his scent lingered on the sheets. It was wrong to be disappointed, she realised. After all, Will was a farmer; early starts were part of his life. She reached for his pillow, cuddling it close, thinking of how shyly he had touched her as they had kissed. A warm glow filtered through her body and her heart beat a fraction quicker as she remembered being held in Will's arms.

As she hugged his pillow, Alison had to acknowledge her feelings; there was no point in denying them. She was certain that she was falling in love. The rational part of her brain tried to tell her it was too soon and that she was confusing her deep gratitude with love, but her heart knew that wasn't the case. It wasn't lust either. Will Barnes was a special man – humble, modest and good down to his soul. Alison found herself drawn to his shy ways, his thoughtfulness, his kindness and above all his tenderness. His soft words, gentle kisses and hesitant caresses had left an imprint on her heart. She couldn't begin to contemplate having to leave him – just the thought of it caused her heart to contract painfully.

She offered a silent prayer that they might remain marooned here at the farm for some time yet, allowing them the space away from the real world to explore their new feelings, to see what might develop without censure – and there would be censure of that Alison was certain. People would not understand her declaration of love for someone she had known for forty-eight hours. How could they? Even to her own ears it seemed ridiculous. She wanted what she had with Will to be untouched by the real world, especially her life with Rob, which was totally unrealistic. Her past had to be faced and dealt with to allow her to move on. Just not yet, she thought. Allow us a few more days before we have to face the inevitable. She closed her eyes and allowed herself five minutes to daydream.

Never one to lie idly in bed once awake, it wasn't long before she became restless and decided to get up. Her muscles and bones seemed marginally less painful today but it still hurt to take a deep breath so she moved cautiously. A glance under the rugby shirt she was wearing revealed that the bruises from the seat belt had turned a multitude of colours. She carefully moved her shoulder, relieved that here at least the pain was much improved.

After she had set the kettle on the range, she slowly climbed the stairs, shivering now she was away from the warmth of the rooms downstairs. Once she had used the bathroom she was drawn to the room she had found Will in yesterday. The pretty wallpaper and bed linen pointed to it being a young girl's room. Alison couldn't help but wonder who and where she was. On the chest of drawers there were two photographs, one of a young woman with her arms around a teenager, the other a wedding photograph with Will stood between the two women. She smiled, he looked so happy. What had Will said about Moira agreeing to marry him? That it was like his birthday and Christmas both together. The older woman had to be Moira. She was far too young to have died. It was strange, she hadn't really thought of her as being young but, confronted by the photograph, her age was brought into sharp relief. Questions about her death formed in her mind; it was only natural to wonder how she had died.

She was a very pretty woman with long, curly hair and dark eyes. Her smile, though, didn't quite reach her eyes and Alison was struck by how sad they were. Was she, even then on her wedding day, regretting marrying Will? Had she even attempted to make the marriage a success? To be happy with him?

Her eyes moved to the image of the young girl. Who was this teenager? There was a marked resemblance to the older woman so maybe she was a younger sister. Like Will, she looked happy. I'm glad, Alison thought, that someone else was as happy as he was that day.

The room was tidy but lived in and smelt of bees wax polish. Treasured possessions were dotted around the room – a teddy rested against the pillow and a poster of Viggo Mortensen was pinned on the door. CDs were stacked on a shelf next to a music centre. A bookshelf was filled with books, on top of which stood a display of china horses and silk rosettes. On the bedside cabinet were two more photographs, one a picture of the woman and one of Will. She picked the photograph of Will up and slowly stroked the glass. He was smiling softly and in his arms he held a sleeping puppy. The photograph was simply stunning. His pale skin was clear, almost luminous, his deep blue eyes shone with some unknown emotion, his dark brown hair, so soft and tousled, begged to be touched. He hasn't a clue how gorgeous he is, Alison thought, unlike Rob who knows he's good looking and wants everybody else to know as well.

She sensed the room was still used; it certainly didn't feel like a shrine. Alison was sure that, whoever the girl was, she was still a part of Will's life. She made her way back downstairs not wanting to pry any further, certain that at some point Will would explain who the women were and where the younger one was.

The kettle that she had set on the range was boiling so she made her tea. Will had left a note on the table explaining where he was and that he would be back at eight to make her breakfast. Alison smiled at his last words:

"Take two painkillers."

The box was even on the table ready. She shook out two pink pills, knowing it would be the first thing he would check she had done.

Making her way back into the living room with her tea, she heard the wild barking of a dog outside. Moving to the window, Alison peered out to see what the noise was about.

Her breath caught in her throat. If she hadn't already been half in love with this quiet, gentle man, the image of him in the farmyard would have set her on the way. His head was thrown back and his face was alive with laughter. It illuminated his features making him appear years younger. Such a contrast to the shy, serious man she had come to know. Her hands itched to take a photograph and capture the joy in his expression.

He was throwing snowballs for the young sheep dog, Winston. She watched as another arced through the frigid, cold morning air, before breaking into pieces when it landed; Winston dashed madly after it, snow flying in all directions, before he came to an abrupt halt wondering where 'the ball' had landed. He ran in bewildered circles looking for it. The other two older dogs sat looking on indulgently at the younger dog's antics. Will's shoulders shook with laughter as the young dog bounded back to him. He patted his chest and the dog jumped into his arms. Alison watched as he showered the dog with love and affection before he lowered him back to the floor. He repeated the game, throwing a snowball in the other direction.

Time seemed to stand still as she watched him having pure, unadulterated fun.

"How often do you do this, Will? Just take time away from the responsibility you wear like a skin? Just have fun and play? Not nearly often enough, I bet," she whispered.

The game continued for fifteen minutes before the need to do some work interrupted him and Will headed into one of the farm buildings, all three dogs trailing after him.

She glanced at the grandfather clock. Quarter to eight. He'd be back at eight to make her breakfast. Taking care of her. But who took care of him? Had anybody ever taken care of him? Somehow she doubted it. Well, that was about to change. She wasn't so sick that she needed waiting on; she could certainly make breakfast for them both.

****

Will paused in the porch; Alison was singing in the kitchen. He recognised the carol from his childhood when he'd gone to church on Christmas Day with his gran. He wondered if she knew she had a lovely voice. He opened the door quietly; she was at the range stirring something on the hob. Winston's whining caused her to stop singing before she had finished the carol. She spun around at the sound, her face flushed at having been caught.

"Oh God, how long have you been stood there?"

"Since 'Earth stood hard as iron'," Will said with a smile.

Alison groaned as her hands flew to her face to cover her flaming cheeks.

"Oh, great."

Will moved towards her and took her hands in his.

"No hiding. It were beautiful. Won't you finish singing it?"

Alison was suddenly nervous, which was odd, as she had sung in public on numerous occasions. This was different though. It was all together more intimate. Will hadn't released her hands and his intense blue eyes were staring down at her.

"Please, lass. For me?"

She moistened her lips which had become suddenly dry. How was she supposed to refuse when he looked at her like that? The answer was she couldn't.

"What can I give him, poor as I am?

If I were a shepherd, I would bring a lamb.

If I were a Wise Man, I would do my part.

Yet what I can I give him: give my heart."

Will pulled her close and kissed the top of her head.

"That were beautiful, Alison, lass. Thank you for letting me listen."

"You're welcome and you're bloody cold, Mr Barnes. Sit yourself down by the range and get warm. Breakfast won't be a minute."

Will looked around. Listening to her sing, he hadn't registered that she had made breakfast.

"You shouldn't have done this, lass. You're still recovering."

"I'm not made of glass; I won't shatter. I was bored and I'm aware that you have to look after the farm alone. You shouldn't have to look after me, not now I'm feeling much better."

Will shivered as a chill passed over him that had nothing to do with the weather. Alison saying she was feeling better reminded him that she would soon be well enough to leave, which was something he really wasn't ready to deal with yet.

"Will, you ok?"

He mentally shook himself.

"Yeah, why do you ask?"

"It's just that you looked worried."

"No, I'm fine."

Alison moved towards him.

"Don't lie. Did you know, big guy, that when you worry you get these three little crinkles on your forehead?" She reached up and touched them. "And they make you look so damn sexy - they really should be illegal. They appear and I get the overwhelming urge to kiss you." Alison reached up, smiling at the blush on his cheeks and then she kissed him. "See, I can't help myself. Now sit down while I dish up breakfast and stop worrying, I'm fine."

Will sat down. She might be fine, he thought, but if she left when the snow cleared he knew he wouldn't be.

"Have you had vocal training?" Will said, desperate to talk about something and not think about her leaving.

"When I was younger, yes. I studied singing and the piano. Don't laugh, but I sing in a choir at home."

"Why would I laugh?"

"Well, it sounds so boring, saying you sing in a choir."

"I don't think it's boring and you sound fantastic. Do you teach music as well as English?"

"No, I surprised everybody by studying English."

"Why were they surprised?"

"Because everybody thought I would teach music, but I believe everybody should be able to read. God, I sound like a prig. It's just that there's a whole world inside the cover of a book and everybody should be able to discover it. I wanted to help them."

Will smiled.

"Do your students realise how lucky they are to have you?"

"I don't know about that." She placed the porridge on the table. "But when I first started teaching I did help a young lad who could barely read and had no interest in school through his GCSE English Lit exam. That was fantastic."

"How did you get him interested?"

"You have to understand that this boy was excluded most of the time. So he was never in class. I gave him specific assignments. I chose books and plays he could relate to. He was from a pretty poor background and belonged in a gang. So I got him reading Romeo and Juliet because, while it's a love story, it's also about gangs. My colleagues thought I was mad; they felt certain I'd be hurt by him. But this kid had nobody going out to bat for him. I did help him and he repaid me by passing the subject. When I'm having a bad day I remember him. I bet I sound so smug. "

"No, you don't, lass. I help young people as well. It does make you feel good."

"Really. How do you help?"

"A few years back the probation service asked if I'd be prepared to give a couple of young offenders work on the farm. Young lads in particular are less likely to reoffend if they have work. I normally have two or three teenagers working for me. I think I mentioned two of them the other day."

"Yes, you did."

"Well, Stuart is the fifteenth young lad I've taken on and Mike is now in college. Most have worked out really well and are now in other jobs."

"That's wonderful, Will, but it must be difficult without them to help at the moment."

"Aye, it is. But there's nowt I can do about it. So I'll just have to get on with the work on my own."

Win whined from his basket.

"Oh, I'm sorry, mate, I stand corrected. Winston, Bess and Drake will help, so I won't be on my own."

Alison smiled.

"No, you mustn't forget the dogs; they're man's best friend after all."

"My only friends," Will muttered as he stood and took his dishes to the sink.

Alison didn't move immediately. She was certain Will hadn't intended for her to hear his last comment. Had she ever heard anybody sound so lonely? She had thought that Will had chosen to be alone but now she wondered if he was actually lonely.

She stood and, picking up the tea towel, moved to his side.

"You wash and I'll dry. Will you be back at lunch time?"

"I doubt it. I have to get up to the higher fields today and check the sheep."

"Ok, I'll pack you some lunch then."

They moved in comfortable silence cleaning the kitchen together. He switched the radio on to catch the news while she made his lunch.

Will watched as she placed sandwiches in a lunchbox.

"You didn't have to make those. I could have done it."

"I don't mind, but I charge for making sarnies, you know."

He smiled at the gleam in her eye.

"You're up north now, lass. We don't eat sarnies – we eat butties. So, what do four butties cost?"

"One kiss."

She moved towards him.

The moment her lips touched his, he was lost. At first her lips were gentle like their previous kisses but then something changed. The kiss became more intense. There was a wildness about it that scared the hell out of him. He'd no idea he could feel this way. He pulled away and, grabbing his lunch, left while he still could.

Alison stared at the door, her heart pounding, trying to understand what had just happened. She pressed her hand to her lips. She had devoured him. A few minutes more and they would have been making love. Was she ready for that? She was so confused she didn't know what she wanted.

****

It was strange that it should feel so good to be this tired. Will wondered if other people ever felt like this, tired but satisfied. He had, as he told Alison he would be, been out all day. He smiled at the memory of sharing breakfast with her. For the first time in a long time, maybe ever, he felt complete. The sensible part of his brain reminded him that none of it was real. She wasn't his wife or partner; they weren't making a home together, but it had been good to pretend even for a short while.

They'd switched the radio on, listening to the news. The country, it seemed, was at a virtual standstill with all public transport suspended. Huge parts were without electricity, water or telephone. Experts were saying that this was the worst winter storm on record and it could take a week or more to reach people who were stranded in the more remote areas, and that was if there was no more snow fall. He'd been relieved by this, not about the people trapped in the snow – countless people would be really suffering; some of whom would possibly die. No, he was relieved that, for a while longer at least, Alison would have to stay with him.

The illusion of domestic bliss had continued when Alison helped him pack his lunch and made him a large thermos of coffee. He couldn't remember anybody making his lunch since he was a child, certainly not Moira. And Sarah, God love her, was no morning person; she could barely get herself ready for college in time for the bus, let alone make his lunch. He'd been taking care of himself for a long time and it was odd to suddenly have somebody else do things for him.

If he'd been unprepared for her help in the kitchen, then he was blindsided by the kiss they had shared before he had left. He could still feel its effects several hours later. It had started like all the others they had shared, soft and gentle, but then something had changed, the kiss becoming more intense, more demanding. Alison's hands had slid under his shirt, exploring and pulling him closer, her hips rocking against his seductively. Will had never kissed like this before. The power of it scared him; he wasn't used to being out of control. He found himself following her lead, helpless to stop. His hands had moved beneath her shirt, touching her bare flesh for the first time. He'd barely touched a woman before and never like this. The tentative caresses through her clothes the night before had in no way prepared him for the petal softness of her skin. He'd wanted to cup her breast as he had done last night but his confidence deserted him and then she'd pulled away clearly as stunned by the kiss as he was. Whatever was happening between them had clearly moved on to another level and neither of them had been prepared for it.

His emotions had been running riot when he'd left the

farmhouse and he'd been glad that he had a lot of work to distract him. It was only now as he made his way home that he had allowed himself to analyse what he was feeling. Was it love? He wasn't ready to admit that even to himself. His past had made him cautious. And as much as Alison had captivated him, he had a built in need to protect himself. The scars that his marriage to Moira had left, although healed, still served as a reminder that he'd once given his heart and been badly hurt. He needed to be certain that Alison's feelings towards him were not confused because of the situation she had found herself in.

There was another reason he was being cautious: his inexperience. It wasn't that he was ashamed of it, he wasn't, well, apart from his first time with Moira. That had been a sordid disaster. No, he wasn't ashamed, but he was embarrassed. He was over thirty. How could he explain that he'd only tried to have sex three times and that each time had been a fumbled mess? How could he explain he wasn't certain that he knew how to make love? God knows he wanted to and, if the kiss they had shared that morning was anything to go by, it was where they were heading. He sighed. He was going to have to find a way to tell her or it would be as disastrous as it had been with Moira.

He had taken the tractor and begun to clear a path up to the other fields, feeding and checking the sheep as he went. As far as the eye could see, the Dales were covered in a blanket of snow. The stone walls that bordered most of the fields had been lost in drifts ten or twelve feet high. The going was slightly easier heading back down than it had been going up as he had cleared a path. Finding the gates in the walls had been difficult and frustrating even for him, and he knew this countryside like the back of his hand. He had lost count of the times he had climbed down from the cab of the tractor. Snow shoes or skis would have been better than his Wellington boots to walk through the snow.

Now that the light was beginning to fade, the countryside took on an eerie kind of beauty. Trees casting long shadows on the snow were silhouetted against the darkening sky. Icicles hung from the branches like glittering jewels. The sun was dipping low on the horizon, leaving a paint box of colours across the sky, from fiery red, to blazing gold and finally to a soft muted pink, all reflected in the dazzling white of the snow. There was not a breath of wind. It was as if the whole world were still, sat in silent wonder, watching nature's fireworks illuminate the sky. There in front of him was the farmhouse; soft, subtle light glowed from the windows like a beacon calling him home. Alison must have lit some candles.

For the first time in a long time, he was actually glad to be going home. Instead of a cold empty house awaiting him, tonight there would be a warm welcoming home. It occurred to him how lonely he had been since Sarah had started her gap year. That had been September and he had spent every night alone at the farmhouse since. He was beginning to see that Alison was saving him just as he had saved her.

He pulled into the yard and let Winston down from the cab. The young dog bounded to the back porch barking loudly. The door opened and light spilled out into the now almost dark farmyard. He glanced up and there she was, standing in the doorway, a smile on her face. She was the image of wholesome prettiness framed within the doorway, and to him more precious than any work of art in the Louvre.

Will quickly checked that the animals in the outbuildings which surrounded the farmyard were alright and secured them for the night before he headed back to the house. No, he corrected himself, he wasn't just going back to his house. He was going back home.

Chapter Eight

Alison was stirring a pot of chilli when she heard Will come into the porch. She turned as the kitchen door opened. God, he looked tired. The memory of the kiss they had shared was making her feel awkward and she was unsure what to say. She didn't know whether to tell him how worried she had been when the light had begun to fade and he had not returned.

"You've cooked tea. That wasn't necessary," he said

She handed him a mug of tea.

"It was the least I could do; you've been working all day."

"I know, but you should have been resting."

"I did rest. How bad is it out there?" she asked.

"Well, there's a lot of drifting and it were really icy this morning. I've not known worse conditions. I cleared a path up through the fields so all the sheep have been fed." As he spoke the words, he wondered if Alison would think it wrong that he had not tried to get to the village.

"Did you lose any more sheep?" Alison asked.

"Six more, which were far fewer than I'd been expecting. They were all together, using each other's heat to stay warm. They're not as daft as they look."

"I'm glad that the losses have 't been too great, but it must hurt to lose even one animal," she said softly.

"Aye, lass, it does. But that's farming - there will always be deaths. The only thing you can do is the best you can. Alison, I'm sorry that I didn't have time to try and go down to the village but I had to check on the livestock."

Privately she was glad he hadn't gone down to the village.

"Don't be so daft; your animals are the most important thing on the farm. It's only right you look after them. I never expected you to go to the village."

"You didn't?"

"No, I didn't." She took his hand. "I'm ok here, aren't I? I mean, do you want me to leave? Am I in the way?"

"No, of course I don't want you to leave. You can stay as long as you like."

"Good." She smiled. "Now, you look tired, so you just finish your tea. I've put water on to heat so you could clean up before tea."

Will glanced at the bucket of hot water on the range.

"Alison, you shouldn't be lifting buckets of water."

"Oh, don't worry, I didn't, I put the bucket on the range and then filled it up using the kettle. It's boiling now so, whenever you're ready, you can take it upstairs and get cleaned up."

"Ok, thank you for taking the trouble. I'm not used to being looked after." He sipped his tea, drawn in by the domesticity. "How have you been today and what have you done with yourself?" he asked.

"Oh, I'm much better. I took some more painkillers and had a sleep this afternoon, not that I'm doing anything to be tired. Then I read a farming magazine."

Will frowned.

"You're doing it again Will, crinkling."

"I should have told you there are loads of books upstairs, I never thought."

"Hey, don't be silly. I'll have a look after tea. Now go get cleaned up or tea will be ruined."

"Yeah, I can tell you're better because you're bossing me about." His shy smile slid across his face as he spoke, his tone teasing.

"You bet I am; now get going," she smiled back.

He climbed up the stairs slowly. He knew it was stupid to be thinking of forever, but he couldn't help wishing Alison would always be waiting when he came home.

The chilli she had made was keeping warm on the range and because Will was still in the bathroom she decided to grab a book to read after tea. She was managing the stairs better now. The bathroom door was closed so she carried on down the corridor, looking in the doors leading off from it until she found the one with a bookcase. She guessed it was Will's room. It looked more masculine than the room he had been in yesterday. The décor was plain and unfussy. She realised that the huge bed was minus its mattress because it was downstairs. He had, it seemed, quite literally given her his bed. She moved to the bookshelf. His reading tastes were a surprise; eclectic summed it up. Classics nestled next to modern thrillers. History books were popular as was poetry and there were several biographies and autobiographies. It was an English Literature teacher's dream. She was about to remove 'A Christmas Carol' when she heard a noise at the door.

Turning, she gasped in surprise and then froze. Will was stood in the doorway. Apart from the bath towel around his hips he was naked. If she was asked she couldn't have said what colour the towel was because her eyes were drawn to his chest. Her mouth had gone dry and she was certain her cheeks were flushed. She should move or say something but she couldn't. Small droplets of water were scattered over his chest. One was trickling slowly down towards his abdomen. The hard physical farm work had made his chest and arm muscles strong and well developed. His abdomen was flat and toned. He'd almost certainly never been in a gym and didn't need to. He was physically stunning. She'd guessed that he was powerfully built when she had run her hands over his back last night, but nothing had prepared her for this perfection. If she were an artist she would want to sculpt him.

Her skin was hot, her pulse and breathing ragged. Red, hot desire and need shot through her. She wanted this man on the most basic human level. She raised her eyes to his face. His eyes were burning and his cheeks were pink with embarrassment. He turned before she could speak or move and fled back to the safety of the bathroom.

He reached the bathroom and slammed the door. He was trembling violently – no matter how hard he tried he was unable to control it. It had started when he had found Alison in his room. At first he'd been embarrassed to be seen in just a towel, but that hadn't lasted, not once he had seen the look in Alison's eyes. He might be inexperienced, but he was certain that what he was seeing was raw, naked passion. Alison's gaze had been transfixed on him. He'd begun to feel panic rising through his body. What if she touched him or went to remove the towel? Memories of that first time with Moira flooded through him. None of the times he had sex did he last long enough, but the first time with Moira it was over before it started. He couldn't face that happening with Alison. He'd watched as her small pink tongue moistened her lips. He'd felt his groin grow heavy. Was his arousal visible through the towel? He prayed not. He swallowed hard, trying to think of something flippant to say but words failed him. She seemed to move slightly towards him. Panic surged through him. If she touched him it would happen again and he didn't want a quick fumble with him unable to control himself. So he turned and fled.

    His heart was hammering and it felt as if it were rising out of his chest up into his throat, dragging the acid from his stomach with it. His breathing was ragged, being torn from his lungs in rapid gasps. The breaths were too fast and too shallow to take enough oxygen into his lungs. Pain began to spread down his arms resulting in tingling in his hands and fingers. Black spots floated in front of his eyes and his sight became blurred and unfocused.

The bathroom had suddenly become unbearably hot and sweat beaded on his brow. Will was terrified. He had no idea what was happening but he was certain it wasn't good. Was it a heart attack or a stroke? Whatever it was he wished it would stop. Nausea washed over him and before he could move he vomited all over the floor. Realising he was going to be sick again he moved to the toilet where the vomiting continued. He retched until his stomach was empty.

In the distance, he could hear insistent tapping on the bathroom door and somebody repeatedly calling his name: Alison. The mere thought of facing her terrified him and his breathing became rapid once more. The room began to spin and a loud buzzing noise filled his head. His mouth was as dry as sandpaper. He was so hot. The knocking on the door became more insistent and Alison's voice held an edge of panic. He felt the colour begin to drain from his face. Although it had never happened before; he knew without a doubt that he was going to pass out. The walls of the bathroom were closing in on him and he began to feel weak and disorientated. He needed help and Alison was the only person here so no matter how humiliated he felt he was going to have to ask her for help. Turning to the door he reached for the bolt, his hand shook and his palm was sweaty which made it difficult to slide it back. Finally he managed to open the door.

Alison's face swam in front of him. Will registered that the look of hot passion had gone; in its place was a small frown that showed how worried she was. He took two steps forward before his legs gave out and he fell to his knees, trying desperately to get some air into his lungs. It seemed the harder he tried the less air he actually took in.

Although the sight of Will falling forwards on to his hands and knees had set her heart rate racing, Alison ordered herself to stay calm. She thought she knew what was happening, though she was having difficulty believing that it would happen to her strong dependable rescuer, but she had to be certain.

She knelt by his side her hand resting on the pulse at his wrist. It was a little fast but strong.

"Will, don't talk just nod or shake your head, ok?" Alison told him quietly.

He nodded slowly.

"Do you have a deep crushing pain in your chest?"

He shook his head.

"How about down your left arm? Any pain there?"

"Both arms," Will gasped.

"Do you have pins and needles in your hands?"

He nodded again.

"Will, I'm pretty sure it's nothing serious. Just hold on a second while I get something and we'll slow your breathing down." She stood slowly and headed downstairs.

It was ironic. Five minutes ago he hadn't wanted to see her and now he didn't want her to leave him alone. He watched her disappear downstairs. If he'd had the breath to call after her, beg her not to leave him, he would have. He felt so helpless and that scared him. He'd always been the strong one. What would happen to the farm if he were sick? Who would tell Sarah? Christ knows she had suffered enough losses in her young life without losing him as well. He felt a trickle of sweat run down his neck, trailing down his spine. This part of the house had been without heat for three days. He should be cold – it was odd that he wasn't.

Footsteps on the stairs confirmed that Alison was returning. The relief he felt was overwhelming. He closed his eyes, trying to control his breathing, while he waited for her to return. Then she was there, her arm draped over his shoulders, speaking softly to him.

"Will, you're hyperventilating. You need to blow into this bag - it will help slow your breathing down."

He opened his eyes. She was holding a paper bag near his mouth.

"You just have to blow, Will. You know how to blow, don't you? You just put your lips together and blow." She smiled, trying to get him to relax.

He tried to place the bag to his lips but his hands were shaking too much.

"Here, let me hold it. You just concentrate on blowing."

They stayed there for several minutes while Will followed her instructions. Alison sat at his side rubbing his back, praying she was wrong. Slowly his breathing returned to normal.

He lowered the bag from his lips.

"You feel better now?" she asked.

"Yeah, I guess. What happened to me?"

"I think you had a panic attack."

Will turned away saying nothing; he was too ashamed to. A panic attack! Was that all? He'd panicked like some useless wimp. What the hell must she think of that?

"You need to get dressed or you'll catch cold. I'll go and get you something for you to put on."

"It's ok, I can manage. You go back where it's warm."

He started to struggle to his feet. Alison placed her arm at his waist to help him.

Will pulled away so ashamed of himself that he didn't want her to touch him.

"I said I could manage. Just go downstairs." His tone was sharp, far more so than he'd intended.

Alison backed away as if she'd been smacked. Tears flooded into her eyes. She turned away, hoping he hadn't seen them and hurried downstairs.

He watched her retreating. Shit, he thought, I've made her cry.

"Alison..." His call went either unheard or ignored as she ran away.

He pushed his hand through his damp hair before hitting the wall in frustration. He hadn't had pain in his chest before but he had now. Pain brought on by the regret of having hurt her. What kind of bastard was he to make her cry? All she'd done was offer to help him and he'd bitten her head off.

Sighing and cursing himself for his stupidity, he went to his room and quickly pulled on his clothes. He had to explain, he owed her that much. How did he do that though? He could hardly just go up to her and blurt out that he had a problem with premature ejaculation. The first thing he had to do in any case was apologise; he'd never made anybody cry before.

Sarah's bedroom door was open and once again he was drawn to it, as if he were somehow closer to her here. He picked up the photograph of him and her. You'd tell me I was a prat, he thought. Which would be right, a little voice in his head told him, so quit stalling and just go down and apologise. If they weren't snowed in he would give her flowers to let her know how sorry he was. A roll of pink wrapping paper in the corner of

Sarah's room stirred a memory and gave him an idea.

Alison stood gazing out of the window, silent tears trickling down her cheeks. She'd told herself that she was being ridiculous, but it hadn't helped. She'd had worse rows with Rob and never cried like this. What was going on with her? Her emotions were shot to pieces. Was it being trapped here? Did it make everything feel more intense and reactions more extreme? Is that why Will had suffered a panic attack? Her reaction to him in the towel had been blatant, she was aware of that. She'd practically dissolved in a puddle at his feet. That didn't explain the look of terror on his face though; most men would have been flattered not scared. Nothing made sense. If she hadn't known better she would have sworn he'd never been with a woman, but he'd been married. This knowledge made her all the more confused. As did his snapping at her. He'd been so patient and kind, so where had that attitude come from? She was damned if she knew.

A slight cough brought her out of her contemplations; she turned slowly at the sound. Will stood by the kitchen counter, one arm behind his back. She wanted to be mad with him but just one look had her dissolving all over again. It wasn't his body this time, although it looked wonderful in jeans washed so many times that they were white in places and hugged his thighs like a second skin and a powder blue jumper that looked like soft cashmere. Gorgeous though he looked it was his eyes that undid her. They were the most expressive eyes she had ever seen. Every thought and emotion was displayed in their fathomless depths. She had never seen such unconcealed misery in a man's eyes before and it broke her heart. What had happened to cause him such pain?

"Alison, lass, I'm so sorry. I never meant to hurt you or make you cry." His voice was little more than a croak. He moved towards her, his hand moving from behind his back and held out a pink paper palm tree. "I don't have flowers," he said with a shy smile.

Her heart flipped, it really was official; she loved him. How could she not love a man who made her a palm tree out of paper because he had no flowers? The tears flowed again.

"Oh God, please stop, Alison. I'm so sorry, so sorry. I'll do anything, please stop, lass."

"They're good tears," she sniffed.

He leaned forward and using his thumb brushed the tears away.

"There are things I need to explain," he told her.

"Will, there really is no need."

"There is but it's difficult."

She nodded.

"Ok, if you insist, but we eat first. I don't do difficult on an empty stomach." She moved to the range and started to take out the food.

"Alright, food first," he agreed. "Oh yeah, and while I remember – wasn't that a quote. 'You know how to whistle, don't you, Steve? You just put your lips together and blow.'" He smiled as he spoke.

"Oh God, now I know you're perfect. You like Bogart and Bacall."

She walked past him into the kitchen.

"Put the flowers in a vase and I'll dish up tea. We can talk classic movies while we eat."

Chapter Nine

He tensed as her fingers gently ruffled through his hair.

"You're supposed to be relaxing," she told him sternly.

"Well, having me stretch out on the sofa with me head in your lap wasn't the best place to start, lass," he grumbled.

"I thought it would be like being on a couch talking to a therapist," she told him cheekily.

He felt his tension slip away.

"If you were a counsellor you'd be guilty of being unprofessional, playing with me hair like that."

She pouted.

"I can't help it. You have all these lovely little waves that are begging to be touched. I love the way it curls," she said, her fingers fluffing through his hair.

"Sarah says it looks like a bird's nest."

Alison looked down at him. She'd been about to feign mock outrage, but his tone and expression made her stop and change direction.

"Sarah, who's Sarah?" she asked quietly.

"Officially, she's me stepdaughter – Moira's daughter. But she is so much more than just that. She's a friend, confidant, and fashion guru." He smiled as he said the last thing and pointed to his hair. "Hence the hair cut. She can and does drive me mad, make me worry, and I'll never understand her. But I couldn't love her more even if she were me own flesh and blood." He smiled as he spoke and his eyes sparkled with emotion.

A stepdaughter. Where was she now, Alison wondered? Had she gone to live with her biological father after Moira's death? If so, that must have hurt Will.

"Where is she, Will? Do you still see her at all?" she asked softly, her hand continuing to play with his hair.

"After her mother died, she decided to stay with me. She's off on her big adventure at the moment. A gap year she calls it. She's in New Zealand, working at some outward bound school." He paused for a moment, smiling again. "She'll be good at that: she was always fearless."

"So Sarah's what, seventeen or eighteen?" Alison tried hard to keep the shock out of her voice; she'd been expecting him to talk about a younger child.

"She's eighteen and she's going on to university next year. She wants to be a teacher." The pride in his voice was evident. "It's daft but I miss her. Since Moira died, it's just been the two of us."

She leant forward and kissed him softly on his forehead.

"Crinkles again," she whispered. "You're not daft; of course you miss her, it's normal. Moira must have been awfully young when she had Sarah?"

"Yeah, she were a child herself. They were more like sisters than mother and daughter."

"It must have been hard on her when she died," Alison said.

"It was, but we helped each other."

"How long were you married, Will?"

"Two years."

Not long, Alison thought, and if Moira had been sick then not easy either.

"It weren't a marriage like yours, Alison."

Alison grimaced.

"I'm not sure what my marriage is or was, certainly not what I thought. Will, before we carry on you need to know that I'm not using you. When the snow has cleared I will file for a divorce."

"Are you sure about that? You shouldn't rush into anything and especially not because of me, lass."

She smiled.

"Do you ever think about yourself first, Will Barnes? Don't answer that because I know you don't. Will, he violated me in the worst possible way. I'm not going back to him."

The smile that spread across his face melted her heart again.

"I'm glad, Alison. For you of course, but mainly for me. I've been so scared that I would lose you before I really found you." She moved to kiss him but he stopped her. "There are things about me you need to know before we go any further."

"Ah, the difficult things you spoke about and why you had a panic attack."

"Don't remind me, I was so ashamed. It was why I snapped at you. I already don't feel like a man and that confirmed it."

"Sorry, did you say you didn't feel like a man? Why on earth would you feel like that?"

Will took a deep breath. His face was pink again.

"Will, whatever it is, just say it."

"I don't know how to make love." He spoke so quickly and quietly that she couldn't understand him.

"Sorry, Will, I didn't catch that."

Oh God, he thought, this was so embarrassing.

"I don't know how to make love."

The words hung in the air. He waited for her laughter, but her voice was soft and gentle when she spoke.

"Are you saying you're a virgin, Will?"

He swallowed.

"Yes, I suppose so. As near as damn it," he whispered.

"You are going to have to explain what you mean, Will."

"Moira is the only woman I have tried to have sex with, and then only three times – it was a disaster. After the third time we never tried again."

"Why was it a disaster?"

"Well, she wasn't interested in me really and I didn't know what to do." He looked away from her before continuing. "I... never managed it. When you were in the bedroom it was obvious what you were thinking and I panicked. I want you, lass, but I really don't know what to do."

Alison sat in stunned silence, gathering her thoughts, knowing that she had to tread carefully. One wrong word and she'd lose him forever.

Will made to move. She was obviously repulsed by his story, so much so that she couldn't even speak to him.

"Where do you think you're going?" she asked as he sat up. "You've done the difficult bit, you've told me."

"What, and you don't think I'm a sad bastard who can't get laid? Or that this whole situation is not really funny? I mean, a thirty seven year old virgin! It's bloody hilarious!" He turned and sat with his head in his hands.

Alison moved to his side, her hands caressing him through the soft wool of his sweater.

"Is that what others have said, Will?"

"God no, I've never told anybody else and I've not been near a woman since Moira."

"And before Moira? How come there weren't women before her?"

He laughed bitterly.

"Other girls? You have to be joking. What teenage girl would have hung about with me? Let alone had sex. I was like a skinny beanpole with a big nose and bad clothes. I lived with me grandparents, money was tight, I had to help out. There wasn't much time for fun. Then me gran got sick. It was a bad time. Me granddad, he went out to work on the farm so I cared for gran. It didn't leave any time for a girlfriend. Not that I minded. I'd do it again – in a heartbeat. "

Of course he would, she thought. Because that's who he was - what he was. A beautiful and generous person, who'd always put other people's needs before his own. She realised then, that he'd never had a childhood or been a teenager.

"It seems to me that it's not that you're no good at making love but that you never had the practice when you were younger. You know, kissing, making out, all that kind of stuff teenagers do."

"No, I never did owt like that. Aren't you going to run a mile from me, Alison?" He turned towards her and discovered his face was inches away from her own.

"No, Will. I'm not." She kissed him softly. "I'm staying right here."

"What are we going to do then because I can't do it? I… always finish too soon."

"Look, you were trying to make love to somebody who wasn't interested in you. No wonder it was a disaster. I mean, did she ever tell you how wonderful you were or show you any affection." Will shook his head.

"And that's the difference. I want you, Will Barnes. I do think you are wonderful and I am willing to bet you will turn out to be a fantastic lover. And do you know what?"

"No. Know what?" Will shook his head, hardly able to believe she wasn't pushing him away.

"I'm going to have a lot of fun teaching you how to make love." She smiled wickedly.

"T-t-t-teaching me how to make love?" he stammered.

"Yes, but first I need you to tell me about your experiences."

"Oh G-g-god, do I have to?"

"Don't worry. Like I said, you've done the difficult thing by telling me. The rest is just details. Just talk me through that first time. How old were you?"

"I was nearly thirty. It were the day she came back. She'd been to see Myles, to tell him about Sarah. I don't think I said, she's Myles' daughter. He'd not wanted to know about her. It was late when Moira came back here. Sarah had gone to bed. She was angry and upset with Myles. Christ knows why but she begged me to shag her."

Alison winced at the term.

"Not very romantic."

"Her words not mine. But I'd loved her for what seemed like forever and here she was offering me the one thing I'd dreamed of. She were in a hurry and started tearing at my clothes and pushing me back on the sofa. I had no idea what she were doing and at first it were exciting. But well, then she touched me... you know... intimately and well, it was all over. She laughed at us. It were awful, I tried to continue but couldn't."

"Hardly surprising it was a disaster given the circumstances. How dare she laugh at you? I know she was your wife, but that was cruel."

"Well, it never got any better."

"Ok, enough of confessions. I think you need to do some things you never did as a teenager. Are you ready for lesson number one?"

"Lesson number one?" he said puzzled.

"Yes, lesson number one: making out on the sofa." She pushed him back against the cushions. "Now, I had a rule, no hands below the waist."

He was so tense.

"Alison... lass, I..."

"Just follow your instincts." She ran her hand down his arm. "Who bought you this jumper?"

"Sarah did, she said I needed updating."

"It's gorgeous. I think your daughter wanted you to find a woman. It sends out a signal."

"It does?"

"Oh yes. It says touch me." She ran her hands over the material. "And it shows off a frankly impressive pair of shoulders." Her hands wandered over him as she spoke. "And the V neck shows a little skin, well, that begs to be kissed." She leant down and placed her lips against his throat.

The kisses were only soft, like the flutter of a butterfly's wing, but they were driving him slowly mad. She pulled him forward.

"Of course, the thing it positively screams is: take me off." Her hands reached under the sweater and slowly peeled it over his head.

It was Alison's turn to swallow. His skin was so pale and smooth, his muscles sharply defined by the hard work he did. His movement towards her was slow, hesitant, but it was him who made it. His kiss started slowly but then became more intense as she slid her arms round his body. Her hands moved softly over his back causing his muscles to ripple.

He groaned and kissed her deeper, his tongue dancing over hers. His hands moved to the hem of the shirt she was wearing, slowly sliding under it, caressing her skin. He pulled away slightly and looked at her face. Her skin was flushed, her pupils dilated. He was staggered. She was enjoying this; it wasn't just him who was turned on.

"Will," she whispered. "Don't stop."

"I want to see you, I want to feel you, Alison," he whispered against her ear.

She guided his hand to her shirt.

"Well, what's stopping you?"

Will knew that this was up to him. She'd given him permission, but it was going to be his decision to take this further. His eyes were held captive by hers. What could he see there? Many things, he realised: trust, understanding, compassion but, above all, desire. He was finding it hard to believe that any woman could desire him, let alone the beautiful intelligent one in front of him. He touched her face, his thumb slowly stroking her cheek.

"Will?"

"Just checking you're real, lass. I'm having trouble believing this, you being here with me."

"Believe it, Will. I'm here and there's nowhere else I would rather be."

His mouth claimed hers in the softest of touches and then he moved trailing kisses along her jaw. He couldn't wait any longer to see her and his hands slid back to the hem of her shirt.

Alison was sure he was actually holding his breath as he slowly removed her shirt; she was certainly holding hers. Heat was spreading through her body; she desperately needed him to touch her. She knew he had to set the pace but this go slow was driving her crazy. His hands trembled as he pulled one button after another undone. When the shirt was open he slid it from her shoulders, placing soft kisses on the milky flesh he'd exposed. How could such soft kisses cause such a burning need? Alison thought, as her hands moved to his shoulders in silent encouragement.

He'd never really seen a woman naked before. Moira had always undressed in the bathroom and the few times they had attempted to make love it had been in the dark. Even when he had removed Alison's clothes, when she'd been hurt, he'd looked away as best he could. The only way he could do this now was to take it slowly. His hands trembled as he pushed the shirt free from her shoulders, their creamy loveliness tempting beyond belief. Instinct took over and he trailed a line of soft kisses along her collar bone. Alison placed her arms around him, her fingers dancing over his shoulders, silently begging for more. He revealed her skin inch by inch until the shirt slid off and he allowed it to drop to the floor, and then he just stared. She was naked beneath the shirt, her bra drying with her other clothes. But it was her face he looked at first. Pleasure, it was alive with pleasure. God, she was beautiful, he thought.

Alison watched as his burning gaze moved down her body. How could she look away? It was as if he were worshipping her. As a woman, she had never felt so desired.

He gasped at the sight of the bruising from her accident.

"Not pretty, I know; I really did a job on myself."

"Alison, why didn't you say? Why let me do this when you must be in pain?"

"I'll be in more pain if you stop and so will you, because I will hurt you if you dare to stop now. It looks worse than it is. Just be gentle and maybe later you can kiss it better." Alison smiled wickedly again.

He leant forward taking her in his arms. Holding her gently against him, he luxuriated in the feeling of her skin against his, so soft and smooth. He lowered her back against the cushions and they lay together kissing endlessly, as his hands gently caressed her back. He discovered her spine was sensitive, especially at the base of her back and the nape of her neck. She seemed to love it when he trailed a single finger down its length. It caused her to stretch and push herself closer to him. He smiled at the sounds of her sighs.

"Do you like that, lass?"

"Oh yes, Mr Barnes, I do."

She moved then altering their positions so he was lying back against the cushions and she straddled his thighs. He tensed slightly.

"It's ok, Will. It's going to be good, I promise," she whispered.

"What if I... you know... finish early."

"If you do I'll just start again. So stop worrying. She lowered her head and her lips began to trail over his chest. Not wet and sloppy but firm and slightly moist. His breath caught in his throat.

"Liking this, are we, Will?" she teased.

"You have to ask," he murmured.

She laughed softly as she continued to rain kisses over his abdomen and back to his chest. Her curtain of hair tickled his skin as she explored him slowly with her clever hands and wicked tongue. His muscles quivered under her touch and he was having trouble breathing.

"It's getting good now, isn't it Will?"

He nodded, unable to speak. Good, that didn't even begin to describe what he was feeling. He lost track of time as she repeatedly kissed and touched his body. The pleasure he was feeling caused him to push himself closer to her. He couldn't describe how good it was or even why. Her mouth was driving him mad. Her bottom was moving suggestively over him and his hips were moving of their own accord trying to get closer to her.

Although he was inexperienced, Will realised, aroused as he was, that if Alison touched him more intimately then he would explode. He didn't want that to happen, not yet, not like this. He pulled away slightly, unable to voice his feelings, his eyes cloudy with confusion. Alison reached up and touched his cheek gently.

"I know you're close, Will," she whispered. "And you're not sure you want to continue. It can be, and at the right time is, wonderful, but I don't think this is the right time for you. Am I right?" She looked at him for confirmation that she was reading the situation correctly.

He nodded slowly, relieved she'd realised how he felt.

"You want the first time to be when we can make love fully. I promise it will be beautiful. Unfortunately I am still too sore for that just yet. I can pleasure you in other ways, make you feel more comfortable..." she paused, a smile on her lips.

He knew what she meant but she was right – he needed his first time with her to be as she'd described.

"I'll wait until we can make love fully," he told her quietly.

"Ok, Will, if that's what you want. Besides, this is a lesson." She paused, grinning impishly. "Part of making out with a girl on a sofa is being left hard, hurting and frustrated and I wouldn't want to leave any gaps in your education," she told him giggling.

"You really are a witch," he said, before joining in with her laughter.

When their laughter had subsided he held her again, stroking her soft skin.

"Alison, you are the most beautiful woman I've ever known. Christ knows, lass, why you're here with me. But I'm glad you are." His kiss was hot and demanding and his hands moved to her hair pushing through the silken strands.

"Touch me, Will, taste me as I have you," she begged.

His hands moved slowly down her rib cage, softly, gently so as not to hurt her. Her skin was like smooth satin against his work roughened palms. What did he do now he wondered?

"Remember, just follow your instincts. I will guide you," she whispered.

"Ok, lass."

Under Alison's words of encouragement, he learned how to give her pleasure with his hands and his mouth. He couldn't begin to explain the power he felt or how much he wanted to do this for her. It was as wonderful for him as it was for her. For a single moment he had doubts that he could give her the kind of pleasure she had given him, but he pushed them aside as he caressed and kissed her. Her hands moved to his head and he felt her fingers raking through his short hair. Her breathing had changed and quite suddenly he realised that she was close to completion. A moment later her release washed over her.

He held her against him while the trembling stopped and her breathing returned to normal. God, it had been wonderful to be able to do that for her. For the first time in his life he felt complete as a man. Her silence was worrying him though. Had he gone too far?

"Lass, are you okay?" he asked.

"I'm not sure I will ever be ok again? I think, Mr Barnes, you are going to be a straight A student. If that was your first time I can't wait to see how good you are going to get with practice."

"It was good then... I mean, you liked what I did... I mean, you did have..." he stopped embarrassed.

"Yes, I did. You're not sorry I didn't wait until we were together, so to speak..." She whispered, a little embarrassed herself.

"No, it were wonderful to be able to do that for you. I've never, well, you know," he said shyly.

"It was a first for me as well. I mean, like that... in that way, just from touching."

Will smiled. She was as embarrassed as him.

"I'm glad," he whispered. "Glad that I was the first."

Chapter Ten

He should have been asleep, Lord knows he was tired enough but he couldn't settle. His mind was in turmoil. Feelings and emotions that he had never experienced before were threatening to engulf him. No other woman had made him feel the things that Alison did. Not even Moira. He'd spent more than half his life believing himself in love with her. Suddenly, out of nowhere, Alison had appeared and he was experiencing feelings and urges that he hadn't known existed, feelings he'd never had for Moira, and he felt disloyal. That was right, wasn't it? After all, she'd been his wife. He sighed as Sarah's words entered his thoughts: 'It were wrong what she did to you. She should never have married you.'

But she had married him and he felt like he was betraying her. Why had he not felt like this with her? Is this how she'd felt about Myles. He'd known about them having sex when they were younger. He'd walked in on them one time at the white cottage. What he had seen was raw, rough passion; if Moira hadn't been demanding more he'd have sworn she wasn't willing. It was the first time that he realised sex and passion had a smell. It had actually made him gag.

He'd run from the house and thrown up in the garden. They'd come out later laughing at him. He tried in his bumbling way to caution against what they were doing, but Myles had sneered and said just because he couldn't get laid didn't mean the rest of them shouldn't have a shag. He turned away at the crude words and the image they brought to mind. Moira had taken him by the arm and told him that she'd die if she couldn't have Myles. The need was that great – her words had been prophetic.

He turned slightly trying to get comfortable.

"Will, is something wrong?"

"I'm sorry, lass, I didn't mean to keep you awake. I'm all of a muddle as me gran would say."

Alison moved so that her head rested on his chest. It was the most natural thing in the world when his arm curled around her.

"My gran would say a problem shared is a problem halved."

"You're going to think I'm daft. I feel as though I'm cheating on Moira."

"No, Will, I don't think you're daft. I think your reaction is probably normal. I'm sure any widower would feel the same way. I'm the first woman that you've been with since Moira. You're bound to be confused."

"It isn't just that. I thought I loved her for more than half my life, but I never felt like this about her."

"Felt like what?"

"It's hard to explain. One moment I feel like I'm floating and giddy, dancing almost, and the next my heart is pounding and my skin is burning."

Alison smiled.

"That's a combination of sexual awareness, tenderness and good old fashioned lust."

"Lust? Are you saying I lust after you?" he asked, shocked.

"God, I hope so. I have a healthy dose of lust for you."

"I don't lust after you. That makes what I'm feeling seedy and it's not."

"No, it's not. It's wonderful and special. Desiring somebody is not a bad thing. Why would you think it was?"

"I saw desire become obsessive to the point it destroyed not just the two people who were in love, but their families as well."

"I don't understand?"

"Moira and Myles, their love was obsessive. They didn't care who they hurt. I think they saw themselves as some tragic couple. They certainly didn't see anybody else."

"I thought you said that when she came back Myles rejected her and Sarah," Alison whispered.

"Oh, he did at first, but he obviously couldn't ignore the attraction they'd always had for each other. He began coming around the farm. Then Moira would disappear for days on end. I heard the rumours, so did his family. His mother showed up and told me to control my slut of a wife and keep her away from Myles."

"Nice woman."

"Well, I confronted Moira, but she denied it. So I ignored the rumours. But then one day she left, not that it was unusual for her to take off. Like I said, she'd disappear for days. But this time she left a note." He felt himself tremble. "Christ, after all this time it still scares me to think of it."

"Then don't think of it," Alison said softly.

"No, I have to because I suspect that you think Moira died in an accident or of some illness."

"Didn't she?"

"No, her death was intentional... She and Myles committed suicide. I found them up on t'moors in an old labourer's cottage."

He felt Alison's breath catch, shocked at his words.

"Oh Will, I'm so sorry, it must have been awful," she whispered.

"It was and not just for me. That's what I meant when I said I'd seen that kind of selfish obsession destroying people. Myles was married; he had a young son. And then there was Sarah. I went onto auto pilot sorting things out."

"You were being there for everybody else. But who was there for you?"

"Well, Sarah was. I guess we helped each other. It frightens me, Alison, to think that I might love you like that."

"You couldn't... I don't mean you couldn't love me, but it wouldn't be that selfish. You don't have a selfish bone in your body."

"I thought I loved Moira..."

"I'm sure you did but you were a teenager and feelings change and develop as we get older."

"Yeah, I suppose you're right." His arm tightened around her. Was it too soon to tell her that he loved her, he wondered?

"Of course I'm right. I'm a woman. We will just see how this, I mean we, develop; take it slowly and keep it simple."

"Do you really want to see how this develops?"

"Yes, I really do. Now we have that settled you need to get some sleep." He felt her lips brush against his skin. "Goodnight, Will."

He pressed a kiss to her hair. "Good night, lass."

She lay silent for a long time before sleep claimed her, wondering what Will would say if she told him that she was already more than halfway in love with him.

****

It was like playing house, albeit a grown up version. Cocooned as they were, it was easy to be drawn into the dream of being partners, sharing a home and a life. Every morning for the past three days they shared breakfast with Will going over what he needed to do around the farm. With no help available, he was putting in long hours every day. While he was out, she rested most of the time, just allowing her battered body to heal. She raided the bookcase to stave off boredom, reacquainting herself with some much loved classics. During the afternoon she prepared the evening meal, looking forward to the sight of Will returning home. She'd never seen anybody eat so much. He'd laughed when she commented on his appetite and told her it was fuel for a working boy.

As much as she loved their meals together, it was the evenings curled on the sofa she had come to love. She was sure she was seeing a side to the quiet farmer that very few people saw. Take now, for example; he was lying stretched out explaining how he'd come to love Shakespeare.

"There were this competition at school. My English teacher made me enter because she wanted me to learn how to speak out loud. I chose Prince Hal's speech from Henry the Fourth part one. You know, the one at the end of the first act:

"Yet herein will I imitate the sun,
Who doth permit the base contagious clouds
To smother up his beauty from the world,
That when he please again to be himself.........
She coached me for weeks trying to get me to speak with a BBC accent but, come the day, I were so nervous I forgot and read it with me broad Yorkshire accent. Christ, she was mad."

"But Shakespeare should be read with accents - it makes it more real."

"Yeah, I agree. And so did the judges. I won first prize. My gran was so proud." He smiled.

"I bet she was. What was the prize?" Alison was proud for the boy he must have been.

"A cup- she polished it every week- and a gift voucher for ten pounds for WH Smiths. I bought copies of Henry V, A Tale of Two Cites and Far from the Madding Crowd."

"Do you still have the cup?"

"No, when my gran died I had the cup placed in her coffin," Will said quietly. "I thought she'd like that."

"That's a lovely gesture. And the books, do you still have them?"

"Yeah, I do, upstairs in the bookcase."

"I think you are my Gabriel Oak and I hope, as he would say:

'At home by the fire, whenever I look up, there you will be. And whenever you look up, there I shall be.' "

"For as long as you need me to be, lass. I will be there."

Alison smiled before leaning forward. She took the book Will was holding from his hands and brushed her lips over his. "Good."

Later, as they lay in each other's arms on the mattress in front of the fire, he told her his work plans for the next day.

"I'm not taking the dogs in the morning, so will you let them out occasionally while I'm gone?" Will asked.

"Yeah, of cause I will. Why aren't you taking them?"

"I'm heading over to a small hamlet just outside Erringdon. It's about two miles from here. They're mostly pensioners out there. I usually call in a couple of times a week to make sure they're alright. I haven't been since the snow. I'll take some milk, eggs and bread over to them. Chop some wood so they don't run out."

"Ah, so that's why you baked all that bread; you weren't just showing off your baking skills, Nigella."

"My baps are better, and tastier than hers, you know."

She giggled at the innuendo. He really was coming out of his shell.

"Also, I need to start and clear the lane leading to the main road." He lapsed into silence, letting his words sink in.

He was talking about the real world encroaching. She wanted to beg him not to go but realised that he had no choice. Instead, she snuggled a little closer and waited for morning.

****

Tears glistened on her eyelashes and a single teardrop trickled slowly down her cheek. Alison sniffed. It had to happen, of course, she realised that. She wasn't a fool nor was she a child who believed in fairy tales. The problem was it had felt like a fairy tale these past few days. Will had been her knight in shining armour, rescuing her from mortal danger, keeping her safe and warm. He'd cast a spell and bewitched her as surely as any fairy tale prince did. She wasn't ready for the magic to end. She wasn't ready for reality to return. Truthfully, she wanted to stay cut off at the farm, isolated from the outside world and the harsh reality she had to face.

The electricity suddenly coming back on had been one thing too many to deal with while she was alone. Will had left early as he had said he would, heading for civilization. When he had said goodbye, he'd wrapped his arms around her as if knowing the pain his words were causing. Then he had kissed her almost desperately, making her wonder if he were as reluctant as she to have the world interrupt them.

The farmhouse seemed empty without him. He'd left Winston, Drake and Bess at home and they seemed unsettled too, knowing that something was different. She'd let them out a couple of times, and while the older dogs had sniffed around the farmyard Winston had run to the gate and lain down as if waiting for him to return. He had come at her call but he'd stopped and looked back. The bond between dog and master was a strong one. She'd knelt down at the dog's side, stroking its silky fur, telling him how much she missed Will as well.

The phone rang at about eleven, the sound strangely alien after several days of silence. She let it ring for thirty seconds or so before answering it, realising that she really couldn't ignore it. She had to let whoever was calling know that Will was ok. It was the local police constable who was obviously surprised at a strange female answering the phone.

"I crashed my car," she explained. "Will's dog found me and I've been here at Highcroft ever since.

"No, I don't need urgent medical attention. I dislocated my shoulder, but Will has put it back in and my bruising is fading now."

She explained that Will was clearing the roads and heading towards the neighbouring hamlet near Erringdon. The policeman knew where it was.

"Well, I'll tell Will you called." She smiled as he told her to take care and then she hung up.

He'd called her lass, just like Will. It was obvious that this was what women were called locally. It was odd though, when Will called her lass it sent shivers down her spine. There was something incredibly intimate about the way he said it, making it sound little more than a whisper, and all the while his intense gaze would be watching her. It was as if those gorgeous blue eyes were caressing her soul.

The phone call had shaken her a little. She could no longer hide behind the communication breakdown that the weather had caused. If the phone lines were working then the electricity would soon be reconnected. As much as she didn't want to confront the issues in her life, she knew there were people whom she loved that would be worried if she didn't contact them. The problem was she was ashamed. She'd, on some level at least, failed at her marriage; she knew that it was Rob who had betrayed her but he wouldn't have needed to if she'd made him happy.

"How do I tell my parents? How do I explain that the life I think I had is a lie?" she asked Win. The dog put his head on her knee as if to say he didn't know the answer, but whatever she did he'd be with her. The answer was of course not to tell them the whole truth, not until she could speak to them face to face.

Alison brushed the tear from her cheek. It had been easier to lie over the phone than she had thought it would be. Her parents thought she was at a teaching conference. It had been easy to let them think it had been in Yorkshire and that, because of the weather, she was staying with a teacher who lived locally. Satisfied that they were alright, she'd put the phone down before the conversation could turn to Rob. For half a second she considered calling and letting him know she was safe, before she decided to let him sweat on where she was.

Finally she rang her head teacher and explained that she had been in an accident, she had dislocated her shoulder and that she would not be back at work for the rest of the week. It wasn't the whole truth but it at least bought her a little more time with Will.

She'd been curled on the sofa, reading, when the lights came back on, one more reminder that civilisation was encroaching. It was this that had set the tears flowing. Sensing her distress, Winston pushed his head into her hands. "Oh Winston, what am I going to do? I have a job, a home and friends away from here."

The dog whined softly.

"The problem is, I've gone and fallen in love with him."

Winston tilted his head to one side, as if he were listening closely.

Another time she'd have found it comical.

"I know it's stupid, I've only known him a few days, but, Winston, I'm sure I love him, surer than I have been about anything in my life."

The dog blinked, his brown eyes soft, and he put his head on her knee. Alison stroked his ears.

"I guess you don't think that's stupid because you love him as well."

The dog climbed up on the sofa, as if they were kindred spirits.

"The thing is, Winston, how do I walk away when the time comes for me to leave and go back to my life?" she whispered, tears trickling down her cheek. "My life isn't mine anymore, its somebody else's.

Everything I believed isn't true. I want this life, Win, I want Will."

Chapter Eleven

He was distracted; Alison had been on his mind all morning. For the first time that he could remember he hadn't wanted to go to work on the farm. Had she felt as he did, when he spoke of clearing the road? He knew that it had to be done. They could not remain isolated at the farm forever and they both had lives and responsibilities. It was just that, before Alison's arrival, he'd been lonely and he didn't want to go back to that.

Locally, he knew that people felt sorry for him, widowed so young and in such scandalous circumstances. After both Myles' and Moira's death he and Sarah had been the subject of much speculation. Conversation used to stop when they entered shops or the local pub. For a long time he'd not gone into Hebden Bridge and even now he still saw pity in people's eyes, not just because Moira had died, but because they thought him a fool to have married her.

He sighed. It was different with Alison. Her opinion of him was not tainted by those events. She saw a very different Will Barnes. She had shown him a side to himself he hadn't known about and although she had only been in his life a short time, he liked the man she was teaching him to be. He seemed to be standing straighter, speaking more freely and generally had more confidence. He didn't want to go back to being the man that folk felt sorry for when she returned to Bath. The way she had responded to his kisses made him think that she had little desire to go back to real life either, but it couldn't be avoided.

He worked slowly all morning, using his tractor to clear away the snow, all the while inching slowly closer to the main road, which cut across the moor, and civilization. It was about eleven when he happened upon Alison's car. His heart went cold when he saw it. The fire damage was obvious. It was a miracle she'd walked away from the accident. He realised that she must have followed the wall down to the farm. It was also a miracle that she had walked in the right direction. All in all she'd had luck on her side that night.

He didn't linger by the car, not wanting to dwell on what might have happened. Instead he pushed on towards the main road. Once there, he realised it would still be several days before any vehicle would get up from the village. He smiled, ridiculously pleased. Alison and he would have a few more days alone yet.

His priority now was his neighbours. So he turned away from the direction of the village and made his way slowly down Spenser Lane now and, although a car couldn't have got past, the tractor was making headway. The people over Erringdon way would be expecting to see him. They were all elderly and he was their closest neighbour and he looked out for them, fetching shopping, chopping wood, making sure they didn't need anything. Up ahead, nestling in a dip in the rolling hills, he could see the cluster of four houses. How picturesque they looked with snow inches deep on the roof and icicles hanging from the gables. Wisps of smoke curled out from the chimneys so he knew the folk who lived there were warm at least. He pulled up and hopped down from the cab, grabbing the supplies he'd brought with him, and started to make his rounds.

He worked his way around each house, finally coming to Doris Bradshaw's home. He'd known her since he was a lad; she'd been friends with his gran. She had no family so he was her only visitor and he always spent more time here. He tapped on the door and then pushed it open;

despite his suggestions she should lock the door she never did and he called her name as he went in.

"Will, lad, is that you? I'm in the living room."

The cottage was small and he had to duck to get through the doorway.

"Aye, it's me, Mrs B. I just thought I'd check you're alright and that you don't need owt. "

The old lady was sat in a wing back chair inside a sleeping bag.

"I'm ok, lad. Snug as a bug in a rug."

"So I see. Have you managed with no electricity?" He knew the old lady had ready meals delivered to heat up in the microwave. He was worried that, with the electricity being out, she'd not had a hot meal.

"Ok, but it's been boring; I miss my soaps and quiz shows."

"What about food? Have you had owt hot?"

"Well, I've heated soup on the hob and had a sandwich for me dinner and tea."

"How about I fix you a meal then? I've brought some supplies," he said.

"You should be fixing a meal for some pretty lass, Will Barnes, not an old woman like me."

Will felt his cheeks colour.

Doris Bradshaw might have been elderly, but she was as sharp as a tack and missed nothing.

"Will Barnes, you're blushing. Have you met a lass?"

"No," he mumbled.

"Don't you lie to me, young man. Your ears turn red when you lie; always have, even when you were a young un. Who is she?"

"What if I told you there is nobody."

"I shouldn't believe you. So I repeat, who is she?"

"There is no she, not how you mean anyroad. A young woman got caught in the snow and so I put her up at Highcroft. That's all there is to it. Now, am I making you some dinner?"

She looked at him carefully.

"Yes, you can fix us both something to eat and then you can tell me more about this house guest who makes you blush and lie to an old woman."

"Her name is Alison Robinson. She's a teacher in Bath," Will said undoing a container with stew in and setting it to heat on the hob.

"She's a long way from home. What were she doing up here in this weather."

Will paused. He wasn't prepared for questions.

"She was on her way to a teaching conference," he said without looking at the older woman.

More lies, Doris thought, but this time she kept quiet.

"How did she find the farmhouse? We're pretty remote out here."

"It found her or rather Winston did. She'd got lost in the snow and crashed her car into the wall of the lower field. She got out and started walking which was when Win found her." He put cutlery and two mugs of tea on the table.

"She's a city girl, then. What does she teach?"

"English." A smile lit up his face as he remembered their chats about books and plays.

Doris didn't miss the smile either.

"Oh, perfect lass for you then. You always had your head in a book when you were a young un."

"I already told you…"

"There's no harm in my having a little dream."

He laughed.

"You're incorrigible. Come and get your dinner while it's hot."

"How old is she?"

"She's in her early thirties. So, she's younger than me."

"Is she pretty? And don't tell me you never noticed, your blush says you have."

"No, she's not pretty...she's beautiful."

"I see." Doris smiled and began eating with gusto.

"That doesn't mean anything other than I noticed she's a beautiful woman."

"Has she noticed how gorgeous you are?"

"Mrs B!"

"Oh give over. You must know that you're what me magazines would call a hunk."

He shook his head in despair.

"Enough."

"Is she married?"

The pause was longer this time

"Separated." It wasn't a lie, Will thought, just not the whole truth.

Doris took pity on him and changed the subject.

He stayed for an hour.

"You be sure to bring your young lady with you when you come next time," Doris said as he left.

He shook his head.

"How many times do I have to tell you she's not my young lady?"

"Will, lad, your tongue says one thing, but your eyes say another and not before time too. Moira weren't no good for you, lad. Grab this girl. You deserve some happiness."

He smiled and waved goodbye and headed back to Highcroft, pondering her words. Was it really so obvious what he felt for Alison? Would everybody know?

The journey back to the farm was slightly quicker than going and he was approaching Highcroft when his mobile phone vibrated in his pocket. It scared the living daylights out of him, the noise strange after so many days of silence. It was Paul, a police constable from Hebden Bridge, checking how things were. He explained that Doris and the others over Erringdon way were alright.

"It's pretty inaccessible up here. I left them with forty eight hours of supplies. I'm going back again day after tomorrow."

"You're a regular Boy Scout, Will. I've been talking to your house guest."

"Alison?"

"Aye. Is she ok? She said she didn't need to see a doctor."

"Well, she'd dislocated her shoulder but I put it back and apart from a few bruises she's recovered well. When the snow clears, I expect she'll be on her way."

"She sounded nice, not from round here though."

"No, she was attending some teaching thing and got lost when the weather turned nasty. She crashed her car. Win found her. She's been lucky."

"Ok, well, must have been nice to have some company, especially with Sarah away."

"Yeah, I guess."

"I was ringing to ask if you could help with road clearing after you've tended your livestock tomorrow?"

"Yeah, sure. It's no problem. I've already cleared a path from my farm to Spencer lane. I'll start from there."

"Like I said, you're a regular Boy Scout. See you tomorrow, Will."

He put the phone back in his pocket. It was strange talking to other people. Strange and oddly intrusive; he was enjoying it just being him and Alison and he didn't want it to end.

He turned into the narrow lane up to the farmhouse. The light was already fading but the farmhouse was well lit - a welcoming sight. He realised belatedly that the electricity was back on. Another sign that the storm was loosening its icy grip. He pushed open the door to the farmhouse and Bess and Drake, tails wagging, ran forward to greet him.

"Where's Win?" he asked, as he fussed each dog. "With Alison no doubt," he continued as he walked through into the lounge.

Alison was curled up on the sofa with Winston at her side. The young dog lifted his head and whined at the sound of John moving towards them.

"Hey, boy, what's up then?" he asked softly.

He dropped to Alison's side; she was asleep but tears had dried on her cheeks. A frown appeared on his face. What had made her cry? Her eyes flickered open and it took a second for her to get her bearings. Once she had, she launched herself into his arms and her tears started afresh. Great gut wrenching sobs.

"Hey, it's alright, I'm here. Whatever it is, Alison, I'll sort it out. Just tell me why you're crying? I hate to see you cry, lass."

"You'll think I'm being so stupid and I am, I know that."

"No, I won't, I promise," he said softly.

"It's the phone and electricity – they're back on. It made me realise that our time alone is almost at an end and I don't want it to be."

"Me neither, lass," he whispered. "But it were bound to happen."

"I know that I have to face things at home. I'm just not ready to." She shook her head as she spoke.

"You can stay here as long as you need to. You know that, don't you?"

"I know. I lied to my parents, Will. I've never lied to them before."

"When did you lie to them?"

"Today, after the policeman...oh I forget to say a policeman rang."

"Paul. I know, he got me on me mobile."

"Oh, that's good. Well, after he rang I thought I'd best let my parents know that I was alright. I must have stood by the phone for an hour thinking how to tell them about Rob. In the end I decided I couldn't, not over the phone at least. So I lied, told them the conference was in Yorkshire and that I was staying with a fellow teacher. I know I lied but at least they know I'm safe. I'll tell them about me and Rob when I go home."

"What about Rob? Have you been in touch with him?" Will asked.

"No, I haven't. The bastard can sweat on where I am." Alison shuddered as she spoke.

"Has he contacted you?"

"Contacted me?"

"Yeah, he may have left a message on your mobile phone. It

was in your coat pocket. It's on the window sill in the kitchen." Will stood up to go and get it.

"Don't, Will, I really don't want to know, not tonight."

"Alison you have to face..."

"I know I do," she interrupted him.

She pulled him back down and reached out to touch his face softly.

"I want us to have this night, Will. I need you to make love to me now; let's forget about the real world, just for tonight."

His eyes darkened; they were more grey now than blue. He stared at her face intently, as if looking for answers to unasked questions.

What did he see there? Alison wondered, as his eyes wandered over her face. Was the love she felt reflected in her eyes? It must be, for the feelings she had for him threatened to overwhelm her. Her heart fluttered in her chest. Did he sense her nervousness, because, as much as she needed him, she knew that once they had made love things would never be the same for either of them and she was nervous.

"Lass?"

There it was again, the half whispered term of endearment that made her heart melt.

"Are you sure that this is what you want...? That I'm what you want?" he asked hesitantly.

"I want you, Will, more than anything."

"You have to be certain. I don't want you to regret this afterwards."

"My mother says that it's not the things that we do in life that we regret the most but the things we don't do. My world has turned on its axis over the last three or four days; all that I knew and believed about my life is a lie. The only things I am certain of are my feelings and need for you. If we don't make love I'll regret it for the rest of my life. Am I misreading things? I thought this was what you wanted too?"

"It is, lass, don't ever doubt it. It's just, Moira regretted me every day we were married and I couldn't bear to see regret in your eyes."

"You won't, Will." He'd stood and stepped away from her after she asked him to make love and she stood now with her arms circling his waist, pulling at his shirt and reaching up to kiss him.

"Protection," he mumbled embarrassed. "I don't have protection."

"It's ok, I have an implant."
She kissed him deeply.

"Alison, wait, I'm filthy. I've been at work all day. I must smell like a barnyard. I need to clean up first." He still sounded embarrassed.

Aware that he needed to slow things down a little, she pulled away smiling.

"You look windswept, rugged and sexy. One day, Will Barnes, we'll make love the moment you walk through the door, but I'm patient, I can wait. Our first time should be in a bed. If you take the mattress back upstairs I'll make the bed while you shower."

He watched as she walked to the stairs, his heart beating erratically. It was really going to happen, she wanted this as much as he did. It was different to how it had been with Moira; *she* was different. In some way, and he didn't know how, he realised that he would never disappoint Alison. That realisation made his doubts disappear and dragging the mattress with him he followed her upstairs.

He put it back on the bed. Alison turned and smiled at him.

"Ok, go have your shower, I'll make the bed. And, Will, when you come back just wear a towel."

He showered quickly, not lingering under the warm spray to enjoy the luxury of hot water for the first time in days. He rubbed himself dry and wrapped the towel around his waist, his hands trembling slightly as much from anticipation as nerves. It was hard to believe that he was here about to make love with a woman who wanted him as much as he did her.

Alison had lit the lamp on the chest of drawers and soft shadows were cast around the room. She was stood at the window, looking out over the farmyard. She'd changed into one of his shirts; it skimmed her thighs, displaying the long length of her legs. He moved behind her, circling her waist and placing a kiss at her temple.

"It's beautiful here, Will, with the farm buildings all covered in snow and the hills behind them. We could be in the Alps."

"Aye, it is, but not as beautiful as you, lass," he whispered as he trailed kisses along her neck, praying he was doing this right.

She turned in the circle of his arms and he took her mouth. Gently and a little hesitantly he began to kiss her, slowly tasting her soft lips, five, six or more times, teasing little nibbles to her lower lip until, on a moan of part pleasure, part frustration, her lips parted, inviting him to take more. He kissed her with greater urgency, his tongue stroking and exploring. Her arms slid around his waist exploring the plains and contours of his back. His hands moved to the back of her head playing with the strands of hair that had fallen loose. Tilting her head back he changed the angle of his kiss, his teeth grazing over her lips causing heat to spread through her. Her tongue slid over his as she returned his kisses with equal passion. He was trembling again, but now it was with desire.

Taking his hand, she led him to the bed and turned the covers back. He swallowed, his mouth suddenly dry.

"Nervous?" Alison reached up and touched his cheek.

"A little," he confessed shyly.

"Remember, just follow your instincts." Reaching up Alison kissed him deeply, the movement causing the shirt to rise up. "What are your instincts telling you to do now?"

"This." His hands moved to the buttons on the shirt and he slipped them free before pushing the shirt from her shoulders. His eyes darkened with pleasure. God, she was beautiful; long and slim, but utterly feminine. Her skin, soft as silk, was tinted the palest peach and just begged to be touched. Will gave in to the temptation, pulling her close, his hands running the length of her back and softly rounded bottom as he pressed soft kisses to her throat and shoulders.

"So beautiful," he murmured against her hair. "You're so beautiful."

His hands glided up her body, their roughened texture spreading heat over her. "Alison, I'm not hurting you, am I?" he whispered.

"No, you're killing me, but please don't stop." Her hands moved to the towel and she paused, aware that she was trembling.

"Now who's nervous?" The teasing tone surprised her. How he had changed over the past few days.

She loosened the towel and let it fall to the floor at their feet. His body was lean and hard from manual labour. Although she was tall, Alison could not help but notice how much bigger Will was than her. He was compellingly masculine, all muscle and sinew.

"Let's take this to the bed."

****

Much later she rolled to his side and they lay cocooned together, gently caressing each other. He turned to look at her, his eyes serious.

"Alison, I.... was it... I mean, was I... Did you... I mean, it were perfect for me, I never knew..."

She smiled, God, he was gorgeous when he went all bashful.

"Well, now you do, and yes it was perfect for me."

He kissed her gently.

"You're incredible, lass. You came into my empty, lonely world and made me feel whole. You showed me things that I never believed were possible."

She smiled softly.

"You saved me as well, Will. If I'd not met you I'd probably forgive Rob, give it another go. But now I won't because you showed me what a self-centred bastard he is."

She smiled gently.

"Me, how did I do that?" The thought of her returning to Rob terrified him.

"You did it just by being you. I know you don't get it, but you are one hell of a package; hard working, dependable, calm, unflappable in an emergency and kind to animals. Add into that all that sex appeal..."

"Sex appeal, me? I don't think..."

"Yes, you. Women round here must be blind. Mind you, I'm glad they are. It's your eyes and your voice I think. You look at me as if I'm the only woman in the world and your voice is as sinful as chocolate and when you call me "lass" I melt. And then there's your body, I belong to a gym and the blokes there would kill for your body."

Her hands were wandering over his abdomen causing his muscles to ripple in anticipation.

"Lass, what are you doing?"

"If you have to ask, Will, your education is not going as well as I thought," she said smiling wickedly.

Chapter Twelve

Rob had difficulty reining in his temper. He was shaking and his knuckles gleamed white because of the death grip he had on the telephone receiver. The bitch was playing with him. Taking a calming breath, he finally answered:

"You're right, Jo, a dislocated shoulder is a nasty injury but I'm just glad it wasn't worse."

"No, there is no point in you coming round. The accident happened in Warwickshire. Ali had gone to visit her parents."

"Yeah, I did warn her about the weather but you know what she's like."

"Yeah, of course I'll give her your love when I speak to her."

He hung up and hurled the glass he'd put down to answer the phone at the wall opposite.

Bitch! Did she think he was a fool? He had left seven messages on her phone and she hadn't returned one of them; seven messages where he had apologised, grovelled, begged and pleaded. How dare she ignore him?

According to Jo, Ali had rung the head of her school and phoned in sick – with a dislocated shoulder to be exact. Anger swept over him quickly, like a forest fire, hot, fast, furious and destructive. How much of what Ali had told her boss was true? How dare she speak to others, let them know she was alright, but not tell him? He'd never had to discipline her during their marriage so far, but he would have to now.

He ordered himself to think; he needed to try and work out what Ali would do. If she wasn't at her parents, he reasoned that she would have contacted them to let them know she was safe. If so, did they know he had cheated on Ali? He realised that there was only one way to find out and that was to contact them. He'd have to be careful how he approached them. If they didn't know about him he didn't want to tip them off. His heart beat erratically as he dialled the number; his life as he knew it hinged on this conversation. His mother in law answered and her first words told him that they knew nothing.

"Rob, how are you coping with Alison being stuck up in Yorkshire?"

He smiled before answering.

"Fine, though I'm missing Ali. I was ringing to check that you and Henry were alright?"

He smiled again as his mother in law told him what a good son in law he was before continuing.

"Yes, we're fine. You must have been worried at not being able to get in touch with Alison. It was good of the teacher in Yorkshire to put her up though. When will she be back, has she said?"

Rob was deliberately vague in his answer, saying it depended on the weather and that it was still bad up in Yorkshire. He promised to let them know when he heard more and then hung up. He would have liked to have asked for a contact number, but that would have looked suspicious. He had at least narrowed down where she was. Which story was true though: the dislocated shoulder or being stranded? He thought for a few moments; the easiest one to check out was the accident. The police would presumably have a record if there had been an accident or have the means to check admissions to casualty departments.

He cleared up the glass and then made a coffee for Claire.

She was in the bedroom, applying moisturizer to her skin following a shower.

"I have a lead on where she went. Fucking Yorkshire. I'm going to the police station and get them looking for her. She's told her mother and boss different stories so she doesn't have to rush back."

"What are you going to do when you find her?"

"Drag her back by her hair and make sure she knows who the boss is. Punish her for thinking she can ignore me. When I've finished disciplining her she won't ignore me again."

"Will you record the punishment so I can screw you while I watch you punish her?

He groaned, wondering if she knew what she did to him.

"Sure, baby. Look, I have to go but I'll be back soon. Will you be ok?"

"I guess so." She pouted. "Bring back champagne so we can celebrate."

"Celebrate what?"

"That you're closer to finding the Stepford wife. I can't wait to see you discipline her."

"I'll bring the champagne. You just be ready for me to screw when I get back."

****

He hated to be kept waiting. He'd thought his request would be treated with some degree of urgency, but the police did not seem to be in any kind of a rush to talk to him. They'd given him a cup of tea and told him to wait.

He hoped Claire wasn't worried about him. Stupid thought. She wouldn't be worried. She'd be trying Ali's clothes on and using her beauty products. He swallowed and blocked the image, not wanting to become aroused in the police station.

The door opened and a police constable came in.

"Sorry to keep you waiting. As you can imagine, it's bloody bedlam everywhere," he said.

"I don't care about that. My wife's missing. She's not answering her phone. You have to find her."

"Ok, sir, I can see you're upset. So why don't I take down some details and then we can try and trace your wife's whereabouts."

He nodded. The anger had been a good thing. It made them think he was really upset. Well, he was, just not in the way they thought.

It surprised him how long it took to make the report. They asked dozens of questions. How was he supposed to know what she was wearing? He'd been screwing Claire. He told them a pair of trousers and a sweater, which is what she usually wore to work. The real difficulty arose when he explained she'd been heading to Yorkshire. He had no idea where to say she was heading for. The first place that came to mind was

Halifax so that was what he said, explaining she was going to look at some proposed places for the children to visit on school trips.

He handed them a photo of Ali; it had been Claire's idea and a good one. The constable was pleased.

"This will help. It may take a while, but we'll be in touch every day to keep you updated. Try not to worry, sir. She's probably in some little hotel waiting out the weather."

"Yeah, I guess so. Thanks for helping and sorry about being angry."

"Think nothing of it."

Claire was waiting in the lounge for him when he returned.

"Did everything go alright?"

"Perfect," he said as he uncorked the champagne. "The police think I'm husband of the year." He walked to the window to draw the curtains.

"You play the devoted husband so well. What would they say if only they knew what a bastard you are?" Claire spoke, coming up behind him.

"They won't know and you like me being a bastard, don't you?"

She reached down cupping him intimately.

"Yeah, I do, but not as much as I like being a bitch. I like the power. You won't give me up - not even for her. Like now, you want me, don't you? You'd like me to take you here in this tidy little lounge. Does she do that, in broad daylight on the lounge floor?"

"Not like you baby, never like you." He turned as she unzipped his trousers and dropped to the floor. God, she really was going to do this while he stood in front of the window. Could the neighbours see? Did it look from the outside like he was just stood in the window or was it obvious what was happening? Ali would never do something like this and as much as he needed the safe security she gave him, he needed this as well. He would find Ali and bring her back - he had to - but he'd still be screwing Claire. She was right, he couldn't give her up.

"Are you thinking of her?" Rob nodded, unsure of how Claire would react.

"Good, imagine it's her doing this."

He gave in then, not caring if he could be seen by the neighbours.

Chapter Thirteen

It was a new and wonderful experience to wake with Alison, naked in his arms. Her head was resting comfortably on his shoulder, her arms and legs twined around him. They had made love twice during the previous evening and night. He had discovered the joys of touching and being touched. At first he had been shy and hesitant but under Alison's patient guidance he had relaxed, giving into the sensual pleasures she had shown him. He should be exhausted but, strangely, he wasn't. He felt vibrant and alive and he wanted desperately to make love before getting up and heading out into the cold. Liar, his conscience laughed at him, you want to stay here and make love all day.

His hands moved slowly down her silken back. Did he dare wake her with a kiss and make love to her? His finger traced a path across the cheeks of her softly rounded bottom. She moved slightly in her sleep, pushing herself closer to him. He kissed the top of her head and allowed his hands to slide once more over her back in soft, gentle caresses.

Alison's head tilted backwards and she opened her eyes sleepily looking at him. He smiled. Drinking in her beauty, before he joined his lips to hers, sighing as her lips parted allowing his tongue to join the tender assault on her mouth.

Had she thought the man was a good kisser? Good? He was a grand master.

"Morning, lass," he whispered, when he finally drew away.

"Wow, that sure beats the alarm clock."

He smiled as he moved her so she lay flush against him.

"Will, what are you doing?"

"You don't know? And I thought you were my teacher."

"Oh, I know," she whispered as he parted her legs with his knees. He slowly pushed into her welcoming body, his thrusts as long, slow and deep as his kisses. In some part of her mind she recognised that this loving was different from what they had shared before. Will was slightly more confident; he didn't seem to need any words of reassurance or guidance. There was a beauty in its simplicity; no long teasing foreplay, no heated words. Just two people joined in the most intimate way. How long he kept up the slow, steady rhythm she had no idea, time lost all meaning. Everything began and ended with him.

It was unbelievable, Will thought. A day ago he'd been certain that he couldn't make love and now he was buried deep inside a woman, enjoying the most amazing experience he'd ever known. Judging by the little noises and gasps of pleasure she was making, Alison was enjoying it just as much as he was. He smiled. He, Will Barnes, was making love to a woman and it was bloody wonderful. With that thought lingering in his mind he let his release wash over him.

It was many minutes before either of them spoke again as they lay in a tranquil, post love making haze, idly tracing patterns on each other's skin as their temperatures and heartbeats returned to normal.

"You are one hell of a pupil, Mr Barnes." Alison stretched like a contented cat.

"It's all down to you, lass, you inspire me." His smile was charming and Alison fell a little deeper in love. "You also tempt me," he continued. "But I have animals that need to be fed so I must get up." He dropped a kiss on her head and climbed out of bed.

"Ok." She put on an exaggerated pout. "I guess you must. You shower and I'll make you some breakfast."

Alison was just putting scrambled eggs on toast on the table when he came down.

"Sorry lass, but I'm going to be gone all day again. Will you be ok?

"Yeah, I'll be fine. What are you doing today?"

"I have to start clearing the lane leading down to the main road to Hebden Bridge. As much as I like it being just the two of us, I need help on the farm and that means getting the road cleared. I'm sorry, lass."

"Hey, don't be, I was just being stupid yesterday. I could do with the road being cleared."

A worried frown creased Will's brow.

She reached up and softly kissed his brow.

"Only so I can get some clothes that fit."

A smile tugged at Will's lips and the frown slipped away.

"That's a shame because I really like how my shirt looks on you." He slipped his hands under the soft cotton fabric as he kissed her softly.

"Behave or you won't get that road cleared." She scolded. "And your eggs will be cold."

****

The mobile phone lay on the window sill. Ridiculous as it was, she would swear it was taunting her. No matter where she moved around the kitchen or the lounge, her eyes were drawn to it, checking it was still there, hoping it might just disappear. Of course it never did. Switch it on, her conscience nagged. You know you have to at some point. I know, she answered herself, just not yet. She wanted to deny his existence for a little longer. She patted the cushions on the sofa. Here there was no trace of him. Until Will had remembered her mobile she had been able to forget about him for huge chunks of the day. Her eyes flicked to the window sill, but now she knew about the phone she couldn't. It was a tangible link to her real life.

Would he have rung? Of course he would. There would be a message, maybe more than one. He'd have left both a text and voice mail. She wasn't ready to hear his voice and she needed no written proof of how screwed up her life was.
She wandered from room to room, unable to settle, always returning to the kitchen and the mobile. It was switched off but, one touch of a button and it would return to life. The silly jingle would cut through the peace of the farmhouse and the

display would tell her about missed calls and messages.

Since when have you been a coward? The little voice in her head taunted. Just switch it on. She moved to the window sill and picked it up. It felt strange in her hand. Who'd have thought that? A few days ago, like almost everybody in the world, she would have been constantly checking for messages and texting. Now she had got used to being without it. Her hand trembled slightly, a sign of how nervous she was.

Gripping it a little tighter, she moved towards the table and sank down on a chair. You can do this, she told herself. She fumbled a little as she switched it on and unconsciously held her breath while she waited for the jaunty tune that signalled it was working. She looked down at the illuminated screen: four missed calls, two voice mails and seven text messages – all from Rob. Christ, he must be desperate to talk to her.

Ignoring the voice mail she began opening the text messages. The first five were grovelling, snivelling apologies. If she'd had a bucket she'd have puked, they were so nauseating. Did the conceited bastard really think that a few 'I'm sorries' and 'forgive mes' was all it was going to take to repair their marriage. The sixth unnerved her; he had obviously found out that she had rung her boss because he wanted to know why she hadn't contacted him. And the seventh just plain scared her. She placed the phone on the table, but she couldn't pull her eyes away from the message.

"I won't be ignored. You have been told."

The tremor in her hands spread through her body until she was shaking from head to foot. She'd realised over the past few days that her life with Rob was a sham, but that hadn't prepared her for those words. She should be thankful they were only written. At least she couldn't hear the tone. The message was menacing enough just reading it.

She had known Rob liked to be in control - they'd often joked about it - how he chose the restaurants and their holidays. But this... this was different. This was threatening. The words violated her as much as his cheating. She was cold, despite the heat from the range. It suddenly occurred to her that she was alone. Will had taken the dogs. She felt sick. It was ridiculous. Rob was miles away in Bath – he couldn't touch her. Even so, she moved to the back door and slid the bolt home.

Tea, she'd make a cup of tea. That would help, didn't it always? No, not really, she thought, but it was something to distract her. Everything seemed different. There was a tension in the air that hadn't been there fifteen minutes before. She was filling the kettle when her mobile rang. She wasn't sure if she screamed first or dropped the kettle, both occurred so close together. She turned slowly and on legs that had suddenly taken on the consistency of jelly she walked back to the table and looked at the phone.

'Rob calling'

She clumsily picked up the phone. There was no way she could speak to him. The ringing stopped as abruptly as it had started. Fumbling, she switched the phone off. She had to, for her sanity. If the phone kept ringing she would be a nervous wreck all day. She wasn't daft; she knew she'd have to speak to Rob, but it would have to be on her terms not his. It was the only way she could deal with it.

She needed to keep busy, that was the trick. Tea, she'd been making tea. She returned to the sink and retrieved the kettle, setting it to boil on the range. After she'd drunk her tea she would clean the house.

She was glad of the familiarity of the task. Cleaning was cleaning no matter where you did it. Will was organised and she found kitchen cleaner, rags and polish under the sink. She amused herself in the kitchen by wondering where all the mismatched china in the dresser had come from: antique shops, jumble or car boot sales. A lovely image flashed into her mind, a daydream really of the two of them strolling around an antique fair, hands linked together as they browsed the stalls, before stopping at a pub by a river for a lazy lunch, before going home to make love in the afternoon.

The image when she cleaned the bathroom was much steamier and triggered by the showerhead being positioned so high it reminded her of how tall Will was. In a flash the image of him naked in the shower filled her thoughts and within seconds she was imagining having mind blowing sex in the shower. She grinned. Cleaning had never been so erotic – if she had worn glasses they'd have steamed up.

Cleaning had also never been so exhausting; that was probably due to the after effects of the accident. It had taken more out of her than she'd realised. She went into his room and lay down on the bed, intending to rest for a minute, but within seconds she was sound asleep.

****

Will stared at the rolling, snow covered hills, a blanket of white as far as the eye could see. Here and there he could just make out the top of the stone walls that separated the fields - stone walls that had been built by his ancestors. He belonged to this land as much as it belonged to him. He'd known it all his life. Even as a small child it had called to him. The history of the place fascinated him; he was awed by the fact that for hundreds of years his family had tended the land, fighting the extremes of the weather, just as he was now. It would have been a hard life – it still was. With the land came responsibility; it had to be tended and looked after. There had been a time, after his grandparents had become sick, when the farm had been neglected. Even now, years later, he still felt guilty. Not that he'd any control over things he hadn't, but since then he had made amends every day. The farm was now prospering and he'd gradually begun to improve his home.

Being a part of the land had always been enough, but it was odd, looking out over the hills, he found himself questioning if it was now. Until a few days ago he'd accepted and made his peace with his lot in life - to be alone. Alison's arrival had changed all that. Things were different; he was different. His land was still important but he realised that, without anybody to share it with, it was diminished. For the first time he looked forward not back. In his will he had left the farm to Sarah, but he had never expected her to stay. She wasn't tied to the land as he was. But now he was thinking about a family, children to carry on his legacy. Alison had shown him he could have that. He sighed. It was ridiculous to be thinking about children and family. He should just relax and enjoy being in a normal relationship. Except, it wasn't normal, cut off and isolated from everybody as they had been. Time would tell, now that real life was returning, if they had a relationship.

On the horizon he could make out a moving vehicle. He assumed it was probably a council road gritter. If he kept clearing the road, in another hour, they'd meet and he and Alison would no longer be alone. He expected the local police constable, Paul, to be with the council workers. Suddenly he was nervous about meeting them. Would they realise something was different? Did he look different? Sarah said he sounded different. He smiled. It had been great to hear from her. Her call had come out of the blue so was a wonderful surprise. She'd been trying to contact him for days and almost wept in relief when he answered. He'd calmed her down and told her everything was alright. It had been good to hear her voice and before long she'd started chatting away about New Zealand. Her enthusiasm was infectious and he'd been in a good mood ever since her call. It had been when she had asked how he was occupying himself while he was snowed in, that she told him he'd changed. He supposed she had heard the hesitation in his answers. He hadn't wanted to lie but it was too soon to speak to her about Alison. He could hardly have told her he was learning how to make love. He'd changed the subject back to her but his thoughts remained on her statement that he sounded different.

The lorry on the horizon was getting closer now. He realised that it wouldn't be long before it reached him. It was stupid to worry about what people might think. So what if he seemed different? He was different and he hoped to God he'd never feel the same again.

****

Rob had texted several times while she had been asleep. There were no more threats, he'd gone back to begging. It was pathetic, really; he sounded like a whiney child who couldn't get his own way. Alison smiled. The way to deal with a spoilt child was to ignore them, she thought, as she switched off the phone.

She spent the rest of the afternoon preparing the evening meal and was just checking the vegetables when the sound of the tractor entering the yard told her Will was back. She decided not to mention Rob's text messages - it would only spoil the evening. She turned as he opened the door, smiling. Her heart flipped over as he walked in. He was compellingly masculine – tall, broad and strong. His jaw was dark with a five o'clock shadow which would have made him look dangerous were it not for the tenderness in his eyes. She moved towards him, eager to be enveloped in the warmth of his embrace.

"I missed you," she whispered as she pulled his head down for a kiss.

"I missed you as well, lass. I spent the day thinking about you and me."

"I thought about you as well."

"Good thoughts, I hope."

She smiled remembering the shower.

"Yes, very good thoughts; daydreams really."

He smiled.

"Daydreams about me? I'm not sure I'm interesting enough to daydream about." He looked over at the cooker. "Do I have time for a shower before tea's ready?"

Alison smiled wickedly.

"Yes, you do."

A more worldly man would have seen the gleam in her eyes.

She waited five minutes before she followed him upstairs. Pausing outside the bathroom long enough to slip out of her clothing, she pushed opened the bathroom door quietly, the noise of the shower disguising her entrance.

He had his back to the shower door and his eyes closed when she entered.

He turned slowly, stunned by her appearance.

"I thought it was time for another lesson." She reached up and kissed him.

"I..." His hands moved down covering himself.

"Hey, it's too late to be embarrassed." She lifted his hands away. "I've seen it all before, remember. Just relax, this is going to be so much fun," she said grabbing the sponge and soap.

"Fun" didn't come close to what it was, he thought an hour later. "Mind blowing" was a better description, the things she had done with that sponge and her mouth. He blushed at the memory of them, but God knows he wouldn't mind doing them again.

His legs weren't quite steady as he came downstairs. She was dressed in one of his shirts dishing up the food she'd prepared. He was in complete awe of her. She was so natural, so at home.

"Hey, perfect timing." When he didn't speak she moved towards him.

"Will, are you alright?"

Was he alright? He had no idea.

"Was it too much? The shower, I mean?"

"No...it was a surprise. I wasn't expecting... didn't know."

"Did you like it?"

"Like doesn't come close. I'm still reeling. That was some lesson."

"Well, I hope you paid attention because there will be a test later in the week and it will be a practical."

Will laughed and pulled her into his arms.

"Perhaps I'd best do some revision then."

Chapter Fourteen

She came awake with a start. It was still dark but she knew instantly that she was alone again. How did he do that, leave without disturbing her? For a big man he moved with almost silent grace. She turned over; his side of the bed was cool so he'd obviously been gone quite some time. The total darkness here was disorientating and she had no idea of the time. She'd noticed on the first night that she'd slept in this room that there was no clock. When she asked Will how he woke without an alarm clock he had just smiled and said that after thirty years of waking at four thirty he needed no clock. Suddenly, as if answering an unasked question, the grandfather clock struck seven, its deep gongs echoing throughout the house.

She stretched, pondering what had woken her, when she heard the back door slam and the dogs barking loudly. That was unusual; they seldom barked. She slipped out of bed and walked to the window. A four wheel drive stood in the farmyard. Was it Will's, she wondered? She pulled on the jogging bottoms she had been wearing and headed to the stairway. She was halfway down when she heard voices.

"Morning Will. You survived without us then?"

"I just about managed it." Will smiled at the two younger men.

"More than can be said for the Renault Clio down on the lane."

The smile disappeared as he remembered how close Alison had come to death.

"Yes, the owner were lucky. Matter of fact, lads, she's been staying here since the accident, waiting out t'storm like and recovering from her injuries."

"You have a woman staying here?" The shock in the voice made Alison smile.

"Yeah, yeah. I know. Incredible, isn't?" Will's tone was mildly sarcastic. "Who'd have thought Silas Marner would help anybody out?"

"Who's Silas Marner?" Stu asked.

"Nobody, it doesn't matter." Will sighed. "What matters is Alison, who is here as I said, is recovering from her injuries."

"Alison?"

"Aye, Alison Robinson, and she's a lady so mind your language, Stu. Cut out the effing and blinding."

"What about Mike? His language is just as bad as mine." The young man's voice whined.

"No, it isn't. Don't worry, Will, I'll make sure he behaves himself. So when are we going to meet Alison?" Mike asked.

"Yeah, what's she like, Will? Young or old, fat or thin? Beautiful..."

"Well, if you turn around you can judge for yourself." Alison said from the stairs.

"Alison, l-l-lass, I'm sorry. Did we wake you?" Will stammered surprised at her arrival.

"No, I was awake and heard the door slam. So Stu, is it? How do I look? Fat, thin, beautiful...?"

"Beautiful... I mean..." Stu broke off as Mike punched him on the arm.

"Idiot! Pay him no mind, most of the time he's harmless. It's just when you're his age your brains are in your trousers. I'm Mike Williams and the idiot's Stu Pearson."

"Alison Robinson. Tell me, Mike, at what age does a man's brain return to its normal anatomical position?"

He grinned.

"Well, I'm twenty two and mines back in place. Of course, some blokes never get it back. Stu was doing well till you appeared. I'm guessing you've set his rehab back six months." Mike laughed.

"I'm flattered; I've never set anybody's recovery back."

Will listened frowning. He didn't know why but he didn't like the easy familiarity and banter between Mike and Alison. A niggling pain settled in his stomach and he rubbed his hand idly over it.

"Are you men hungry? Shall I fix breakfast?"

"God, you cook. Marry me now! Me girlfriend can't even boil an egg," Stu said.

"Don't you think I'm a little old for you, Stu?"

"He's probably hoping you can teach him a thing or two," Mike laughed.

She laughed.

"How do bacon butties sound?"

"Not for me," Will said sharply. He turned to face the two younger men. "When you've had a brew you can see t'pigs." Will realised he was being abrupt but he couldn't help it. He didn't know why but he just had to get out of the kitchen.

Alison watched as he hurried back outside.

"You've not improved the boss' temperament much, Miss Robinson," Stu said with a smile.

Mike reached up and gently clipped the younger lad on the head.

"No speaking ill of the boss. You've a lot to thank him for. Pay no mind to Stuart, Miss Robinson. Will's a good bloke, he's just not used to company. Since Sarah left, you're his first visitor."

"Only since Sarah left? Be honest. Will has never had visitors. When we were kids, me mates and I were terrified of him. When he used to come down to school to see Sarah, we'd all run off and hide." Stu said.

"He's shy, Stu; that doesn't make him bad. Honest, the boss don't talk much and you'll likely not see him smile, Miss Robinson, but he's got a good heart."

"It's Alison," she said quietly. "I'll make the tea and butties," she said, looking at the door Will had gone through.

She made the tea half listening to the two younger men chat and half thinking about Will as she did so. What had come over him, she wondered? She didn't recognise the surly man who'd stomped off out of the kitchen and she couldn't pretend she wasn't hurt by his not wanting breakfast with her. She'd enjoyed his company the past few mornings before he'd left for work. His behaviour this morning was at odds with the man she thought she knew. Well, she thought, I'm not letting him behave like a bear with a sore head. She poured the tea into the mugs and placed them on the table.

"I'll take Will a cuppa. Where will I find him?"

"You'll need a coat – its brass monkey weather out there. Sarah's coat is on t'porch and there's some wellies out there as well. You can use those. I expect the boss 'll be in t'stable, talking to Aragorn and Arwen." Mike said.

"Aragorn and Arwen? Who are they?"

"Sarah's horses. He always goes over there when he's troubled. I reckon he feels close to her when he talks to them."

"Oh, right. And the stable is where?" Alison asked. "I've not been outside yet."

"It's t'building opposite. Be careful walking over, it's slippery outside."

Thanking them, she headed out to the porch and wrapped up against the weather.

****

The horse shuffled about nervously, its tail swishing wildly. He was not used to the tension that was radiating from the man cleaning out his stable. He shied away from the stall, neighing anxiously, as the man stomped about.

Will tossed fresh hay into the stall with unnecessary vigour, trying to understand where his anger had come from.

"You're scaring the horse."

Muttering an oath, he turned.

She was stood at the door, bundled up in Sarah's coat.

"What are you doing out here, Alison. It's bloody freezing." His tone was far from pleasant.

"I know it is. That's why I brought you a mug of tea. I didn't realise you kept horses."

"I told you I didn't want owt."

"What's the matter with you this morning?"

"What's t'matter with me? You are the one who is ..."

"Me! What have I done?" Alison asked incredulously.

"Flirting and batting your eyes..."

"Flirting with whom?"

"With Mike. You and him..."

"Me and Mike...?"

"Yes, you and him. You were practically crawling all over each other."

"Crawling..."

"Aye, I were thinking about telling you to get a room."

Alison froze. She felt like she'd been slapped. The colour drained from her face, but she was damned if she would let him see her cry.

"Is that right? I could have sworn I was at least three foot away from him. It's amazing how the green eyed monster distorts the facts. Well, when you've taken your head out of your ass maybe you would take me down to the village so I can get a room." She turned and walked away letting the tears roll down her cheeks.

Will threw down the rake he'd been spreading straw with.

"Damn."

The horse snorted.

"You don't have to say owt either; I know I'm a bastard."

The horse snorted again and shied away.

Will reached up and patted the horse's neck.

"Steady on, big fella." The horse calmed under his touch. "I don't know what's the matter with me, lad. Me guts are tied in knots and I'm so angry with everybody. Is that jealousy?"

The horse whinnied softly and nodded his head.

"When did you get to be so wise? They were just larking about, that's all. I know that. I'm being bloody stupid. I'm supposed to be a grown up, but I feel like a kid left out of a game."

He led the horse back into the stall and offered the carrot he had in his pocket.

"See, I may be grumpy but I'm not forgetful. Now, I best see to your lady before going to apologise to mine"

He led the mare out of the stall and ran his hands over her flank, smiling as he felt the movement of her unborn foal.

"Is all well in there, lass?"

The mare blinked serenely and neighed softly.

"That's good. You'll be a wonderful mother won't you, Lady Arwen?"

Will cleaned out her stall with quiet efficiency, leading her back in when he'd finished. She accepted her treat before gently butting her head against his shoulder.

"I know, lass, I best go and find her and try and explain."

Before heading into the house, he called to Mike who was feeding the pigs.

"Take Stu up to top field and see to the sheep up there. I've loaded the trailer ready."

"Ok, Will. Should we come back down for us dinner?" He glanced at the house.

"You worried you might be in the way?" Will said with a smile.

"Something like that. We didn't mean owt, you know."

"You've been listening at the stable door again?"

Mike smiled and nodded.

"She seems real nice, Will. You could do a lot worse."

"Thanks, Mike, I'd appreciate if you kept this to yourself for a bit. It's early days yet. Come back at one. I'll make some soup and butties."

Having given the two workers their jobs for the day, he knew he could not put off going into the house any longer.

He found her sat in front of the fire, lost in her thoughts, seemingly mesmerised by how the flames curled and danced. If she heard him enter she gave no indication. He sighed. This was not going to be easy. He looked at Win who was curled at her side. Even his dog was ignoring him.

"I guess it will take more than paper flowers to earn your forgiveness?"

Alison turned her head.

"Yeah, it will. What the hell came over you?"

He shook his head.

"I don't want to give you excuses. No matter what, there are none. I'm sorry."

"I don't think they would be excuses. I need to understand, Will."

"I don't understand myself. It was like being back with Moira and Myles again. The banter you and Mike shared was similar to their joking about. I was always excluded – Christ, it hurt. I loved her so much and she barely knew I existed. I watched you with Mike and thought 'not again'. Then the hot sharp pain in my gut returned, pain which I haven't felt since I used to see Moira and Myles together. I never knew what it was, but now I realise it was jealousy. I was jealous, Alison."

"Part of having a relationship is dealing with things like jealousy. You have to deal with it."

"What do I know about relationships? I've never been in one. We're kidding ourselves, you and me."

"Kidding ourselves? About what?"

"I don't know..." Will waved his hand around the kitchen. "These last few days, me and you, playing at happy families, it's not real. It's not having a relationship. A relationship – who am I kidding? I'm no good at sex and I'm no good at conversation. I'm not smart or funny. Face it, you'd be bored in less than a day."

Alison's heart bled for him.

"They did a real job on you, didn't they, Moira and Myles? They knocked and slighted you at every turn, destroying your confidence. The sad thing is they are still doing it and you're letting them."

"I'm letting them!"

"Yes. When was the last time you went to the pub and socialised? Don't answer. I can guess – before Moira and Miles died."

A small smile tugged on his lips.

"You're wrong, it were when Sarah left for her gap year... Before that it was at Moira's wake."

The delivery was droll and the timing perfect; could he not see he was funny?

She smiled.

"You know, Will, Silas Marner..."

"Oh God, you heard that?" he asked.

Alison nodded.

"Silas Marner wasn't alone; he was lonely. I think you're desperate for company, but you control your contact with society so you can't be hurt again."

"How do you mean?"

"The people you help – pensioners, troubled young lads and injured tourists out on the moors – none of them can hurt you. Why?

Because you don't let them get close enough."

"I don't know how to let anybody close."

"But you do...you have... me. You have let me get close. That's why you were jealous. I don't know if we can make a relationship work, Will, or if at this stage we should even be thinking like that. What I do know is that I would like to explore what has started here."

He sank to her side.

"I thought I'd blown it."

"No, you haven't." Alison curled against his chest. "You smell of hay and horses."

"Sorry," he whispered.

"Don't be. It's a good, honest smell. I didn't know you had horses. It occurred to me, when I walked back, that I really don't know much about the farm. Is there any chance of a guided tour?"

"Sure, but you need to wrap up; it's bloody cold out."

"I'll borrow Sarah's coat again if that's alright."

Will nodded.

"It's fine, lass."

"I really need to get a couple of things to wear. Not that your jogging pants aren't comfy - they are – and roomy as well."

"I could take you to Halifax on Friday if you like."

"Can you spare the time?"

"Aye, if the roads are clear, it should be ok. Besides, you need to see a doctor and get that arm checked out. We can do that first down in Hebden Bridge and then head into Halifax."

"Do I really need to see a doctor?"

"Aye, we need to be sure that your arm is ok."

"All right, if you insist, and thanks for the trip to Halifax. Now, how about that tour you promised?"

"Ok, but just the farmyard today; it's too cold and dangerous underfoot to venture further afield."

"Ok, you're the boss."

****

It was a new feeling, certainly not one he was used to, pride. Seeing the farm through Alison's eyes he could see all he'd achieved and he was proud. For a long time, while he'd been caring for his grandparents, he'd not had the time to maintain the place. Back then he'd lived from day to day and the place had fallen into disrepair. After their death he'd worked like a madman to rebuild the farm. He'd sold a small piece of land

and invested the money in the farm. Gone were the dilapidated farmyard and outbuildings. Walls had been re-pointed and rebuilt. The roofs on the stables and outbuildings had been replaced - not that the new tiles could be seen beneath the thick covering of snow, but they were there - and the animals housed in those buildings were well cared for and thriving. Slowly he'd turned the farm around.

It was when they turned back to the house that Alison realised something for the first time. The house was not stood alone.

"Will, what is all that?" She pointed to the building adjoining the farmhouse. "I didn't realise you had neighbours."

He followed her gaze.

"I don't, lass. That's t'rest of t'house."

"The rest of the house? You mean that is part of your house?"

"Aye, 'tis the main part of the house. It's not been used since my parents died. I'm restoring it."

"Restoring it?"

"Aye, it were a wreck. My grandparents abandoned it after my parents died. It's a long way from finished. Do you want a look?"

"Do you have time?"

"Aye, I do."

His smile was boyish and charming. If the farm was his life, then restoring his family home was his baby. He took her hand, eager to show her what he'd been working on, and led her back to the house.

"Leave your coat on; that part of the house will be cold. I've not got the heating on," he told her as he pulled a bunch of keys from the drawer in the kitchen. He walked to the door leading off the living room that she'd wondered about the other day.

It wasn't a cupboard – it was a corridor. Alison followed him along it, coming to a standstill at the end of it in stunned surprise. The corridor had opened out into a beautiful hallway. Pale, wintery sunlight streamed in through elegant windows either side of a grandiose front door. Small particles of dust could be seen dancing on the air, a sign that this part of the house was empty. The floor beneath her feet was a rich, golden oak and looked as if it had recently been sanded and sealed. The majestic staircase that rose up to the second floor had also been restored. She moved over to it, running her hand along the bannister, silently appreciating the texture and patina of the wood. The scent of wax and varnish filled the air and she inhaled deeply. The pale cream walls reflected the light, giving the place a golden feel. More light spilled in through an arched shaped window on the landing, the brightness making one want to explore further.

"Lass, do you like it?"

"Oh, Will, it's beautiful. Show me the rest." She was excited now like a child in a toy shop. There was still work to be done. Alison realised that several of the rooms had just been stripped back to their bare bones. As she poked around, Will explained his plans.

"The house is Georgian. Do you remember me saying that the land were given to the family as a reward for saving the life of the local landowner's child?" Alison nodded. "Well, the house came with it. It hasn't been occupied for thirty years or more, and even then there wasn't the money to do any repairs. The whole place was so sad and dilapidated. I felt I owed it to my ancestors to fix it up, making it a home. Gran and granddad only ever lived in the kitchen wing. I've a lot still to do but hopefully it will be a proper home again."

Judging by the work he had already done, it would be a magnificent home, a family home. This place should ring with the sound of children laughing. Did he realise that subconsciously he was showing the world what he longed for – a family?

"I'm sure it will be stunning." She squeezed his hand. "Thank you for sharing this with me."

"You're welcome, lass, and you're bloody cold as well. We best go back into the warm."

She nodded, having another look at the hallway as they passed through – hoping it wouldn't be the last time she saw it.

Chapter Fifteen

Alison couldn't believe that Will considered the road away from the farm passable. As far as she could tell it was still treacherous. Certainly only a four wheel drive would ever attempt to drive down it.

Sensing her unease, Will reached over and touched her hand.

"Once we're off this lane the road is better."

"Ok, I'll take your word for it..." Alison's words died away. Will's eyes followed her stare.

"Bloody hell, is that my car?"

"Aye, lass, it is. This is the junction with t'main road. You must have run into the corner of the wall. It was damn lucky you walked along this part of the wall and not the other way."

She shivered. If she'd followed the other wall, she'd have gone higher on to the moors, walking to certain death.

"Don't think about it, lass," Will said, sensing she was realising how close she had come to dying.

"I realised in my mind that you saved my life; this just brings home how lucky I was."

For a while, they travelled along what appeared to be the top of the moors. The view was an unending panorama of snow covered hills. Alison had never seen anything like it – not in the UK at least. There was a sweeping, majestic solitude to it, as if the land was primitive and new. The snow carpeting the earth was virgin and untouched. She felt like an explorer discovering some strange, new world.

"Breathtaking," she whispered.

Will smiled, pleased that she was so taken with the view. This was, after all, his land and his home. It was strange he hadn't realised how important it was that she liked it until he had seen her reaction.

"Aye, lass, it is that."

The road began to head downhill and followed alongside an area of dense woodland.

"Does the wood have a name?"

"'Tis Hardcastle Crags, it's National Trust land. It's a grand place – good for walking. If you keep an eye out, you'll see Gibson Mill down in t'valley. It's a visitor centre now but it used to be a cotton mill. I'll take you walking one day during the summer and show you the crags."

Alison smiled at his words, thrilled. He was thinking about the summer with her.

They were approaching Hebden Bridge now and Alison's first thought was that it was larger than she'd imagined. Buildings of local stone were built into the wooded hillside and roads meandered down to the town centre. Water seemed to be at its centre and she was enchanted by the charming bridge that crossed Hebden Water.

"It had a big birthday last year - 'twere five hundred years old. The town celebrated in style."

"Wow, five hundred years! If only the stones could talk, imagine the stories they could tell."

"Aye, Heptonstall and Hebden have seen major changes over the years." He pulled into the car park of the doctor's surgery.

"Here we are, lass. The doctor you're seeing is Ben Chambers. Local people call him young Dr Ben. This was his father's practice for years."

"Would he be known as old Dr Ben?"

"No, around here he were known as God. He was what you'd call an old school GP. He told you things and you didn't question him, ever. Ben is... human." Will smiled.

"We'd best go in. Even if he is human I doubt he'll be pleased if I'm late."

****

She'd have been amused, had she not been the subject of the speculation, by the undisguised interest in her being with Will. As was to be expected, following the recent bad weather, the doctor's surgery was crowded. When they had entered there had been a steady hum of voices, as patients chatted while they waited their turn to be seen. Once she had checked in, however, and people realised that she was actually with Will, the chattering stopped. It was as if every eye in the place was fixed on her. It felt as if a hole was being burned into her back as she filled in the temporary registration form at the desk. The receptionist took the form off her and scanned the details before asking her to take a seat. Was it her imagination or had the receptionist said her name a little louder than was strictly necessary, she wondered? Whether she had or not the whole waiting room now knew her name.

Will was obviously as aware of all the attention as she was. His discomfort was acute. Over the past few days, the stooped, unsure man who didn't hold his head up had begun to change. As he had relaxed in her company and become more confident, his posture had become straighter and he'd stopped looking at the floor as he was walking. Now, within seconds of entering the waiting room, the stooped man was back. As he sat down she realised he was trying to make himself look smaller and less noticeable. He'd chosen a seat tucked away in the corner. He had sunk back in the chair, with his shoulders curled forward and his head lowered, avoiding eye contact with anybody.

The wait was interminable, with each minute seeming like an hour. Alison wanted to hold Will's hand, just to reassure him, but that would just embarrass him even more. She was staggered at the naked curiosity etched on the faces of everybody in the waiting room. Looks were exchanged and elbows nudged; it was like being under a microscope, and every time somebody new entered the surgery the scrutiny began afresh.

Alison sighed in relief when her name was finally called.

"Are you ok, lass? Do you want me to come with you?" Will said, quietly.

Alison smiled softly at the use of the endearment. Was he aware of how intimate he made it sound? Glancing at the faces in the waiting room, others were.

"I'll be fine," she murmured.

The doctor smiled as she entered.

"You look like you've been in the wars, Mrs Robinson."

"Yeah, I'm lucky Winston found me, otherwise I'd have died."

The doctor nodded.

"Will said when he rang. Fate was smiling on you that day, Mrs Robinson. Will and Winston are both valuable members of the Calder Valley search and rescue team. We'd best check you over. See what kind of job Will made of patching you up."

"Ok, but do you think you could call me Alison? I'm trying to forget that I'm married."

The doctor frowned slightly, but didn't ask her to elaborate.

"Well, I'm Ben Chambers. I volunteer with Will in the S&R team. So I hope he followed my training. He said you were hypothermic when he found you?"

"Yeah, I don't remember that, but that was why he delayed treating my arm; he had to get me warm first." Alison told him as she slipped her arm out of her shirt.

"Ok, well, let's take a look at you."

His examination was gentle, but thorough. Not only did he check her arm but he checked her ribs, sternum, breathing as well as her circulation.

"All right, Alison. You can get dressed again." He disappeared behind the curtains.

He was sat at his desk making some notes on his computer. When she reappeared he turned to face her.

"Will seems to have done a top job."

"He's a wonderful man. I mean... he's been wonderful. "

Ben Chambers glanced at the young woman opposite him. A slight blush tinged her cheeks. Was there more to her words than just being thankful to the man who'd rescued her?

"I want you to have an x-ray to just check there is no other damage and then you will need a period of rehabilitation with the arm. We don't advocate immobilisation anymore. Gentle exercise and movement is the key."

"Yeah, Will said that I had to try and move it a little."

"He'll be after my job next," Ben smiled. "Do you mind if I call him in and let him know what a good job he's done? Likely it will embarrass him, but it has to be said."

"He won't like that. He's the most humble, modest man I've ever met," Alison said with a smile.

There was that look again. Ben was sure that there was more to her comments than met the eye. He opened the door and called Will into his room. Judging by the look on Will's face as he stood up, whatever was going on, it was clearly not one sided.

"Everything is ok, Will," he said as he closed the door. "I didn't mean to worry you. I just wanted to commend you for doing so well."

As Alison had predicted, Will brushed the praise aside.

"'Twere nothing. I... did nothing... anybody would have done the same."

"Not everybody would know what to do, but I can see it embarrasses you so we shall move on. Alison needs to have an x-ray on her shoulder." He turned his head to address her. "Once I have the results I'll write to your GP and he can refer you to an orthopaedic surgeon where you live."

He'd have had to be blind not to see the look that passed between the two of them. He'd reminded them with his words that Alison had a life away from Yorkshire.

"Thank you, Dr Chambers," Alison said, her eyes not leaving Will's face.

"You should probably take a couple of weeks off work. Will said you were a teacher. I can provide a sick note." He pulled a pad from his drawer and signed it.

She turned to look at the man. What had he seen? What did he think was going on between her and Will, she wondered? Well, whatever it was, the note in his hand was a two week gift and she accepted it gratefully.

"Thank you again." Alison stood and walked to the door.

"Will, can I have a moment?"

Alison looked at the doctor for a second and then touched Will's hand.

"I'll wait outside."

Ben waited until she had closed the door.

"Will, don't be offended by what I'm going to say."

"If it's likely to cause offence, best you don't say owt."

"I've known you since we were at school and, because of the work we do with the S&R, consider you a friend and I don't want to see you hurt."

"Alison... this is about Alison isn't it? Alison would never hurt me."

"She may have no choice. She has a husband..."

"Her marriage is over. The man is a bastard."

"What he is or isn't doesn't alter the fact that he is her husband. I've seen how a marriage with three people in it damn near killed you. A poor friend I'd be if I didn't warn you."

"Alison is not Moira and I'm not the man I was then."

Ben regarded the man stood opposite him.

"No, I guess you 're not. Well, I wish you luck. She seems very nice."

"Aye, she is, but 'tis early days yet so I 'm not reading owt into anything. I'll see you at training later this week." Will shook hands with the doctor and left the room.

****

Alison sat watching as Will went and bought the drinks. It was strange, the moment they were away from Hebden Bridge his demeanour changed. Without the scrutiny and speculation, his confidence had returned. How relaxed he looked, so different from the self-conscious man in the doctor's surgery. He turned and smiled at her. Even that's different, she thought; his smile was natural, reaching his eyes. He was wearing jeans and the blue v necked sweater he'd worn the other night when they'd made out on the sofa. He'd no idea how gorgeous he looked. She smiled as the girl on the checkout flirted outrageously with him as he paid the bill and almost laughed out loud as she checked out his butt as he walked away.

"What are you smiling at?" he said when he sat down.

"I'm just thinking that I'm the envy of nearly all the women here. They're all wondering how I've managed to grab such a great looking guy," she said.

"They are not," he muttered.

"Trust me, Will, they are."

"Well, that's easy. The reason you have me is because you're such a beautiful person who doesn't mind my faults," he informed her.

"Yes, and one of your faults is putting cheesecake in front of me. Here I am unable to exercise, so I have to watch my figure, and you buy me a calorie laden lunch," she complained.

He smiled and looked over her long, slim frame.

"You eat. I'll watch your figure?"

She laughed.

"And you don't think you're funny."

After lunch they strolled around the town centre, their hands linked comfortably together. They window shopped until a lingerie shop caught Alison's eye.

"Lass, while you go in there I'll nip and get my hair cut," he said backing away.

"Not up to handling sexy undies yet, big guy?"

"Not in public anyway," he said with a smile.

She reached up and touched the curls at the nape of his neck.

"Don't have it cut too short."

"I won't."

"How about a goodbye kiss?" she whispered against his ear.

"What? Here in public, lass?"

She smiled.

"Aye, lad, here in public. Deep breath now."

Her face was inches from his and she could see amusement enter the clear, azure depth of his eyes and the tiny crinkles crease at their corners. The corners of his mouth lifted in a wide smile. A smile that was lethal.

It was the humour of the mock Yorkshire accent which made his inhibition vanish. "Shoulders back. You ready? "

She nodded.

His lips lowered to hers – soft and tender, they gently explored her mouth. His hands framed her face, his thumb gently caressing her soft skin, the movement in time with the soft kisses he was bestowing on her mouth. She loved it when he cupped her face; it was so personal to touch somebody else's face; it made her feel as if they were the only people in the entire world.

After what seemed like an eternity he gently pulled away. He hadn't meant to kiss her like that, not in public but, the moment he touched her, he was lost. The world just slipped away.

"Wow, farm boy, that was some kiss. I feel like Bridget Jones, stood in the snow, kissing Mark Darcy – well , except that I'm wearing more than just my knickers." Alison's voice interrupted his thoughts.

"Mark Darcy?"

"Chick flick, which obviously passed you by. Look, is that Marks and Spencer up there?"

He nodded.

"Ok, I 'll meet you there in forty five minutes."

"Ok, don't be late."

"I won't... and, farm boy, you kiss better than Colin Firth."

****

She was certain her jaw hit the floor. All she could do was stand and stare. She certainly wasn't capable of coherent speech and the ability to move had deserted her. People pushed past her, grumbling that she had chosen a stupid place to stop. Before she'd entered the store, she'd been wondering if he'd be easy to see among the crowds of shoppers. Easy? – Her eyes had been drawn to him from the moment she had stepped through the door, and now she couldn't look away.

She'd thought him good looking before and had actually loved his shaggy, curling hair, but nothing had prepared her for this simple haircut. It was short but it was still possible to see its natural waves as it swept across his head. What she hadn't been expecting was how it was cut to curve around his ear and down his neck. It altered his face and, stood in profile, as he was now, she could see the plains and angles of his jaw and cheeks. Even the nose he claimed to hate was more regal.

A hand pushing at her back gently propelled her forward. Once in motion she had to continue moving and she was soon at his side. He turned towards her and went to speak.

Reaching up she touched his lips with a finger to silence him.

"Shush, I need to savour this moment." Her eyes roamed his face and her hands moved to finger his newly cut hair. Keeping the atmosphere light she whispered against his ear. "Nice haircut, farm boy."

He blushed slightly.

"Farm boy? Is that my new nick name?"

"Do you mind?"

"No, I don't mind. I never had a nice nick name – plenty of horrid ones though: beanpole, concord, super beak, HH which stood for humungous hooter, lofty long conk, and Willy no mates are some of the ones I remember."

Her heart ached for the lonely little boy he must have been.

"Well, farm boy, you've had the last laugh. Take it from me, you're bloody gorgeous."

He blushed again and changed the subject.

"That's an awful big bag for the scraps of lace they were selling in that shop."

"They always put sexy items in large, posh bags," she said, hoping he couldn't guess she was being less than truthful. She'd bought a dress and wanted it to be a surprise and she didn't want him seeing it before she put it on.

He glanced at his watch.

"It's been a long day. You must be tired, lass."

"A little. I just need to pick up a couple of things from here and then we can head home if you like."

He smiled. Home, she was speaking of the farm as home.

"Aye, lass, let's go home."

Chapter Sixteen

Alison inhaled the fragrant scent of the flowers, before placing them on the table. She tilted her head and studied it critically. Was it too much? No, she decided; she wanted tonight to be more than just a meal at the end of the day.

Everything was ready - all she needed to do was put on her dress. She'd spent the entire afternoon indulging herself, firstly by filling Will's enormous bath, adding a capful of her favourite bath foam and soaking for the better part of an hour. Then she'd pampered her skin with moisturising body butter, body butter that she and Will had put to such inventive use the night before.

Her hair had been a huge problem. The pain in her shoulder meant that all she could do was pin it in a simple twist. A fancy style was out of the question since she couldn't lift her arm above her head for long enough to pin it elaborately.

Standing in front of the mirror in Will's room, she was pleased that her skin looked soft and more radiant than it had in days. The bruising, though fading, was still very evident. She sighed. It was of no use worrying; there wasn't anything she could do about it. She reached for the new underwear, fingering the silk and lace before putting it on. There was something utterly sexy about matching silk and lace underwear – especially if it were black. She smiled, liking what she saw in the mirror. It made her feel like some powerful goddess.

The dress was simple, timeless and elegant. A shift of black satin, overlaid with lace, with a V neck that ended just above her cleavage and a hem that ended just above her knees. She'd bought sheer black lace hold ups and plain black stilettoes to complete the outfit. It was more money than she should have spent, but, as Coco Channel had said, all women should own a little black dress. Turning in front of the mirror, she smiled once more. As her mother would say – she'd do.

The noise of the tractor entering the yard drew her to the window. As she had hoped, Will went off to the stable to check on the horses. Smiling, she went down to put the finishing touches to her surprise.

****

Will didn't like surprises. The ones he had received in his life had seldom been good. In truth they had been disastrous and he was always left to face the consequences. Is that why his hands were trembling as he buttoned the shirt Alison had left out on the bed? Was he worried about what she was up to?

The house had been quiet when he had returned home and Alison had been nowhere to be found. At first he'd panicked, certain she had gone, but then he had found the note on the table, instructing him to go upstairs to the bathroom. The bath had been filled and, judging by the amount of fragrant foam on top of the water, she hadn't stinted on the bubble bath. The fragrance wasn't flowery though; it was decidedly masculine. Since he had no male grooming products apart from shaving foam and deodorant, he realised that Alison must have bought this when he'd taken her shopping.

Another note stood propped against a mug of tea, telling him to relax in the bath and then join her downstairs in fifty minutes. The tea, he discovered, was hot which meant that she was not very far away. It was strangely exciting to know she was near and to follow her instructions. He stripped off, lowered himself into the hot bath and lay wondering what she was planning.

The week that had passed since they had first made love had been an awakening of sorts. Not just a sexual awakening but a social one as well. How long had it been since anybody his own age had shown any kind of interest in him? Not the farm, but him as a person? Alison did, and when she listened to him it was as if he were the only person in the world. Not that they agreed on everything; they didn't. In the evenings they had debated many things, each proving willing to defend their own point of view.

They had a shared love of words and in Alison he had found a kindred soul to share the crossword with and the scrabble set had seen more use in the past few days than it had in years.

With the electricity back on, they could have watched TV all night but it was usually late when they switched it on, mainly to catch the news. They had settled into a routine. Some would no doubt call it simple or boring, but it wasn't for him; it was the perfect life.

A life with Alison – Lord, how he wanted that. For the most part he'd enjoyed yesterday, especially when he had taken her into Halifax shopping. They had strolled around like any young couple spending the day together. She'd linked hands as they had walked, leaving him to wish that she would never let him go. The kiss they had shared had been bliss.

He'd no idea where he'd found the confidence to kiss her in public like that. Certainly, if they had been in Hebden Bridge, he'd never have done it. He'd felt under a microscope in the doctor's surgery. Two years had passed since Moira and Myles' deaths, but he could still stop conversation simply by walking into the room. No, he'd not enjoyed the trip to Hebden Bridge, but everything else had been great. He'd felt like a regular guy out with his girl. He smiled at that thought. He *had* been a regular guy out with a girl. The smile had widened – who'd have thought it?

Even walking around Tesco had been wonderful. They had squabbled and joked over what was put in the trolley and who was going to pay. She'd put some food items in that had intrigued him but, when he'd gone to pick them up, she'd slapped his hand away saying they were for a surprise. She'd spent ages selecting some toiletries saying his were ok for a strapping bloke but she needed some fragrance in hers. He'd been about to grumble about the time when she'd handed him a tub of body butter. He'd blushed to his roots when she had whispered where she'd be massaging the scented cream. She had kept the promise too. His body still tingled at the memory of her hands massaging the cream into his skin. There wasn't an inch of his body she hadn't touched. He'd picked up the tea and sipped slowly, remembering how he'd returned her massage with one of his own.

He wanted this fantasy to continue but had no idea how to ask her. They'd only known each other days; so why did it feel like forever? How did they even begin to plan a life together? He couldn't leave Highcroft - it was the only home he had and there was the responsibility of the land. His family had worked it for generations and, at times, it had been hard, but it had been by their blood, sweat and tears that the farm had survived all those years and it should not be allowed to die out.

Did he have the right to ask Alison to move her life to Yorkshire? Did she even want to? She'd told him she would not be returning to her husband but that didn't mean she would want to stay here. She had friends and a job she loved in Bath. Could he expect her just to leave all that? He'd got out of the water then, not wanting to think of her leaving.

She'd laid his clothes out on the bed and on top of them was an invitation to dinner at Chateau Highcroft. The enticing smell of food was wafting up the stairs; his fifty minutes were almost up. What if this was a farewell meal, their last before she left? Pushing the thought aside, he finished buttoning his shirt. A bottle of aftershave stood on the chest of drawers next to his comb. He smiled. Alison had a lot in common with Sarah; it seemed they were both trying to turn him into a new man. He hoped that the two women would have an opportunity to meet as he was certain they would be friends. He uncapped the aftershave and cautiously sniffed the contents. The smell surprised him: it was clean, sharp and masculine. He shook some into his palm and patted it to his freshly shaved cheeks, wincing at the sting of the alcohol. A quick comb through his hair and he could delay no more. Switching off the light, he headed into the hall and down the stairs.

Alison glanced at the table for the hundredth time. Her nerves surprised her; she wanted everything to be perfect. Candles flickered, casting a soft glow around the room. The small posy of flowers she had placed on the table scented the air with a subtle fragrance that mingled with the aroma of the food she had prepared. Glasses and cutlery glinted in the candlelight. She'd borrowed the music centre from Sarah's room and a Chopin concerto now played quietly in the background.

She smoothed her hands down imaginary wrinkles in her dress. Will had never seen her in a dress. She smiled. He'd barely seen her in her own clothes as she'd been wearing his all week. She'd seen the dress and known immediately that she wanted Will to see her in it. She'd wanted to dress up and look feminine for him. Had a man's opinion ever been more important to her? Feminists across the country would lynch her if they knew that she was dressing to please a man. Something told her, though, that no woman had ever done that for Will, made themselves beautiful just for him and nobody else.

The words that she had not yet spoken, feelings that she had yet to declare, had to be shared tonight. She had to tell him that she loved him and that scared her. It was funny how love made one both powerful and vulnerable at the same time. She knew Will liked her and was grateful she had come into his life but that wasn't necessarily love. Love and trust were things she suspected he had barely known and she had to accept that her declaration of love might be too soon. And yet she also knew that, no matter the risk to her own heart, she had to tell him. The snow was melting and the roads were passable; they could no longer block out reality, and with that came choices. In her mind she had already chosen. But her choices depended on Will, so she had to tell him how she felt and what she wanted.

His footsteps sounded on the stairs, a reminder – not that she needed one - that the evening could no longer be delayed. Taking a deep breath, she turned and waited for him to come into the room.

His first coherent thought was that she was wearing a dress, not just any dress but a classic black number. It would have been demure had it not hugged and caressed all her curves and displayed her endlessly long, lean legs – legs clad in sheer stockings. She was even wearing high heels. His eyes skimmed up her body and rested on her face and he almost forgot to breathe. Gone was the pretty girl next door look he had grown used to and in its place was a sultry temptress. The make-up she had used made her eyes dark and sensual, her lips full and begging to be kissed. Her hair was done up in a simple classic twist that could have been austere but for the soft tendrils that hung loose, framing her face.

"I'm afraid to touch you, lass," he said, moving towards her. "Yet... powerless to stop." He stroked a single finger down her cheek, touching the tendril of hair that grazed it, before brushing the softest kiss on her lips. Her pulse fluttered and she could feel his breath against her skin before his lips caressed the soft spot below her ear.

"You approve of the dress then?" she whispered.

He slowly circled her.

"Approve? You are so stunning that you fair take my breath away. I'm puzzled though. What's the occasion?"

She swallowed nervously before she spoke.

"You are... what I mean is... I wanted to thank you for everything you have done for me."

His eyes darkened. A scowl flitted across his face before he had chance to control his emotions.

"That sounds like goodbye. Is it, lass? Is it goodbye? Are the fine clothes and fancy dinner a parting gift? Because, if they are, I don't want them. I don't want your gratitude, Alison."

He turned away, suddenly afraid to be near her, ashamed that she might see the sheen of tears in his eyes.

Realising her words had been badly misjudged, Alison reached out to him.

"Gratitude is not what I'm offering, Will. Not that I'm not grateful - I am. I would be to any man who rescued me from the snow. I didn't do all this though because of that. I did it because I wanted the evening on which I told you that I loved you to be special."

He turned at her words, afraid to believe what he had just heard.

"And I do love you, Will. And I am so scared that you will think it is too soon or that I am mistaking what I feel and that you will send me away..."

"Send you away? How could I send you away, when for days I've been thinking of how I could ask you to stay?"

He cupped her face in his hands.

"I love you, Alison. Please stay with me. Without you my life is barren and empty. I know that you have things you have to sort out but when you have, please come back home to me." His kiss was hot, almost desperate. "Please, Alison. Without you, I am nothing."

Tears shimmered in her eyes at his words.

"You are far from nothing, Will Barnes. You are everything. And just you try and keep me away." She kissed him softly.

They stood kissing for several moments before reluctantly drawing apart.

Taking him by the hand she led him into the kitchen.

"I wanted this night to be perfect so I cooked something special. Let's eat while we make plans and then I want you to make love to me."

If it hadn't been obvious that she had gone to a lot of trouble with dinner, he would have carried her upstairs and made love to her there and then, but she had, so he sat down at the table. It looked lovely with the crisp linen, shining cutlery and crystal goblets, an extension really of his hostess' innate good taste. The flowers in the vase were giving off a delicate perfume, but the thing he liked the most was the candle light. It was strange how different she looked in their soft light. Her luminous skin, that was several shades darker than his fair white, glowed gold. Her eyes normally so soft and gentle, burned brightly with desire. He was sure the salmon she'd cooked was full of wonderful flavours but none compared to the taste of the kiss she had given him as she'd served the food – hot, sweet and sinful. Even the way she was drinking wine was seductive. He watched her bring her glass to her lips as she sipped the golden liquid. She closed her eyes as if enjoying that first moment of the grape on her tongue, moistening her lips after she savoured the flavour of the liquid. God, she was driving him mad.

Later, when they moved through to the living room, Will reflected that everything about the evening had been perfect and that, for the first time, a surprise had turned out to be a good one. He smiled contentedly and sipped his coffee.

"A penny for your thoughts," Alison said, smiling as well.

"I reckon they're worth more than a penny, seeing as I'm thinking of making love to you."

"Well, when are you going to stop thinking and start acting?" she teased.

He stood up and crooked his finger.

"What? Now? This minute?" she whispered.

"Yes, lass, I can't wait another moment longer."

She moved into his arms but was taken by surprise when his hands moved to the zip on her dress.

"What, here and now?"

He nodded.

"This second, right here."

He slowly lowered the zip and pushed the dress from her shoulders, kissing the honey toned skin he revealed. His eyes darkened with desire at the silk and lace he exposed. He pressed a kiss to the hollow at the throat and feathered kisses with his lips and tongue along her collarbone. His hands softly and gently began to caress her breasts through the silk and lace of her bra. A sigh left her lips, followed by a murmur of pleasure as he returned his mouth to hers and kissed her time and time again.

"How does this undo?" he asked, as he fingered the lace of the bra.

"A clasp at the front," she whispered.

"– May I?" he asked shyly.

"God, yes," she whispered.

His hands moved hesitantly to the fastening and they fumbled slightly as he undid it. They slid up her rib cage and he gently cupped her breasts as his thumbs slowly brushed over her nipples before he slid the bra from her shoulders. He slowly moved them down her body in feather like touches and found the edge of her panties. Hooking a finger under the hem, he slowly inched them down.

Once she was naked, he lowered them to the rug in front of the log burner. "You are so beautiful," he said as he stroked her face.

"So are you, but you have too many clothes on."

"Well, that's easily remedied." He grinned cheekily as he undressed.

She lay back on the rug, drinking in the sight of him.

"What do you want, Will?" she whispered as he returned to her side.

"You, I want you."

She brought her lips back to his.

"You have me. Always."

Chapter Seventeen

Rob had never considered himself a violent man. Congenial, affable, agreeable and good natured were all adjectives commonly used to describe him. But Ali's disappearance had made him furious. He wasn't used to feeling like a fool. And Ali was playing him for the biggest of fools. Did she really think she could just run away from him? That he would just let her go?

Being alone was fuelling his anger. It was strange; he'd never really been alone in the house for any length of time before. When Ali went away on a teaching course he'd invited his mistress around. Lately that had been Claire, but there had been others. He wasn't used to the solitude and he had no idea what to do with all this spare time he had, except brood over the two women who had gone. Claire had left as well. Usually that didn't bother him. Normally they made plans for when they were going to meet again and he just went back to his life with Ali. But now there was no Ali. Bitch. She continued to ignore his calls and so far the police had no idea where she was. He never wondered where Claire went or what she did when they weren't together. But now, because he was alone, he did. It occurred to him that he knew little of her life.

He sighed. This time alone was giving him too much time to think – to plan his revenge. He would not be ignored. He was spending the silent hours planning what he would do to her, when he found her. Bring her back here to their home, that was for certain. She'd have to be taught a lesson; discipline, that was the answer.

He got up and poured himself a generous measure of Scotch. He'd been spending time thinking how he would teach her a lesson. If she'd have just come straight back home, he'd have bought flowers, maybe taken her away for a romantic break – rekindled things so to speak. But now things were different. Ignore him! How dare she?

Before he recapped the scotch, he took a decent sized swig straight from the bottle, enjoying the heat and fiery kick as the amber spirit burnt a trail down his throat. Yes, he thought as he sat down, Ali would have to be reminded about who was the boss. He'd fuck her; that would remind her that he was the boss. They'd always been good together. It wouldn't be enough though. She would have to learn her place. Maybe he would tie her up? That would show her he was her master. Spanking her on her buttocks and legs appealed to him. Yes, hitting her so hard that she would whimper in pain. And then he'd screw her. He felt himself grow hard at the thought. He reached down and freed himself from his trousers. The anger that coursed through his veins was a big turn on and, as his imagination ran riot, he masturbated. Yes, he thought with satisfaction, she would learn who the boss was.

The phone call came later. It was the police inspector. They had a lead on Ali's whereabouts. Her credit cards had been used in Halifax and so they were checking with West Yorkshire police if there had been any reports on where she was staying.

The frustration he felt at her absence eased slightly. They were closer to finding her now. She couldn't hide for ever. All he had to do was be patient.

****

"Are you sure you want to do this, lass?"

They were driving over the moors, towards Erringdon.

"What, visit with your neighbours? They're just pensioners, aren't they?

"Aye, they are."

"Well, if I'm going to be a part of your life I have to meet your neighbours ... your friends."

He turned to look at her, a stunned expression on his face.

"What's that look for?" she said.

"It's nowt, lass. I just have to pinch meself when you say things like that. I keep thinking this is a dream."

"No, it's no dream. I'm here and I want to meet your friends and neighbours."

"Aye, that'll take all of five minutes... I've not got many friends. Remember. Willy no mates, that's me. Me neighbours, well, they can be kind of nosy."

"They're pensioners, Will, I'd expect them to be nosy."

"Especially Doris; she can prise out any secret. I swear she learnt her interrogation techniques during the war. I wouldn't be surprised if she were an agent for Churchill's secret army." He smiled as he spoke.

"You forget I'm a teacher. I stand up in front of thirty teenagers every day. One little old lady doesn't scare me."

They were approaching the hamlet now. It was, Alison could see, very isolated, just a small collection of cottages, grouped in a semicircle.

They worked their way around the semi-circle of houses. Will was obviously very popular with these people, who seemed genuinely delighted to see him. He chatted with each of them while he replenished wood for fires and delivered bags full of groceries – in two houses he put them away as well. In all of them he collected lists for the next week's shopping. Alison's presence was met with surprise, but it wasn't like the morbid curiosity shown down in the village. They had clucked and fussed over her when she told them about her accident but weren't intrusive.

Doris' house was last. Will explained she'd been a good friend of his gran's and would expect them to stay for lunch. At the other houses he'd knocked and waited to be let in, but here he tapped the door and pushed it open, calling out as they went in.

"Mrs B, it's only me."

They went into a small, cluttered living room.

"It's about time you showed up, young man. I saw you spend forty minutes with Netty Wilson, making me wait until last."

Will winked at Alison.

"Hush your scolding me. I brought you a visitor. Alison, this is Mrs Doris Bradshaw."

"I'm pleased to meet you, Mrs Bradshaw. Will speaks very fondly of you." Alison held out her hand to the old lady.

"That I doubt." She peered at Alison through thick lensed glasses, like a wise owl weighing something up. "You've nice manners, I'll say that much for you." She took Alison's hand in a quick handshake.

Will smiled. Doris was the epitome of a blunt Yorkshire woman.

"What are you grinning like an idiot for, Will Barnes? Haven't you groceries to put away?"

He smiled again.

"Aye, Mrs B, I have... And Mrs B, go easy on her, ok?"

He winked at Alison again before he went into the kitchen.

"Well, take your coat off and sit down, lass. We don't stand on ceremony here tha knows."

Alison slid her coat off and sat down in the chair on the other side of the fireplace.

"You're a tall, lanky thing, but Will's a big lad so that's alright. You could do with some meat on your bones. But you youngsters always do."

"I've not been called a youngster in a long while."

They'd exchanged the usual pleasantries about home and families when Doris raised the subject that had brought her to the farm.

"Will said you crashed your car in the storm?"

Alison frowned at the memory.

"Yes, I was lucky Winston found me."

"What were you doing up in Yorkshire? It's a long way from Bath," Doris asked.

"I was just driving. Like I said, I was lucky that Will was around to help me. He's been so kind."

Doris looked at her thoughtfully.

"Aye, he is. Sometimes he's been too kind for his own good. Folk sometimes abuse such kindness – take it for granted. Are you going to do that?"

"Will knows how grateful I am. I'd never take that for granted."

"It's not your gratitude he wants, though - the lad's in love with you. Are you in a position to return that love?"

"Will said you were forthright."

"Oh, I am. Especially about people who mean a lot to me. What were you running away from?"

"Sorry?"

"When you crashed, what were you running away from? You said that you were just driving, but that doesn't make sense. You were on a remote part of t'moors in a dreadful storm; you must have been running from something...or somebody. Was it your husband?" At the look of shock on Alison's face Doris continued. "Will told me you were separated."

"Did he?" Alison glanced at the kitchen door.

"Aye, but that's all he said, lass. I'm not just being nosy. Will means the world to me. I'm his godmother and I've seen him badly burned by a woman before."

"Moira." Alison nodded. "I know about what happened - Will told me. I'd never hurt him, Mrs Bradshaw."

"No? Maybe not intentionally but you do have the power to hurt him." The older woman looked at her closely. "What about your husband? Would he hurt him?"

"Rob. Let's leave him out of this."

"But you can't, can you? Were you running away from him?" The question was asked gently and that was her undoing.

"I caught him cheating on me. I had to get away. I wasn't thinking straight."

"Are you thinking straight now? About Will, I mean? I knew you were different when he spoke about you. Likely he fell in love at first sight. Like I said, he has a huge capacity to love and he's been hurt before. If you hurt him like Moira did, I'm not sure he'd survive."

"I wouldn't. I couldn't."

"You could. Have you slept with him?"

"That's none... No comment."

"I'll take that to mean yes. Young people today are always in a hurry."

"I can't believe I'm discussing this with you. Will was right, you are one hell of an interrogator. You said Will is in love with me. Well, I've news for you. I'm in love with him as well."

"Are you? Are you sure you're not reacting to the emotion of the last few days?" Doris asked.

"I don't think so. All I know is that I feel more for him than I have for any other human. Is it wrong of me to give us a chance? See where things lead?"

"No, Alison. Is it alright for me to call you Alison?"

She nodded.

"It's not wrong. You seem like a lovely lass. If I'm concerned, it's just because I want my lad to be happy. He should never have married Moira. You know, he didn't tell me his plans until the wedding were over. I think he knew I'd try and stop him. She weren't no good for him. A more selfish creature you'd never find. Except for that Myles – they were made for each other."

The old lady's tone had become angry.

"Will explained about them. I know his history, Mrs Bradshaw. I'll tread carefully."

"Will you, lass? He may seem gruff and reclusive but that's nowt but an act, protection against the pain he's suffered. He deserves love... the forever kind of love."

"Mrs Bradshaw, I don't know if it will be forever. I thought my marriage was forever and look what has happened there. It's early days yet. What I will say is, there is nowhere I would rather be than here with Will. There is a lot for me to do, not least sort out my marriage, before I can talk forever. For now we are taking things slowly. Keeping it simple, if you like, and seeing where it leads."

Doris Bradshaw nodded satisfied.

"A simple kind of love," she said smiling.

"Yes, that sounds right, simple and uncomplicated. I've had enough complications."

"You'll do, lass, you'll do. I reckon you best call me Doris, it's what my friends call me,"

Lunch was a lively affair, with Doris, as old people are wont to do, embarrassing Will with tales from his childhood. They left a couple of hours later, promising to return on Wednesday.

"She thinks the world of you, Will. I thought she was just a neighbour, but she's family, isn't she?"

"I guess so. Gran and she grew up together. They were bridesmaids for each other, godmother to each other's children. Both suffered the tragedy of losing those children far too young. When gran died, I promised I'd look out for her. She liked you, lass, and that's no mean feat. She doesn't make friends easily."

"Is that why she didn't come to your wedding to Moira, because she didn't get on with her?"

"She told you that, did she? She'd have told me not to wed her, so I didn't tell her. I can't regret my marriage. If nowt else, it gave me Sarah."

He lapsed into silence and Alison sensed he didn't wish to talk about his marriage anymore. They were on the top part of the moors now. The snow in the fields was still feet deep. A small house up ahead caught her attention. It could be a lovely home but was just falling into disrepair. She was about to ask about it when Will slowed the Landrover and climbed out.

"Stay there. A sheep is stuck – I'll just go and free it." She watched as he vaulted the wall by the road.

They'd stopped opposite the house and, unable to resist, she got out of the car and went to have a closer look. It always made her sad to see houses like this with boarded up windows and slates missing from the roof. It was small, little more than a two up, two down cottage, surrounded by the same kind of stone wall that bordered the fields here about. Who had once lived here, she wondered? A gate hung limply on its side and she stepped past it, into what should have been a pretty garden.

"Alison, don't go in there." Will's voice stopped her.

"I won't go in the cottage. I'm just looking at the outside."

"I'd rather you didn't."

"Why? It's just an old cottage?" She said, walking further into the garden.

Will cursed as she walked around the corner. Wild horses wouldn't drag him into that garden.

He heard her call his name once, but he ignored it.

It seemed an eternity before she reappeared but, in reality, it was only a few minutes.

"This could be a beautiful little home. Who does it belong to?" she said, coming out of the garden.

"I've no idea."

Will climbed back into the Landrover and pulled off, almost as soon as she was settled, eager to be away from the place.

"I'm surprised you don't know who owns it. I wonder how long it's been empty and who lived there before it became deserted?" Alison said, looking back at it as they drove away.

"It's just a dreary, old cottage."

"But it could be a lovely home. All it would take is a little imagination. You should think of finding out who owns it and adding it to your holiday cottages maybe," she carried on.

"I don't think so. Can we just forget the place, please?"

"Why? It could be perfect?"

"If you had my memories of that place you'd want to forget it too. I don't want you tainted by it. So please drop the subject."

"Sorry," Alison whispered quietly.

They drove on in silence, Alison too stunned to speak and Will trying to get his emotions under control. They pulled up in front of the farm house. Will got out and headed into the barn, leaving Alison sat in the Landrover. She stayed seated, not knowing what else to do – the farmhouse was locked up and Will had the keys. She sighed. This was the problem with a new relationships; the potential for misunderstandings was enormous when you didn't know very much about each other. Her mind replayed events but she couldn't see what she'd done wrong.

A small tap at the window brought her out of her contemplations. She undid the door.

"Come on, lass, let's get you in where it's warm. I owe you an explanation." She took his hand and let him lead her to the farmhouse. He didn't speak immediately, preferring to make some tea instead, using the time, Alison suspected, to work out what he was going to say. He was worried, she realised, the three small crinkles that had appeared on his brow a sure sign he was upset. He was avoiding eye contact. Something else she'd learnt he did when he was upset. From the occasional glimpse she had of them, they had gone from a bright periwinkle blue to a dark, stormy grey.

He put the tea in front of her. He didn't sit, preferring to stand and pace about.

"The cottage on t'moor, I own it. It's an old shepherd's cottage."

Alison waited, knowing there was more.

"If I could I'd wipe it from the face of the earth I would, but demolition costs are too high."

She looked puzzled.

"'Tis their cottage, Myles and Moira's, I mean. They used to meet there. We found it when we were kids. It was abandoned even then. I suppose it's where Sarah was conceived. I walked in on them once. I didn't understand the heat or their passion, it just seemed dirty. After Moira came back I suppose they just fell back into using it..."

He paused, thinking how to continue.

"It's where I found them. They were lying together - entwined, you could say. I'll never forget how still they were. How cold and still. Both of them looked so young and beautiful. Is it odd to think of them as beautiful? Even Myles? They were more like a sculpture than people. I've heard it said that people who've died look like they are asleep but they didn't. They looked frozen – almost suspended in time. I've not set foot inside it since they died. I couldn't even go back in when the police arrived."

Her cheeks were wet with tears. It was impossible not to be moved by what he was saying.

"I'm sorry, lass, for speaking as I did. I know it's been five years but I can't face it. I know I have to but..."

"No buts. You only have to face it when you are ready to."

"You don't think it's daft?" He sat down at her side.

"No, of course not. I've my own demons to face and I don't know how I'm going to. And they're not half as tragic as yours," she told him.

"Together. How about we face our demons together?"

"That sounds like a plan, Mr Barnes."

****

The police rang just after lunch the next day. They'd found her. She'd been in a car accident and had been stranded at a farm just outside Hebden Bridge.

Chapter Eighteen

It was late when he arrived in Yorkshire. Temperatures had fallen again, making the deserted roads slick with ice. His convertible BMW was just not cut out for the weather conditions. He'd asked at a local garage for directions to Highcroft Farm.

"It's way up on t'moor. Only a fool would go up there tonight, especially in that car. You'd total it before you reached Heptonstall. Come back in the morning and I'll draw you a map."

Reluctantly, Rob found himself agreeing. It was annoying, but, if anything happened to the car, he'd be seriously pissed off. He booked into a hotel in the centre of Hebden Bridge. He could wait one more day. He'd missed the evening meal so, after a quick shower, he headed into town.

Rob supposed there were people who loved places like The Fleece – he just wasn't one of them. He liked modern, sleek bars, where happy hour lasted all night and the disco blared in the corner. The pub was old and the décor looked older.

The tables that were scattered around the bar were solid chunks of wood, scarred and stained from years of use. Sagging sofas sat alongside traditional stools. The beams were original, solid, huge chunks of aged oak, blackened with four hundred years of smoke and grime.

To the side of the giant inglenook fireplace was a large wicker basket filled with logs, fuel for the blazing fire that had been lit. The flames were reflected in the polished surfaces of the horse brasses that hung around the solid stone chimney. In fact, Rob noticed that there was brass everywhere, hanging from the ceiling, on the walls and in the fire places. Kettles, jugs, chargers and bed warmers, all gleaming and shiny, were hung everywhere. Rob supposed some would call it lived in but to him it was just cluttered.

The bar ran the length of one wall and was again of some sort of solid wood, Rob didn't know what. He was a granite and chrome lover, not a wood and brass one. The bar was as traditional as the real ale it served. Several pumps on the bar advertised local beers, brewed in the centuries old way, so that the hops hung on the tongue. Rob didn't drink real ale either. He ordered a Jack Daniels and turned to look around the pub while the landlord got his drink.

It was busier than he'd expected and Rob commented as

much when the landlord bought his drink over.

"Aye, it's the first night that most folk have been out since the snow and it's a darts night."

Rob handed over the money for his drink.

"You're not from around here – what brings you to Hebden Bridge?" the landlord asked, curious about the stranger.

"My wife crashed her car in the snow. She got stranded at a farm nearby. Perhaps you've heard of it? Highcroft?"

"Will Barnes' place. She'll be glad to see you then."

"Why glad? She seemed very grateful to Mr Barnes." Rob lied. He'd no idea if Ali was grateful or not.

"Will were never much of a social person, didn't talk much, but since his wife died he's become almost a recluse. Highcroft is a grim place as well; old man Barnes let it fall into rack and ruin."

"Old man Barnes?"

"Will's grandfather. Highcroft has been farmed by Will's family for years. When his parents died, the farm went to Will. I don't imagine he'll make much of a go of it. Not got the brains."

Rob smiled to himself. If Ali had been 'roughing it' with a crusty old widower she'd probably be pleased to see him.

"And when were the last time you were up at Highcroft, Steve? Not recently, I'll wager?"

Rob turned to look at the man who had come to the bar. He was in his fifties, with thinning hair.

"Don't listen to him, mate. Will, he'll have looked after your wife alright. My son is on a placement from college to Highcroft. Will's done some alterations to the house and the farm's thriving. Steve's right in one way – Will don't say much but he's a good farmer." The man took a sip from his pint. "Funny though, Will didn't mention a house guest to my Mike when he rang to say roads were passable. I haven't seen Mike today though."

"Dave, how's Will got money to do Highcroft up? The place was pitiful last time I were up there." The landlord leaned on the bar, intent on catching up on the gossip.

"I imagine it's from the money he gets from the holiday cottages on the farm. I mean, they must be right lucrative."

"Holiday cottages?"

"Aye, he converted an old barn into three cottages. Sarah was in charge of them. You know, cleaning and so forth. I suppose, now she's away, he'll have to advertise for somebody to clean when the season starts. How come you don't know about the cottages? The holiday makers must have been in here last summer?"

"If you remember, the missus and I went to Australia for four months last summer, to see her brother. We got tenants in here, didn't we? I suppose he caters for the walkers and ramblers. I can't say I'd want to stay out at Highcroft though, cursed place."

"Cursed?" Rob asked.

"Well, sad more like. It stands to reason that it would be, with the double suicide that happened up there."

"Suicides! My God, that's terrible. Were they local people?"

"Aye, they were. Myles Bishop and Moira, Will's wife. They killed themself up in a ruined farm cottage; lovers' pact. Will found them. Sent him a bit queer, I reckon."

"Queer? How?" Rob asked uneasily.

"Well, he shut himself away; rarely comes into the town anymore."

"He were in town yesterday," another customer chimed in. "The wife saw him. Is your missus a tall, slim blond?"

"Yes, that sounds like Ali." Rob nodded.

"Well, he took her to see young Dr Ben."

Rob thought on his feet.

"Oh yeah, Ali said she'd seen a doctor. So, this Mr Barnes, he doesn't mix in much then?"

"Will? Nope, he's as reclusive as that Howard Hughes bloke. If your girl's like mine, she'll be missing a natter. Will, he don't say much," Steve said, handing a pint to the man who joined in the conversation."

"Gossiping again, Steve, eh?" A younger man approached the bar. "I'm Paul Wellings, local bobby, we spoke on the phone. Your wife is in good hands with Will; he's a good bloke. She was lucky 'twere him that found her. He volunteers with search and rescue so he knew what to do about the hypothermia and the dislocation."

"Yes, well, that's the impression I got from Ali. That she'd been well taken care of."

"All this talk of Will reminds me that my lad, Mike, wants to take Will a bottle of whiskey as a Christmas gift. It's difficult to know what to get him - he's not into things that most young blokes are. Can you sell me a bottle?" the older man asked the publican.

"Young? I thought he was a widower?"

"He is, but he's only your age or younger, in his thirties anyway."

Rob clenched his jaw as anger spread over him. She'd been shacked up with some young, single farmer. Rob didn't like that – no, he didn't like that at all. He forced a smile onto his face and spoke to the policeman.

"So, you've seen Ali. Does she look alright? Only, I know what she's like about playing things down."

"Oh, I haven't seen her. I spoke to her on the phone. I thought she was young Sarah to begin with."

"Sarah?" That was the second time he had heard her mentioned.

"Will's wife Moira's daughter, but then I remembered that she's on a gap year."

"He has a daughter?"

"Well, nobody knows if he was the father. Moira never said, not publicly. She were only fifteen when she fell pregnant. Whoever the father was, he's lucky not to be serving time for rape." The landlord placed a pint on the bar for the local bobby.

"Now, you have no evidence that was Will. So mind your tongue." Paul Wellings hated idle gossip.

"You don't think it odd how he dotes on young Sarah? I mean, he sure acts like her father," the landlord said defensively.

"The lass has been through more than any girl should have to at her age. She'd have been in care if it hadn't been for Will." Paul Wellings glared at the landlord before he headed over to watch the darts match that had begun.

Rob waited until PC Wellings had moved away before he spoke.

"So you think Barnes knocked up this girl when she was a fifteen?"

"Well, it was no secret that he was in love with her – besotted. Of course, she wasn't interested. Moira only had eyes for Myles. When she was fifteen, Moira and her mam disappeared. When she came back with the child, folks speculated who the father was. There was talk that Will had, you know, taken her by force. It would have been just after her dad died. He used to work up at Highcroft. Can you imagine a vulnerable girl saying no to an older man? Not that there was any proof that he'd raped her. It was just odd that Will should marry Moira and take care of Sarah. He must have known that she didn't love him. What possible reason could he have had?"

"Well, if he had raped Moira and the girl – Sarah was it? – the girl was his daughter, that would be a reason. Maybe he felt guilty or Moira blackmailed him. And the girl, Sarah, she's away at the moment?" Rob drained his glass and nodded that he'd like another.

"Aye, Australia I think."

"So, he's out at the farm on his own? Apart from Dave's..." he glanced towards the man who was now watching the darts match, "Dave's son?"

"Oh, I don't think the farm workers stop out there," Mike said.

Anger again built up. She really was alone with him. He sounded like a right sad bastard.

"What's he like, then?"

"Who? Will? Big and broad, 6 ft. 2 inches at least. A bit scruffy. Quiet and brooding, my missus says."

"Who do I say is brooding?" A petite woman appeared at the landlord's side.

"Will Barnes. This bloke's wife has been stranded at Highcroft during snow."

"Oh, he broods all right. He has a scowl that'd cut you dead. He's a good looking lad, mind you, in a dangerous Heathcliff kind of way." She sighed. "I bet he's bloody gorgeous when he smiles."

Rob's hand tightened on the glass he was holding as he thought. So this Will Barnes was young and good looking. He'd better not have looked at his wife. If he had, he'd kill him. He swallowed the Jack Daniels and asked for another.

"You must have been worried about her, lost in all the snow."

"Yes, I was. It's good to know she's been in safe hands."

"I wouldn't mind being in Will Barnes' hands. I'd be putty, but I'll have to make do with Steve here." The landlady laughed.

Rob smiled. If the people at the bar had known him, they'd have realised the smile didn't reach his eyes.

He lingered a while longer, drawing up a picture of Will Barnes in his mind, before he headed back to his hotel room to wait for morning.

****

Alison sighed. She was curled at Will's side, her head resting comfortably on his chest. His arm was draped around her and his hand was idly stroking her arm. He was just as relaxed as she was. How far he'd come in a week. She recalled that second night when he'd hesitantly asked if he should sit with her. He'd been so shy and awkward. He was still shy, but the awkwardness was fading. She was reluctant to destroy the atmosphere, but she had to. There was no hiding from it.

"Will?"

"Yes, lass."

"It's time, isn't it?"

"Time? Time for what?" he replied puzzled.

"It's time for me to face up to my future. I spoke to a solicitor today."

"Did you? What did he say?"

"Oh, he didn't say a lot, really. I told him what I wanted to discuss and I made an appointment to see him."

Will sighed.

"When are you going?"

"Monday. I'll come back on Friday. I mean, if that's ok? I don't want to go but I have to start sorting things out at home."

He sighed. He knew it was coming but that didn't make it hurt less.

"I know you do, lass. How are you going to handle it? I mean Rob."

"I'll go to my parents first. Explain what has happened."

"Are you going to tell them about us?"

"Do you want me to?"

"It's up to you, lass. I'll understand if you don't want to." He didn't want to pressurize her.

"Then I'm going to tell them. They need to know how important you are to me."

"Won't they say it's too soon?"

"Probably, but I'll just remind them that I'm a grown up. I hope they'll come with me to Bath. I'm sure they will. There's so much to do. I suppose tomorrow I'll have to make a list. Did I tell you that I'm big on lists?"

"No, you didn't. But I can see you would be. You're so tidy and methodical."

She gave him a dig in the ribs.

"Do you mind? That makes me sound like the biggest bore around."

"Sorry, lass, but you are. I just bet all the books on your bookshelves will be arranged by genre and author."

She laughed, acknowledging he was right.

"And your hair and clothes are so tidy, they make me want to ruffle you up a bit."

"Later. Stop distracting me. I'll go and see the solicitor on Tuesday, get the ball rolling, so to speak. Then I will need to look for somewhere to stay. I can't carry on living in that house. I'll have to go into school as well, let them know when I'll be back at work. I should be able to return here on Friday."

The reality of the situation hit him then. This was going to have to be a long distance relationship, at least for the time being; especially during the school term when she'd have to work. He didn't like it but he would have to accept it.

"I'll have the kettle on waiting for you, lass." He gave her a soft squeeze of reassurance. "And I'll arrange it so I can spend one day a week in Bath with you."

She tilted her head to look at him.

"You'd do that for me?"

"Of course I would. If we're going to make this work, we both have to make the effort. And I really want us to work."

She smiled at him.

"It won't be forever Will. Once I get things sorted out, I'll look for a job up here."

"You'll do that for me?" He repeated her words incredulously.

"I've nothing to keep me in Bath. But it'll take a while to sort things out."

"I can wait for as long as it takes."

"Well, with that settled, you can ruffle me up a little if you like."

She took his hand to lead him upstairs but, instead, he knelt down in front of her and reached for the pins that were holding her hair in place, watching intently as it tumbled loosely to her shoulders. When he'd finished, his hands pushed through the silken strands before he pulled her towards him and lowered his mouth to hers. Gently and a little hesitantly he began to kiss her, slowly tasting her soft lips, five, six or more times, just teasing little nibbles to her lower lip until, on a moan of part pleasure and part frustration, her lips parted, inviting him to take more. He kissed her then with more urgency, his tongue stroking and exploring. Her arms slid around his waist, moving under his shirt, stroking the plains and contours of his back. His hands were at the base of her neck, playing with the strands of hair that had fallen loose. Tilting her head back, he changed the angle of his kiss, his teeth grazing over her lips causing heat to spread through her. Her tongue slid over his as she returned his kisses with equal passion. It was incredible to believe that a few short days ago he'd claimed he was rubbish at kissing.

He pulled back and smiled before he lowered her to the floor in front of the fire.

"I'm growing partial to this rug," he whispered.

"So am I, farm boy, so am I."

They undressed each other, slowly kissing the skin they exposed as each article of clothing was discarded. In the glow of the fire, Alison's skin took on a golden sheen. Will pulled the cushions from the sofa and laid her down against them. With one single finger he traced a line from her ear down her jaw. She trembled slightly as his lips followed the same path. His hand stroked the soft skin of her neck before moving down to cup her breast, his touch causing soft sighs of pleasure to be torn from her lips. His hands moved lower, stroking her flat abdomen and curved hip and finally the soft skin of her thighs. Alison lifted her hips towards him.

"Will, please, I want you."

"Shush, you can have me – later. I want to give you this. I want you to remember this – to remember me, and to come back to me. Promise me," he whispered.

"I promise."

His mouth and lips moved lower, following where his hands had led, and brought her to a shimmering release. He held her close while her breathing returned to normal.

"And now, lass, we go together."

Later, curled in bed, Alison couldn't help but think how great things were. She had her plan now. In her mind she had worked out how she and Will could make their blossoming relationship work. She couldn't wait to offload the baggage of her marriage. Everything was perfect and nothing was going to spoil what she and Will had. Nothing.

****

He turned restlessly in the darkness. Three a.m. Time was moving slowly and, unusually for him, Rob couldn't sleep. Anticipation, he supposed. Every nerve ending seemed to tingle and his thoughts were racing. He shouldn't worry, morning would come soon enough. He would soon have his wife back and if Will Barnes had so much as looked at her he was going to be very, very sorry.

Chapter Nineteen

He'd never tire of looking at her. Out here, in the fresh morning air, her cheeks were pink and, below the edge of the dark red knitted cap, her eyes sparkled. She'd kept him in bed until six o'clock, not that he'd put up much of a fight, which had left him behind with the chores. She'd insisted on helping him out.

"After all, if I'm going to live up here I want to know what I am letting myself in for," she'd told him as she'd pulled Sarah's Wellington boots on.

He still couldn't believe that she intended to move to Yorkshire, once everything was settled back in Bath. His smile widened at the thought of being together with her.

She was leaning over one of the pig pens.

"What do they normally eat?" she called back to him.

"Your fingers, if you reach over with no food in your hand."

He laughed as her hand shot back.

"When the snow's cleared they'll forage for food, but for now I'll supplement their diet with dry pellets, though I think they'd prefer your hand."

"So, pig rule number one: don't put your hand in the pig pen unless you have food in it."

"The most amazing thing about the pig is that the only part you can't eat is its squeal." A mischievous smile lit up his face. "All its meat can be consumed –feet, offal, even its ears. I remember, when I was a lad, me gran used to boil the head and mash it down..."

A snowball hitting him in the middle of his chest made him smile even more.

"That is disgusting." She looked back at the pig and shuddered.

"No, it's right nourishing. It's called brawn and you..."

A second snow ball hit him in the face.

He shook his head.

"You do realise that is war?" He scooped up some snow.

"Now, Will, remember I'm injured."

"You should have thought of that before." The snow ball arced through the sky and, although she tried to dodge, it caught her on the shoulder.

The battle that followed was accompanied by laughter and barking as the dogs joined in with the fun and games.

It was fifteen minutes later that she called a halt to the fight.

"Enough, I quit and you win," she said breathlessly.

"Do I get a prize?"

"Like what?"

"This." He bent and kissed her softly. "Your nose is cold."

"As is yours," she replied.

They linked arms and headed towards the stable.

"Are you going to introduce me properly to the horses?"

"Sarah's pets," he said, pulling open the door. It was one of those moments when he wished he had a camera to hand to capture the moment. Her smile was dazzling.

"Shire horses. Wow, I know I saw them briefly the other day but I was preoccupied; I obviously didn't register that they were Shire horses. My God, they're huge, I never realised how big they are."

"Aye, Aragorn is 17.3 hands and his lady, Arwen, is 16.2. Gentle giants though; they wouldn't hurt a fly and they'd work their heart out for you."

Just like you, Will Barnes, Alison thought.

"Sarah rescued them. They're at risk of becoming extinct."

"Extinct?"

"Aye, a lot of our traditional breeds are dying out. It's down to intensive farming methods and EU regulations. They mean less diversity."

"You don't imagine animals becoming extinct in Britain."

"No, especially not farm animals. Sarah had no idea what she was starting when she begged me to buy these two. I've invested in a lot of rare breeds. I'm trying to preserve my heritage."

The larger of the two horses neighed impatiently.

Will smiled and moved forward and reached up to stroke the horse's nose. "Morning, lad. Did you think I'd forgotten you?" The horse neighed in reply. "Ah, well, I know I'm late. But don't you think I have a good reason?" He glanced at Alison and the horse seemed to follow the direction of his gaze.

"Come and make friends, Alison. If you give this old softy an apple or a carrot you'll be friends for life."

Alison moved forward, fascinated by this view of Will – so calm and gentle, his voice so soft and quiet, different to any tone he had used before. He handed her the carrot and placed it on her palm.

"Offer it to him, but keep your palm flat." She did as he said and the horse gently took it.

"My God. But you are a beauty, aren't you?" she said stroking his nose and neck. "You say these are Sarah's pets?"

"Aye, we rescued them. Shire horses, like I said, are an endangered breed. They were going to be put down when they were foals. Sarah heard about it. She shows them and they work for a local carriage company. Come and meet his lady."

The other horse was smaller but not by much. Will again spoke quietly as he gently ran his hands over her flanks.

"All well, is it, girl?" The horse looked at him with soft, velvet brown eyes and whinnied softly. "She's telling me not to worry so. You're in foal, aren't you, Lady Arwen? And me and your man like to make sure you're ok."

Alison offered a carrot to the mare.

"Men. They just don't realise, do they, Lady Arwen, that pregnancy is just normal for us girls. When is she due to deliver?"

"In early May, by my calculations. I've not taken part in a foaling so I'm anxious. It's like being an expectant father."

An image flashed into her mind of a blue eyed little boy playing with this giant of a man. He'd make a wonderful father.

"They've not been out since the snow so I'll just take them out into the paddock and then muck out the stalls." He slipped a head collar over the mare's head and handed it to Alison.

"Don't worry, she'll just follow me and Aragorn."

They stood watching the horses run free for a moment before returning to the barn.

They worked together for an hour, although Will wouldn't let Alison do too much. It was simply lovely being together. Alison had just thrown a hand full of straw at Will for jokingly ordering her back to the kitchen to make a cuppa when a familiar and unwanted voice spoke from the stable doorway.

"Well, there's a sight I never thought I'd see: you, Ali, in a stable." He glanced at Will who had turned at the voice. "Stephen Robinson. Everybody calls me Rob. I'm Ali's husband."

"What are you doing here, Rob?" Alison asked coldly.

"I've come to take you home."

"I have no home with you. Go away."

"Ali, we need to talk, but not here in front of him."

"I have nothing to say to you but, even if I did, Will could hear every word. He knows what you did and what you are. Just go away."

Rob felt his anger rising.

"Does he now? And just how close are you and Will? Did you let him inside your knickers, Ali?... Like some whore?"

"Get out of here. The only whore is the woman you had in my bed."

"I'm not leaving without you," Rob said as he stepped towards Ali.

"I'm not coming with you. I've spoken to a solicitor."

"There will be no solicitor. You're my wife. Did you think you could ignore me, Ali? Ignore all my calls. You're coming home, back to your rightful place at my side."

"Why don't you just turn around and go back where you came from?" Although Will's voice was quiet the tone was firm and authoritarian.

"Not without Ali."

"I think you should..."

"Well, what you think is irrelevant. She's my wife."

"I stopped being your wife when you took another woman into our bed. Now go away."

Will moved to her side and put a protective arm around her waist.

"Alison wants you to leave."

Rob looked at him carefully.

"You've been helping yourself to my wife, haven't you? She may have let you shag her as a thank you, but she's my wife and I will have what is mine."

The three dogs began to growl, sensing something was wrong.

""You three, quiet!" Will commanded. The growling stopped, but the dogs' teeth remained bared. "I'm telling you to leave. This is private property." Will stood still, not moving from Alison's side.

"Ali, do you know what he is? He's a rapist and a paedophile. Ask him about his wife, about her having a kid when she was fifteen years old. What kind of sick freak shags a fifteen year old? I'll tell you, one who wants what his best mate had. He couldn't have this Moira so he raped her. It's why they committed suicide. Ask about his daughter and how he barely leaves the farm. Gossip is, he sleeps with her as well. He's a sick bastard. So you're coming with me."

Alison felt Will tense at her side; pain was raw and evident in his eyes.

"No, you're a liar and a bastard. Now leave."

"It's true. The whole town knows it. It's why he rarely goes there."

Alison looked at Will, silently telling him she didn't believe a word Rob was saying.

"That's bullshit. Just go away, Rob."

Rob took a pace forward.

"Not without you."

The step forward did not go unnoticed.

"Alison is going nowhere. I'm asking you one last time. Leave my property." Will took a pace forward, just to let Rob know he'd seen his movement.

Rage swept over Rob as he realised Ali was not going to come with him. She was going to stay with some dirty, unkempt farmer.

"Come with me, Ali, or I'll kill you."

Will moved forward, presenting himself as a target, shielding Alison with his large frame.

"Nobody is killing anybody," Will said quietly.

"Oh, I am. First I'll kill you, you bastard, and then her. Did you think I'd stand by and let another man touch you? You whore."

Alison was trembling now. Who was this man? This animal?

Where was the calm, sophisticated Rob she knew?"

A spade stood propped against the stable wall and Rob grabbed it, swinging it wildly. There was no thought to his actions – no plan. For a big man, Will could move nimbly and he found it easy to avoid the swinging spade. He was much quicker than his attacker and he stepped forward and grabbed the spade; being bigger and more powerful than Rob, in seconds he had wrenched it from his hands. He threw it away into one of the stalls. Pinning Rob's arms behind his back he marched him to the door of the stable.

"I don't want to hurt you. I don't want the bother. I just want you to leave." Will spoke firmly, as he pushed Rob towards his car.

Anger, much wilder and stronger than he had ever known, consumed Rob, and a red mist of hate descended.

"Do you think I'll just walk away, Ali?"

He ran at Will, knocking him backwards into the barn. Using his forearms, Will parried the blows, not wanting to fight. But Rob would not be halted and the blows kept coming. Once more he overpowered him, restraining him by pinning him against the steps leading to the hayloft, telling him again that he had to leave. Rob forced his elbow backwards into Will's ribs, causing him to gasp and stagger backwards. Sensing that Will was winded, Rob ran forward like a ram and knocked him to the floor before pummelling punches to his head and arms.

"Stop it, just stop it!" Alison screamed as the men rolled over.

Realising the only way to stop it was to really hit Rob back, Will began to return the punches.

Rob used his feet and kicked Will away before staggering to his feet. He went to grab Alison's arm but Will was quicker.

"Alison, get out of here. Go up to the house. Lock the door and call the police," Will shouted, as he pulled Rob away.

The dogs began to bark wildly but somehow Alison knew they wouldn't attack unless Will told them to.

"Alison, get out of here," Will shouted again.

But she was rigid with shock, paralysed with fear and unable to move. All she could do was watch, horrified. Vaguely she heard a car pull up in the farmyard and the two farmhands jumped out as Will and

Rob crashed out of the stable, fists flying.

The sound of bone on skin, and grunts from the men as blows were landed, shattered the younger men's laughter.

Will's punches were hard and Rob's face was bloodied from a cut above his eye. Left, right, his fists flew in quick jabs and full bodied punches that caused Rob to stagger and fall. Thinking quickly, he tangled his legs with Will's and pulled him to the ground as well. Over and over they rolled, covered in mud and snow. Knowing he had to end this, Rob's hand closed around a broken brick.

Seeing what he was about to do, the two young farmhands shouted out a warning.

"Will, watch out!"

A split second later the brick connected with Will's skull; pain erupted and blood splatters flew from the wound. He vaguely saw Rob's hand rise again and then pain exploded once more as the brick hit again. Stars appeared in front of his eyes and he fell forwards, Alison's screams ringing in his ears.

The two young farmhands dragged Rob off and locked him in a spare stable before running back to Will.

"Will? Will, can you hear me?" Alison crouched at his side. Blood was pouring from the head wound, running down his cheek and forming a scarlet pool in the snow beneath his head. She felt a cloth being pushed into her hand; she accepted it gratefully and pressed it against his scalp, trying to stem the bleeding. Looking up, she realised it was the young lad, Stu, who'd handed her the cloth. He was shocked, that much was obvious from his pallor and the way he was struggling to hold back his tears.

"Thank you for the cloth, Stu. We need to call an ambulance now. Can you do that?" she said, blinking her own tears away.

"Mike's already doing that."

"Good, that's good. We need to get him out of the cold." She looked about to see where Mike was. She could see him by the gate, his mobile in his hand.

"It won't be long, Will; help's on the way," she said looking down at him.

Will's lips moved slowly in a whisper, as if he was trying to explain something. He could only manage to get two words out before he slipped into unconsciousness.

"Tell Sarah...."

She wanted to scream, cry or shout, but none of that would help Will. With hands that were shaking, she fumbled at his wrist to find a pulse. Was it there? It was difficult to tell. She unzipped his coat and rested her hand against his chest. Relief flooded over her as she felt it rise and fall – he was breathing.

Realising they had to get him inside, she yelled to Mike for help.

They lay him on the kitchen table in the recovery position. "What did the emergency services say, Mike?"

"They're sending the air ambulance. I told 'em it would be alright to land in the paddock."

"They can't. The horses... The horses are out there."

"Me and Stu, we'll get them in. Will you be ok on your own for a few minutes?"

"Yes, go on, I'll be fine."

The house was so quiet; even the dogs had stopped barking. Drake and Bess stood either side of the door, as if on guard duty, and Winston lay by the table. He'd tried to climb up on it to get next to Will but she'd pulled him down. The only sound was the clock, ticking solemnly, marking the passing of time. What was taking so long, she wondered? Surely she should be able to hear the helicopter by now? Every minute was vital. She looked at Will. He hadn't moved, not an inch. Hopeless and helpless that was what she felt. She took his hand – there was nothing else she could do.

Chapter Twenty

Blood. Belatedly she realised, she was covered in Will's blood. It stained her hands and clothes. She could smell it – a strange, sweetly, sickly, metallic smell. Iron, she supposed. It was odd, she hadn't really registered it before. God, she was a mess. She ran her hand through her hair. No doubt there was blood in there as well.

Why did it have to be so God damn quiet? What was this place? Some kind of relatives' room, she supposed. She'd preferred the hustle and bustle of the Accident and Emergency department. At least there had been distractions from other patients there. Not that her mind was focused on anything other than Will. It had been since she'd seen the brick come down on his skull.

She'd heard it said that some accidents seemed to happen in slow motion. She'd never really understood what people meant when they'd said that but, she did now. The fight, until that point, had been fast and furious but, from the moment Rob picked up the brick, everything had slowed down. Not just Rob's actions, but her reactions as well. It was as if her brain had struggled to compute what was happening and was playing the scene in slow motion so that it could work it out. Her legs initially felt as though they were shackled to the floor. No matter how hard she'd tried, she'd been unable to move. When she could finally move, it was as if she were walking into a strong current that was intent on pushing her back. Somewhere in the distance she'd heard Mike's shout of warning. But even that had sounded wrong – slow, distorted, like it was being played on the wrong speed.

  Mike and Stu, God bless them, had been marvellous. The way they had tackled Rob, with no thought for their own safety. And then, having the presence of mind to lock him in the tack room of the stable had been magnificent. They'd remained so calm and then called the emergency services. Was Rob still in the tack room, she suddenly wondered? What did she care if he was? The only person who mattered was Will. Why didn't somebody come? A glance at her watch told her it had been more than two hours since they'd brought her in here. Two hours of staring at the magnolia coloured walls. They'd given her a cup of tea but it had long since gone cold. She couldn't have swallowed a single mouthful without being sick. Intermittently, she'd got up and walked about but it hadn't helped. If anything, it had only made her anxiety greater.

She'd never felt so alone; she had done since the moment the air ambulance had lifted off. It hadn't occurred to her that she would not be able to go with Will to hospital, but the helicopter medic had explained that there wasn't room for her in it. She'd stayed rooted to the spot until the helicopter had long since disappeared. It was Mike who'd led her back to the house – dear, sweet, perceptive Mike who'd realised that she'd needed to follow the air ambulance. He'd told the police as much and they'd brought her, here, to the hospital. Sergeant Wellings had said he'd be along to take a statement but he hadn't arrived yet.

She asked herself why they didn't come. "You already said that," a voice in her head chided. She knew why. Of course, their priority was Will. Will - he'd been so still. Like a statue. The injury had to be serious. Nobody could be that still unless they were badly hurt. She'd listened as the paramedic had spoken over the radio. She presumed it was to somebody at the hospital – updating them on Will's injury. Something about a Glasgow coma score. She'd no idea what it meant but the look on the paramedic's face said it was serious.

He'd had the look - that grave, controlled look of concern and compassion that medical professionals seem to acquire. He'd spent a few minutes, explaining what was going to happen to Will, where they were taking him, so on and so forth. She'd tried to tell him it didn't matter, all that mattered was Will, but he said he had to explain, give her some details.

It was approaching lunch time. Occasionally the smell of hospital food wafted in and she could hear people outside the door. She must be quite near the hospital canteen. Don't think of food, she ordered herself as a wave of nausea washed over her.

She leant back in the chair and closed her eyes, willing the nausea to pass. Acid was churning in her stomach, causing hot burning pain. Good, she told herself. It was no more than she deserved for involving Will in all this. It was all her fault that Will lay in a coma. She shouldn't have ignored the messages from Rob. She'd initially felt threatened by them but then dismissed them. Rob, after all, had no history of violence, so she'd never suspected he would do this. But she should have realised that her life with Rob wasn't what she'd thought. Rob wasn't who she'd thought. She should have realised, and at least shown Will the text messages she'd been receiving. Oh God, what if he died?

Silent tears slipped from beneath her lashes, small rivulets of salty water, that fell in a steady stream down her cheeks and splashed onto her hands. It was taking all her willpower for them not to become gut wrenching sobs. She wouldn't lose control like that, not in public.

The door opened suddenly, the interruption startling her. She dashed the tears away with the back of her hand. Whoever it was wouldn't be fooled, but at least they wouldn't actually see her crying.

"Mrs Robinson?"

She turned at her name. A police sergeant stood in the doorway.

"I'm Paul Wellings. We spoke on the phone the other day and I was up at t'farm."

She sniffed and stood up.

"Yes, I remember."

"I'm sorry to intrude but there are some questions that I need to ask you about what happened today."

"No, that's alright, I... I know you have to ask."

"Is there any news about Will?"

"No. When I got here the nurse told me they were assessing his injuries and somebody would come and see me when they knew something more."

Paul nodded.

"Your husband... Stephen?"

"Rob, he's always known as Rob."

"Well, he says that he was just defending himself, that Will attacked him..."

"He's a liar!" Alison interrupted him.

"Ok, let's start from the beginning." He withdrew his notebook.

"Well, that would be when I caught him in bed with some other woman."

It was odd but it was a relief to tell somebody. She hadn't expected it to be. Maybe it was because he just sat and listened without passing judgement.

"You do realise that this is his word against yours? He's saying that he caught you with Will," Sergeant Wellings said, when she had finished telling him what had happened.

"No, he didn't. He came up there threatening me. Will tried several times just to make him leave. He wouldn't listen. Then he threatened to kill us."

"Like I said, Mrs Robinson, it's his word against yours. He says he thought you were at a conference and that he found you and Will having intercourse."

"No, he didn't."

"So you are saying that you are not having intimate relations with Will?"

She blushed.

"No, that is not what I'm saying. Will and I... we... look, it's all new. But Rob never found us in bed. We were mucking out the horses, for crying out loud. Rob threatened me. I should have seen it coming after the text messages."

"Text messages?"

"Yes, Rob left several messages. Some of them were very menacing. I suppose I should have told Will about them but I didn't want to taint what was happening between us."

"The text messages – I don't suppose that you still have them?" Paul Wellings asked quietly.

"I do. They would be proof, wouldn't they, that Rob came here to hurt me?"

"They would."

She reached into her bag and handed him her phone.

"It's odd. When you arrived I was thinking that Will wouldn't have been hurt if I'd shown him the text messages."

"Mrs Robinson, you're not to blame and..."

He stopped as the door opened again.

The nurse, who had shown Alison into this room, had come in accompanied by a man in theatre scrubs.

"Mrs Robinson, I'm Mr Chappell, consultant neurosurgeon. I understand that you're a close friend of Mr Barnes."

Alison nodded.

"Are there any family members that I can speak to?" he asked.

"As far as I know, Mr Barnes - Will - has no blood relatives. His stepdaughter, Sarah, is his next of kin. But she's out of the country, in New Zealand."

Alison looked to Sergeant Wellings for confirmation.

"Aye, that's right. Sarah's been contacted, but it'll be twenty four hours or more before she can get here."

The surgeon sighed. He looked solemn and serious.

"Mrs Robinson, in the absence of Mr Barnes' next of kin, and as you are a close friend, I need to explain what we need to do for him."

She tried to take in everything he was saying, tried to remember it for when Sarah arrived. They were going to have to take him to theatre, something to do with the pressure on his brain caused by a subdural haematoma, whatever one of those was. She must have looked puzzled because he started to explain what he had meant.

"When Will suffered the blow to the head, it resulted in a small tear of one of the blood vessels in his brain. This has bled and a clot has formed causing pressure in the brain. We need to do a craniotomy which involves temporarily removing a flap of the skull. I will then remove the clot and attempt to stop any bleeding. This will reduce the swelling and then I'll replace the skull flap with a metal plate or wires."

She was shaking now, it was impossible not to. This was the stark reality of Will's condition being laid out in front of her. He was critically ill and it scared her.

"The surgery is complex. There is no guarantee that I will be able to stop the bleeding. He could die while under the anaesthetic. There is a chance of permanent and irreversible brain damage. The one thing I haven't got is time to wait for his daughter to return."

The woman in front of him seemed too stunned to speak. He

wasn't sure she understood what he was saying.

"Mrs Robinson, do you understand what I'm telling you? It's important that you realise how seriously ill Will is, important that you acknowledge that I have told you just how serious this is."

She nodded and swallowed hard. Her mouth had suddenly gone dry. Her words, when they came out, were little more than a croak.

"Do you need me to sign anything? A consent form, permission slip or whatever?"

"No. Because Mr Barnes is unable to consent for himself, I'll operate with him unconsented."

"Ok."

"It's going to be a long wait, several hours. You may want to go home.

"No, I couldn't. I have to be here."

"Alright. I will come back and speak to you when I've finished." He turned to go.

"Mr Chappell?"

"Yes."

"I ... thank you for being so honest and for what you are doing for Will."

The surgeon nodded and then disappeared.

"You know, he's right. You should go home and get some rest," Paul Wellings said.

"No, I have to be here. Not just for me, but for Sarah. She needs to know he's not alone. I want you to tell her."

"I will, but who is here for you?"

"I've rung my parents. They're on their way here."

"Alright, I have to go. I would stay but I have to go and charge Robinson. I'll need you to sign a statement, but I'll come back and do that later."

"Ok, thank you."

He left then and suddenly she was alone once more. Her long vigil had begun. A short while later, another nurse came into the room, with yet more tea; she didn't stop or speak: she just left directions for the canteen and chapel, with the cup and saucer. Alison had no need for either. The thought of food was still making her feel sick and she'd never needed to be in a church to pray.

****

She was curled up asleep when her parents arrived several hours later. The tears had come then – great, gut wrenching sobs. It was many minutes before she got control of her emotions and her parents did the only thing they could – hold her. When she'd stopped, her Dad handed her a hankie and she wiped away the tears.

"Thank you," she whispered.

"What has happened? Can you tell us now? You were so vague on the phone."

As she spoke she realised that her life sounded like a scene from some seedy soap opera. Her parents sat in stunned silence as she told them about Rob's betrayal and how she had run from what she had witnessed at her home in Bath. If they wondered why she had not run to them they did not question her about it, realising if they interrupted the flow of words she might not be able to carry on. The violence of the attack shocked them.

"Where is Rob now?" her Dad asked quietly, keeping his anger under control for fear of scaring the two women.

"In custody. He's been charged with causing Grievous Bodily Harm." It was surreal, Alison thought. A week ago she wouldn't have thought Rob possible of such violence. They said a week was a long time in politics – it was a long time in her life as well.

"And Mr Barnes' family? Where are they?"

"The only family he has is a stepdaughter, Sarah. She's on a gap year in New Zealand. I got her number from Will's phone. Paul Wellings spoke to her earlier; she's on her way back."

Her dad placed his arm around her shoulder.

"I understand that you'll want to wait here until she returns; once she does, we'll take you back to Stratford."

"Back to Stratford? I can't go back to Stratford. There's something I haven't told you...about Will. I love him. I know what you're going to say. How can I love him after a week? Well, I do love him and there is not the slightest doubt in my mind that he loves me. I have to be here when he wakes up."

Her parents studied her for a moment. They couldn't begin to understand all that had happened in the past week. But they could hear the simple truth in their daughter's words.

"Ok, sweetheart, whatever you want is alright with us."

The day moved on slowly. No amount of cajoling or persuading could induce her to move from the relatives' room apart from a trip to the relatives' bathroom, where she had a quick shower and changed into some fresh clothes that her mother had brought with her. Periodically, someone gave her a mug of tea or coffee, not that she really wanted one. She was still unable to face food. Her Dad was worried about this, constantly muttering about needing to keep her strength up. But her mum had understood and told him to stop fussing.

She glanced at the clock; it was a typical NHS clock, plain and unadorned. How long since there had been any news, she wondered? No news was good news, they said, but it wasn't when the man you loved was in grave danger. Why, in times of trouble, did time move so slowly? Like every second was an hour? Another glance at the clock confirmed it was only 5 minutes since she had last checked.

Her parents remained at her side, not questioning her love for this man. They would have to have been blind not to realise the depth of her feelings or how shattered she was. They had been her rock – holding her when she wept, listening when she wanted to talk and offering silent support when she had wanted silence.

It was very much later when the door opened once more. In the doorway was stood the neurosurgeon.

"Mrs Robinson, he's out of theatre and in intensive care. You can see him for five minutes and then you have to get some rest. No arguments." The surgeon held the door open.

"Dad, will you come with me? I don't think I can do this on my own," Alison whispered.

She was glad, afterwards, that she had asked her dad to go in with her because her knees had buckled at the sight of Will. She would have fallen had it not been for his support. As long as she lived she would never forget the noise of the ventilator, its rhythmic hissing so strange and alien, so frightening, even though she knew it was keeping Will alive. Tubes seemed to be coming out from everywhere and wires seemed to lead to an astonishing array of machinery, all beeping and alarming, and in among it all was Will. He seemed so small and shrunken, lying still and unmoving. Alison had never seen anybody look so pale and lifeless. His usually flawless skin was grey and clammy; dark circles had formed under his eyes and his dark brown hair was covered with a stark white bandage.

Mr Chappell explained what they'd done.

"We will keep him in an induced coma for a few days, to allow the brain to rest, and then we will try and bring him round. I'll leave you be for five minutes." He walked away to the nurses' station.

Alison took Will's lax hand in hers. He never moved. All she could do was bend over and kiss his cheek.

"I'll be back, I promise," she whispered.

Chapter Twenty One

Sarah smiled. The day, thus far, had been perfect. She glanced sideways at the young man she was with. Did Brian think so too, she wondered? It was strange; she seemed acutely aware of him today, in tune with him almost. Whenever she reached for his hand, which was often, it had been there. She'd found herself sneaking peeks at him all morning when he wasn't looking, like some lovesick puppy. It was great, spending a few hours alone, just the two of them, instead of being a part of the crowd. Was that why things felt so different? She glanced at him again. Was he aware, she wondered, of the shift in their relationship? Or was it only her?

She'd been intrigued by him right from the beginning. He was that most attractive of things – an older man. At twenty three he'd finished his University degree whereas she had yet to begin hers. He was taking a gap year to celebrate completing his PhD in Marine Biology, while she was celebrating passing her A levels. It had been a surprise when he'd asked her out. He'd seemed so urbane and sophisticated, at least compared to her. She'd wondered how he'd enjoy roughing it. But right from the word go he'd been in his element. He was popular with everybody and more than one girl had made a play for him. Sarah hadn't, believing him to be out of her league. Maybe that was why he'd asked her out. Well, whatever the reason, they had clicked and had been together for a couple of months.

Things had been progressing slowly between them over the few months they'd been in New Zealand. She'd had boyfriends before, but none who had been serious enough to break her heart over or lose her virginity to. Her upbringing had made her wary of intimacy, especially once she had discovered the details of her birth. Without even being told, Brian seemed to understand her need to take things slowly.

They hadn't kissed properly on the first few dates, just a quick peck on the cheek at the beginning and end of the evening. In fact, their first kiss hadn't been on a date at all. It had been after her first time at leading on a night hike. She'd been so pleased to lead her group back to camp without any mishaps and he'd been waiting with a huge grin on his face. The kiss had started innocently enough, just a light brushing of the lips, a token to say well done. But then he'd pulled back, a question in his eyes. She'd only nodded slightly but it had been enough. She was lost the moment he kissed her again. How could a simple kiss do that? He'd been soft and gentle, yet insistent and demanding, coaxing her lips to part and then deepening the kiss. After what had been like an eternity he'd pulled away and led her to a secluded spot, away from prying eyes.

They had spent the day in Wellington on the tourist trail. It had been educational, wandering around the Museum of New Zealand. And she'd realised a geeky dream when they'd visited the Weta Cave. She'd barely been able to conceal her excitement at being surrounded by props from Lord of the Rings. Brian had finally dragged her away and, as punishment, made her walk up to the botanic gardens. The view from the top was stunning, taking in all of Wellington, and they'd finished by riding the old cable car back down to the quayside.

He'd said something about finding somewhere to eat, and that was where they were heading now.

"What are you smiling about?" Brian asked.

"I was just thinking what a great day this has been."

"It's not over yet." He bent and kissed her. "Today is our two month anniversary so I booked a table here." Brian pointed to a restaurant just ahead of them on the quayside

The Dockside, as it was appropriately called, was popular and the meal they had there was the perfect end to the perfect day.

It was late when they returned to the outward bound school. Like other instructors, they were being put up in chalets that were away from the main house.

He'd been quiet on the journey home and Sarah wondered again what he was thinking. He walked her to the door of her chalet. Taking her in his arms, he placed a soft kiss on her forehead and then trailed his lips down the contours of her face and neck. Light soft touches that caressed her skin. He paused before he brought his lips to hers, a question in his eyes. His kiss was gentle and delicate and nowhere near enough. Sarah pulled him closer, begging him for more. At her request Brian deepened the kiss, his tongue teasing and exploring. Sarah sighed and returned his kisses with a passion not woken before. Her hands moved to the hem of his shirt; sliding underneath, she caressed him, slowly running her palms over the contours of his muscles so firm beneath her touch. He ended the kiss the same way he had begun, by slowly trailing kisses back up towards her hair. It was then that she knew. He was leaving the next step up to her. Did she want this, she asked herself? In the space of a heartbeat, she realised she did.

"Stay with me tonight," she whispered.

"Are you sure?"

"Oh, yes. I'm certain."

****

For a moment Sarah wasn't sure what had woken her up, but then she realised it was somebody knocking sharply on the door.

"Just a moment," she called pulling her nightdress on.

Who could be knocking at this time of night? A sense of apprehension washed over her. As she opened the door she couldn't help but think something was wrong. Mr and Mrs Williams, her boss and his wife, stood there in their pyjamas, the shocked look on their faces enough to tell her that something terrible had happened.

Mrs Williams spoke first, gently explaining that there had been an urgent phone call for her. It was something everybody dreaded, she thought, an unexpected phone call in the middle of the night.

"Sarah, it's Will, your stepfather, he's been hurt in an accident. I don't know all the details. But he's been taken to a neurosurgery unit."

Quite suddenly she felt strange, different to how she had ever felt before, light headed, unable to focus. The sensation spread over her, accompanied by the most intense heat. Sweat broke out all over her body, causing her nightdress to become damp in minutes. Wave after wave of nausea washed over her, until she could fight it no more and she stumbled to the bathroom where she was violently sick.

It was Brian who helped her to the main house. Mr Williams had taken a contact number and it was Brian who dialled it for her when he realised that she could not manage it because her hands were shaking too much. He'd also taken the phone off her when she had broken down and calmly listened to Sergeant Wellings' view of the accident. He explained that Will had been attacked and that he had been airlifted to Leeds infirmary. He hadn't been alone – Alison was with him. Sarah had no idea who Alison was. PC Wellings had described her as a friend, but the name had meant nothing. He'd pulled no punches, explaining that Will's condition was considered critical and it was unsure if he would survive. At the end of the conversation, Brian had thanked him and replaced the receiver, and then he'd just held Sarah close as he explained what the police had said.

"Mrs Williams, could you make some tea? I think we could all do with a cup," he said when he had finished, "while Sarah decides what she wants to do."

She wiped away her tears and spoke very quietly.

"I know what I want to do. I want to go home."

****

Sarah sat rigidly in her seat, staring blankly ahead. The strange numbness that had settled around her, when she first heard the news, was acting like a barrier against the reality of her situation. Everything and everybody else in the world was moving at a normal speed, while she had come to a standstill, barely able to move or speak. She had felt like this twice before in her life and that had been twice too often. Memories of two other people flooded her mind. She prayed, as she had never done before, that Will would not be dead like them.

Brian had told her she should try and sleep, that the journey would pass quicker if she did. He'd even covered her over with a blanket and his hand had never left hers. Sleep eluded her though, as she knew it would. It was strange; her mind was racing, even if her body had come to a virtual standstill. A million unanswered questions kept repeating themselves over and over again.

Sarah felt Brian's hand squeeze hers gently. She was worrying him. Shocked and immobile as she was, she could still acknowledge that he was deeply concerned. Like me, she thought, he is too young to be dealing with these events. He'd been brilliant, making the travel arrangements, packing her bags. It had obviously never occurred to him that she should deal with this alone. She had sensed from the beginning that Brian was different from the other boys she had known. His actions of the past twenty four hours had confirmed how special he was. She smiled slightly, glad that he was with her, glad that she was not alone.

Brian glanced at her and not for the first time wished she would rest. Dark circles had appeared under her eyes and her cheeks were too pale. He was worried she would collapse before they reached London. He had realised how much Will meant to Sarah, even before the phone call. She'd explained how he had looked after her, following her mother's death. He had been there for her during her darkest hours. He was, Sarah had said, the reason she had turned out halfway decent. Now she was faced with losing him. Brian wished he could, in some way, ease her distress, but he had not the first idea where to begin. Nobody close to him had even so much as had their appendix out let alone been really seriously injured. It hadn't been so bad back in New Zealand – then there had been practical things to be done – but here on the interminable flight back to the UK he felt utterly useless.

"How are we getting to Leeds from the airport?" Sarah asked.

He'd already told her once but he'd noticed that she kept repeating the same questions, as if she was having trouble remembering what she had been told.

"My parents are going to pick us up and take us directly to Leeds."

"That's very good of them. Why would they do that for me? I'm just a stranger."

Brian sighed.

"I told them how special you are, Sarah, and how much I care about you, so they just want to help. You know how special I think you are, don't you?"

"Yes, Brian, and you are special to me as well; it's just that at the moment I can only think of Will. The not knowing, the being out of telephone contact is killing me."

"I know it is but, Sarah, if you don't rest you'll be no good to anybody."

"I know, but me mind is a whirl; I keep going over things – things about Will."

Sighing, Brian did the only thing he could think of. He encouraged her to talk.

And talk she did, about everything and nothing, until exhaustion finally overwhelmed her and she slept.

Chapter Twenty Two

Was it odd, Alison wondered? After just two days she seemed to be getting used to this strange alien world. She knew now without being told that there were times when she would have to leave Will's side to allow the staff to do their jobs. At the moment it was the physiotherapist who was with Will. The little relatives' lounge with its neutral coloured walls, jolly prints and artificial flowers had become a second home. It was rare to be alone in here. Other patients' visitors flitted in and out throughout the day. To begin with, none of them spoke to her. They just offered smiles of sympathy. But, once she'd been there twenty four hours, strange friendships developed, friendships that were born out of shared experiences and from the knowledge that they were all members of an exclusive club – a club nobody wanted to be a member of.

She was losing track of time. Here there was no day or night, merely routine. Routine that had to be adhered to. It was odd that she had lost the concept of time, because the clock was like a God in the unit. Observations were recorded every half an hour, medicines were given and infusions changed at certain times. At the prescribed times, therapy took place. It might be two hourly, it might be four hourly, but it was always time specific.

All the things they did to Will were called 'care interventions'. She knew that was what the nurses called it – the term was used on Will's care plan. Care interventions: everything they did, from emptying his catheter bag to giving him drugs, was a care intervention. In between times, she sat at his side. The problem was she couldn't get close – not really. The IV lines, pumps and machinery were an impenetrable barrier. She'd had to seek permission to touch him. Not that she needed it; she just didn't realise it was safe to.

She didn't recognise him. It was like a stranger lying on the bed. Why was that, she wondered? She pondered that thought for several minutes. It was because his eyes were shut, she realised. They were so expressive, revealed so much about what he was thinking. Not being able to see that made his face appear like a mask – a shrunken mask, nothing more than plains, hollows and shadows. Every time she returned to his bedside she was shocked anew at how sick he looked, his normally luminous skin so paper thin and grey. The tape that secured the ET tube in place was cutting into his skin and his lips were dry and cracked. Frail, that was what he looked. She acknowledged it was an odd adjective to describe a man who was so tall and strong. It was as if he had been felled. Even the way he was lying was at odds with everything she knew about him – so still and straight, flat on his back and completely immobile. A total contrast to how he had curled himself against her just a few precious days ago.

    She held his hand, but even that felt lifeless. The sedation he was under was high because they wanted him to rest and heal. She'd started having conversations with him. One sided though they were, she had to believe he could hear her. She had told him how he couldn't die, how she needed him and how he made her life complete. She talked of things that she still wanted to share with him. Almost always she apologised for causing his injuries and invariably the one sided chat ended with her begging him to wake up and return to her.

    Alison was not alone - her parents had remained at her side. If they thought she was stupid to believe herself in love after so short a time, they had said nothing. Their support had been unwavering. It seemed that no matter what she had needed, they had given it — a shoulder to cry on when she wept, a friendly ear when she wanted to talk and peace and quiet when she wanted to sit in silence. They'd sorted out the practicalities of hotel rooms and food at regular intervals. In truth, she couldn't have managed without them.

It had been her turn to make the tea during this break and she carried it over to the sofa.

"I've booked two rooms for Will's daughter and the people who are bringing her up from London," her Dad told her as she sat down.

"Thanks, Dad. I don't know what I would do without you. When are they due here? I've lost track of the time."

"According to the young man who spoke to Sergeant Wellings, they should be here sometime this afternoon."

"Good. I'll feel better once Sarah arrives."

They'd almost finished the tea when Sergeant Wellings arrived. He told them that Rob had appeared in Leeds crown court and had been remanded in custody for one week.

"He is still insisting that Will started the fight."

"No, he didn't. All Will did was ask him to leave. Rob started the fight because I wouldn't go with him."

"He's claiming Will started the fight because he accused him of raping his wife when she was a young girl."

"He accused Will of that, and being a paedophile before they fought. But Will only hit him in self-defence."

"These allegations your husband was making will come out in court. He'll use them in his defence."

"Why, they're utter rubbish. Christ knows how he even found out about Sarah and Moira."

"I think that was my fault. He had the police searching for you. I told him where you were and that I'd thought that you were Sarah when I rang. Perhaps if I'd known the story I wouldn't have said owt to him."

"I know. I should have said about the text messages," Alison said miserably.

"Well, there's no point crying over spilt milk. At least you didn't delete them."

"No, but it doesn't make me feel any less responsible though. What I really don't understand is why Rob thought Will had raped Moira."

"That'd be folks in the pub. Rob were in there, the night before the attack, asking questions. Some people in the pub were gossiping about her."

"Nothing changes down The Fleece then. Will and me, still the subject of gossip and tittle tattle."

Both Paul and Alison turned towards the voice. Sarah stood in the doorway. Alison recognised her from the photographs back at Highcroft. At her side was a young man, and an older couple stood behind them.

"Sarah, love, come and sit down. This is Alison, she were with Will when he was attacked."

The young girl nodded.

"How is he?"

"He's had surgery to stop the bleeding and drain the haematoma. There was a lot of swelling so Mr Chapel, the surgeon, has kept him in a medically induced coma."

"Sorry, what does that mean?"

"It means they are keeping him in a coma using drugs. He remains critical, but he survived the surgery." Alison spoke quietly, wishing with all her heart that she could have met this young woman in some other circumstances.

Sarah sank to the chair.

"Paul, you said on the phone he'd been attacked? I don't understand. Who'd want to attack Will?"

"We've arrested a man, Stephen Robinson..."

"Rob's my husband," Alison interrupted the policeman. "Will was defending me."

"Will was defending you? Your husband did this to Will?" Sarah was aware she sounded like a parrot.

"Yes," Alison said quietly.

"You're not from these parts, are you?"

"No, I live in Bath."

"Bath? If you don't mind me asking, how did you meet him? It's odd he's not mentioned you or owt."

"We only met last week. I crashed my car in the snow. Winston and Will found me. He saved my life."

"Where does your husband come into this?"

"I had left him after I caught him cheating on me. He came to take me back by force if he had to. Will stopped him from hurting me."

Sarah nodded slowly.

"That sounds like Will. I'd like to see him now." She looked at Paul Wellings.

"Right, I'll speak to the staff."

"Thanks. Mrs Robinson, it has been good of you to wait with Will, but you must want to get back to your life."

Alison froze. Now what? She had effectively been dismissed.

"We won't leave till the morning; it'll be dark soon and the roads are still bad. My parents have booked you into the hotel just down the road. If you give the staff your room number they'll be able to contact you during the night." She had no idea how she was talking or if it made sense at all. She just knew she had to say something. "If it's all right with you, I'll pop back tomorrow before we go."

"Yes, of course."

Alison nodded and gestured to her parents that she was leaving. They'd barely taken five steps out of the room before her Dad stopped her.

"Alison, what are you doing? Go back and explain that you love Will."

"I can't, Dad. You heard her - she doesn't want me there. "

"That's because she doesn't have the full picture about you and Will."

"Did you see her face when she realised that it was my husband who'd done this? No, it's better I leave. Go back to the hotel; I'll be along soon. I just need some time alone."

Her father made to protest but his wife stopped him before he could. She reached up and kissed her daughter's cheek.

"If that's what you want. Come on, Henry."

Alison didn't leave the hospital. For a while she walked the corridors, pacing up and down, before finally finding herself in the hospital chapel. She wasn't particularly religious, but the peace and serenity of the chapel enveloped her and for a short time eased her hurt and pain. She didn't blame Sarah; the young woman had no idea how her words had wounded. At least here she felt close to Will.

****

"Are you ok, Sarah?" Brian asked.

"I don't know. It sounds so bad. It'll be better when I can see him and speak to somebody."

"Well, like Alison said, he came through the surgery much better than was expected. So that's positive," Brian said.

"Do you think it odd that she stayed here? I mean, it's not like she knows Will."

"Perhaps she felt she had to stay, guilt or something."

"Yeah, that could be it, I guess..."

Sarah stopped talking as the door opened.

"Dr Ben!" She jumped up and gave the GP a huge hug. "Have you seen Will? How is he? What's happening?"

"Sarah, this is Mr Chappell. He operated on Will."

"Hello, Miss Bradshaw. Shall we sit down? I'll go through things and explain where we are at and what's happening next."

Ben glanced around the room.

"Where's Alison? The nursing staff said that she was in here?"

"Oh, she was. She explained what had happened and now she's gone back to the hotel," Sarah said.

"That's strange. She has always waited to see either me or the consultant anaesthetist before going back to the hotel," Mr Chappell said.

"Well, I suppose because I'm here she didn't feel it necessary. I mean, she only stayed until I got here."

"I got the impression that she was Mr Barnes' girlfriend," Mr Chappell said looking at the young GP.

"No, you're mistaken. They only just met. I guess that she felt obligated to stay until we arrived," Sarah said.

"Oh, I'm sorry; that must be my mistake. Well, if you come with me, I'll take you to see him and explain everything."

"Brian...?"

"Do you need me to come with you?"

She nodded.

"Yes, please."

****

Sarah couldn't hear the words that the consultant was saying. The humming that had started in her head when they entered ITU was so loud that it was drowning out his words. In any case, it wasn't Will he was talking about. The man lying on the bed didn't look anything like Will. She'd even said as much, but they hadn't believed her. They told her it was because of the equipment, that it made people look different. The consultant just kept talking. She wished he'd stop. How could she make him stop? That wasn't Will. She didn't need to know all of this. Will must be back on the farm. That was good. He'd hate it here; it was far too hot and the air seemed stale, as if all the oxygen had been used up. Will liked fresh air – he often said he'd shrivel up if he had to stay indoors. She knew how he felt, especially now. She needed fresh air. She started to move away, only vaguely aware of her name being called. It was odd; darkness seemed to invade the room.

She'd forgotten how quick night fell this time of the year. Night time. That must be why she was so tired. She'd be better when she'd slept. Then she'd find Will. She felt strong arms encircle her and a voice telling her she'd be alright.

She'd fainted – how embarrassing. These people had really sick people to look after and she was keeping them away from their work. She tried to sit up, but Dr Ben stopped her.

"No, just lie still for a little while."

"Don't be silly – it was just hot in there."

"Sarah, Dr Chappell seemed to think that you were denying it was Will. It is him, lass. You do understand that, don't you?"

"It doesn't look like him."

"I know it doesn't, but it really is him."

"I know it is. I just don't want to believe it."

The door to the relatives' room opened.

"We're sorry to disturb you, but we wondered if Alison had come back here?"

"No, did she say she was going to?"

"She never came back to the hotel. She said she needed some time alone but that was two hours ago."

"I don't understand why she left when Sarah arrived?"

"I told you, Dr Ben, I don't suppose she felt it was her place to stay. I mean, Will is just a stranger who happened to be in the wrong place at the wrong time," Sarah said sitting up.

"Sarah, that's not quite true. While Alison never discussed her relationship with Will, when he brought her to see me, it was obvious that there was more going on than just him rescuing her and being a Good Samaritan. Will confirmed that – told me it was early days, but that he and Alison wanted to be together."

"Together, as in being a couple?"

Aye, that's right, lass."

"But they'd only just met. Are you saying Will told you he loved her?"

"Yes, that's what I'm saying."

"Oh my God, I sent her away. Why didn't she say owt?"

"She didn't want to hurt you. Thought you had enough to deal with," Alison's mother said quietly.

"Well, she can't be far. We'll find her."

****

She had no idea how long she'd sat there, but the chapel was in darkness when the door opened.

"Your family are going frantic with worry."

She started at the sound of Sarah's voice.

"I...I lost track of time. How did you find me?"

"This is where I would come if I couldn't be close to Will. Why didn't you tell me, about you and him?"

"Who told you? Did my parents?"

"No, they didn't. It was Dr Ben. I think you've met him?"

"Yes, he checked my shoulder was alright. But I don't understand..." Alison stopped puzzled.

"Will told him that he was in love with you. I'm guessing that it wasn't all one sided."

"No, it wasn't. I love him, Sarah... I know it hasn't been long and I don't expect you to understand, but I do love him. God, it's my fault he's hurt. I'm so sorry. You must hate me. I promised him I wouldn't leave, but, I'll understand if you want me to go."

"No, I don't want you to go."

"Thank you."

Sarah studied the woman opposite her.

"Will is easy to love, easy to hurt as well. I do believe you love him but, Alison, you'd best not ever hurt him. He's been hurt too much."

"I know he has, but he won't be by me, I promise."

"I'm glad to hear that because, if you do hurt him, I will have to come after you with a rolling pin."

"Ok, I've been warned. It's lovely to meet you. Will's told me a lot about you."

"Nowt good I hope. That'd be boring. Well, I think we best go back before they send out a search party for me as well."

They walked back to ITU and continued the vigil together.

Chapter Twenty Three

Was this place real, Will thought? If it were, he'd no idea why he was here or even where here was. Grey, it was just an unending sea of grey. He wondered if it was the fear of this strange place that had rendered him immobile. He was, without a doubt, more terrified than he had ever been in his whole life. He wanted to run as far and fast as he could but his legs felt like they were shackled to the floor. All he was able to do was look straight up. Logically, he realised that he must be lying on his back which meant the grey above him was what? The ceiling or the sky? Not the sky, he decided. If he were outside, he would be able to feel the breeze on his skin.

It should have been peaceful but he couldn't rest. Not knowing this place was unsettling him and then there was the certain knowledge they'd be back. He wasn't sure how long it had been since they last appeared; he just knew they'd be back. Heads, floating heads. Human heads; sometimes they were male and sometimes female. They just appeared. He could never see their bodies just the heads, suspended above him. Sometimes they would come close to his face and a blinding light would shine in his eyes. He tried to move away when they did this, pushing himself back into the surface beneath him, willing whatever he was lying on to swallow him.

The worst thing about the heads was they seemed to have an ability to stop him breathing. They'd appear and something would happen and it would feel as if his throat was closing. He could feel himself gagging and coughing and then, as quickly as it started, it would be over. But never for long and then it would happen again. To begin with, he tried to fight against it. But, he couldn't move, not even his head and, in any case, he'd discovered that trying to fight it made the whole experience much worse. He was also terrified that, by fighting the heads, they'd get annoyed and cut his airway off completely.

What was just as frightening was, they didn't speak in any kind of language he understood. How stupid a thought was that, as if a floating head was ever going to speak in English? The whole scenario was like some ghoulish nightmare. Yet, somehow he knew this was real and not some dream. The sounds they made were slow and distorted, nothing more than incomprehensible gibberish.

The heads always disappeared as suddenly as they appeared. He tried to work out how often they came but time had no meaning here. It was just infinite and endless. In between the visits from the floating heads he felt as if he were drifting, lulled along by a rhythmic, metronomic sound.

The worry of the farm was never far from his mind. He had to get back home. Who was seeing to the animals? He was just getting the place back on its feet. The years of nursing his family had taken their toll. The loan he'd had to take to buy new livestock had to be paid on time. He just did not have the time to be idle. If only he could get up and leave, but, no matter how hard he tried, he couldn't. He began to panic then. He was trapped in this strange twilight world with no means of escape.

****

"I came to Halifax with Will a couple of days before the accident. We had coffee in here then as well. It never occurred to me that you and he used this café," Alison said.

"Aye, we have done since we first moved in with Will. He used to treat us to milkshake and cakes when he came to do his banking," Sarah said sipping her coffee.

"The waitress was flirting outrageously with him when we were here. I'll never forget how embarrassed he was. I swear, even his ears turned pink."

"That'd be Will all over. He's kind of shy. Can I ask a personal question?"

"I suppose so."

"Who made the first move? I mean with Will being so shy."

"I suppose it happened when I got stuck in the bath," she said laughing at Sarah's face. "I know, it was so stupid. He ran me a bubble bath and I got in alright but because of my arm I couldn't get out. He was so sweet, fetching me a long t shirt and standing with his eyes closed while I put it on while in the bath. It was to spare my blushes. The problem was, the moment we touched, it was electric. I suddenly became aware of him as a man not my rescuer. "

"And Will?"

"I think, if we'd not been snowed in, he'd have run a mile, but he had to stay and face his feelings. The rest, as they say, is history."

"I'm glad. Will has never had any luck with women. Me mam doesn't count."

"Will told me a little about your mum. I'm so sorry that you had to lose her when you were so young."

"Aye, well, it was a long time ago. I had Will to take care of me..." Sarah's voice broke as she spoke. "I don't know what I'm going to do if he doesn't come through this."

"Hey, come on. No thinking like that. Didn't we say yesterday that he seemed more awake?"

"Yes, but the anaesthetist and the surgeon both said that there was no change in his conscious level."

"Oh, what do they know? Patients have been proving doctors wrong for years. Seriously, who is better placed to say whether Will is more awake? You, who's known him for years, or them?"

"You don't think we were just wishing he was more awake?"

"No, I don't. I'd swear on my mother's life he was trying to listen to what we were saying."

Sarah sipped at her coffee, thinking.

"The medical bods, they told us we had to get some time away. I think that's because they know Will isn't going to recover," she said.

"No, I was speaking to Mr Chappell. He feels that it's quality time with the patient that's important. You have to look after yourself, Sarah, or you'll be no good to Will. The visitors from the S&R will be a change for Will as well. And you'll be able to reassure Will that Mike and Stuart are looking after the farm well. If there's one thing I've learned it's how much the farm and the land mean to him."

Sarah nodded.

"That's true, and that Mrs B is alright. He'd fret about that."

"I was thinking as well. Will likes word games. I think that, when we're at the hospital, we should do the crossword but read the clues to him. Maybe somewhere in his mind he can hear us so we should include him. I'm going to read to him – Far from the Madding Crowd, I think."

"Ok, shall we go shopping then? You can pick up the book."

"While we shop, you can tell me all about Brian. He must be a special young man to fly all the way from New Zealand with you."

"He is. I suppose, having quizzed you about Will, it's only fair that you get to question me."

The afternoon was a pleasant one. Sarah was, Alison realised, a thoroughly lovely young woman. No wonder Will was proud of her. It wasn't difficult to understand why. The hours away from Will's bedside recharged the batteries and they returned to the hospital in better spirits than they had left.

****

Somebody was reading; he could hear them and finally the words were making sense. He wanted to cry with relief. For days he'd lain listening to the babble of gibberish, thinking he'd never hear English again.

The owner of the voice must be holding his hand because he could feel the fingers move against his palm. It was a small hand; very much smaller than his – softer as well. A female hand, he realised. Whose though, he wondered? The voice was neither Moira's nor Sarah's.

He liked her reading choice. He'd not read Far From the Madding Crowd for years but he found comfort in the familiar story. After days of being in this strange place, it was fantastic to finally recognise something, even if it was just words in a novel. He wanted to thank the person but speech remained beyond him. No matter how hard he tried, no words came out. So he did the only other thing he could think of - he squeezed her hand. God, he was weak. His hand barely moved. Had she even noticed? He concentrated hard and moved it again. Why did he have to think so hard to move his hand? Normally, if he needed to move his hand, he did, and with no real thought. Maybe this place had different gravity to the earth. He laughed at himself. How stupid. He didn't believe in alien planets or characters like Superman, Ming the Merciless or Luke Skywalker. He needed to see more of where he was. Maybe then he'd understand. For the first time in days, he was able to move his head. It was difficult and hurt like hell but he turned it towards the voice that was reading.

****

Sarah was looking at the paper and half listening to Alison reading to Will when it happened. Alison had paused mid-sentence and when she looked over to see why she'd stopped reading she saw Will turn his head. She'd never be able to describe the moment in a million years. There were too many differing emotions entwined with each other. All threatened to overwhelm her and one glance at Alison's face showed she was experiencing the same emotional overload.

"I'll fetch his nurse," Alison whispered, hardly daring to believe what she witnessed. She stood up, surprised that her legs felt so unsteady. Everything around her faded into the background, except for the nurse stood at the nurse's station.

"It's Will - he's waking up."

The nurse smiled indulgently. Relatives often thought this, only to be wrong and then disappointment kicked in. But as she approached Will's bed she realised that what Alison had said was true. He was taking a lot of spontaneous breaths and he was moving with control, following Sarah's instructions.

"Bleep Mr Chappell and find Dr Ellis," she called to a colleague at the desk.

The next few hours were in turn emotional, exciting, uplifting, frustrating and frightening. The doctors had warned them that Will would not return to normal immediately, and he didn't, but it was obvious that he was slowly becoming more aware of his surroundings.

It was late afternoon when he spoke. He'd slowly watched the world come back to something like normal, finally realising he was in a hospital. Nothing made sense. He'd no idea why he was there. And then there was Sarah. He'd lain trying to understand what had happened to her. But he couldn't, so eventually he had to ask.

"Sarah?" his voice, raspy from the tube, whispered her name as a question.

Never had a single word been more welcome.

Sarah reached for his hand, bringing it to her face before she slumped forward, crying for all she was worth.

Alison watched as sobs shook the younger girl's body. Tears spiked on her own lashes as she said tremulously: "They're good tears. She's pleased to see you, really."

Will stared at the young woman, stunned. Something was very wrong; he recognised the woman's voice as belonging to the person who was reading earlier but he had no idea who she was. His eyes moved to Sarah. He thought the nightmare was over but it wasn't.

Alison realised something wasn't right; it would have been impossible to miss the look of shock on Will's face.

"Will, what's the matter? Are you in pain? Shall I fetch a nurse?"

Sarah sat up at her words.

"Will?"

He wasn't sure what was happening. He was terrified – even more than when he had been in the grey world. He wanted to know what had happened but at the same time he was scared to find out. He looked at the two women in front of him, staring at him expectantly. But how did he explain what he didn't understand himself? What did he say? The first thing that came into his head.

"Sarah, what happened? You're... different."

"How do you mean, different?
"Older."

"Well, maybe that's because I've been away in New Zealand for a few months. I feel older somehow and you've given me a few grey hairs this week."

New Zealand! His head began to hurt. A man approached the bed. He seemed vaguely familiar and then he realised he was one of the talking heads from his dreams. A doctor, he supposed. Will looked at him.

"Are you a doctor?" The man nodded.

"Yes, I'm Mr Chappell. I operated on you."

Operated on? Why? What happened to me, Will wondered? His hand brushed the bandage on his head. That could wait. Right now he had to know about Sarah.

"Can you...?" Will swallowed, his mouth dry as parchment

"Here, have some water." Mr Chappell pushed a button on the

locker and Will felt the head of the bed raise up. He placed a cup in front of Will's mouth. Will took a few sips. It felt strange to swallow, as if his throat was swollen.

"Please," he croaked. "Tell me... Sarah... she's older... why?"

"How do you mean, older?"

"I mean that she went to school as a thirteen year old this morning and now she must be at least eighteen."

Chapter Twenty Four

Post traumatic amnesia they called it. Yet another medical condition Alison had no desire to know about. She stood alone in the corner of the room - just an observer, really. Anxiety washed over her, its tendrils invading both her heart and mind. She should have realised that this might happen. The doctor had warned them that Will might be confused and disorientated when he woke up. She'd been expecting that and had prepared herself for it even. She'd always known that she would have to explain about Rob and the accident – had been ready to do just that – but then he'd spoken. Confusion was one thing; complete loss of memory was another. Will had no recollection of the last five years. No recollection of her.

In among everything that was going on it occurred to her that she was the only person who'd realised that. Nobody else had picked up on the simple fact that he'd met her during those five years. Initially, the doctors had asked them to leave so that they could carry out some tests. Sarah had been visibly shaken by this development and Alison hadn't thought it the moment to point out to the young girl that Will would have no memory of her. The problem was, there just hadn't been a right time.

Mr Chappell and the anaesthetist had come and explained what Post Traumatic Amnesia, or PTA as they called it, was. Alison wanted to scream. She was sick of all the bloody abbreviations. Couldn't these people speak in proper words? It seemed that, as a result of the head injury, Will had lost the ability to recall the day to day events of the last five years. He had quite literally woken up believing it was 2006.

They explained that, over the next few days, they would be carrying out a series of repetitive tests at regular intervals to determine whether he was able to retain any new information at all.

Sarah had voiced what everybody was thinking.

"You mean, he may not be able to retain any new information?"

"That is the worst case scenario, but yes. We won't really know for a few days. So, you need to cross that bridge when you come to it."

"What about the memory he has lost? How likely is it that he will regain it?" Alison asked, quietly.

"There is no definite time scale. Will definitely has a retrograde amnesia at present. He may well recover most of that memory over the next few weeks or months. However, what you have to realise is that memories tend to return like pieces of a jigsaw puzzle. And, like a puzzle, the pieces return in random order. When assessing the severity of a head injury in general, it's fair to say that, the smaller the degree of retrograde amnesia, the less significant the head injury."

"Oh, my God..."

"Sarah, "Brian said, quietly. "That's not new information; we already knew Will had suffered a severe head injury. This kind of just confirms it. We can deal with this. You have been dealing with this."

"I think you should go back in to Will – he wants to see you again, Sarah. And right now he needs something familiar."

The words were like a slap – hard and sharp. He wanted to see Sarah, not her. Stupid, she thought. How could he want to see her? He didn't even know she existed. She waited for the others to realise what this meant for her but they didn't. Mr Chappell had continued speaking.

"You may notice a marked change in Will's behaviour and you need to be prepared for it. He may be very confused, agitated, distressed or anxious. This mild, quiet man I've been hearing about may become both verbally and physically aggressive. You have to try not to get upset by this as it will just make him more confused and anxious."

"I can't imagine him being aggressive."

"Well, let's hope he isn't. Before you do go back to see him, he keeps asking about Moira who, I understand, is his wife."

"Yes, she was. She was my mother. She died two years ago. Oh, good God, he's going to have to be told, isn't he?"

The consultant sighed.

"Yes, he is."

They debated not telling him immediately, but a nurse had appeared saying that Will was getting very agitated about his wife.

Sarah and the consultant had broken the news. She'd gone in with them but had retreated to the corner where she now stood. Her heart bled for him. She'd never seen a man crumple so completely; if he'd been stood up he would surely have fallen. His already pale feature skin turned the colour of putty and shock, pain and disbelief were all etched on his features.

Will looked from one to the other. It was difficult to take in what they were saying. His hearing had suddenly become strange. There was a buzzing in his ears – everything that Sarah was saying seemed distorted, like a record being played on the wrong speed. Pain hit him in his chest and stomach, hot, sharp, and constant. He couldn't breathe. The blood seemed to be haemorrhaging from him, as if he had a gaping wound. He was so cold. He looked up at Sarah, almost begging her to say it wasn't true.

"Dead?" he whispered, as if trying to understand. "Were we in a car accident?"

"No, Moira... Moira, she died two years ago, Will," Sarah said.

"What? No... no... no... that can't be right. Two years! It isn't true. Please... tell me it isn't true."

"Will..."

"It can't be true; we just got married. Oh God, this isn't happening. It's just a nightmare like the talking heads were a nightmare. I haven't woken up."

"Will, you have woken up. I know it's difficult to understand and I won't begin to claim that I know what you're feeling but everything Sarah has said is true."

He broke down then. He seemed to visibly shrink, sinking back into the mattress as if he wanted it to swallow him. The sob came suddenly, an inhuman sound torn from the depth of his soul, his keening cries echoing around the room. The doctor stood immobile. He had no words of comfort to offer - surely none existed? Will turned his head away in grief and despair, crying, rocking and trembling, unable to comprehend anything other than the fact that his beautiful Moira had gone, and, with her, his whole world.

Dr Chappell whispered something to the nurse and, moments later, a drug was added to Will's IV line. After a few moments he seemed to calm a little and Alison realised it must have been a sedative of some description. Once Will had quietened, the medical team left them alone - alone to come to grips with what had happened.

Silent tears trickled down Alison's face. She wanted to go to Will, to comfort him. But she was now nothing more than a stranger; any move on her part at this point in time would almost certainly distress him further.

Looking over at Sarah, she realised her tears were for her as well as Will. She'd come to really like the young woman and knew this must be like losing her mother all over again. Looking at Will and her as they took and gave support to each other, she realised that they looked like a unit – something she was not a part of. It hit her then; right now, she wasn't needed. Indeed, her presence might actually be hugely detrimental to Will. They needed time alone together so they could grieve. She glanced at Brian. The young man remained at Sarah's side, his arm around her in quiet, solid support. Alison was glad he was there for Sarah – like a link between the past and the future. She was going to need him over the coming weeks.

She slipped quietly away and made it several steps down the corridor before she had to stop, overcome by the emotion of it all. She leant against the wall but her legs wouldn't support her so she slid down the wall to her haunches. It was strange; she didn't really cry - she was beyond tears. She just began to shake, her body gripped by tremors that she just couldn't control.

She wasn't sure how long she was there before she was found. It seemed like hours but, in reality, it was probably no more than fifteen minutes. It was Ben Chambers who found her.

"Alison?"

She looked up as he crouched down by her side.

"Here, put your arms around my shoulder and I'll help you up."

Her legs protested at the movement, after being crouched for so long, and she needed to hold on to Dr Chambers as they went back to the relatives' room.

He sat her down on the sofa.

"God, you're like ice." He disappeared but returned quickly with a blanket which he wrapped around her.

"Has something happened to Will?" he asked, once he'd finished.

"Yeah, he woke up and spoke to us."

A smile broke on the doctor's face.

"That's good news…" He paused, looking at Alison's pale face. "Or it should be."

"He woke up thinking it was 2006. He has no memory of the last five years."

"Oh, Jesus!"

"Yes, Sarah's with him. They had to tell him about Moira. It was bloody awful."

Ben nodded.

"That must have been hard. How did he take the news?"

"How do you think? He's distraught. Moira's the only woman he ever loved."

"What about you? He loved you."

Alison remained silent so Ben pressed on.

"Did the medics ask you to leave so they could explain about you to Will?"

"Explain about me?"

"Well, if he has no memory of the last five years, he won't have any memory of you, will he?"

"To be honest, that hasn't occurred to the medics or Sarah yet."

"Are you saying nobody has made that connection yet?"

"No... and that is as it should be. The focus has to be Will and his needs. I left because the family needs time to grieve alone..."

"And then you collapsed alone in a corridor because nobody cared about you?" Ben was angry.

"No, this isn't about me. It's about Will. In his mind, he's still in love with Moira. I left because I thought the shock of being told about me might cause him harm."

"I understand that, but somebody should have realised what his memory loss means for you."

"And they will, once they have dealt with Will's immediate needs."

"What are you going to do now?" Ben asked, his anger subsiding slightly.

"Oh, you know, that British thing, have a cup of tea and wait."

****

Will lay with his eyes shut, trying to come to terms with what had happened. He didn't feel as if a chunk of his life was missing. Perhaps he would, once he was allowed home. Sarah had explained all about Moira's death. He couldn't begin to understand how difficult that must have been for her. He still couldn't believe Moira had gone. It didn't seem possible. And she'd committed suicide. He should have seen the signs, done something to prevent it. He couldn't comprehend that he must have asked all these questions before, grieved like this before.

"Was Moira buried or cremated?" he asked suddenly.

"Cremated. We scattered her ashes up on the moors," Sarah said quietly.

"I'm sorry, Sarah. Making you relive this. It's selfish of me."

"No, don't think like that. You're the least selfish person I know. You always have been. A bang on the head isn't going to change that. If you need to know anything else about Moira, just ask."

"To be honest with you, Sarah, I need a break from sad things. I'd like to know about you. I mean, look at you, all grown up and left school. And perhaps you'll introduce me to your friend?"

"I don't want to tire you," Sarah said.

"You won't."

They talked for about fifteen minutes before Will realised that, despite his protests, he was tired. He tried to hide it but Sarah realised.

"That's enough for today. You should try and get some sleep."

"Ok. Sarah. You will come back, won't you?"

"Yes, of course. First thing tomorrow morning."

"Good. Perhaps you can read me some more of Far from the Madding Crowd?"

"Oh, that wasn't me. It was Alison..."

She stopped speaking, realising that Will was asleep.

She turned to speak to Alison.

"Brian, did you see where Alison went?"

"No. Perhaps she went back to the relatives' room."

"Why would she do that?"

"Well, you and Will, you had a lot to talk about. She probably didn't want to intrude."

"Or maybe she realised that Will can have no memory of her and thought it best to leave," Ben Chambers said from the doorway.

Sarah turned slowly towards him as his words sank in.

"Oh, shit." She glanced back at Will. "How can I not have registered that he won't know her?"

She stepped out into the corridor.

"Where is she? Where did she go?"

"She's waiting in the relatives' room."

Sarah went to head in that direction but Ben caught her arm.

"Sarah, I know this is hard for you with Will and his memory but, behind the brave act that Alison is putting on, she's frightened."

"Frightened of what?"

"Frightened that Will may never remember her and that he will blame her for the accident that did this. She won't say that but she is."

Sarah sighed. How could she have been such a fool?

"Ok, thanks Dr Ben."

She walked to the door of the relatives' room and pushed it opened. Alison was stood at the sink, washing up cups. There were two other people sat talking. People Sarah didn't recognise. Alison turned to see who'd opened the door. She looks tired,

Sarah thought. It was funny that she'd not noticed before.

"How is he?"

"Exhausted. It's a lot to take in. He's sleeping now."

Alison nodded.

"He'd say that while he's sleeping he's healing," she said with a soft smile.

"Yes, he would. Do you feel up to a walk? I fancy a drink and there's a pub just down the road."

"Yeah, that sounds good." She dried the cup and placed it in the cupboard.

The pub Sarah had mentioned was only a short walk away and they were soon sat with a drink.

"I'm sorry, Alison, for not realising what Will's amnesia means for you."

"What do you mean?"

"That he doesn't remember you."

"You were focused on Will. That is as it should be," Alison said, quietly.

"No, I should have realised and so should Dr Chappell. You love Will and, from what Dr Ben and Mrs B have told me, you were the best thing to happen to him in a long time. They also both believe he loves you. If Will doesn't remember you then we will just have to remind him."

Alison was touched by the sincerity in the younger woman's words.

"Thank you, Sarah. Your words mean more than you can ever know. Selfish as it is, I'm terrified that he won't remember me and what we shared."

"It's not selfish. I'm scared too. I think it's normal to feel like this and I'm willing to bet that over the next few days we will get frustrated and even angry with him as well," Sarah said taking a sip of her wine.

"How did he take the news of Moira's death?"

"It was strange. He reacted how I expected him to when it happened. Normal grief, if grief can ever be normal. What I mean is that, when it happened, he didn't have time to grieve; maybe now he can. Everybody should have time to grieve."

"You're a wise woman for one so young, Sarah."

"She's not that wise or she'd realise her man is starving," Brian said with a grin, thinking it was time to lighten the mood and remind them that Will was recovering.

"Food, it's all they think of." Sarah gave him a punch before she handed him the menu.

"I was going to buy champagne, but, keep abusing me, and I won't."

"Champagne?"

"Yes, I know it's a long way to go but we should celebrate Will regaining consciousness."

"I don't know…" Sarah said slowly.

"I do. Brian's right. We should celebrate the positives, not dwell on the negatives," Alison said. "After all, he has come back to us."

"Ok, get your wallet out then, Brian," Sarah said. "You're buying."

****

He woke early. Panic gripped him to begin with. This wasn't his room and it wasn't his bed. It took less than a minute for him to remember where he was and only a minute more to recall that he'd no memory of the last five years. Pain hit him then – Moira was dead. Sarah had told him. Not the young girl who he remembered but a sophisticated grown up version. There was so much he missed. So much he had to get back.

The room wasn't completely dark. A dim night light glowed in the ceiling and he could hear the sounds of movement outside his door. He tried to sit up and get out of bed but he was so weak that all he managed to do was trigger the alarms on the monitor he was attached to. Will's heart lurched in his chest as panic rose. What was it? Why was the machine alarming? He felt the same, not ill, just shattered; surely they shouldn't alarm because he was tired. The high pitched bleeping sliced through the silence in the room and brought a nurse running through the door.

She reached up to the monitor and cancelled the alarm.

"Good morning, Will."

"Did I do something to set the alarm off?"

"You moved, that's all. It's one of the things that frighten ITU patients when they wake up, the alarms."

He nodded.

"Would you like a drink?" She poured him a glass of water.

His hand trembled as he held the glass and water spilt on the sheet.

"Sorry, I feel so weak."

"Don't worry, its normal," she said, helping him with the glass. "The day staff will be around in a while. They will help you have a wash and get you ready for your day," she said when he'd finished drinking. "So just lie back and relax."

She'd gone before he could ask what she meant by his day.

Later, as the nurses bed bathed him, he decided that if he'd realised what helping him have a wash entailed he'd probably have refused. He was a shy, private man – always had been – so when the nurses stripped him off and proceeded to wash him, he wanted to die from embarrassment. He lost count of the times they told him to relax. Relax! How could he? Nobody had ever seen him naked, not even Moira, and certainly nobody had touched him as the nurse was doing now. The wet cloth rubbing his private areas and top of his thighs was warm, but that didn't make it less embarrassing. They rolled him onto his side and washed his back and bottom, removing a faeces soiled pad from under him. He wanted to die. Humiliation swept over him – he'd messed the bed. What must they think? Should he apologise?

"I'm... sorry... I didn't know I..."

"It's ok, Will, when you have been as sick as you have the body functions get altered. It won't be permanent."

He nodded.

"Do you feel like some breakfast?"

Did he? He wasn't hungry but he hadn't eaten since regaining consciousness so he realised he should try.

His limbs were still as heavy as lead and the effort of putting even one spoonful in his mouth was too tiring so that the nurse fed him. Even then he could only manage a quarter of the bowl and half a cup of tea.

"Have a rest now; you must be tired. Mr Chappell and Dr Ellis will be coming round shortly."

Rest, it was all he was doing. He hated inactivity but the nurse was right: he was exhausted and, within minutes, he had dozed off.

The doctors woke him a little later.

"How do you feel today?" Mr Chappell asked.

"Exhausted. All I do is sleep. And uncoordinated. Me arms and legs won't do what I want them to."

"Even though you're out of the coma, your brain is still healing. It will take a while for things to return to normal. The good news is that your short term memory is working well and you're retaining new information. How about your memory of the last five years? Is that still a blank?"

"Yes, it is. And no matter how hard I try I can't recall anything."

"Difficult as it is, you mustn't try so hard. As I explained to your family, it's likely it will return in fits and starts."

"I don't remember the accident and I didn't think to ask, but how did it happen?"

"You were assaulted. The police will be able to explain more. I've given them permission to talk to you today. I'm sure they'll be along later. Meanwhile, your family are waiting. I'll tell them they can come in."

The surgeon disappeared.

Assaulted? Will frowned. Who'd want to attack him? It didn't make sense. Nothing made sense.

The door opened and he smiled as Sarah appeared. It was still a shock to see her all grown up but at least he recognised her from yesterday. She was accompanied by the young man who'd been with her. Brian, his name was Brian. The consultant was right, he was retaining new information. They were followed in by a tall, blond haired woman who he remembered had been with Sarah yesterday. Beyond that he didn't recognise her. If she hadn't been wearing jeans and a plaid shirt he'd have thought she was a member of staff. Who was she, he wondered?

Sarah reached the bed first and brushed a kiss on his cheek.

"Morning, Will. How are you today?" she asked.

"Awake and I remember yesterday. The doctor says that's good." Will didn't sound like he thought it was good.

"It is good. He also said you still couldn't remember the last five years?"

"I can't. He said I mustn't try too hard. It'll just come back."

"Well, I'm sure it will. There is somebody you need to meet."

The blond woman stepped closer to the bed. She was very pretty, Will registered, and older than Sarah, so it was unlikely she was a friend.

"Will, this is Alison... She's your... your girlfriend."

Chapter Twenty Five

Will realised his silence must be hurting her, but he really had no idea what to say. He'd no recollection of the woman in front of him. Nor did he want any. Sarah said she was his girlfriend. He'd almost laughed out loud at the word. He might have lost his memory, but he doubted much had changed about his character in the last five years. He'd never been good at talking to lasses – certainly not one as pretty as this one – and he'd never had a girlfriend. Not even Moira had been his girlfriend. Moira – she was the biggest problem. He loved her. And while he accepted she was dead, he couldn't accept that he'd betray her memory. But he must have, because the proof was in front of him. This woman, Alison, she represented his betrayal.

He should have questions to ask, things he should want to know, but there was nothing. All he wanted was for her to go, so he could ask Moira's forgiveness. He had no idea, though, how to ask her to leave. So he closed his eyes instead. He really couldn't face looking into her eyes.

"Would you like to know how you met?" Sarah asked.

No, he thought. I don't want to know. It wouldn't change anything.

"It was so romantic. You rescued her during the snow storm. Well, you and Winston did," Sarah carried on.

Winston, he thought. Somebody else he didn't know.

"Winston's one of your dogs, Will. You work together with the search and rescue team." His eyes opened at the sound of her voice. It was the voice that had read to him while he was in a coma. He realised he had to say something. It would be wrong not to acknowledge her at all.

"It's lucky we were able to help." His voice was dull, devoid of emotion.

"It was. I'd have died without you. We were cut off at the farm for days," Alison explained.

"It must have been a bad storm." His voice remained flat and emotionless.

Alison wasn't sure what scared her most, the tone of his voice or the look in his eyes. The look in his eyes she decided. When he'd been unconscious she'd thought him a stranger because she couldn't read his expression. Now he was a stranger because she could read them – and there was nothing there. No sign of recognition, no emotion, no life and it frightened her.

He might be showing no emotion but he was waiting for her reply.

"Yes, the roads have only just really cleared."

"Only just cleared... so we've only just met," he said.

"Yes, only three weeks ago."

"Right," he said and lapsed back into silence again.

"You took Alison to The Spotted Teapot café, just like you used to take me when I was younger."

"Did I?" It was impossible to miss the lack of interest in his voice this time.

"Sarah and I went out to the farm the day before yesterday. Mike and Stu, the lads you employ, they're looking after everything really well," Alison said, trying to move the conversation on.

"Mike and Stu, two more names I don't know." Frustration laced his words.

"I know it's hard, Will, but maybe if we tell you about things that are happening in your life, it will trigger a memory," Sarah said.

"I'm sorry, Sarah. It's just so damn hard. I'm in mourning for my wife and you present me with a girlfriend. I can't do this... I can't, not now." He closed his eyes.

Alison stood shakily. She had to go, this was just making things worse for Will.

"Where are you going, Alison?" Sarah asked, seeing her stand and walk to the door.

"My being here is hurting Will, something I would never do. I'm going to go, but with your permission, Will, I'd like to come back every day and spend half an hour talking about what we have shared since we met. Sarah's right, by talking to you, we may trigger your memory."

He supposed he owed her that much.

"I guess that would be ok," he said without looking at her.

She left then, blindly hurrying along the corridor, and bumped straight into Mr Chappell.

"Ms Robinson, are you ok?"

"Why wouldn't I be? The man I love doesn't even remember me - doesn't want to be in the same room as me. But it's no reason to be upset."

"That bad."

"I'm sorry, you're not to blame."

"Look, my office is just here. Come in and sit down for a moment. I'd like to talk to you."

He opened the door and led her in. His secretary was sat at a desk.

"Joyce, would you mind making us some coffee?" he said, as he led her through to his office.

Alison watched as the efficient Joyce poured two cups of coffee from a machine in the corner of the office.

"What is it about you medical bods and offering drinks to relatives?" she asked when Joyce placed the coffee in front of her.

Mr Chappell smiled.

"I think it stems from the need to give some physical sign of reassurance without being emotionally involved. Offering a drink is a visible way of helping."

"Yes, you can't get emotionally involved," Alison remarked somewhat bitterly.

"No, we can't. If we did, we couldn't function," he replied.

She regarded him for a moment.

"Yet you ask us to hold our emotions in check so we don't upset the patient."

"You think I ask the impossible?"

"Yes, I do. We're not trained like you."

"No, I suppose not. I wanted to apologise for not realising that Will wouldn't remember you. It was a bad miss on my part."

"Why does everybody say that? I'm not the patient?"

"No, but we have to look after family and friends as well. You will need support. I take it the visit didn't go well?"

"No, it didn't. I hurt Will more by being there," she sighed. "We have agreed that I will visit just once a day for now."

A worried frown crossed the surgeon's face.

"I've seen it before, a loved one not remembered or treated with complete indifference; it doesn't make it easier to watch. So much for keeping my emotions under control," he said with a wry smile.

"Well, I suppose you can't be without your emotions all the time."

"No. In this situation, Ms Robinson, all you can do is wait. I know that's easy for me to say."

"What am I waiting for, Mr Chappell?"

"Well, I guess either till he regains his memory or accepts his condition and that you were a part of his life."

She sipped her coffee.

"You forgot one other scenario."

"I did?" He looked at her carefully.

"Yes. What about waiting for him to tell me to leave for good? That, whatever we had has gone and he doesn't want it back."

"I won't lie and say that doesn't happen."

"And when it does, what then?"

"I guess you cry a little and then move on. Listen, Ms Robinson, if that does happen, and I'm not saying it will, you will be strong enough to deal with it. I have seen that strength every day since you have been here. In the meantime, take it one day at a time."

She finished the coffee.

"I'll have to, it's not as if I have much choice. Mr Chappell, I haven't said it enough, but thank you. You really do a difficult job fantastically well."

She stood up to leave.

"And by the way, never let your secretary go. Out of all the meaningless cups of coffee I've been offered in this past week, yours was the only one that was really drinkable."

****

Nobody could say that she was a quitter. She went to the hospital every day just as she said she would. It was a month after the accident and, physically, Will was progressing well.

He was now on a rehabilitation ward and he could walk, wash and dress independently. Psychologically, things were not so good. He was prone to periods of deep depression and he was constantly frustrated by the lack of progress with his memory.

Sarah was gearing up for his discharge home and they all hoped the familiar surroundings of the farm might trigger something. Sarah, the physiotherapist and occupational therapist had taken Will on a home visit. She'd offered to go with them but Will hadn't wanted that.

It hadn't hurt that he'd not wanted her there. She was beyond being hurt. After the first week of her daily visits to him, numbness had settled over her, like a protective shell. She hadn't felt anything since. She was existing in a strange limbo land where everything that was real and meaningful was just out of reach. She could see it but not have it.

She stood for a second, gazing at the hospital entrance. It would be strange not to come back here once Will was discharged. She could have walked to his ward blind folded, she had made this journey so many times. She pushed open the door to the ward and walked the short distance to Will's bed. Sometimes Sarah and Brian would be there but today he was alone. He's too thin, she thought. She wanted to reach out and touch him, but knowing that it would not be welcome she just sat at his side. The other bed in the room was unoccupied and so it was just the two of them.

"Hi, Will. How are you today?"

He looked up from the book he was reading and sighed. Was the woman a glutton for punishment? Every day he treated her with complete indifference, but still she turned up like the proverbial bad penny.

Alison would have to be blind not to see the expression in his eyes. He didn't want her here. She brushed it aside and listened to his reply.

"I'm ok, thank you. I expect Sarah has told you that the home visit went well. I can go home tomorrow."

"Yes, she did say the visit went well. Apparently, Winston wouldn't leave your side the whole of the time you were there."

"No, no, he wouldn't." He smiled fleetingly. "He seems like a great dog."

"Yeah, he is. You don't remember, I know, but he stayed with me until you came and found me. I have never been so glad to see anything so much in all my life as your dog."

"I'm glad we could help."

Alison realised that his words were meaningless - he was just being polite; he wasn't glad at all. If he were honest, he probably wished the whole event had never happened.

"And Mike and Stu, did you see them?" she said moving on.

"Yes, they're keeping things ticking over at the farm. They're good lads."

"You must have seen all the changes you made at the farm," she said.

"Yeah, I didn't recognise the place." Frustration crept into the flat tone.

"You should be proud of what you've achieved," Alison told him.

"Should I?" he said softly.

"Yes, I remember the tone in your voice and expression on your face when you explained how you took the lads on, gave them a sense of purpose. And then there's the home you're creating. What you are doing out there is beautiful and inspiring. So, yes, you should be proud."

"What's the point, when I have nobody to share it with?" The moment he said the words he realised the hurt they would cause but he couldn't retract them. He didn't want to retract them.

Alison looked at him carefully, refusing to let his words penetrate her protective shield. He flinched and looked away.

"No, Will, don't turn away. You will look at me while I speak to you. I am tired of talking to the back of your head. At least extend me the courtesy of facing me."

Shocked at the tone she used, he turned to look at her.

"Even taking me and our plans out of the equation, you have Sarah to share your home with."

"Sarah is growing up and moving on. I should be sharing my home with Moira."

"Moira died, Will, and that was tragic..."

"Don't you dare speak of Moira! You didn't know her. I loved her - she was my whole life. I wake up and discover she's dead and everybody expects me to forget her in a second. Well, I can't. I won't."

"Will..."

"No, it's time for me to say what I want. I'm sick of doing what everybody else tells me to. I agreed to your coming to talk to me, Alison, in the hope I could remember you. But it's been a month and there's nothing. Do you know why? Because I don't want there to be anything. I look at you and I feel disgusted – disgusted that I would cheat on Moira. At home, yesterday, there was nothing of her. Your things were where hers should have been. God, it made me so angry. I want them gone. I want you gone. Do you understand me? Get out of my life, you don't belong in it."

"Will!" Sarah froze in the doorway.

Alison stood slowly.

"It's ok, Sarah. This has been coming." She turned to look at him. "I shall never forget you, Will Barnes, and I am more sorry than you will ever know to have caused you pain. Before we made love..." She smiled wryly at the shocked look on his face. "Yes, we made love... before the first time, you asked me to be sure that I would have no regrets. Well, I don't, Will. If you remember nothing else about me, remember that I didn't regret you, not for a second."

"Alison..." Sarah moved towards her.

"Don't, Sarah, please. This is for the best. I'll go back to the farm now and move my clothes. It will be too late to leave Yorkshire so I'll book into the hotel in Hebden Bridge and then head back to my parents tomorrow. I'll ring you, Sarah, to let you know I got home safely."

She turned for a final time to face Will.

"Goodbye, Will." She bent over and brushed a kiss on his lips and then walked out of the hospital.

****

She'd never know how she managed to get out to the farm and collect her things without falling apart. She wandered aimlessly around Leeds for a while before she realised she was just prevaricating and rang Ben Chambers and asked him for a lift.

Mike and Stu were nowhere to be seen and for that she was grateful; the fewer people she saw the better. They must have the dogs with them and she was glad about that too. Seeing Winston would be too much to bear.

She wanted to remove her belongings quickly, but it was as though her brain was dictating that she should move slowly so she could take in all the details of a home she'd come to love. Every room in the farmhouse held a special memory and she found herself touching things as she moved from room to room, as if to physically imprint them on her memory.

Will's bedroom was particularly hard and in there she didn't linger. She just gathered her clothes and returned back downstairs.

"Are you all done?" Ben asked as she reappeared in the kitchen.

"Yeah, I just have one last thing to do."

She reached into her bag and pulled out the copy of Far from the Madding Crowd she had been reading to him the day he woke from the coma. She paused to write a brief message inside the cover.

"My Darling Will,

Because you cannot remember all we shared, I will, for both of us. And, if ever there comes a time when you want to know, I will be waiting.

Love Alison xxxxx

Placing it on the table, she turned in a circle, having one last look at the place before she left, locking the door behind her. She held the key in the palm of her hand for a second before she pushed it back through the letterbox.

She didn't speak to Ben on the way to Hebden Bridge. She just sat with her eyes closed, willing herself to hold it together until she reached her hotel room. Occasionally, she peeked out from under her lashes at Ben as he drove along. She wasn't fooling him, with her I'm alright act, not for a moment. His face was tense and lines of worry creased his brow.

The journey to Hebden was over quickly and they were soon pulling up in the car park of the hotel.

"Alison, before we get out, there's something I have to say... No, don't interrupt me. For what it's worth, I think Will is a fool. You were the best thing to ever happen to him. I'm sorry you feel you have to leave and I really hope that in time he remembers you and that it's not too late."

"Don't judge him too harshly, Ben. And promise me that you will remain his friend. It will ease my pain to know he has a friend here in Yorkshire."

"Aye, lass, I will."

He helped her carry her bags to the hotel and then left her alone.

Once she was up in her room, she picked up the phone.

"Room service? Can you please send a bottle of scotch up to room twelve?"

The pain that she'd held at bay for so many days now threatened to consume her. She hoped the alcohol would act as an analgesic. She was trembling and the knock on the door made her jump violently. She opened the door and took the bottle from the man on the other side, mumbling her thanks before shutting the door quietly.

She fumbled with the bottle top, as she was trembling so much, and some of the scotch spilt as she poured it into the glass. She tossed the first shot down in one go, eager for it to burn a trail to her stomach and numb the pain. It didn't help so she tried a second measure. But, although she got the fiery kick, the pain still remained.

She was rocking now, as if the motion might move the pain on. The wetness of tears falling on her hands made her realise she was crying. It was as if her heart had shattered into a thousand pieces. If somebody had told her, she wouldn't have believed it possible to feel such pain and still be alive. She'd broken down then, crying noisily. Her body convulsed with pain – one moment curled in a ball and the next thrashing about, angry at the world and everybody in it. How long she cried for she wasn't really sure but it was dark when she headed through to the bathroom. God, she looked a mess. Her normally golden skin was parchment white. Dark circles ringed her eyes and her hair was a tangled mess. Her throat was raw and she drank a glass of water to ease its soreness. Her body ached and so she stripped off and stood beneath the hot spray from the shower; but this brought memories of its own and soon tears were falling again. She slid down the shower wall, her legs unable to hold her and sat huddled on the floor until the shower turned cold.

Eventually, when the cold penetrated, she struggled shakily to her feet and got dried. Returning to the bedroom, she poured another glass of scotch, this time to warm her up, and then crawled beneath the blankets, eventually falling into a fitful sleep several hours later.

The next morning she checked out and climbed into the hire car her insurance company had arranged and drove away from Yorkshire. And away from Will.

Chapter Twenty Six

It was good, Will decided, to be keeping busy. It was six months since his accident and he was physically at least back to normal. The spring lambs were ready to be weaned from the ewes and they were being moved on to fresh, new pasture. Mike, Stu and a new boy, Pete, were separating them from their mothers. The men's banter and laughter was ringing in the air and the dogs were bounding around, eager to help.

It had taken time, but gradually he had begun to feel at one with the land. It had not been easy. So much had changed at the farm. Changes he'd been responsible for but couldn't remember making.

He'd spent hours walking the moors, thinking of Moira. Treading the path of grief, slowly and finally the pain of her passing had eased. He'd spoken to Ben about why it had hit him so hard. The young doctor had no real answer, but he did explain that when Moira had died that he hadn't taken time to grieve properly; he'd been too busy supporting everybody else and maybe that was why he was feeling her death so keenly now.

They were being watched by two young holiday makers. He'd sat them up on the wall, out of harm's way. Every now and again his thoughts were interrupted by their questions. It was odd – around young children he wasn't self-conscious at all. If only it were as easy around adults. The boys' parents were making their way from the cottage to where the boys were sitting and he felt tension creep into his muscles.

"I hope they're not being a nuisance, Mr Barnes."

He shook his head and muttered that they weren't.

The family were staying in one of the holiday cottages. That had been a surprise. He owned holiday cottages. He'd realised at once that an old barn had been converted. Sarah had explained how the income from the cottages was being ploughed back into the farm.

He'd had one of the few memory flashes he'd experienced while being shown the cottages. It had been of him and Sarah painting the walls, laughing at how she had got more on her than the wall.

Winston bounded over to Will, eager to be introduced to the newcomers.

"Mam, this is Winston. And besides his work on the farm he's a search and rescue dog. During the bad weather before Christmas last year he rescued a woman from the snow. He's a real hero, isn't he, Mr Barnes?" the younger of the two boys said.

"Aye, he is," Will said, wondering which of the farmhands had told the young boy that. For it certainly hadn't been him.

"Well, I think you've bothered Mr Barnes enough today. Say 'thank you'. We have to get going if we're going to the castle."

"Thanks, Mr Barnes. Can we come back and see Bess, Drake and Winston later?"

"I guess, so long as they're not working."

They headed off amid the sound of cheers and laughter, promising to come back later.

"You're awfully good with them, you know?"

Will turned at the sound of Sarah's voice.

"Am I?"

"Yes, you should have kids of your own."

He raised his eyebrows.

"Like that's going to happen."

She looked at him, sternly. He knew she was thinking that he'd had the chance of that with Alison. God, she'd been angry with him the last day at the hospital, demanding to know where he got off being so cruel.

He'd told her that it was being cruel to be kind. Far better to cut her loose than give her false hope. She told him that was complete bollocks and that he was just being cruel.

"Are you and Brian going to see her this weekend?"

He laughed at her shocked expression.

"Did you think I didn't know you were still seeing her?"

"I thought we'd kept it quiet."

"I hear you and Brian discussing it and sometimes when I walk in the room the conversation stops suddenly. There are also the train tickets to Bath that you leave lying around."

"I'm not going to apologise for seeing her, Will. When you were in a coma she was like the big sister I never had."

"I'm not asking you to apologise. I just don't want either of you getting your hopes up that I'm going to want to see her again."

"Oh, don't flatter yourself, Will Barnes. You're not that irresistible."

He smiled.

"Aren't I?"

"No, you're not. And, in any case, happen you'll have to see her next week."

"Next week?"

"At the trial. She's being called to give evidence. The barrister told us, do you remember?"

He remembered alright. Ever since he'd found out she'd be giving evidence he'd been trying to think of a way he could avoid being in court.

"Of course I remember, Sarah."

"And have you remembered the charity quiz down at t'Fleece tonight?"

"Yes, but that doesn't mean I want to go," he grumbled.

"There's no reason why you shouldn't. It's been ok in there since I put them straight on a few things, hasn't it?"

Will smiled. Put them straight. She'd done more than that. She'd been like a hellcat. He'd been out of hospital about a month when she'd announced they were going down to the pub for a drink. He'd no desire to go down there but she'd insisted. It was time, she said, to set the town right about a few things. Protests from him had been brushed aside. He was too good a man to be the subject of such malicious lies, she'd told him. He'd hugged her close. This was a secret they had shared since Moira's death; her suicide note had explained everything and he didn't want Sarah to feel that she had to say anything, especially not for him.

"It's not for you, not really," she'd said." I need to do this for me. Once it's out in the open then I can finally move on. The only thing I ask is that you are with me when I tell everybody."

"You don't even have to ask, Sarah. Of course I will be."

The landlord had greeted them the moment they had gone into the pub.

"Will, lad, it's grand to see you back on your feet."

"No bloody thanks to you, seeing as it were your filthy gossip that put him in the hospital," Sarah said loudly.

The landlord went red and stammered that he didn't understand.

"Speculating, weren't you, with the bastard who attacked him? Spreading dirty rumours about Will, making Robinson think that Will was a rapist and a paedophile. That's what he called him before he smashed his head in with a brick. Is that what you all think? Is that why, whenever Will comes into town, he's treated like a leper?" She turned in a circle, looking at everybody, making sure she had the attention of the whole bar before she continued. "Will didn't rape Moira; he isn't me biological father."

Murmurs went around the bar. "Myles Bishop was. And before you call me mam a trollop or a whore you'd best understand this: she loved Myles. If it weren't for her dad dying things might have been different. But he did die and she was taken away. When she came back, after her mam died, Myles were married to somebody else. He was a weak man, Myles. He didn't want me. He only wanted Moira. To start with, she didn't want that and so she married a man she knew loved her – Will. You know the rest. Moira and Myles, they needed each other but they didn't feel they could be together, not in this world at any rate. So they killed themselves.

Will picked up the pieces, helped me rebuild me life and turned a debt ridden, poverty stricken farm into a thriving business and, more importantly, a home. Something I'd never had. I won't acknowledge Myles as me Dad. The only Dad I've ever known is Will. And it's thanks to him I'm the woman I am today. All of you'd best stop your gossiping and leave Will alone. He's way out of your league.

Thanks to this malicious tittle tattle, Will suffered a severe head injury and has lost more than you will ever know. It'd be tempting to leave

Hebden Bridge but why should we? Highcroft has been in Will's family for years. We want to move on, put this behind us. I know the gossip is fuelled by just a few and I'm not one to bear a grudge so we're going to buy a drink and sit in that corner and enjoy a quiet evening. Stop by and say 'hi'. We'd like that."

She'd been trembling when she'd finished. Brian had told her to go with Will and sit down, that he'd get the drinks. Of course, the gossip had abounded for a while, but, within a month, it had settled down and the town had gathered to help, especially when the first lambs were born.

He still wasn't comfortable socialising. It was so damn difficult. In a small community like this, people were always talking about things from the past and, if it was in the past five years, he hadn't a clue. They would suddenly remember he had no memory and get all embarrassed. It was easier to stay here at the farm, but Sarah would never let him.

"Will, you've gone awfully quiet on me. You're not gonna back out on me, are you?"

"No, I'll go."

She smiled, relieved.

"So, what time is Brian arriving today?" he asked.

"About three o'clock." She glanced at her watch. "God, is that the time? I have to tidy my room and change the sheets on the bed and take a blanket off. After all, I'll have Brian to keep me warm."

Will felt himself blush. That was one of the hardest things to adjust to. Sarah was a grown woman but he still had to remind himself that she wasn't thirteen, especially when she was sharing a bedroom with Brian.

"That is too much information, young lady. I'm your dad, remember."

Yes, Sarah thought, and I thank God every day that you are.

Brian arrived an hour later. Will liked him – it was impossible not to. They were as different as chalk and cheese. Brian was urbane and outgoing while he was quiet and withdrawn but, unlikely as it was, they'd hit it off. In the early days of his recovery, he'd spent hours with the young man, either talking about global events of the past five years that he'd missed, or playing chess or backgammon. He'd also rolled his sleeves up and helped around the farm and was deeply interested in the rare breeds that Will was introducing. But the thing that had impressed him most was how he'd taken the news of Sarah's birth and her parent's death.

People could be judgemental about such things, Will knew that first hand, but Brian had been wonderful. After Sarah had told him, he'd simply held her in his arms.

"Some parents," he told her, "some parents do their utmost to fuck their kids' lives up. I'm sorry that you lost your mum so early in your life and that the man who fathered you was so weak and pathetic. Sorry that this town has treated you badly because of your birth. But none of those things matters to me. What I mean is that it doesn't change what I feel about you. If anything, it makes me love you more."

Yes, Will thought as the young man came towards him, Brian was good for Sarah.

Despite Will's anxiety, they went to the pub that night.

"So, what time are you two leaving for Bath tomorrow?" Will asked after the quiz had finished.

"You finally told him?" Brian said, pleased. He'd hated the clandestine nature of the trips to see Alison.

"Not exactly," Sarah confessed. "He's known all along."

The shocked look on Brian's face made him laugh.

"Neither of you should think about becoming spies – you're both useless at subterfuge. So, what time and when are you coming back?"

"We're leaving here at about eleven and then we're all travelling back up on Sunday, ready for the trial Monday. Alison has booked into a hotel in Leeds." Seeing the uncomfortable look on Will's face, she hurried to reassure him. "Don't worry, not the same one we're going to be staying in."

He nodded. He was dreading the trial. His barrister wasn't going to call him to give evidence. What would be the point? He still had no memory of the accident. It was strange. The pain he always felt when he thought about his memory loss was less intense now. It normally made him so angry and frustrated but, sitting there in the pub, he realised that it was futile wasting energy on trying to gain those years back and, by trying to, he was in danger of wasting the rest of his life. The trial, no matter what the outcome was, had to be the *start* of the rest of his life.

****

Alison was fastening her briefcase when her headmaster came into her classroom.

"I'm glad I caught you before you left, Alison."

"If you've come to try and persuade me to stay on after the end of term... again, the answer is the same as the last time you asked me." She glanced at her watch. "Which, Mr Collins, was only two and a half hours ago... No."

Matthew Collins smiled at his head of English.

"It's my prerogative... no, duty, to ask you to stay. It's demeaning, I know, for me to sink as low as begging, but needs must. However, that is not why I'm here. I came to wish you good luck for next week."

"Thank you. It seems so strange. As if it's not my life, but an episode of Eastenders or Emmerdale that I've fallen into. I never imagined that violence such as this would ever touch my life."

"No, I don't suppose any of us expect that. How will you feel about seeing him again?"

"Who, Rob? It isn't him I'm worried about seeing. He doesn't have the power to hurt me anymore. The divorce is final and I've changed my name back to Marshall. In short, I'm done with him."

"So, who is it you're worried about seeing?"

"Sorry?"

"You said it wasn't Rob you were worried about seeing. So it must be somebody else."

"I forgot how well you listen. I should have known you'd pick up on that. It's Will Barnes that I'm worried about seeing."

"I thought you were in contact with him?"

"No, I haven't seen him since December when he was discharged from hospital. He asked me to leave. I've kept in touch with his stepdaughter."

"Obviously there's more to what happened between you and him than a simple rescue."

"There was, but that's in the past. There's no point in thinking 'what if'."

"So, why take up a teaching post in Yorkshire?"

"I fell in love with more than a man. It's a beautiful part of the country. I wasn't really looking for a new job. It just came along and, the next thing I knew, I was being interviewed. Is it the right thing to do? I don't know. All I know is, I have to do this. I want peace and I haven't found it here."

"I hope you find it as well, Alison."

"So do I." She glanced at her watch. "I have to get going. I'm picking up Sarah and Brian at the station. I'll speak to you Monday and let you know what's happening."

"Ok, take care and try to have a relaxing weekend. I suspect you'll need it."

****

The station was crowded and it took a few minutes for her to spot Sarah and Brian. It was strange that, despite the 15 year age gap, they had become good friends and she really looked forward to the young couple's visits. Waving to them, she moved forward to meet them.

"How was the journey?"

"Awful. The train was really crowded. Is something going on this weekend?" Sarah asked.

"Yes, there's a big Jane Austen festival here this weekend. I thought, if you liked, we could catch some of the events."

"I'd have stayed with Will, if I'd have known this was going to be a Mr Darcy love fest," Brian teased.

"It's not. It's a Sense and Sensibility fest. I have tickets for a performance tomorrow night."

"Yes, that sounds great. I think you're quite like Edward Ferrars, Brian," Sarah said.

"I suppose he's the boring, annoyingly good one?"

Alison linked arms with them both.

"He is but he gets the girl, so that's ok," she told him smiling.

The journey to Alison's rented house didn't take long.

"I'll put the kettle on, while you take your things upstairs."

She was pottering in the kitchen when they reappeared.

"So," she said, turning as they entered. "Where does Will think you are this weekend?"

"He knows that we're here with you," Sarah said.

"Really!"

"He has apparently always known. We're not nearly as good at being secretive as we think we are."

"And what does he think of you being in touch with me?"

"He's worried that we're both hoping that he'll change his mind about meeting you."

Alison went silent, pouring the tea as she thought about Sarah's words.

"I hope you know that I've kept in touch with you because of you, Sarah, not Will."

"I do know that and I told Will as much."

She nodded.

"I have news. It doesn't change anything about how I feel about Will and what I expect from him, but I've been offered and have accepted a new job, as head of the English department at Brighouse High School, near Halifax."

"I take it you mean Halifax, Yorkshire, not Nova Scotia," Brian said.

"I do."

"Is that wise, Alison? Won't you be opening yourself up to more hurt?" Sarah asked.

"Possibly. But I'm not happy here. When I headed up north for the interview it was as though I was going home. I don't know, I felt at peace."

"I hope it works out for you then. If it's what you want. And you'll be close enough for me to visit when I'm at university. We can go clubbing."

"Clubbing! I'm not sure about that. That's enough about me anyway. How are your plans for the summer going? Are you still going to back pack around Europe?"

"Yes, we are. We leave on June the first," Brian said firmly.

"That tone brooks no arguments," Alison commented.

"No, both him and Will are bullying me on this," Sarah said.

"No, that's not it. Will wants you to live your life and stop treating him like a child. He had a head injury and has recovered," Brian said patiently.

"But he hasn't. He still has next to no memory of the last five years," Sarah said.

"No, he hasn't. But he's accepted it and wants to move on. Sorry, Alison, if that's harsh."

"It's not harsh, Brian. It's realistic. He's right, Sarah, you have to move on. We all do. I'm hoping the trial will allow us to."

Sarah sighed.

"I know you're right. Talking of the trial, are you ready for it?"

"As ready as I'll ever be. I'm anxious, but the barrister tells me I have nothing to worry about. To be honest, I just want it over."

"Well, it will be soon. Let's forget about it until Sunday and enjoy the weekend," Sarah said.

Alison nodded her head, but she knew she couldn't forget it. This trial was basically her word against Rob's. All she could hope was that she was strong enough to see it through, for Will's sake as much as for her own.

The weekend passed quickly; it always did when Brian and Sarah visited. But this time, instead of driving them to the station, they drove north to Yorkshire. Sarah had explained they were staying in a different hotel to her.

"I'm sorry, Alison, Will wouldn't be comfortable staying in the same hotel as you."

"Hey, no apology necessary. I'll drop you first and then go on to my hotel."

"Thanks. Will was going to drive himself to Leeds, so I said we'd meet him there. "

It took five hours to reach Yorkshire. It amazed Alison, as it did every time she had made this trip, how she had last November driven so far in the snow without any idea where she was going. She pulled in at Sarah and Brian's hotel.

"Will you be ok?" Sarah asked.

"I'll be fine, don't worry."

"Promise to ring me later?"

"Alright, I'll phone later. Now go on in. Will's waiting for you."

She watched them go into the hotel and then drove off to her own – off to wait alone for tomorrow to arrive.

Chapter Twenty Seven

Alison felt slightly sick, caused, she supposed, by the inevitable nerves. She was glad that they'd parked a little bit away from court house, as the walk was helping her to calm down. Her parents had arrived first thing that morning and were walking either side of her. The barrister had told her he'd meet her in the reception area, just inside the main doors of the combined court centre. She wasn't sure what she was more nervous about: giving evidence or seeing Will again. Logically, it should be giving evidence, but it wasn't.

They were approaching the court centre, a modern brick built complex, and the nausea became worse. Alison could see some steps leading up to a glass entrance way. She stopped and looked up at the door.

Seeing her dad starting to climb the stairs, she called for him to stop.

"Dad, just give me a minute. I need to collect my thoughts."

"Take as long as you like, sweetheart," her dad said quietly.

How does this work, she wondered? Would Will be there? Waiting just the other side of the door? Or would she not see him until she was called in to give evidence? It was the not knowing that was unsettling her. Taking a deep breath, she decided to prepare herself mentally for him being on the other side of the door.

"Ok, I'm ready."

There were eight steps leading up to the entrance way; Alison counted them silently as she climbed them. Her hand trembled slightly as she placed it on the glass of the revolving door to push it open.

"Are you ok, darling," her mum asked.

"I'll be ok, once I've seen him. I can't put it off any longer, mum. Let's go."

Her legs felt like jelly. Alison was certain everybody must be able to see them shaking. She came to a standstill, almost as soon as she came out of the revolving door. Will was stood fifty feet away. He was with Sarah and Brian, talking to a man she recognised as Mr Watson, the barrister. Will looked as though he'd lost weight, but maybe it was the suit he was wearing that made him appear thinner. He was facing slightly away from her so he didn't see her entrance. Had it really been six months since she'd seen him? Faced with him, the months just fell away. It was as if they'd never been apart. She wanted to move towards him, to take his hand in hers and feel his fingers curl around hers. But she didn't move – not a muscle. It would not be welcomed.

Brian saw her first and he placed his hand on the barrister's arm and indicated that she was there. She waited for Will to turn and face her. It took a moment or two and she wondered if he, like she had, was mentally preparing himself. When he did turn, there was no big Hollywood revelation scene. She hadn't expected one. He still had no memory of her. Instead, he offered a small, polite smile but made no attempt to move towards her. Sarah waved but she didn't come over. Alison understood that her place, today, was at Will's side. The barrister said something to them and then he walked over to Alison.

"Good morning, Miss Marshall. Are you ok?"

"Well, not ok as such, but better than I thought I'd be. How are Will and his family holding up?"

"Understandably, they're anxious. They are as keen as you are to put this behind them. Mr Barnes feels guilty that he cannot give evidence, but, as I explained, the fact that he can't because of the head injury, is evidence enough that he was the victim of a brutal attack. Have my clerk and the solicitor explained court procedure?"

"Yes, Mr Ross has gone through things. I know that I'll be waiting on my own until I'm called to give evidence."

"That's right, but hopefully it won't be too long. I have to get a move on. Just remember what we discussed in my chambers and you'll be fine." He shook her hand and then disappeared in the direction that Will, Sarah and Brian had gone.

Alison watched him go, thinking it was fine for him to say she'd be alright, he wasn't going to be the one in the witness box.

Once she had reported in, she was shown by an usher to a small ante room to wait. They'd hoped she wouldn't have to wait for very long but, having never been in court before, she had no idea what they classed as a long wait. To her, it seemed interminable.

The room she was in was small, little bigger than a cupboard, and airless. The walls were blank, save for the no smoking sign. There wasn't even a clock – not that she needed one; she was glancing at her watch every five minutes or so. Her parents kept the conversation going but she barely joined in. She was too busy going over what would happen in court. It was odd, given that she was thinking about going in to give evidence, that she was startled by the door opening and an usher telling her they were waiting for her.

She stood slowly and, stopping only briefly to hug her parents, she followed the usher into the court.

****

Not comfortable with being the centre of attention, Will had always been a keen observer and here in court it was no different. When they had first entered the court, the thing that had struck him immediately was how clean everything was. The scents of beeswax furniture polish and carpet freshener hung in the air. The wood of the benches, dock, witness stand and chairs all shone. The windows gleamed and, where the rays of the sun beamed in, no dust motes hung in the air. Sterile, it had all seemed so sterile. That was until other people entered the court. He'd observed them all. The other players, as he thought of them – the barristers, the judge, members of the jury and the public. Now, while they waited for Alison to take the stand, he found himself studying Stephen Robinson closely and what he saw was a stranger. He'd anticipated that.

After all, he'd no memory of the attack. He had, though, expected to feel something – anger, pity, shame even – but he didn't. In some way he was disassociated from everything, as if he was watching a play or film.

Stephen Robinson made no eye contact with him. He'd probably been advised not to. Will was struck by how sophisticated he looked. Which begged the question: why had such a sophisticated man carried out such a violent attack? Or had he, as his solicitor maintained, acted in self-defence? He trembled slightly. Had he attacked this man first? Sarah must have felt his shiver, for he suddenly became aware of her hand touching his.

The door opened suddenly and Will turned his head to watch Alison Marshall enter the court. Just as he had been, when he first saw her in his hospital room, he was struck by how pretty she was. Pretty and very different from the woman he'd ordered to leave. She was stronger, calmer and more self-composed. Gone were the casual jeans and jumper and in their place she wore a smart, navy blue suit. He wondered, as she walked slowly to the witness stand, if she was really as cool, calm and collected as she looked. No, he decided, she wasn't. But she was putting on a good act. He had no idea how he knew that. There was just something about the way she stared resolutely at his barrister, Mr Watson, and nowhere else, and most especially not at him or her ex-husband.

Her voice was quiet but calm when she took her oath. Her hand steady as she held the card from which she read the oath. Will glanced sideways at Stephen Robinson, who was anything but calm. As he had heard Alison confirm her name, his hand had curled into a tight ball and a muscle in his face had begun to twitch. He was angry. Something had happened that was unexpected. What was it? Will didn't get it until Mr Watson called her Ms Marshall. It was her name. She'd changed her name and Stephen Robinson didn't like it all. Had the jury seen his reaction, Will wondered? It certainly hadn't been one of calm sophistication.

Alison had begun giving her evidence and he turned his attention to what she was saying. It was the first time he'd heard the details of the attack. Again, it surprised him that it didn't make it seem more real. Mr Watson led her through her evidence with a great deal of skill. Her answers were complete but concise and had he been on the jury he'd have been impressed.

She was told by the judge to remain in the witness box.

The defence barrister stood up, a wry smile on his face.

"Ms Marshall, wouldn't it be true to say that you are the only witness to the fight that took place between Mr Robinson and Mr Barnes?"

"Well, Mr Richards and Mr Henderson saw the end of it."

"But not the beginning?"

"No, they didn't see the beginning."

"Now, you claim that my client attacked Mr Barnes because you wouldn't return home with him?"

"Yes, that's right."

"And why wouldn't you return home with him?"

"I was seeking a divorce from him. I'd discovered he was having an affair."

"An affair? May I ask with whom?"

"I don't know her name. I just caught them in our bed."

"Ah, so we only have your word that my client was having an affair?"

"No, that's not all. He sent me text after text begging me to forgive him."

"Ah, yes, the text messages. They don't say why he wanted your forgiveness, do they, Ms Marshall?"

"No, no they don't."

"You've told the court that you were at the farm because of being in a car accident. An accident Mr Barnes rescued you from."

"Yes, that's correct."

"And that was the only reason that you were at the farm?"

"Yes, Will kindly took me in because the roads were blocked."

"But the roads weren't blocked when my client came to get you. Were they?"

"No," Alison answered.

"No. And you had actually been to town the day before and gone back to the farm."

"That's correct."

"I don't understand. You and Mr Barnes were strangers. Why not book into a hotel?

"Will, Mr Barnes, he offered me a room until I was well enough to travel."

"Is that all he offered you?"

"What do you mean?"

"Several witnesses say that you looked very close when they saw you in town together."

"Well, we had become friends by then," Alison said, trying to remain calm. Mr Watson had warned her that the defence team would get personal.

"Just friends? Come now, Ms Marshall. It was more than that, wasn't it?"

"Yes, we had become good friends. The best I'd ever had. He'd saved my life. I'd have died had he not found me. So, something special had developed between us."

"By special you mean intimate, don't you? You and Mr Barnes were having a sexual relationship, weren't you?"

Alison was too shocked to speak.

"Answer the question." Mr King's tone was demanding.

"Your Honour, Mr King needs reminding that Ms Marshall is not on trial here and neither is Mr Barnes. Whether they were in a relationship at the time does not alter the fact that Mr Robinson attacked Mr Barnes," Mr Watson intervened.

"Your Honour, the fact that they were having an affair is relevant as I will demonstrate," Mr King explained.

"I will allow that, Mr King, but Mr Watson is right. Please remember that Ms Marshall is not on trial here."

"Of course she's not, your Honour. So, Ms Marshall, were you and Mr Barnes having a sexual relationship?"

"We were..."

"Just yes or no?"

"Yes."

"Mr Robinson claims that he confronted you over your affair and that Mr Barnes attacked him."

"No, that is not what happened. Rob attacked Mr Barnes when he asked him to leave."

"So you keep saying. But that's not true. My client was defending himself against an attack by a much bigger person. He used the brick as the only way to stop Mr Barnes."

"No, that's not what happened."

"I submit that when you realised Will Barnes was unconscious you concocted a web of lies to protect your lover and to hurt your husband."

"No, everything I've said about the fight is true."

"I don't think it is. My client discovered you had been having an affair."

"No, I'd only just met Will."

"Again, so you say. But I think that you are lying. You had come to Yorkshire to your lover and got stuck in the snow. When my client came to find you, he discovered the affair. He was attacked by Mr Barnes and had to defend himself."

"No, we'd only just met. It was Rob who had the affair, Rob who threatened me and Mr Barnes."

"Do you make a habit of having sex with men after you've just met them?"

Will was horrified. The defence council was tearing her to shreds over and over again. He stopped short of calling Alison a whore, but only just. Anger burned through him. He was sure that she didn't deserve this treatment.

"Your Honour, Ms Marshall's sexual habits are not on trial here."

"Agreed. Mr King, you will withdraw that remark."

"Sorry, your Honour."

Alison looked at the man, knowing he was anything but sorry.

"But your plan with your lover backfired, didn't it?" Mr King said.

"I didn't have a plan. Rob threatened me, both by text messages and in person. He then attacked Will," Alison said tiredly.

"Your plan was to get your husband sent to prison so you could be with Will Barnes. The amnesia was a bonus because he doesn't remember the accident. He can be portrayed as the innocent victim."

"He is the innocent victim. He didn't do anything wrong."

"That may be true. My client says Mr Barnes attacked him, but because of your lies he is on trial. You are the guilty one, aren't you, Ms Marshall?"

"I haven't lied. I've done nothing but tell the truth."

"So you keep saying. Your plan has backfired though, hasn't it? You are not with Mr Barnes anymore, are you? Why is that?"

"It didn't work out."

"It didn't work out because Mr Barnes has no memory of you, does he?"

"No, he doesn't."

"You didn't stay and fight for your lover, did you? Was that because you didn't want to be saddled with a man who was brain damaged?"

Alison felt like she'd been slapped.

"Members of the jury, you will disregard that question. Mr King, you had better conclude your questioning of the witness immediately. She's not on trial."

"That's alright, your Honour, I have no further questions."

"Mr Watson, do you have any further questions?"

"Just one or two, your Honour." He smiled reassuringly at Alison.

"Ms Marshall, the defence have made a lot of your relationship with the victim of this violent crime. It did develop quickly. Why do you think that was?"

"There were lots of reasons. Will Barnes is the kindest, most generous man I have ever met. I was emotionally battered by the knowledge of my husband's betrayal. We were stranded in the snow so things progressed differently to how they would have otherwise. I fell in love far quicker than I would normally have done."

"You fell in love with Mr Barnes?"

"I did." She looked at him for the first time. "Will is easy to love. It was new and we realised there were complications to be sorted out but we had made plans to stay together as a couple."

"Yet you are not together now?"

"No, we are not. Will has no memory of the last five years. When he came out of the coma, he still believed he was married to his wife, Moira. She had died several years ago. Will had to grieve for her all over again. I left because he asked me to. He didn't recognise or remember me. My being there was hurting him. I

love him too much to ever hurt him –
so I left."

"Thank you, Ms Marshall."

Will sat in shocked silence. He wasn't aware he was holding his breath until Sarah told him to breathe. Her simple declaration of love had stunned him. How could he not have known?

Alison sat in the canteen. The judge had asked her not to leave the court building in case they needed to speak to her again. She didn't say much; she just sat and listened to her dad rant about how disgusted he was about the way she'd been treated. She hadn't expected it to be so bad. She felt like she'd been through an emotional wringer. She could have gone back into court to listen to Rob's evidence but she didn't want to hear his lies. It was after five when the usher told them that the case had been adjourned for the day and that they could leave. The trial would resume at 10.00 a.m. tomorrow morning. Thankfully, she left the court centre and returned to her hotel.

****

Sarah watched Will push his food around his plate. He'd been awfully quiet since they'd returned from the court, and now he was brooding over his evening meal.

"Will, is something wrong with your chicken?"

"What?" He glanced at his plate. "No, it's fine."

As if to prove his point, he put a fork full of food in his mouth.

"Sarah, you know where she's staying, don't you?" he asked quietly.

"Know where who is staying?"

"Ms Marshall... Alison. I need to see her."

Sarah was almost speechless. "Why do...?"

"Please, Sarah, don't ask questions," Will said, interrupting her. "I don't know the answers. I just know that I have to see her tonight. I don't want her going to sleep before I thank her."

Sarah observed him closely.

"Before I tell you where she is, you have to promise me you're not going to hurt her. She's been hurt enough, first Rob betraying her and then you telling her to leave. And if that wasn't bad enough, there was what that bastard did to her in that court room. She's fragile, Will. She pretends to be tough but she isn't. So, if you hurt her I'll come after you with a rolling pin."

"I'm not going to hurt her," he said with sincerity.

"The Cosmopolitan Hotel. She's staying at the Cosmopolitan Hotel."

****

He had no difficulty finding a taxi and the journey took less than ten minutes. The Cosmopolitan, a large modern hotel, was the complete opposite to the charming Victorian place they were staying in. He stood outside the hotel for a few minutes, wondering what he was going to say. He really had no idea why he was even there. As he had said to Sarah, he just knew he had to see her. With that thought in mind, he walked into the hotel.

Alison put down the phone. It had been her parents checking that she was alright. She hadn't wanted to eat out with them and, while they had said they understood her need to be alone, it hadn't stopped them being concerned. She'd reassured them that she was fine and she was feeling better. The warm bath and glass of wine had eased some of the tension in her shoulders. She had slipped into her satin pyjamas and was just scanning the TV channels when she was disturbed by a knock at the door. Puzzlement at who it might be turned to shock when she opened the door and saw Will stood in the doorway.

Chapter Twenty Eight

Will's mouth went dry. God, he really hadn't thought this through. He wasn't good at making conversation at the best of times and definitely not with a beautiful woman who was stood in her night clothes. And not just any night clothes. Alison's were of some slinky material that caressed her skin and screamed: Touch me. He could feel colour staining his cheeks. She must be thinking him a complete idiot. He ran his hand through his hair. What was he doing here?

Alison's breath caught in her throat – he was blushing. Oh, how she had missed that blush. He looked so shy and unsure. As if he didn't know why he was stood at her door.

"Will?"

"I... I'm sorry, I shouldn't have come...should have called. You're ready for bed. I... I'll..."

"Why did you come?"

"I... I had to see you..." he stopped.

"Well, now you have seen me, do you just want to turn around and go?"

"I... I wanted to talk... to ask if you were alright. After today, I mean."

"Then you'd best come in, don't you think?"

"But you're… you're in your pyjamas."

"If it makes you uncomfortable, I'll get dressed again. Come on in."

Will glanced up and down the corridor.

"It's ok, we're grownups. You can come into my room or we can go down to the bar if you prefer… I'll definitely have to get dressed if we're going to do that. My satin pj's might shock them down at the bar."

Will stepped into the room. It was spacious, with a seating area as well as a bed. It was ridiculous for them to go downstairs.

"Here is fine and you don't have to get dressed…I mean, you're covered up," he said and blushed again.

"Ok, if you're sure?"

"Yes, it's ok."

"I was about to have a nightcap will you join me? Or are you driving?"

A nightcap was probably not a bad idea. He could do with some Dutch courage.

"No, I'm not driving," he said.

"What'll it be then? Whisky? Brandy?"

"Whisky'll be fine."

She opened the mini bar and poured two drinks and took them over to the seating area.

"My parents paid for this room; they wanted me to be comfortable."

"Aye, it's a right posh place," Will said, hovering by the door.

"Come and sit down, please."

He walked across and, avoiding the sofa where she was seated, he lowered himself into one of the chairs. For a moment he sat studying the floor. Alison sipped her drink and waited for him to feel comfortable enough to speak.

"What they did to you in that court room, it weren't right, lass. I'm sorry you had to go through that," Will said quietly, not lifting his eyes from the carpet.

Alison's hand trembled as she put the glass down and tears glazed her eyes – tears which she blinked rapidly away. He mustn't see how his words were affecting her. But she couldn't help being emotional – he'd called her lass. He'd called her lass! Just the way he had done when he'd rescued her.

"I'm sorry it were you who had to take the stand. It should have been me."

She reached out and took his hand in hers.

"How could you?" Alison asked puzzled.

"I don't know, but I should have found a way. I should have been able to remember the fight. Instead I sat in court like some halfwit."

"No, Will, that's not true. You were the victim of an awful crime. The jury will see that. You have to believe they will see that."

"They as good as called you a whore, lass. And I did nowt to stop 'em."

"What could you have done? Even if you could remember, they'd still have turned this into some sordid sex story. They'd have to; it's the only defence Rob has."

"But it must have hurt you... the things they said."

Alison watched as Will's thumb softly stroked her hand. How many nights had she lain awake dreaming of his touch?

"It did for a while, but then I realised I was allowing that barrister to make what we had sordid by dwelling on his words."

"Is that why you didn't come back into court?" he asked.

"Partly, and I didn't want to listen to Rob's lies. He'd have made everything about you even dirtier than the barrister. I didn't want that. You see, I know what we shared, Will, and it wasn't dirty or tawdry; it was... it was beautiful. You were beautiful."

He blushed again.

"I wish I could remember..." his voice trailed off.

All Alison could do, was stare at him.

"Sorry... I..." Now she was the one stammering.

He looked up for the first time and smiled.

"Thank you."

"Thank you for what?" she asked puzzled.

"For being as nervous as I am."

"Why are you really here, Will? Don't say it's to check that I'm ok."

"I really don't know. I saw you walk into court and saw nothing... other than a beautiful, poised woman. I felt nothing."

"Will..."

"Let me finish. I saw them hurt you. You tried to hide it and most people in that court room wouldn't have known. But I did. It was there in the depth of your eyes. I couldn't understand how I knew, I was just certain they had. Then you said you loved me. I didn't know... When I woke... you never said. Why didn't you tell me?"

"You were grieving for Moira. It wouldn't have been fair to you," she said simply.

"What about you? Was it fair to you?"

"I didn't matter."

"You should have mattered. I'm so sorry. Sorry that I can't remember you and our relationship. Is that what we had – a relationship?"

"It was what we were hoping would develop. I think that what we had was just a simple kind of love... the best kind of love."

He sighed.

"I was sat having me tea with Sarah and suddenly I just had to see you. I said I didn't know why, but now I think I do. I want to remember about us and I need you to help me."

"Why?"

"Because you said you would." He pulled out the copy of Far from the Madding Crowd.

"You read my message," she whispered.

"I did. When I first saw it, I hated you for writing it. I wanted to deny your existence. I wanted to throw the book away. But I couldn't. I read it again. In my head I heard your voice reading to me – just as you were when I woke from the coma." He smiled at her. "I never told you, did I, lass? That yours was the first voice I heard and understood when I came out of the coma."

"No, you didn't." Her eyes were bright with unshed tears.

"I'm sorry, I should have."

"No, please don't apologise." She touched a finger to his lips. "Never apologise."

"I don't know what's happening here. I don't want you to get your hopes up... about us, I mean. I don't know what future we have. But I want to know about our past."

"Well, I'm just the woman who can tell you about it." She stood and refreshed the drinks.

Once they were sitting comfortably, they chatted about how they'd met. Alison was relieved at how he relaxed and smiled when she recalled some of the silly things they'd done.

"I've never been good with girls so I don't understand how things progressed like they did," Will said puzzled.

"Well, we weren't normal from the beginning. I mean, you got me naked within minutes."

She laughed at his stunned expression.

"It was only because I was hypothermic. You had to warm me up. You even told me you hadn't looked when you undressed me."

"It's still quite a leap from first aid to being... being intimate."

Alison sighed wistfully. He was back, her shy, sexy farmer.

"Well, as Hot Chocolate said: 'It Started with a Kiss' - a totally amazing kiss."

"No, there is no way I just kissed you, I don't know how."

"Well, I will admit I may have jumped your bones but you played a very active part in the kiss."

He shook his head.

"This is so surreal. I'm finding it hard to believe that we... that we were... I... mean, that we had..."

"That we had sex? Is that what you're trying to say?" Alison asked gently.

"God, this is embarrassing."

"Yes, we did have sex."

"Did I... manage..." He paused. "Oh, why do I want to know? It will have been a disaster."

"Will, listen to me. It wasn't a disaster. It was perfect. You were perfect."

"I couldn't have been. I don't know how..."

"No, you weren't very experienced, but we had fun practising," Alison winked at him.

Will shook his head.

"It doesn't even sound like me."

"You have to remember, it was the worst winter weather on record. We were snowed in. Had we not been, things would have developed differently. More slowly, I guess. But we couldn't run from our feelings; we had to face them."

"And I would have run, for sure. Or if she'd been around, I'd have asked Sarah to look after you."

"You must be so proud of her?"

"I am. I still can't believe that she wanted to stay with me after Moira died."

"She told me you were the reason she did so well at school."

"I'm sure I didn't do owt," Will said embarrassed.

"Oh, I'm sure you did. Whatever it was, she thinks the world of you. She threatened me with a rolling pin if I ever hurt you."

"Oh, she's right fond of that threat. Before I left to come here, she said if I hurt you she'd hit me with the rolling pin."

"Will, just so you know, I don't think you'd ever hurt me."

"You're very kind, lass, but I know I did..."

"No..."

"Yes, I did, when I asked you to leave. I shouldn't have..."

"You had to do that, Will. There were things you had to learn about and accept without me around. I'd have slowed your recovery."

"You mean Moira?" Will said.

"Yes, I do. You had to mourn her and say goodbye to her and let her go. Until you had done that you couldn't move on with your life."

"I notice you don't mention yourself."

"No, that's up to you."

He nodded.

"I know that. I said that when the trial was over I'd get on with my life. I don't know if the trial will be over tomorrow but would you... maybe you'd like... we could..." He took a deep breath. "Would you like to go out todinnerwithmetomorrow?" he finished in a rush.

God, he was adorable.

"I'd love to."

"I understand if you don't want..."

"Will, I said I'd love to."

"You would!"

"Don't sound so surprised."

"Sorry, I'm no good at this."

"You're doing fine."

"I'll pick you up at seven-thirty. Is that ok?"

"Yes, that's fine."

"Maybe tomorrow, if you decide to come into court, you'd like to sit with us."

"Yeah, if I do, that would be good."

"Well, I should go. You were going to bed when I arrived three hours ago... Oh hell! I'm sorry, lass. Keeping you talking for three hours."

"It's ok, honestly."

She opened the door.

"Goodnight, Alison."

If he hadn't paused Alison wouldn't have done anything. But he did pause, as if unsure if he should say or do anything else. In that instant she reached up and brushed the lightest of kisses on his soft lips.

"Goodnight, Will."

Chapter Twenty Nine

As she often did, when she stayed in a hotel, she had lain awake for ages before she fell asleep. Only it hadn't been the strange room and hard bed that had kept her awake but thoughts of a man; a man whose sudden appearance at her hotel door had thrown her completely off balance. Mentally, she had prepared herself for meeting Will when the case against Rob came to court. She'd played it out in her mind several times and never once had she imagined he'd come to her room. Yes, Will Barnes had certainly surprised her. But more than that, he'd charmed her all over again with his shy blushes and stammering speech. She knew she shouldn't get her hopes up but it was impossible not to, especially when he called her 'lass'. And he'd asked her out to dinner, hadn't he? It was this fact that had kept her awake. Why would he do that if he wasn't thinking about trying again? She'd fallen asleep at about three o'clock, still pondering the dinner invitation.

She glanced at her reflection in the mirror. Did her lack of sleep show? Maybe a little, but the wonders of modern make-up would take care of it. Her nerves were another thing.

She had butterflies the size of elephants in her stomach. This was worse than the morning after the night before. What should she say when she saw him? How should she act? There were no rules for situations like this. He'd probably be more nervous than her, she reasoned.

At least she couldn't get worried about what to wear. Her options were limited. She'd already decided to wear a fitted, plum coloured suit before Will had arrived last night and that was what she had put on. She twisted her hair into a simple elegant twist and secured it with pins.

The first person she faced wouldn't be Will. It would be one of her parents. She was meeting them for breakfast before going to the court. She'd decided that she would do as Will had suggested and go into the public gallery and sit with him. So, she was going to have to tell her parents about Will's visit. They were waiting for her in the dining room.

"Hello, sweetheart, did you sleep well?" Her mother asked her, unknowingly giving her the opening she needed.

"Not really. Will came to see me last night," she said, pouring herself a cup of tea.

A knowing look passed between her parents.

"What is that look about?" Alison asked.

Her mum smiled serenely.

"I told your father yesterday that Will's feelings for you weren't from in the past."

"Mum, he still doesn't remember me," Alison said cautiously.

"No, I understand that. But yesterday, when you were giving evidence, I watched him a lot. He was very upset at the way you were being treated."

"Well, that is one of the reasons he came to see me – to apologise. He is so guilty that he can't give evidence."

"That's hardly his fault," her Dad said. "And the jurors all know why he isn't giving evidence. Sometimes not being able to speak is helpful."

"How do you mean?" Alison asked.

"Well, what the jurors are left with is the image presented to them of a young, hardworking man who has suffered a terrible head injury. They won't see his recovery. All they know is he's not able to give evidence because of that brain injury. It's a powerful image in their minds."

Alison nodded.

"I suppose it is."

"That's not all, Alison. The jury aren't blind. They will have seen the way Rob reacted to the questions about your relationship with Will. He tried to mask his anger but couldn't. Will spotted that as well. It might be a good idea for you to be in court while he finishes giving his testimony. He's not as cool, calm and collected as he likes to think he is," Henry Marshall said.

"Well, Will did suggest that we sit with them if I went into the court today."

"How long did he stay for?" her dad asked.

"Three hours. It was gone one when I went to bed."

"What were you talking about for three hours?" Henry asked, surprised that Will had stayed that long.

"He asked me to tell him about us. He was ready to hear about it, I suppose."

"How did that go?" her mum asked.

"Good, I think. He's invited me out to dinner tonight."

"Really? I told you..."

"Please, Mum. Don't read anything into a simple dinner. I'm not."

"No, you're right, sweetheart. Here's breakfast. I'll say no more."

****

"You need to know what?" Sarah was sure she'd slipped into a parallel universe.

"I need to know the name of a good restaurant. Somewhere classy."

"Will, you don't do classy."

"I know," he muttered, "but I bet she does."

"She? Do you mean Alison?"

Will looked embarrassed. He hadn't intended Sarah to hear that.

"Yeah, I mean Alison."

"Oh my God, you asked her out on a date!"

"It's just dinner, not a date."

"Are you going to let her pay?" Brian asked.

"No, of course not," Will said.

"Then it's a date."

"This is so great. You and Alison are going out on a date. I'm guessing that last night went really well."

"Sarah..."

"What time did you get home? It must have been late...Or perhaps it was early?" She wiggled her eyebrows suggestively.

Will blushed.

"No, I didn't stay the night. We just talked."

"About what?"

"About what happened when she was snowed in with me."

Sarah sighed.

"So you just talked. You didn't recreate any of those special moments. A kiss maybe."

Will prayed he didn't blush again. Could the soft touch that Alison had placed on his lips be classed as a kiss?

"A gentleman would never kiss and tell. Shame on you for asking, Sarah," Brian said, sensing Will's discomfort.

"Ok, I'm sorry. But this is just the best news ever."

Will sighed.

"It's just dinner. I still don't remember her. This doesn't mean we're going to get back together."

"I know that. But when you spend time with her you'll realise how wonderful she is and then, who knows?"

"Sarah, I know that's what you want but Alison and I... we both know that there may be no future for us. So, please don't get your hopes up."

"I won't, I promise. But why did you ask her out to dinner?"

"Because it got late and there was more I wanted to know. That's all." He hoped Sarah would accept that explanation. He wasn't ready to share the real reason with anybody just yet. "So, where do I take her to?"

"Brown's is supposed to be good but she might read something into going somewhere so special. I'll ask at the desk; they may know somewhere. What time did you say you'd pick her up?" Sarah said.

"Seven –thirty."

"You have your breakfast and I'll go and sort it out."

Will watched her hurry away.

"I forgot what a whirlwind she is. It's probably best that I don't tell her I asked Alison to sit with us in court."

Brian smiled.

"Yes, keep that to yourself, Will."

****

Will had to smile at Sarah's reaction to Alison and her family coming to join them in the public gallery. She'd been beside herself with excitement. She'd even arranged how they should sit, like some heroine in a Jane Austen novel, organising everybody so that the two people she wanted to get together were seated next to each other. So he found himself sitting between Sarah and Alison. He'd been introduced to Alison's parents but his shyness and the surroundings stopped him from really talking to them.

They hadn't been seated very long when Mr Watson arrived. Will wasn't sure why but there was an air of excitement surrounding him today, as if he had a secret that nobody else knew. Normally he was calm and placid, but today he was twitchy and nervous, eager for the day's proceedings to begin. Will's suspicions were confirmed when he was passed a note saying there were new developments. He wondered what they were, but before he could ask the judge appeared and the trial recommenced.

Henry Marshall had been right. Stephen Robinson hadn't liked Alison sitting next to Will in court. He'd gone puce with barely controlled rage when he'd come into court and seen them sat together. Everybody had expected the prosecution barrister, Mr Watson, to spend a lot more time cross examining Robinson, but he'd actually been quite brief. Spending a little time confirming that Alison's testimony about having fled to Yorkshire was because she'd caught him having an affair was a lie and that he'd not planned to come up and hurt her as had been suggested.

It was after Robinson had returned to the dock that the developments became apparent. Mr Watson waited for the defence to say that they rested their case and then he stood.

"Your Honour, the prosecution would like to call Claire Morris."

"Why was this witness not called before, Mr Watson?" asked the judge.

"She only came forward yesterday, Your Honour. She is here to refute testimony already given."

"I'll allow the witness."

The defence barrister was on his feet immediately.

"Sit down, Mr King; you will have the opportunity to cross examine the witness."

Will looked at Alison.

"Do you know who this woman is?" he whispered.

"No, I don't..." As the door to the court opened and a young woman entered, Alison's words faded.

Will was aware of tension creeping over Alison as she sat beside him. He turned to look at her concerned.

"Alison?"

"It's her, the woman I caught Rob in bed with."

"Are you ok? Do you want to leave or owt?" he asked quietly.

She shook her head, but was grateful when he curled his hand around hers.

Will supposed that some men would think she was a stunning woman with her sleek, ink black, glossy hair, scarlet lips and nails. But he didn't. There was something dead about her eyes, as if she had no soul. She reminded him of a scorpion and he wondered what sting she was about to deliver.

Claire Morris – such an ordinary name for the marriage wrecker she was, Alison thought. It really should be something more exotic. It was weird; she didn't want to be here in court witnessing this. She felt sick, listening to the disgusting details of the affair this woman had been having with Rob, but it was as if she had no choice but to listen.

Mr Watson was asking about the day in November when Alison had caught her having sex with her then husband.

"Yeah, it was bloody hilarious. She stood there like she was paralysed. Not that I blame her; we were putting on a hell of a show and I don't mind an audience."

Alison felt her dad's arm slip round her shoulder at the same moment as Will's hand tightened in hers, both men offering silent support as she listened to the woman's vile words.

"What did Ms Marshall, or Mrs Robinson as she was then, do when she found you?"

"Well, like I said, she watched until Rob climaxed, then she screamed and ran out. Then she got in her car and drove off."

"Did she return at all that day?"

"No, it was the first day of the big snow. Within hours the country was at a standstill. I couldn't leave and go home – the weather was so bad I had to stay with Rob."

"What was Mr Robinson's reaction to his wife finding you together?"

"Well, on the one hand he was pissed off that she'd caught him, but the thought of her watching us made him horny as hell."

The courtroom erupted as both the defence barrister and Rob jumped up shouting. It took at least five minutes for things to calm down.

"Miss Morris, could you please moderate your language in my courtroom. And, Mr King, one more outburst from your client and I will have him removed to the cells. Do I make myself clear?"

"Yes, Your Honour," Mr King muttered.

"So, Mr Robinson was angry?" Mr Watson continued.

"Yes, he was."

"Did he say what he would do when he found out where she had gone?"

"Discipline her."

Alison's mum gasped. What did she mean by discipline? The barrister was asking the same question.

"You know, tie her up, smack her about a little bit. Then have non-consensual sex. That sort of thing," she said.

Alison was trembling. It was all proving too much to take in. How could she not have known what Rob was like?

"Lass, let me take you out," Will whispered.

"No, I'm ok."

"Mr Robinson told you he was going to do this?"

"Yes, he said he'd record it so that we could screw while we watched it."

"You fucking bitch!" Rob shouted, jumping to his feet.

"Officers, restrain the prisoner and take him down to the cell," the judge ordered.

"That's what you get for ignoring me, for denying I exist, you bastard!" Claire Morris shouted back.

"The witness will be silent or she will find herself in contempt of court."

Once silence resumed the judge nodded for Mr Watson to continue.

"So, Mr Robinson discussed these threats with you?"

"Yes, and that's not all. He e-mailed me from Yorkshire to say if he found her with Will Barnes he'd teach them both a lesson."

"Do you have a copy of the e-mail?" Mr Watson asked.

"I do, yes."

"I have just one more question for you, Ms Morris. Why did you come forward today?"

"I may only be a mistress but I call the shots. He dropped me cold and nobody does that to me. Or if they do, they pay. He had to pay."

Will shuddered. The woman really wasn't normal.

"Thank you, Ms Morris." Mr Watson sat down.

"Mr King, would you care to cross examine the witness?"

"If it pleases your honour, defence counsel requests a short adjournment to discuss these developments with my client."

"Very well, we will adjourn for thirty minutes."

Chapter Thirty

Rob was found guilty. Things moved fast after Claire Morris' testimony. The defence counsel didn't question her. There would have been no point – the damage was already done. Within three hours of being asked to deliberate the case, the jury had returned a guilty verdict. Alison hadn't been jubilant, but relieved as they read out the result. The judge dismissed them and then told Rob he would be brought back in one week for sentencing, warning that he would be given the most severe punishment the law would allow.

The whole ordeal was now behind her and, although it would be a long time before she forgot the woman's chilling words, it was time to move on. Tonight was the beginning. Was she wrong to pin so much hope on one meal? No, she thought, I'm human.

Alison glanced around the Cross Keys restaurant, not at all surprised that he'd chosen somewhere traditional. The exposed brick and wooden beams were solid, dependable and homely like the man opposite. He was wearing the blue sweater that Sarah had given him. She smiled as she remembered that the last time he'd worn it she'd given him his first lesson in making love.

"You're smiling – it must be a relief to have the trial over with," Will said before sipping his pint.

"Yes, it is, but it's not why I'm smiling."

"Oh, so why were you smiling?" he asked.

"I was thinking how well suited you are to the surroundings here."

"Really? So I look like a real northerner who likes real ale and open fires?"

"I was thinking it looks solid, strong and dependable – like you."

"That makes me sound boring."

She smiled again.

"No, never boring. Have you been here before?"

"No, the hotel recommended it to Sarah, so she booked the table."

"Did she tell you to wear that jumper as well?" Alison asked softly.

"Yes, is there something wrong with it?"

"No, it's lovely, but you should know that it means Sarah is playing matchmaker."

"I know she is, but why does the jumper signal that to you."

"We have history where that jumper is concerned and Sarah knows how much I like it."

"So, I've worn it before... when we were together?" he asked, wishing he could remember.

"Well, kind of..." Alison paused, wondering how much she should say.

"Kind of. What's that mean? I don't understand."

"Well, I suppose I let you wear it for an hour before I removed it."

It was unfortunate that he'd just taken a mouthful of his beer, because her words caused him to choke.

"Is the beer not to your liking, Will?"

"The beer's fine. It was what you said that made me choke."

"Sorry, I couldn't resist," she said with a smile.

"It's alright for you, but now I have to sit through dinner, knowing that you've seen me naked," he said embarrassed.

Alison smiled again, letting her eyes travel the length of his body, from head to toe.

"Don't sweat on it. You looked mighty fine. Shall we go up to the dining room?"

"Did you talk to me like this before?" Will said as he stood.

"Yes, I did, and after a few days you talked to me in the same manner."

Will shook his head in disbelief. He just couldn't imagine ever behaving as Alison described.

The dining room of the Cross Keys was on the first floor and, as they climbed the open plan staircase, it occurred to Alison that it had been refitted recently.

"This place is wonderful," she said as they sat down. "Did you notice the name of the dining room? It's called the James Watt room. Maybe he was connected to the pub in some way."

"James Watt once hired a room within the pub for a few months. It's said it was because he wanted to spy on fellow engineer Matthew Murray and steal secrets by getting Murray's workers drunk. I'm Rosie, your waitress for the evening," said the young woman who'd showed them to their seats and was now waiting to hand them their menus.

"Wow, history and good food, what more could we ask for? Thank you," Alison said. "Tell me, has this place been renovated recently?"

"Yes, it were a wreck. It was always an inn but was closed years ago."

Will watched silently as Alison chatted with the waitress about the menu – she was so beautiful. The red dress she was wearing, though simple and demure, hinted at her curves. She'd done something different to her hair. It fell to her shoulders in spiral waves. He wasn't used to paying compliments but somehow he'd have to find the words.

Having discussed the menu with the waitress she opted for the goat's cheese salad to start and the lamb which the restaurant was apparently famous for.

"What will you have, Will?" she asked, looking up from the menu.

"I'll have the Gloucester Old Spot to start and I'll have the lamb as well, thank you." He turned to look at Alison. "Would you like some wine?"

They agreed on a bottle of Pinot Noir and the waitress nodded and disappeared.

"I'm not good at dining out, all those fancy words on the menu. I don't know what half the words mean. I only know I've ordered pork because I'm a farmer and know that a Gloucester Old Spot is a pig," Will said.

Alison smiled.

"And you're such a good cook as well."

"You know I can cook? Of course you do. Well, it was a bloody shock to me. When I went home Sarah explained I'd done all the cooking. I had to learn all over again.

Thank God for all those cookery books."

"You once told me you'd cooked us tripe because I called you Nigella."

"I hadn't, had I?" Will was horrified.

"No, but you thought it was funny telling me you had."

"Well, let's hope the food is better than tripe," he said.

"I'm sure it will be. This whole place is lovely," Alison said, looking around.

"Yes, it is. But the loveliest thing in the room is not part of the restaurant, it's you."

Alison blushed at his words, praying that they meant he was changing his mind about them.

They were eating their main course when Will asked her about what her plans were, now the trial was over.

"I always said the trial was going to be the end of that episode in my life. I've sold the house in Bath and am renting at the moment. I couldn't go back to where Rob and I lived," she said.

"I know. Once Sarah confessed she and Brian had stayed in touch with you, she told me about your new home."

"I have the rest of this week off, on special leave, and then two weeks more at school before the summer holidays."

"So you'll be going back to Bath. When will you leave? Tomorrow?" Suddenly he wasn't sure he wanted her to go.

"No, not tomorrow. I have some business to attend to in Halifax and thought I'd sort it out while I'm here."

"Business in Halifax?"

"Yes. I wondered if Sarah had said anything to you, but I can see she obviously hasn't."

Will looked puzzled.

"I've got a job in Halifax from September, as Head of English Language at a local secondary school. I'm going to look for somewhere to rent tomorrow," Alison told him.

"You're moving to Yorkshire?"

"Yes, I was interviewed at Easter."

"But Yorkshire?"

"Bath is not home. I don't think it ever was."

"I thought you'd go to Stratford. That's where your parents live, isn't it?"

"Yeah, but I can't go home to mum and dad because I screwed up my life. I have to deal with it."

He reached over and took her hand.

"You didn't screw up your life, lass... Rob did."

"I should have known what he was like. How could I not have known?"

"He presented an image. Some folks do that. You're not to blame."

"I do keep telling myself that. Maybe one day I'll believe it."

"You will, because it's the truth. So, why Halifax?" Will asked.

"Do you want an honest answer?"

Her dark eyes searched his face.

"What I mean is, can you handle the honest answer?"

"I don't know if I can, but I need you to be honest."

"I don't expect anything from you, Will. Please don't think I have done this to put some kind of pressure on you, I haven't. The job came up when I was at a real low point. I'd packed up the house, sold my half of everything. I'd no idea what I was going to do, really. So I thought: what the hell, I can't be unhappier in Yorkshire and came up here for the interview. The moment I got here I knew this was where I had to be. Even if there was never going to be any future with you. I realised that

I could still find some measure of peace up here."

"Do you honestly want a future with me?" Will asked.

"I want what makes you happy, Will. I've realised we can't have what we had before. Too much has happened. Too much has changed. Everybody knows that you're not the same but neither am I. The accident has changed us all, you the most significantly, but Sarah and I as well. If you decide you want to see me socially, it would be different and new and I'm ok with that. Equally, if you decide that you don't want to see me at all, then I think I'm strong enough to cope with it."

"I said to Sarah that when the trial was over there would be no looking back. If we do see each other again could we take things slowly?"

Alison held her breath, wondering if he was just thinking out loud or asking her a question.

"Could we, lass? Take it slowly?" he repeated.

"We can take it at any speed you like," Alison whispered.

"I've never dated anybody. I don't know what to do," Will told her.

"We're on a date tonight and you are doing just fine," she told him. "Just relax."

"I'll try. How do you like the lamb?"

"It's wonderful. Everything's wonderful."

"So what should we do for our next date then?"

"How about doing something simple, like going to the cinema? Is there a cinema in Hebden Bridge?"

"Aye, there is."

They were finishing up the coffee when they stopped talking films. Will was staggered at how easy it had been just to talk to her.

"Shall we walk back to my hotel? It can't be far. We weren't in the taxi more than five minutes on the way here," Alison said.

"Aye, if you'd like to, lass. I'll just pay t'bill."

She went to give him some money.

"No, it's alright, lass, this is my treat."

The town centre wasn't as busy as it would have been if it had been the weekend.

"Is it ok if I hold your hand, lass?" Will asked shyly as they left the restaurant.

"Oh, yes. That's a rule of dating," she said, linking hands with him.

They strolled back to the hotel, occasionally stopping to look in shop windows. She'd suggested the walk to prolong the evening but they still arrived back at her hotel all too soon.

"I'd invite you up for a nightcap but you said you wanted to take this slowly and if we go up to my room I might jump your bones," she said.

"In that case best not risk it," Will said with a smile. "Thanks for a lovely evening. 'T'were the best date I've ever had."

"I'd take that as a compliment if you hadn't told me it was the first date you'd been on," Alison said, laughing.

"True. And you can tell I've no idea how to end it."

"A kiss, is customary. But you may think, on a first date, that'd be rushing things."

Will sighed. It was so strange; she'd kissed him before and knew what to expect but he didn't. She was stood quite still but within touching distance. Leaving the next move up to him. Her perfume was intoxicating him and, throwing caution to the wind, he bent and touched his lips to hers. The kiss was soft and tentative at first, as he gently brushed first her top lip and then the bottom one. Her sigh of pleasure made him deepen the kiss and pull her close. Bathed in moonlight, they stood in each other's arms and kissed for several moments. Just when Alison thought she would dissolve at his feet, he pulled away. He touched her cheek gently.

"I should go or I'll forget my own take it slowly rule."

"Ok, thank you for a lovely evening. I'll call you tomorrow when I get to Halifax."

He kissed her one more time and walked away towards a waiting taxi.

The doorman held open the door.

"I trust you had a pleasant evening, Miss," he said, with a twinkle in his eye, as he opened the door.

"I did. It was the best night of my life, the very best."

Chapter Thirty One

Alison sighed contentedly as she drove along. Summer was coming to its end and August was slowly ebbing towards September. The days were slightly shorter and the sun seemed slightly lower in the sky. It was strange: in the city she probably wouldn't be aware of the subtle change but here, in the dales, the seasons were much more defined and autumn was just around the corner. The leaves on the trees were starting to turn gold and the spring lambs were almost fully grown. Even the light was different, depending on the time of year.

Alison knew, when she looked back in years to come, that she would think of the summer as a journey. She wasn't alone on the voyage; she had Will at her side and together they were discovering things – about themselves and each other.

Will's recovery was pretty much complete. He was working full time on the farm and the headaches that had plagued him after the accident had settled. He'd even accepted that his memory was probably never going to return. It had been a dark day when the neurologist told them. The strange thing was, before seeing the doctor, they'd discussed it and come to the conclusion it wasn't going to return, but that didn't help when the consultant told them he was certain that Will wouldn't get those years back. She even thought he might send her away again but he didn't. He'd needed a couple of days alone, to get his head around the news, but then he'd visited her again.

They'd been taking things slowly – as Will had wanted. To begin with, they'd only seen each other once a week. But that had become more frequent once she had moved to Yorkshire. They'd enjoyed exploring the delights of the dales in summer. There had been two concerts, an arts festival and several trips to the cinema. It was, she supposed, an old fashioned courtship. He'd come to dinner at the house she had rented in Hebden Bridge quite a few times but never stayed the night. Sometimes it was hard to believe that they'd ever been lovers. Not that she'd ever forget. Sometimes, when they were kissing, she'd longed to take things further but she'd agreed to take it slowly and so she was letting him set the pace. She'd learnt a couple of things about herself: firstly, she had amazing patience and secondly, cold showers didn't work.

Her patience wasn't just confined to making love. She had been desperate to visit the farm, but she hadn't wanted to just turn up there. Instead, she waited until Will invited her. And it had been a long wait. Three months had passed since the trial. His suggestion that she spend the long bank holiday weekend with him on the farm had come out of the blue. But she had jumped at the chance. Now, here she was, driving through the beautiful countryside towards Highcroft. She couldn't wait to see the farm and the animals again. She wondered if Winston would remember her and what Arwen's foal was like.

As she pulled into the farmyard, she was struck by how different everything looked, with the late afternoon sun shining on the stone walls of the farmhouse and surrounding buildings. The last time she'd been here snow still covered the ground and roof tops. Now they were bathed in late afternoon sunshine. Switching the engine off, she sat for a few moments, silently contemplating everything that had happened since she had last been here.

The sound of a dog's bark brought her out of quiet musings. Drake. She smiled at the sheep dog; he'd always been the guard dog of the three dogs Will owned. His barking must have alerted Will, as it was supposed to, because he suddenly appeared from out of the barn. God, he looked wonderful, Alison thought, compellingly masculine and rugged in his work clothes. He'd put the weight he'd lost back on and she could tell by the way his clothes clung to his body that the hard work on the farm had built up his muscle tone. It was strange how much more noticeable his size and build were today. It must be the different clothing.

She got out of the car and moved towards him, smiling, but before she could go more than a few steps she was stopped by the mad dashing about and excited barking of a smaller, younger collie. Winston. She dropped to her haunches to stroke and pat the excited animal, which was in turn trying to lick any part of her he could reach. Emotion overwhelmed her. He remembered her! Tears spiked on her lashes. She tried to brush them away but it was futile. So she gave in and let them fall unchecked.

Will didn't initially realise she was crying. He walked towards her, intent on telling the dog to calm down but, as he drew closer, he could see her tears.

"Alison, lass, are you ok?" he asked, not understanding why she was crying.

She looked up at him and smiled tremulously through her tears.

"He remembers me...I thought...I...thought I'd... never see him... again. I... didn't t-t-think I'd ever see this place again either. Oh, I need to get a grip. I must look a real state. I'm so sorry for being silly. It's just that, without Win, I wouldn't be here."

Will reached down and helped her stand up.

"You're not stupid and you don't look a state – in fact, you look wonderful," he said, using his thumbs to brush away the tears before giving her a kiss of welcome.

She knew she was supposed to be letting him take the lead and setting the pace but the moment his lips touched hers a flame ignited. She was suddenly plundering his mouth, taking more than he'd ever offered. She should stop. She'd scare him off. But, Lord knows, she couldn't.

Will was stunned. He'd no idea a kiss could be so intense. How could it be so different? There was an urgency about it that he didn't recognise – a hunger. He wanted this passion, this rawness, and it shocked him, but he was powerless to pull away – he didn't want to pull away.

Winston's frantic barking and jumping eventually penetrated the private world they'd slipped into and they pulled apart. Alison, too scared to speak or to make eye contact, stared resolutely at the ground. What had she done? She felt his finger tip under her chin and reluctantly she looked up.

"Wow." He whispered.

Wow was good, wasn't it? Alison thought, trying to judge his reaction.

"I...Lass, there are things I need to say, but I have to finish with the horses. Why don't you go on into the house and I'll be in shortly."

"Ok, I'll put the kettle on, shall I?"

"Aye, I won't be long."

****

The house was the same or at least the part he was living in was. She put her bags in Sarah's room and then, wondering if he'd done anything more to the main house, she decided to explore.

She hadn't expected there to be much change and there wasn't on the ground floor. Upstairs, though, there was a surprise; the master bedroom was not only completed but in use. She'd opened the door of the landing, expecting to see an empty room, decorated possibly, but certainly not furnished. She'd walked in before she'd considered if she should.

It was a beautiful room – bathed in sunlight, which streamed in through the long elegant sash cord windows. The intricate cornice and coving were freshly painted and the walls had been finished in golden tones. A window seat ran the length of the wall, overlooking the front of the house, and the room was furnished with beautiful solid oak furniture. Through an open door she could see a dressing room and en-suite bathroom. It was simply elegant and lovely.

She sank down onto the padded window seat and looked out over what would be a beautiful front garden, once the house was fully renovated. She smiled. It pleased her that Will had continued making the old farmhouse a home.

"Lass, are you in here?"

She turned as Will opened the door.

"Sorry, I probably should have asked before coming up here but I wanted to see if you'd continued with the renovation," she said, smiling at him.

"Well, as you can see, I have."

"I was surprised to see this room furnished. Is somebody using it?" Alison asked.

"Aye, me, I'm using it. It's my room," Will explained.

"Why did you move from the other room above the kitchen?"

"Don't laugh when I tell you, will you?"

"Why would I laugh?" Alison said puzzled.

"I were embarrassed being just down the corridor from Sarah and Brian. I mean, they were sharing a room and... well, it embarrassed me. So I cracked on with this room to spare me blushes and give them some privacy."

"I suppose that it was another reminder of the years you'd lost; suddenly you've a daughter who can legally have sex."

"Not only was she old enough to but she was actually involved with somebody. It took some getting used to, I'll tell you... especially as far as I remember I've never...well, you know," he said quietly.

"Yeah, I know."

"I'd... I'd like to change that."

Alison was glad she was sitting down because, if she hadn't been, she'd have fallen over.

"Sorry, what did you say?"

"I brought you here so I could sleep with you." The words tumbled out so quickly. Alison wasn't sure she'd heard him properly.

"Did you say you want to sleep with me?"

"Oh God... this is difficult. Yes... I want to sleep with you...I thought you wanted the same... especially after the kiss."

"The kiss when I arrived?"

"Yes, it were different. You were different. You didn't hold back. I mean... I don't know what I mean, really. You always seemed to be letting me set the pace but just then you didn't."

"No, you're right, it was different. I lost control. I haven't wanted to rush you. But I do want you."

He smiled relieved.

"I want you too. I even went and saw Ben. He gave me some pamphlets and recommended a couple of books."

"You went to see Ben!"

"You said you knew that me and Moira... didn't... well, have a very good sex life. I needed some kind of advice. I wanted it to be special for you, lass, not a disaster."

Alison couldn't believe what she was hearing.

"It must have taken some guts to talk to Ben? I... you did that for me?"

"Well, yeah, but he weren't surprised. I mean, he's known me since school. Alison, I know we've made love before, but I don't remember it... I'll never remember it. To all intents and purposes I've never done this... Sex, I mean. I've read the books and pamphlets, so in theory I know what to do, but I don't have any experience. So, it would help if you'd just take charge. Make the first move so to speak."

"I should just take charge?"

"Yes... I mean, I've condoms in the bedside cabinet. I'm not completely unprepared. I know the mechanics but..." he broke off, too embarrassed to continue.

Alison's heart dissolved. It was going to be alright. She finally believed it. She smiled.

"I'm to do what I want with you?"

"Yes," he whispered.

She crooked her finger and beckoned him forward.

"Do you mean right now?"

His throat went dry and he had to moisten his lips before he spoke.

"If you want to."

"Oh yes, I do want to."

Once he was in front of her, she reached up and slowly unbuttoned his shirt and pushed it from his shoulders until it dropped to the floor. Slowly she walked around him, her fingers softly grazing his skin as she moved. She looped her arms loosely around his waist. A pulse fluttered at his neck and she pressed her lips to it in a soft kiss.

"Breathe, Will," she teased softly.

"I don't think I can."

"Sure you can. Just in and out; take it nice and slowly." She kissed the fluttering pulse again. "It's your turn to undo my shirt now."

"It is?"

She kissed his lips softly.

"Yes, it is."

His hands trembled as he slowly undid the buttons of her blouse, revealing tempting glimpses of white lace that made his mouth go dry. He slowly slid the blouse from her shoulders and let it join his on the floor. He paused, unsure what to do next.

"Will, don't think, just act. Instincts are usually good."

"I want to taste you. Your skin looks so soft." He realised, as he was speaking, that he didn't need her permission. He could just take this. He lowered his head and trailed kisses along her collar bone to the soft skin at her neck. His hands moved to her back and he pulled her close. He stroked his finger along her cheek before he cupped her face in his hands, lowered his lips to hers in a soft tender kiss, teasing and tasting, until, on a moan of pleasure, her mouth opened as he deepened the kiss, wanting more, his tongue sliding in and exploring. He could feel her hands caressing his back, her gentle touch causing his muscles to ripple in anticipation. Pulling her closer, his hand moved to the nape of her neck and his fingers played with the silky strands of her hair as he changed the angle of his kiss, his teeth scraping over her lips. Her tongue slid over his as she returned his kisses with equal passion.

Alison sighed with pleasure; she'd missed this.

Emboldened by her response to his kiss, Will gently began to caress her breasts through the silk and lace of her bra. Another sigh left her lips, followed by a murmur of pleasure. His hands trembled as he slipped the straps down over her arms.

"It undoes at the back," Alison whispered. Reaching behind, she unhooked the bra and allowed it to fall to the floor.

"You are so beautiful, lass," Will said, swallowing hard.

"Please touch me, Will."

He gently cupped her breast and his thumb slowly brushed over her nipple. His touch was exquisite. Heat spread over her as she gave herself into his wondrous touch. He moved his hands in featherlike touches down her abdomen until he found the zip of her trousers. Slowly he inched it down, causing her trousers to slide over her hips and pool at her feet. He lifted her up and carried her over to the bed and lay her down.

"Is this alright?"

"Well, apart from you having too many clothes on, it's wonderful."

"Oh, well, in that case, I guess I'd best finish what you started." He quickly removed the rest of his clothes and lay down by her side.

"Did the book and pamphlets help with what comes next?"

He took her in his arms.

"I think so, lass."

They made love slowly, exploring each other's bodies, doubts and shyness forgotten. At that moment, there was nothing and nobody else in the world, just the two of them. Time lost all meaning; they were fluid in each other's arms, limbs entwined as pleasure washed over them and they shared the most intimate act of all.

She was curled against him, her head an unfamiliar weight on his chest. How had he not known that making love could be like this? Nothing in his life had prepared him for the simple beauty of it.

"Was it always like that for us, lass?" he whispered against her hair.

"Like what?"

"It'll sound corny, but like we have touched the stars."

"Yes, it can be different, as you'll discover, but it's always special." Her hand slowly traced a pattern on his chest."

"Do you remember, outside, I told you I had things to say?"

"Yes..." she said cautiously.

"Well, the most important one is that I love you."

"You do?"

"Yes, everybody told me I would. They said if I gave you a chance I'd fall in love with you again... because I did love you, didn't I, lass? I mean, I don't remember that. I just somehow know that I did."

Tears shimmered in her eyes.

"Lass, are you crying?"

"Yes, but they're good tears. I love you, Will. I never stopped loving you."

She kissed him softly and rolled so that she was knelt astride him.

"Do you remember how I said each time was different?"

"Yeah?"

"Want me to show you?" She said with a wicked grin.

"What? Again? So soon?"

"Right now," she whispered, before she kissed him.

****

She couldn't sleep so she'd slipped from beneath the covers and gone down to the kitchen to make some tea. Winston stood up and stretched as she came into the room, moving to sit with her as she drank her drink.

She reached down and stroked his silky ears.

"This is like old times, Win, you and me sat talking. Well, me talking and you listening. It's been the most perfect weekend, lad."

The dog wagged his tail as if agreeing with her.

"And I don't just mean the sex either. Just being here and working alongside Will, it's all been perfect. Seeing the farm in a different season, oh, and seeing Aragorn's and Arwen's foal, Boromir." She scratched the dog's head. "And did I mention you? I know I've to go back to my house, but

I can come back here anytime. I can come home, Win."

"Is that what this place is then, lass, home?"

"For a big bloke you don't half move quietly," she said, turning to face him.

"Sorry. Is it home?"

"Well, actually anywhere you are is home." The moment she'd said it she started to laugh. "Please, stop me; I'm turning into a one woman cliché."

"It's all those classics you read. Well, I'm glad you like it here," Will said, pleased.

"I do, Will, I really do. Can I come back?"

He wanted to ask her to stay forever but he was worried that it was a little too soon.

"Aye," he smiled. "I have to say aye 'cause you've already told my dog you'd be back."

"Were you eavesdropping on my private conversation with your dog?" Alison teased. "Yes I was... Alison, I'd like you to come back. I need you to come back."

"He's done it now, Win. He won't be able to keep me away," she told the dog.

"Win, you should tell her I don't want to keep her away – not anymore."

She smiled at his words.

"I know you don't."

"I'm sorry it took me so long to realise how much I love you."

"Don't be. I'm doubly lucky; you fell in love with me twice."

"Talking of love, if you come back to bed I'll help you unwind." He smiled wickedly at her.

"Oh, and how are you going to do that?" she asked.

"Well." He pulled her close. "Come upstairs and I'll show you."

Epilogue

Alison was glad that they'd taken her car. Will's Landrover, while more practical for travelling on the country lanes, was far from comfortable and, with the heater on the blink, they'd have been cold. The temperature had fallen over the last week and she doubted it was above freezing. She'd been happy to hand him the keys to her car - he was more familiar with the roads than she was. It was interesting watching him drive. Like everything else he did, there was a quiet competence about the way he handled the car. He drove confidently without being flashy; the hands that lightly gripped the steering wheel were relaxed. Elegant hands, she realised, even though he worked hard with them. His movements to change gears were calm and unhurried. Despite knowing the route well, his eyes seldom left the road as he concentrated.

"You're staring at me, lass."

"How do you know that?"

"I can feel you watching me."

"I was just thinking that you even make driving sexy."

He laughed.

"How does anybody make driving sexy?"

"I think it's because you give off an air of casual confidence. It's like you are at one with the machine."

His shoulders shook with laughter.

"Oh, lass, I couldn't be sexy, even if you gave us a manual with step by step instructions in it. I'm a Yorkshire sheep farmer."

"Oh, I don't know. When you gave me that massage an hour ago you were pretty damn sexy," Alison said, smiling at the memory.

"Stop teasing, woman." He glanced at her. "Was it alright, lass, what I did?" he asked shyly.
"Will Barnes, are you fishing for compliments again? It was bloody wonderful. You are the best kept secret in The Dales." Alison reached over and touched his cheek softly, aware that he still needed reassurance. "And I love you."

Will smiled; he'd never tire of hearing her saying she loved him. And since she'd moved in with him at the beginning of December it was almost always the first thing she said every day.

He'd been so worried about asking her to move in. But fortune favoured the brave, so they said, so he'd plucked up the courage to ask. He smiled as he remembered. It had been the last Sunday in November.

She'd been talking about whether to renew the lease on the house she was renting or to look for somewhere else.

"How far are you willing to travel?" he asked quietly.

"Why? Do you know somewhere I might like?"

"Well, how about here?"

She launched herself at him. He honestly thought she flew through the air. He'd caught her in his arms, laughing.

"Really!"

"Well, you're here most weekends and at least one night in the week. I may as well put up with you the rest of the week. I mean, you're not a bad cook."

She hit him and then kissed him.

"I thought you wouldn't ask me and I had no idea how to ask you."

"And I was afraid to ask in case you said no. But it's time, lass, for us to be together."

She'd agreed it was and they'd spent the last couple of weeks moving her belongings to Highcroft.

"You're smiling. What are you thinking of?" she asked.

"The day I asked you to move in."

"Regretting it already?"

"Well, only when you come to bed with cold feet."

"Do you realise this is the first time we have gone into Hebden since I moved in with you?"

"Yeah, the gossips will have a field day."

"And the church will be filled with as many gossips as the pub."

"Do you want me to turn around and go back?"

"Don't be daft, let them gossip. Anyway, I'm singing in the choir, I can't back out now."

Will smiled. She'd been practising for the carol service for weeks, her lilting voice ringing out around the farmhouse as she worked. She'd even sung while collecting eggs and feeding the chickens.

"Well, I hope you're in fine voice. I imagine t'church is sure to be packed, folks love a carol service."

****

Will was right – the church was packed. He'd been surprised when he'd been shown to an area of reserved seating, until the woman who was sat next to him explained that they always reserved seats for family members of the choir. Her son had been with the choir for ten years, she explained.

"Is it your wife who's in the choir?"

Will looked at the old lady and pondered how to explain who Alison was. She wasn't his wife but she was more than his girlfriend. He smiled when he thought of what she'd become.

"Alison's my partner," he explained.

"Oh, the new lass. Fred, my son, says she has a lovely voice."

"Well, the chickens on t'farm think so but t'pigs aren't so sure," he said, smiling.

"Farm? I thought Fred said the new girl was a teacher."

"Aye, she is. But we live out on my farm – Highcroft."

"Highcroft? Are you Flo Barnes' kin then?"

"Aye, she were my gran." He held out his hand. "Will Barnes."

"Sally Weston. It's lovely to meet you, lad. I knew your gran well. I grew up in Heptonstall and went to school with her. I was sorry to hear that she'd passed on. It was a mutual friend, Doris Bradshaw, who told me."

"I know Mrs B well."

"Of course you do. You must be the Will she speaks of in her letters. I moved to Halifax years ago but we still keep in touch by letters. Not modern, I know, but computers are beyond me and there's nowt like finding a letter among the bills."

Will smiled.

"No, that's true."

"You'll come to the hotel for a drink after the concert, won't you?"

"Aye, Alison mentioned it. We'll not stay late though. My day starts early on the farm."

"I bet it does. We'll chat later then, young man, and you can introduce me to Alison."

****

Alison smiled. Will was never difficult to spot in a crowd, being so tall and broad. He was in demand. Fred Weston's mother had introduced him to everybody and now he was surrounded. There would have been a time when he'd have run a mile from this situation but, although still quiet, these days he was much more comfortable socially. Ben Chambers appeared at her elbow.

"It's like looking at a different man. You've been so good for him, Alison."

"We're good for each other. I thought I saw you at the concert," she said, reaching up to kiss the young doctor's cheek. He'd become a really good friend in the months after the accident and they often met up socially.

"Well, you were raising money for the hospice and I'm on the board of trustees there. You sang beautifully, by the way."

"Thank you, Ben. That's sweet of you to say." She kissed his cheek again.

"Honestly, Ben, don't you think it's time you found a girl of your own instead of kissing mine all the time?"

"You nabbed the best one around." He shook hands with Will.

"Yes, I did. Are you on your own?"

"No, dad's here somewhere; probably boring somebody to death about the state of the NHS."

They talked to the young GP and mingled for a further hour before they headed back up to the farm.

"What were you talking to Ben about when I interrupted you?" Will asked as they went back to the car.

"He said that I'd been good for you but I corrected him and told him we were good for each other."

Will smiled.

"That we are, lass. That we are."

****

Will was nervous; it was strange - he hadn't expected to be. It was Christmas Eve and Alison was in the kitchen fixing a night cap. He moved to the window, staring out over the farmyard before drawing the curtains. No snow this year but the ground was covered in a hard white frost that sparkled in the moonlight. The renovations to the house were almost complete now, but they still seemed to settle in this sitting room in the evening. The smell of pine filled the air from the tree they had cut and decorated that afternoon. Presents were piled underneath; Santa, it seemed, had come early. The lights sparkled in the darkened room but he didn't put the main light on, liking the way the fire and tree lights softened the atmosphere. They were alone in the house.

Sarah and Brian were spending Christmas day with Brian's family, before travelling up to Yorkshire on Boxing Day. He smiled. Sarah's gift was under the tree or at least part of it. She'd surprised him on her return from Europe by asking him to take her to the cottage where her mother had died. He'd no memory of finding Moira and Myles but he hadn't been inside the cottage since the accident. They'd gone out the following Sunday, just the two of them. Brian and Alison seemed to realise that this was something that father and daughter needed to do alone. It was the first time Will had gone into the cottage since Moira's death. He felt nothing, but having no memory of discovering Moira here, he hadn't expected to. He'd watched Sarah for signs of distress but there were none. In fact she was smiling.

"Will, this house should be lived in. It could be a beautiful home. I thought it'd be a sad place but it's not. It were the only place Moira were happy. When I've finished college I'd like to buy it from you. Promise you won't sell it."

He'd promise not to sell to anybody else, but he'd no intention of selling it to her either. Under the tree was an envelope with a key and deeds to the property. He hoped she'd be pleased.

Sarah and Brian were collecting Alison's parents on the way up so there would be a houseful on Boxing Day. Henry and Ruth had been frequent visitors to Yorkshire since their daughter had moved up from Bath. Judging by the plans Alison had made and the baking she'd done she couldn't wait for everybody to arrive. But for now it was just the two of them and he couldn't be happier.

Happy didn't do justice to how he felt. Blissful was a better word.

Finally he was at peace and content with his life. Everything was almost perfect. He fingered the box in his pocket and if tonight went according to plan it would be perfect.

He turned as he heard Alison come through from the kitchen, Winston at her side as usual.

"Oh, Will, the tree looks lovely."

"It's not as grand as the one in the hall of t'main house," he said.

"I don't care. It looks beautiful."

"As do you, lass." They'd been to church and Alison's hair tumbled against the cherry red cashmere cardigan she wore. Tiny pearl buttons trailed down the front and the soft wool clung to her curves.

He pulled her gently towards the fire and glanced up at the mistletoe that hung from the beam.

"I like Christmas," he murmured, "and all its traditions."

His kiss was persuasive, demanding and devastating. Alison slid boneless against him. What this man could do with a simple kiss should be illegal.

He stepped away and, not taking his eyes from her face, he went down on one knee.

Alison felt her breath catch in her throat and her heart began to beat erratically. How had she not seen this coming? Will's hand moved to his pocket and he placed a small box in her hand.

"Alison, lass, will you marry me?" he asked softly.

She smiled. There were no flowery words, just honest simplicity – like the man he was. The man she loved. She touched his cheek and lowered herself to his side.

"Yes."

She undid the box. Inside was a rose cut diamond cluster ring. It was obviously old and probably very valuable.

"'T were my grandmother's. If you would rather…"

"It's perfect, Will, just perfect. Please, would you put it on?"

He slid it on her finger, holding his breath, praying it would fit. He needn't have worried. Will watched as she tipped her hand this way and that, watching the light catch in the stones.

He placed a soft kiss on her lips.

"Thank you, lass. Thank you for making me the happiest man in the world."

"You're welcome, you gorgeous fool. It works both ways; you've made me the happiest woman in the world."

"I should have thought of champagne and flowers," he whispered.

"I don't need them, all I need is you."

His hands moved to the buttons on

her cardigan.
"Well, that I think I can manage."

Made in the USA
Charleston, SC
02 May 2012